About the author

S. J. Ridgway was previously head of studies in the NHS. With a degree in biology, she applies her interests in genetics and criminology to writing crime fiction. Her husband, a retired CID officer, acts as a resource together with a network of professionals in this arena. Visiting close relatives in Australia and New Zealand triggers plots for stories. She is a member of several writing groups, and gives talks on writing crime fiction. *The Autumn Murders* is the second novel in the series, a third one is currently being planned. She volunteers in health-related organisations, and uses social media for networking purposes.

The Autumn Murders

S.J. Ridgway

The Autumn Murders

Vanguard Press

VANGUARD PAPERBACK

© Copyright 2018
S.J. Ridgway

A CIP catalogue record for this title is
available from the British Library.

ISBN 978 1 784653 47 7

Vanguard Press is an imprint of
Pegasus Elliot MacKenzie Publishers Ltd.
www.pegasuspublishers.com

First Published in 2018

Vanguard Press
Sheraton House Castle Park
Cambridge England

Printed & Bound in Great Britain

Acknowledgments

Thank you to everyone who has given advice and support on the development and accuracy of this novel, including:

Stuart Gibbon, crime writing consultant. My husband Derek, retired CID officer. Steven Booth, crime writer. Staff of the library and archive department, the Caird Library, National Maritime Museum, London.

Chapter 1

The curtain twitched at the second floor window in the lodging house across the street as I stepped out that late August evening. Ethel Redberry was watching me. Ignoring her as usual, I could still feel the steel of her dark blue eyes penetrating my back. Nonchalantly I strolled along the pavement, cocooned in my own quiet world. Cut off from the noise and stench of Victorian London, its people, the traffic and the animals; I lumbered on.

Turning the corner, I stood watching Ethel through a crack in the stone wall. Heading in my direction, she clutched that long faded brown shawl across her head and shoulders – hiding her unkempt blonde hair, and the slight bustle at the back of her dress.

I slipped out of sight into an alleyway, and, extracting my pocket mirror, I watched her. Closer, and closer she came – fog-like vapour issuing from her nostrils as her gait quickened. As she neared my hiding place, I turned up my collar, ambled out of the alleyway, and strode on as if oblivious to her presence.

As I glanced over my shoulder a few yards on, she darted into the alleyway I had previously vacated; the tips of her shoes – traitors to her presence.

I ventured on – she in pursuit. Turning corner after corner, overshadowed by tenements, I eventually met my quarry – an unfortunate woman, peddling her body as others did in the area. With agreement on terms, we strolled off together as lovers might – Ethel following some distance away.

The scene was set in a convenient gateway – my stage. Ethel – my audience. The unfortunate – my prey.

As my knife slid across the unfortunate woman's throat, there was a simultaneous muffled scream from the alleyway where Ethel was hiding. Seconds later, I heard the anger and fear of her footsteps, as Ethel ran back towards the sanctuary of her lodging house. *What would she do then,* I wondered as I finished my work on the unfortunate's body?

***

Ethel did nothing, said nothing, but after that event she followed me again and again. My fourth venture, on that November evening, was no exception. Until, that is, I met Mary: an unfortunate. Instead of the usual alleyway, yard or square, we headed for a courtyard and then to the comfort of Mary's room. There was no stage this time. Ethel – no audience, but a witness to Mary's sweet singing voice.

Leaving Mary's body just before dawn, I opened her door and escaped into an empty courtyard. Returning home, I was not surprised to see Ethel watching me from her usual vantage point.

No sooner had I washed and changed, and was sitting comfortably in my armchair by the fireside, when the doorbell rang. Ethel was standing there, wrapped in that faded-brown shawl.

***

Inspector Paul Evans scrutinised every gesture made by Superintendent Cadema Sharma as she switched off her mobile phone and sat upright behind her desk. Only her rank, and status as an SIO in the Met, gave her the authority over him.

Of course Evans liked women, but only in a sexual context. And they had to be younger than he was at thirty-four. Cadema was different. Despite being three years older, she was a widow, inaccessible, and displayed the persona of a tiger when necessary. Nevertheless, he was attracted to her. He liked her coy smile, her dark penetrating eyes, and the way she brushed her long black hair across her shoulders and tossed her head when she was about to say something she was uncomfortable with. Sometimes he wanted to reach out and touch her, or even ask her for a date, but knew he would be rebuffed.

When she was angry, he hated her. And lately, she was always angry – especially towards him. So, when she called him to her office to tell him that the Belton case was going to be reopened, he was ready for reprisals.

'But, Ma'am, it's over two years since Bernard Franklin was convicted of the murder of Madeline Belton. I did a bloody good job in putting him away,' said Evans as he shuffled his body in the chair, folded his arms and began to grind his teeth.

'Two years and three months, to be precise,' said Cadema assertively. 'I'm not disputing the work you, together with the rest of team, did then. Nor am I undermining the three recent murder cases you've all solved. But the Belton case is being reopened, and that's the end of it.'

Had it really been that long? Cadema questioned her memory. How the time had passed since she returned from India, minus a spouse. Despite being "presented", as her mother called it, to at least four prospective husbands. She had managed a condescending smile, and politely declined their offers. Now all she wanted to do was concentrate on her work, and forget about her mother who was probably playing the lonely hearts card somewhere in India. She shook her head.

'Are you okay, Ma'am? You seemed to…'

'Of course I'm okay,' said Cadema frowning.

'Good.' He paused and took a deep breath. 'I appreciate your appraisal of my work. But surely you can tell me why the case is being reopened.'

Cadema leaned forward – examining Evans' contorted face, the stress lines, that had not been there six months ago, and the thinning brown hair with tints of grey. He leaned back in his chair – his blue eyes narrowed. She took a deep breath.

'I am unable to answer that at present. All I'm asking you to do is find one of the files from the case, that's not too much to ask, is it? Or do you have more important things to do?'

'No, Ma'am, I'll find the file. It'll just take some time, that's all,' he muttered and shuffled awkwardly in the chair.

Despite what Cadema had said, he'd been in the job long enough to know that all the police service needed were loyal and dedicated officers who were intelligent enough to "bend the rules" and never get caught. When he had a suspect, they were always guilty, all he had to do was prove it. Bending a few rules here and there had always been productive; as with Bernard Franklin's conviction. Now he certainly didn't want that case reopened. It would be an insult on his ability as a detective. And most of all he didn't want other, more senior officers, to discover that the case was far from sound. So there was no choice, he had to find the file and remove any incriminating evidence, before giving it to Cadema.

'Well if you haven't got the time, I'll ask someone else to do it,' Cadema bluffed.

'Excuse me, Ma'am.' He swallowed. 'I didn't say I was too busy. Just that it's not going to be easy, especially since all those files have been moved to Drayton Street and mixed with the ones from Aldgate.' His voice echoed around the sparsely furnished office, as he stood.

She remained seated; *he had taken the bait.*

'I know that, so let's hope you'll find it quickly. I want this Belton case closed as much as you do. And since there's no other pressing work to do, make it your priority. We don't want to be downsized like other divisions have. So get on with it, will you?'

'Yes, Ma'am.'

'I'll give you twenty-four hours, is that clear?' He nodded. 'There's no time for procrastination. Twenty-four hours and that's final.'

'But...'

'No more buts; just do it. You can take Sergeant Marriott with you, that'll help to speed up your search.'

Evans gave a grimace of a smile, nodded, coughed, and said the file would be on her desk as instructed. Although he wanted to do the search on his own, there was no point in arguing. Besides, Marriott was only a sergeant and could easily be deployed elsewhere in the archive room, while he searched for the file himself. When he found it, the sergeant wouldn't even see it.

As Evans left Cadema's office he almost collided with Sergeant Marriott who was about to knock on her door.

'You're just the person I want. Follow me,' said Evans.

Giving Marriott no time to answer, he charged along the corridor. Marriott caught up quickly, much quicker than Evans had expected.

'What have you been eating for breakfast then?' said Evans sarcastically, and a little out of breath.

'Just the usual cereal, yogurt and toast, Sir.'

'I meant it rhetorically.'

'Sir?'

'Never mind, we're on a mission,' said Evans, gaining his posture after taking several gulps of air and walking at a slower pace than before.

David Marriott strolled by his side. In the three years since joining the CID, he always followed orders. When he first arrived, his family had come first, but since the divorce, his priorities had changed. Now he was devoted to the job and studying hard to pass his inspectors exams. His slim, tall frame gave him the look of an athlete, although he rarely had time for the gym these days. When DI Evans asked him to accompany him to the archives building, he was elated especially as Evans was usually aloof and seemed to prefer to work alone.

***

By the time they had reached the car park, Evans had finished explaining to Marriott what they were about to do. Finding the allocated unmarked car in the compound, Evans slid into the driver's seat, buckled up, and revved the engine just as Marriott closed the passenger's door.

'At least this one'll go when you put your foot down,' Evans bragged – revving the engine again – smiling at the thought of a chase, even when there wasn't one.

Despite being in an urban area, and the wet roads, his body lunged as the car tyres screeched round bend after bend. The traffic parted as if a giant hand had swept them aside as he drove through red lights with the two-tones on. A woman on a pedestrian crossing managed to jump back out of the way – her shopping bag crashing to the ground.

'Don't you think we had better slow down, Sir? Someone may be killed,' Marriott's voice rasped out as he crouched further down in his seat.

'Nonsense. Anyway, who's driving this thing?' Evans' voice yelled out. Marriott remained quiet – his eyes tightly shut.

Ten minutes later, they had reached their destination. Leaving the car smelling of rubber, they approached the shabby 1960s, flat-roofed building. Evans swiped the security lock with his card, and they entered the unmanned building.

Evans stood in the corridor listening to the drone of the air conditioning and taking in the damp air. Marriott stood beside him waving his arms about to activate the lights. Moving along the corridor in unison, they entered room nine. It was some ten metres wide and fifteen metres long with concrete pillars dotted around. Rows of stacked cardboard boxes, some of which reached the ceiling, looked precarious in the half-light. Seeing some familiar labels over to his right, Evans turned to Marriott.

'You go and look over there to your left. I'll be over here,' Evans pointed. 'Just let me know if you find anything.'

Marriott's head was at ceiling height as he turned towards the dimly-lit area where Evans expected him to work.

'Yes, Sir, but it may be difficult to find anything. And I'm not sure about all those boxes, they don't look safe to me,' said Marriott in an anxious, and almost pleading, voice.

'For goodness' sake, that's all I need, a whingeing sergeant. Anyway Health and Safety have no doubt done their assessment, so get to it will you?'

Marriott lowered his head, nodded to Evans, then gingerly moved down the room towards the shelving on the opposite wall. His journey hindered by the stacked boxes.

'It looks as if the removal men have just dumped these here, hope it's safe,' said Marriott, steading one of the stacks as it wobbled.

'My heart bleeds for you,' Evans muttered.

Edging forward, Marriott noticed an old wooden trunk tucked away under a low shelf. Pushing, pulling, and sliding several stacks of boxes to one side or the other, he managed to reach it. Then, precariously perching himself on a cardboard box, he studied the outside of the trunk. He estimated it to be about eighty centimetres in length, sixty in depth, and some fifty in height. The wood was splintered in places with many minute holes where its previous residents had vacated. Two corroded iron latches were in the locked position at the front. He reached forward to touch one of the latches, then stopped. Was there someone coming? He listened, but all was quiet. Reaching for the latch again he jumped as a car alarm went off somewhere outside. Holding his breath, he looked around.

'Looks as if everything's been here for decades,' he said, loud enough for Evans to hear. There was no answer. Stretching his neck, he looked above one of the stacks; nothing. Could he open the trunk? The corroded latches told him otherwise. They would certainly creak, or even snap. And he didn't want to alert Evans' curiosity. Besides, he was looking for a file, not an old wooden trunk. There may be other opportunities to open it, but not now, and certainly not when Evans was about.

'Where are you, Marriott?' Evans bellowed. 'I've found the file, so let's go.'

'Coming, Sir,' Marriott replied, and then tutted. On his retreat, he pulled some of the stacks back to their original places. Looking back, he couldn't even see the gap he had made which led to the wooden trunk.

Marriott was out of breath and wiping his forehead with a tissue when he reached Evans.

'Christ, you look a bloody mess with all that dust,' said Evans, holding a file in his hand. 'Now I've got this, I'll take you back and drop this off later.'

'I could take it to Superintendent Sharma if you like?' replied Marriott in a concerned voice.

'No need, I'll be seeing her later, so I'll give it to her then.' Evans lied, but was not about to let anyone have the file until he had scrutinised the content and dealt with anything that would incriminate him.

***

Evans drove sedately back to the station. Marriott sat quietly in the passenger seat, curious about the file – he decided not to ask about it. Neither did he mention the wooden trunk. After all, Evans had a reputation in taking charge of anything that was remotely sensational. This was especially the case if it involved subordinates, or if it would expedite his movement up the ranks. He would certainly take over if the wooden trunk turned out to be important – and of course, take the credit for it.

Dropping Marriott off, Evans said goodbye, placed the file in the boot of his own car, and drove off.

When Marriott met Cadema in her office for the briefing on the last case, he had already decided not to mention the trunk. Instead, he would return to the archive room alone as soon as he had the opportunity. Then, if it turned out to be insignificant, he could forget it and move on.

'I have the feeling something is troubling you,' said Cadema frowning as she examined Marriott's features. There was a hint of grey in his otherwise brown hair she hadn't noticed before. The smile lines around his eyes were prominent now. And although he was over six feet tall, he looked much shorter than he had done when he arrived at the division. But when he spoke to her, he was as enthusiastic and keen as he always was.

'Nothing's troubling me, Ma'am. It's just that I've been busy with this report you wanted.' He handed it to her.

'Good, this looks in order. So how did you get on with DI Evans in the archive room?' Marriott coughed, fidgeted in his chair – his face blank. 'Come on, you can tell me in confidence.'

'Ma'am.' He fidgeted again. 'I think he found what he was looking for and said he would give it to you when he comes in.'

'I see. Thank you, Sergeant, you can go now.' Cadema smiled – as if happy with the situation.

Marriott frowned as he left the room, knowing she wasn't happy about something.

Chapter 2

Cadema was never arrogant enough to think she had done a good job, and the last case was no exception. She was paid to do her duty, to protect the public; her obligation to society. So she moved on to the next case with her usual vigour knowing that, once the decadent behaviour of her team was well spent at the *George and Crown*, they would be back to work as usual, no doubt some sporting a hangover.

The workplace had been far too hectic during the last twelve months for Cadema to attend social events. Instead, most of her evenings were spent at work. Only occasionally did she have time to see her friend, Doctor Julia Lilly. And that was mainly to discuss Julia's latest pathology reports. Now that there were fewer constraints on her time, and that the Belton case was simmering in the background, at least for a few days, it meant that she could indulge in a meal out. Besides, she wanted a break, and Julia, with her bubbly personality, was the tonic she needed. After speaking to Julia, she booked the table.

It was a late October evening when Cadema's taxi pulled up outside their favourite Indian restaurant. Paying her fare, there was no sign of Julia as she ran towards the door. Early as usual, Cadema turned to shake the water off her umbrella and saw Julia running towards her. Simultaneously they rushed into the restaurant, put their wet coats on the hook, turned towards each other, then giggled as they gave each other a polite kiss.

'Great to see you again, Julia.'

'Likewise. I was beginning to think you'd left the country – again. Your mother's still away I presume?' said Julia as she watched a waiter walking towards them.

'As always. I think she's going to stay there well into next year.'

'Still trying to find you a suitable partner, is she?' Julia smiled, but the conversation was interrupted by the waiter who, after a greeting and saying it was good to see them again, escorted them to their usual table, took orders for drinks, and left.

'You know I don't intend to marry again – not after… Anyway let's not go down that road,' said Cadema brushing a strand of wet black hair from her face.

'Sorry I didn't mean to…'

'That's okay – I'm just… So what about you? What have you been doing lately?'

'Nothing really. How's work at the Met these days?' asked Julia as the waiter arrived with the glass of Merlot and sparkling water they had requested. Taking the order for their meal, the waiter left. 'Cheers Cadema.' She lifted her glass of wine above the central candle.

Cadema mirrored the action with her glass of water, and leaned forward.

'Busy as usual. But it's been ages since we had time to do this. I've hardly had time to think. And sorry, I haven't even thanked you for the work you did recently.' Cadema watched as Julia shuffled in her chair – her face flushed.

'Just doing my job, but don't forget, you did all the hard work. Anyway, that aside,' Julia smoothed her bobbed blonde hair behind her ears, 'we must do this again.'

Cadema nodded, then sat back watching the waiter place the dishes of food on the table. 'Thank you,' they said in unison to the waiter. He nodded and then left.

'This smells delicious,' Julia sniffed. 'Can hardly wait to tuck in.' She frowned as a group of noisy women were seated a couple of tables away. 'Looks like we made the right decision in coming early?'

'You're right. But why only one glass of wine – you usually have two?'

'It's the publicity about the link with wine to cancer, and my recent scare. Anyway, it's best not to take chances, so I don't drink during the week these days.' Julia dished some curry onto her plate.

'That's very commendable, but there's something I need to tell you about.'

'That sounds ominous. Has there been another murder?' Julia took a fork-full of curry, chewed and swallowed. They both leaned forward.

'No...' Cadema was interrupted by the waiter asking if their meal was satisfactory as he placed a jug of water on the table.

'The food is perfect as always,' Julia smiled.

The waiter nodded, said, 'Enjoy' and then retreated as the two women leaned forward again.

'Now, where were we?' enquired Julia.

'You asked if there was another murder, and no there hasn't been. Besides you know I would have called you if there had been. But you need to be aware we're reopening the Belton case,' Cadema whispered.

'Why? Surely Bernard, what's his name?' she frowned.

'Franklin, Bernard Franklin. He's serving life for the murder of Madeline Belton. But there's new evidence. Once it's been checked out, he will probably be released,' said Cadema taking a mouthful of curry then leaning back in her chair.

Julia forked a piece of chicken around her plate, then looked at Cadema. 'So do you have any other suspects? Thomas, perhaps?'

'No. Although Thomas did murder four women during that time, he was never a suspect in the Belton case. Anyway, as you know he's in Broadmoor, and will never be released. Looks as if we're back to square one with the case.'

'But you must have some ideas?'

'Nothing tangible. Hopefully we will find the answers soon.'

Normally Cadema would have discussed work issues with Julia – tonight was different. She had decided not to mention Evans and the file she had asked him to retrieve. After all it was a delicate matter, a personnel issue perhaps – she had to maintain confidentiality, especially if there was an enquiry. No, she would have to handle it herself without Julia's help.

Cadema gave a nervous cough and looked at Julia. 'Let's not talk shop any more, but please tell me about your new partner. You sounded interested in him when we spoke on the phone.'

'You know how it is,' Julia began.

'Not really – explain,' Cadema teased.

'Well you read the man's profile on the screen, see his photograph and he seems the perfect match. But when you meet him, he's rubbish,' said Julia as took another sip of Merlot.

'So, is this one rubbish?'

'I didn't say that.'

'Then tell me what you're really saying. You know I don't understand internet dating. I've never indulged.'

'As I said, this one's different. His name is Raymond. Quite spoilt by his mother no doubt, but with a mind of his own.' Julia reached into her bag and pulled out a photograph she had printed from the on-line dating agency. 'Not bad to look at, ha? Good teeth with two amalgam fillings, hairline a bit high, broad shoulders, and relatively fit.'

Julia's usual medical description of people, thought Cadema.

When she took the photograph from Julia she could see it was of a young man of about thirty, clean shaven, golden hair and smiling eyes. He looked attractive and for a microsecond she felt a little jealous.

'He looks nice, but I thought you were looking for a new job, not a man?'

'I was just browsing,' Julia shrugged. 'Anyway I'm still looking for a new job. Nothing's turned up. A professorship is not easy to find these days.'

'Well I wish you all the best, but if you do find another job, I'll miss you.' She handed the photograph back. 'How long have you been going out with him?'

Julia blushed, and drained her glass. 'Just the one date so far. I'm seeing him again tomorrow evening at my place. I'm cooking him a meal. By the way he's a solicitor. Works for Jones, Jones and Sons near New Cross.'

'That sounds exciting, hope it goes well.' Cadema smiled awkwardly, not knowing what else to say.

'I'll let you know, but don't tell anyone else as there's no need for them to know unless it turns out to be a long lasting relationship.'

'I'm discretion itself, you know that.' Cadema had just finished gesticulating that her lips were sealed when the waiter handed them the bill. Outside, they agreed to meet in two days' time. By then, Cadema hoped to have more information on the Belton case.

Chapter 3

It was four in the morning when Marriott looked at his bedside clock for the third time during the last hour. But every time he tried to sleep, all he could think about was the trunk. Lying there, he decided which excuse he would use to free himself from duty that morning. Then he would have the time to return to the archive room. If the trunk was empty, it didn't matter. Conversely, if it contained something of interest – he had no idea what. But if it did, he would have to tell Cadema, even if it meant being disciplined for lying about his whereabouts.

By eight o'clock he had finished breakfast. As usual, he was dressed in his pressed suit, his shoes well polished, and ready for work. But with an alternative plan in his mind, he donned his overcoat. Then opening the cupboard under the sink, he took out a screwdriver and other tools, and slid them into his overcoat pocket.

Reaching for his mobile phone, he sent a text message to Cadema:

'Sorry, Ma'am, won't be in 'till later, not sure what time. Family business. Will call you soon.' Pressing send, he switched it to silent and dropped it into his jacket pocket.

***

As he approached the archive building, he could feel his heart thumping – as if an alien were trying to get out. Pulling up his overcoat collar, he scanned the area. Nothing.

He moved on, then jumped as a cat darted across his path and scurried away under a gate. Feeling hot and clammy, he undid the top button of his overcoat. Guilt surged at the back of his throat – burning. Should he turn and walk away? No, he was committed now.

Eventually reaching a side door, instead of the front door which he had done with DI Evans, he took his electronic pass from his pocket – hoping it wouldn't work. When it did work, he shrugged, moved forward, took a last look across his shoulders, and entered the building.

The corridor was darker than he expected as he stood waving his arms – waiting for the lights to come on. A few seconds later, much longer than he had remembered from before, the whole place was well illuminated.

Unfamiliar with his surroundings, he scratched his head and moved towards a faded map hanging from a nail on the wall. Cleaning the dust off with his hand, he could now see the internal layout of the building. After studying it for a moment, he walked on along the labyrinth of corridors with his arms gesticulating, like a demented mole looking for somewhere to surface.

Stopping for breath, he stood in the darkness remembering the time when he was doing his first degree. As a competition, he and his fellow students had taken it in turns to jump up as high as they could in the library to keep the lights on. It was fun at first, but once the novelty had gone, it became a tedious exercise. Just like it was now. He gesticulated again.

Around the next bend, he finally located room nine – open and unmanned. *The cutbacks*, he reasoned. But at least this time they were in his favour, no one to disturb what he was about to do. Then, turning the light switch to permanent, he ventured further into the room. He hated working alone, even though, technically, he worked alone when DI Evans was there.

Looking around, he headed to where the wooden trunk had been. Then, threading his body between stacks of cardboard boxes as before, he pushed some aside, while steadying others.

On reaching the area, he took a tissue from his pocket and wiped the sweat from his brow. He was about to replace the tissue when he noticed it was not only wet but also streaked with dust. He shook his head.

The trunk was much further under the shelf than he had remembered – as if it had been deliberately hidden again. He looked around – nothing unusual. Stooping on his haunches, he tried to pull the trunk out from under the shelf, but it was much heavier than he expected.

'Ouch,' he said, feeling a pain in his back, which then travelled down the back of his left leg; like lightning heading for earth. He waited for the worst to happen, then smiled as the pain disappeared as quickly as it had started.

Standing again, he removed his overcoat, massaged his back with his hands, and waited. Feeling better now, he crouched again, leaned forward, took hold of the trunk by the latches, and pulled. It slid out much easier than he expected, causing him to lose his balance and land backwards on his coccyx – no pain.

Kneeling over the trunk now, he wiped away the dust which had hidden the torn and battered leather top. He stopped.

Was there someone near, someone watching him? He held his breath and crouched. His eyes wide and oscillating looking for signs of movement; nothing. Steadying his hands, he felt hot – almost faint, then dread. As if he were violating another world, or raiding the newly discovered tomb of a pharaoh. A world where he shouldn't be. But he had made the choice; there was no turning back now.

Waiting for a few seconds, which felt like millions, he looked around. It was safe to continue. He took hold of the latch on the right-hand side of the trunk and pulled. It refused to budge. Standing up, he shrugged. Then, turning to his overcoat which was draped across a cardboard box, he foraged in one of the pockets and extracted a can of lubricant spray and screwdriver.

He crouched again, held his breath and sprayed both latches, then waited. Trying the latches again, they would not budge; as *if there is a greater force from within*, he reasoned. Then, dismissing the idea, he forced the screwdriver into the right-hand latch. Snap. The sound of shearing rusted metal echoed in his ears. The other latch creaked and groaned – the snap was louder this time.

As Marriott lifted the lid, he held his breath – fearful of inhaling some putrid-stagnant air from a time when London's sewers ran down crowded streets. There was no foul smell, just dank air. The lid fully open, he slowly shook his head at seeing, what looked like, an assortment of old clothes. Nevertheless, he decided to treat the trunk as he would a crime scene.

Taking the latex gloves, his dictaphone and mobile phone from his pockets, he placed the items on one of the cardboard boxes. Then, donning the gloves, he used the camera app and took a photograph. Replacing the phone next to his dictaphone, he stood facing the open trunk like a surgeon waiting to operate. Using his thumb and forefinger as forceps he gingerly grasped what seemed to be the shoulders of a badly-stained and faded garment. As he slowly extracted it from the trunk, lifting it higher and higher in the process, he eventually realised it was a full-length dress. Draping it over a couple of cardboard boxes, he reached for the dictaphone and began.

'This dress looks like a prop for a period Victorian drama,' he whispered. 'It's too faded to tell what colour it was, but I think it was once pale-blue. There are copious brown stains, probably dried blood, around the neckline, which has made the fabric, in that area, very stiff.' He moved his hands around the dress and tilted his head. 'I can see several holes in the bodice and other parts of the dress. Some areas are threadbare, while others show signs of being mended,' he whispered in a different tone now, as if he were at a funeral and needed to respect the dead.

He switched off the dictaphone, lifted his phone, and took another photograph. Then, arching his back, he rolled his shoulders, wishing he had brought some pain killers with him.

Hands free again, he began to examine the other garments in the trunk. Then he picked up the dictaphone again and began to speak:

'These look like an assortment of women's underwear, and a faded brown shawl,' he frowned. Unsure of what to call the underwear, he decided not to describe them. Instead, he lay the garments on top of the dress, turned his attention to the trunk again, and began to describe what he could see:

'There is an old picture frame, some fifty by fifty centimetres in width and height, and two and a half centimetres thick.' He stopped recording and placed the dictaphone to one side. Taking a deep breath, and slightly bending his knees, he carefully extracted the frame from the trunk. Turning it over, he gasped and his his heart fluttered at the sight before him. Clearing his throat, and gently lowering the frame back into the trunk, he took a deep breath and started to record again:

'This is astonishing.' He took a tissue from his pocket and wiped his forehead. 'I'm looking at a framed copy of the *Illustrated Police News,* dated Saturday, September the twenty-second, 1888. It contains a collage of eleven sketches of people in various scenes. One has a crowd of people with a man brandishing a dagger. One is of a horse and two men. Another resembles a *Punch* cartoon depicting zoo animals.

'There's nothing too shocking, until you read the headline in the centre of the frame saying: "*Latest Details of the Whitechapel Murders.*" Below this, in the centre of the frame, is a sketch of a woman, it states that it is: "*Annie Chapman, both before and after her death.*"' Marriott stopped speaking, took a couple of photographs, and wiped his brow again.

Standing in the silence for a while, he imagined how terrified Annie must have been at the hands of the most notorious murderer Whitechapel had ever known. How she must have dreaded having to roam the streets to earn her living, only to meet her killer on that fateful night. And how, even now, women were still doing the same thing. He shook his head, shuddered and thought of what he should do next.

Should he continue to empty the trunk, or return the things he had removed without venturing to the bottom? He stood pondering this and trying to rationalise his answers. But there were many more questions to consider. Who had put the trunk there and tried to hide it? Who had placed the items in it and why was there such a mixture? Did the dress and the other clothing belong to Annie Chapman, or to one of the other women depicted in one of the scenes? He didn't think it was Annie's as the dress was small – size ten perhaps? Annie, judging from the sketches, would have taken a much bigger size – fourteen at least. The dress had come from a crime scene, but the framed *Illustrated Police News* had obviously not. So why was this in the trunk?

Many more question were spinning in his head as he continued with his search. If he could find something that might explain where the trunk came from, that would be helpful. He could then tell Superintendent Sharma. Hopefully, she would support him in finding answers to his questions.

After deciding not to remove anything else from the trunk, he pushed items aside until he reached the bottom. Here his fingers found a small parcel, tied up, he imagined, with string – he pulled.

Standing erect, he was now holding a bundle of police pocketbooks. He took a deep breath, looked around and listened. All he could hear was the drone of the air conditioning and the sound of wet tyres on tarmac. Some feet were running outside. But, although he waited for a while, he could not hear anyone in the building.

He looked at the pocketbooks again. The urge to examine them far outweighing his logic not to. After all, this crime scene was long gone. Removing one from the bundle, he thumbed through it. Stopped; then began to read the records pencilled by a police officer at the time of the murders.

As he read, his hands shook. He couldn't go on. Instead he methodically returned each item to the trunk, and closed the lid. It was only then that he realised he was still holding one of the pocketbooks.

His eyes scanned the area as he slid it into his pocket. Then, pushing the trunk under the shelf, and pulling some of the cardboard boxes in front of it, he picked up his belongings, retraced his steps, and left the building.

Driving home, he ruminated about what to do next. The trunk was certainly intriguing. And every time he thought about the pocketbook, his heart quickened. But he didn't think it would reveal the identity of the killer; why should it?

If the police couldn't find the killer back then, what chance would there be now? None whatsoever.

***

After showering and dressing for work again, the telephone rang. Picking it up, he heard Cadema's agitated but concerned voice.

'Marriott, when will you be coming in?'

'I'll be there in fifteen minutes. Yes, everything's okay; I'll give you my report as soon as I see you.' His polite goodbye ended the call.

Marriott stood for a moment; his thoughts gnawing at his conscience, his mind itching to read more from the pocketbook. Once he'd done this, he would return it to the trunk without anyone knowing.

He picked up his phone and dialled Cadema's number.

'Now what, Sergeant Marriott?' Gone were her concerns, she sounded angry now. 'I thought you were coming in?'

Marriott stood to attention. 'I'm on my way. But I need to tell you something first.'

'Go on, I'm listening,' she sighed.

He cleared his throat, then explained what he had found in the archive room.

'So that's where you've been? I was wondering what had taken you so long.'

'I can explain…'

'Don't bother,' Cadema exhaled loudly. 'We'll talk about it when you come in. Anyway, about the trunk, what do you expect me to do about it?' She sounded sceptical.

'Well, it's from 1888. And who knows, there's may be something tangible there that'll help to solve those murders?' Marriott's voice had reached fever pitch now, almost manic, his eyes bulging.

Cadema held the phone away from her ear, and went quiet – DI Paul Evans had entered her office.

'Look, Sergeant, we haven't got time for cold cases, just leave it. Anyway, we'll discuss it when you come in. Do you understand?' she said, then gestured to Evans to take a seat.

'Yes, Ma'am, see you soon,' said Marriott, wishing he hadn't mentioned the trunk, especially over the telephone.

***

'What's that all about, Ma'am?' asked Evans. 'I'd hate to miss anything important especially if it relates to one of my subordinates. So what's Marriott been up to this time?' He frowned and edged his chair forward, leaned back and sprawled his legs under her desk.

'Nothing really, only some file from way back. It's not significant to our investigations. Anyway he'll soon be here. So what did you want me for?'

'Just came in to hand you this file you asked for on the Belton case. And to tell you I'm out for the rest of the day, and will see you tomorrow.'

'Thanks, Paul.' She gave a coy smile as she took the file from Evans. Then tossed her hair from her shoulder.

Evans had made the most important alterations – the ones that would have implicated him in the injustice he had created. As he began to leave, he frowned, and turned to speak to Cadema again.

'Before I go, Ma'am, what did you mean by "Only some file from way back"? I hope Marriott isn't going behind my back and jumping rank again? He knows he has to go through the proper channels.'

'Look, Paul, you have enough to do as it is without getting involved in anything else. You just get on with your own work and I'll get on with mine. As for Marriott, he's only doing what I've asked him to do,' she lied. Evans looked at her with the usual contempt in his eyes, as he left her office.

Glancing at Marriott as they passed on the stairs, DI Evans deliberately pushed his shoulder against the sergeant's arm and mouthed something to him. Marriott staggered, grabbed at the handrail, and then sat on the stair with his head lowered. Dazed but standing again, he watched as Evans disappeared from the building. Then he gingerly climbed the remaining stairs and entered Cadema's office.

'At ease, Sergeant, take a seat and tell me what you've been up to.' Cadema smiled as he sat, a little uneasily, on the chair in front of her. 'Are you all right?' She frowned and leant forward.

'I'm okay, Ma'am, just a little trip up the stairs; nothing serious, I'll live,' he grimaced.

'That's okay then. But you look a little pale. Here take this.' She handed him a plastic beaker full of water she had poured from a bottle.

'Thanks, Ma'am.' Marriott's words struggled from his lips. Finishing his drink, he coughed and then shuffled in the chair.

Cadema sat upright again, her keen dark eyes waiting for his report. He knew she wouldn't be fooled into anything. So he was direct and succinct in explaining what he had discovered.

She leaned forward. The frown on her face slowly disappeared.

'Look, David.' Her voice was calm. 'It all sounds very interesting, and I can see how enthusiastic you are about it. But as I've already said, we don't deal with cold cases in this department. Nevertheless, once we've finished our current investigation, I'll see what I can do about the trunk.'

'But, Ma'am, what if someone else finds it, and takes over the investigation?'

'There isn't any investigation, so don't be melodramatic. Anyway, we could leave it for another hundred years and what will it matter; everyone involved is dead? And it wouldn't be in the public interest to waste money, would it? So let's get on with our current work.'

'Yes Ma'am, but can we keep it a secret, at least for the time being?'

'I should say no, especially when you lied about where you were going. But I realise your motive was genuine, so I'll say no more about it. But if I find out that you've gone behind my back again, you'll be in for disciplinary action. Do I make that clear?'

There was something in the way Cadema spoke to him, and the slight twinkle in her eyes, which gave Marriott the impression that she wasn't really serious. That she knew he wouldn't leave it alone. He guessed that she wouldn't have done either, when she was his age.

But things were different now; she had Chief Superintendent Norman Grimes, to answer to. Grimes had the reputation of being single-minded. He wouldn't tolerate deviations, not even with high profile cases, and certainly not with a woman in charge. If Grimes got wind of what he contemplated doing, he would discipline him and Cadema too.

Despite everything, Marriott was determined to continue with his own investigation of the murders from 1888 as soon as he could. He even thought of circumnavigating the police service and doing the investigation for a PhD which he had always wanted to do. And since he now lived alone, he had more time than ever to continue with his academic studies. But deep inside he still wanted to work with Superintendent Sharma. She would know what to do and how to do it. She had the right connections to open doors that would be closed to him. On the other hand, now he had a good subject to study, he remembered what his old Master, Professor Fentuss, had said to him when he went to collect his Master's Degree,

'Don't forget, David Marriott, you will always be welcome to do your PhD with us.' It was said as if it were an order. But he hadn't forgotten, and even though Fentuss had died recently, he knew his old university would be interested. And with a good research proposal, he would be accepted without any problems. He thought of the new title he would have, "Doctor Marriott", and smiled to himself.

***

Marriott sat at his computer screen and typed in "Ripper 1888". He watched as the search engine went ballistic. He turned it off. No, it was useless, potential PhD students had to use primary sources. That meant, police archives, court records, police and suspects statements, forensics, what little, if any, there would be during that time, and witnesses...

But where to start? He scratched his head. There were many more questions to consider. He leant back in his chair, stretched his aching back and began to recall the times, as a boy, when he had consumed every one of Sherlock Holmes cases. Then remembered the phrase, written by Sir Arthur Conan Doyle in *The Sign of Four*:

"When you have eliminated the impossible, what remains, however improvable, must be the truth." Marriott decided to apply this concept to his own investigations. And perhaps, who knows, he may find the truth.

Chapter 4

DI Paul Evans poured himself a drink of his favourite single malt and tried to forget the file he had given to Cadema. Pacing the floor, he picked up the two-day old *Times* newspaper, glanced at the headlines, and threw it back into the paper rack. Gulping his drink, he felt the muscles in his neck tighten. Then a sharp pain in his back made him think of the mythological burning arrow. He turned and picked up his notes on the Madeline Belton case. Skimming through the pages, he found the photograph of Bernard Franklin, then smiled at a job well done, despite having to fabricate some of the evidence to secure the conviction. He began to reflect on the case.

Bernard had denied having met Madeline Belton let alone given her a lift in his car. Evans knew he was lying, his sort always did. But there was no way Bernard could dispute the CCTV evidence which showed Madeline getting into the front seat of his car the night before her body was discovered. Neither was it a coincidence that Madeline happened to have Bernard's DNA on her skirt. Coincidences like that just don't happen. When he confronted Bernard with this, he reluctantly made some excuse about being with his girlfriend Sue, and having sex with her in the front seat of his car. Later, and without saying anything about it, Evans had, through his usual informants, found out that a prostitute called Sue, had disappeared. Bernard had grimaced when Evans told him this.

'No, I don't believe you. My Sue isn't like that. She's a nice girl and she loves me,' Bernard had pleaded. 'Just find her and talk to her, she'll vouch for me that evening. We just got carried away and had sex in my car. That must have been how the DNA got onto the passenger seat and onto Madeline's skirt when I gave her a lift later that evening. Just ask Sue, she'll tell you. Madeline was still alive when I dropped her off.'

Evans had listened to Bernard snivelling story more times than he could remember. But despite some preliminary searches, the elusive Sue could not be found. So there was no alibi for Bernard. And, as Evans had already decided that he was guilty, he called off the search for Sue, who was, to him, a figment of Bernard's imagination – contrived by a guilty mind.

Evans drained his glass as he slammed the photograph on the table, walked over to the sideboard and poured himself another drink. Pacing the room, he thought about the statements in the files.

In one of the files, Evans had said that he interviewed Sue, and that she denied seeing Bernard or having sex in his car. He signed her statement to this effect.

'Anyway,' Evans reasoned, 'who in their right mind would ever believe that Bernard would let Madeline out of his car? A predator is always a predator. Bernard didn't have an alibi, so he was guilty. DNA proved it – case closed.'

Yesterday he had retrieved the statement from the file he had found in the archives room and later watched the incriminating statement burn. He added another one which said that Sue could not be found. Then handed the file to Cadema. Now he was worried. What if Bernard hadn't committed the murder? If he had not, then who had?

There were no other suspects. And he didn't think Thomas had murdered her as the modus operandi was different. Madeline had been bludgeoned to death with a hammer and died soon afterwards. Whereas the others were felled, had their throats cut open, and then ejaculate left at the scene. There was no mutilation to Madeline's body, so there was no doubt in his mind; Bernard had murdered Madeline.

So why was Cadema reopening the case? What other evidence did she have? Was she keeping something from him? Perhaps the illusive Sue had turned up and decided to give Bernard an alibi? Or had someone else confessed to the murder? He had to find out.

Whatever the scenario, he knew he would have been disciplined, or even prosecuted, if Cadema discovered his false statement. Thank goodness, he had the forethought to destroy it – now she would never know.

Pleased with his actions, he managed to get the best night's sleep he had for ages. He was standing in the bathroom ready for his morning shower when Cadema telephoned and asked him go straight to her office the moment he arrived. He smiled, sang in the shower, dressed, and then headed for the police station.

***

'Please take a seat DI Evans,' said Cadema in a solemn, authoritative voice as she sat behind her desk accompanied by Chief Superintendent Norman Grimes. Her eyes focused on the two files on her desk. The buff-coloured file was the one Evans had given her the previous day. The other file was in a green folder.

'I expect you've read the file I gave you,' said Evans, sitting uncomfortably in a chair facing the two officers. 'Hope you are now satisfied that there's no reason to reopen the case, Ma'am.'

'As a matter of fact I have read it.' Cadema's voice was officious as she picked up the green file from the desk. 'Do you know what this is, DI Evans?' Her voice sounded accusing – the question rhetorical.

'No, Ma'am, but it's not the one I gave you.' Evans fidgeted – his face burning. His gaze met Grimes', whose grey eyes and face matched that of an executioner. Evans swallowed.

'I'll tell you what this green file contains,' said Cadema. 'It contains the initial file from the Belton case. The one I had copied before sending you to retrieve the file from the archive room. The buff-coloured file here, is the one you gave to me to read after you took it home with you,' Cadema spoke slowly with emphasis on every word. 'Do you understand what I am saying?'

'Yes, Ma'am, it's quite clear.'

'Good, so you do not have to say anything else now, but I am suspending you from duty, pending further enquiries. When we meet again you are advised to have a representative with you. You will receive a letter to this effect tomorrow. Please leave your warrant card on the desk as you leave.'

Cadema sat back in her chair as Evans shot a glance at her without saying anything. He coughed, stood up, and nodded to Norman Grimes.

'Thank you, Ma'am,' said Evans. Then, placing his warrant card on the desk, he turned and left the room.

Chapter 5

Cadema could not understand why DI Evans had difficulty in locating Sue (Bernard Franklin's supposed girlfriend), and why he had lied about interviewing her. Over two years later, her officers had no difficulty in tracing Susan Tilly through the usual police channels and informants. Now Susan was sitting in the police station wondering what the police wanted her for.

'It's Susan Tilly, isn't it?' said Cadema as she walked up to her. Susan nodded in confirmation – chewing her nicotine gum. 'Do come into my office and take a seat. Can I get you a cup of tea, Miss Tilly?' They both sat down in unison.

'Please call me Sue. So what's this all about? I've done nothing wrong, 'ave I?' She pulled at her highlighted blonde hair and snorted the phlegm at the back of her throat.

The makeup Sue wore reminded Cadema of photographs she had seen of Marylyn Monroe. The woman now sitting in front of her was no film star. Instead, her plump five foot three frame, and her poor oral hygiene, together with her faded yellow dress, gave the impression that Sue, and her clothes, had seen better days. However, as she watched her periodically tug at her short skirt and pull it over her knees, Cadema realised that there was at least some modesty in the girl.

'We are just following up some loose ends on a case of ours. How do you like your tea?'

'Two sugars and strong as it comes,' Sue shouted over her shoulder to DC Rosemary Clarke who was sitting near the door. Clarke nodded an acknowledgement as she left the room

'I'm not saying you've done anything wrong,' said Cadema, 'I just need to speak to you about Bernard Franklin. I understand you know him?'

'Node him, I did. But I haven't clapped eyes on him for years now. Not since I heard he'd been banged up for that murder,' she snorted. Cadema handed her a tissue. 'Thanks.'

'It's the murder of Madeline Belton I want to talk to you about.'

'I never 'ad anything to do with that,' Sue shuffled in the chair and tugged at her skirt again.

'Don't worry, you're not a suspect. All I want to find out is whether you were with Bernard Franklin on the evening of the fourteenth of September, that year?'

'Excuse me; I can 'ardly remember what I was doing last week, let alone then.'

'I know it may be difficult. But please try if you can.' Cadema felt she was wasting her time especially as she expected Sue would not be a person to keep a diary. But she was used to handling people like Sue, and was careful not to put words into her mouth.

'Do you mind if I tape our conversation, just for the records,' she asked calmly.

'No, that's okay.' Sue shrugged but kept her head low, avoiding eye contact. 'Christ, I'm busting for a ciggie, this gum's no good, soon loses its flavour?' Sue spat the gum into the paper tissue she took from the desk, put it into her handbag, and then took out a packet of cigarettes.

'Sorry, it's a non-smoking area,' Cadema retorted. Sue tutted, raised her eyebrows, and replaced the packet into her handbag. 'Just try and see what you can remember.' Cadema needed to think of something that would trigger Sue's memory. But her mind was blank.

'What day did you say it was?'

'Friday the fourteenth of September, when we had all those floods up north. The next morning Madeline's body was found on Putney Heath. I think it may have been your birthday.'

'Oh, I used to tell all my clients that, especially when I wanted a drink. But Bernie didn't d…' Sue looked shocked at her own words and stopped speaking.

'What were you going to say, Sue? Don't worry you're not in any trouble yet. But you may be if you withhold anything that may be useful to the case.'

'All right. Yes I do remember reading about the murder. And I may have been with Bernard, but he weren't my boyfriend. We just met and we did it in his car. Once a month I recall.'

'And September the fourteenth? Did you see him then?'

'I could have, but I'm not sure.' Sue looked at the ceiling. 'Hang on a minute – there was something familiar about that date. Nothin' you've said mind. But it does ring a bell. Ah, yes.' She sat thinking.

'Go on, Sue, I'm listening.'

'Not sure now but it was probably the night that girl was murdered. I seed him then. Five o'clock as usual. We had sex in his car. Yes, now I come to think of it, it was definitely that date. It was the day my little-un, Mary, came down with the measles. Right sick she were. But I couldn't let me client down – especially Bernie. So I left her with Josie, a friend. Just for a couple of hours mind. Later that night I took her to A and E – touch and go it were. Thank goodness she recovered. Now she's as bright as a button. But you can't be too careful with kids, they go up and down quickly, don't they?'

'I suppose they do.' Cadema shook her head. 'There's just one other thing. When Bernard was arrested and tried for the murder, why didn't you come forward to give him an alibi?'

'I didn't know he had been arrested. You see I was with Mary. When she came out of hospital I went back to me Mam's. She took sick and died. It were the drink, the doctor said, what did it. I stayed at her place to sort things out. I'm still there but never have time to read the papers, and hardly watch TV. So I didn't know until your lot showed up and asked me to come here.'

'So you can definitely say, without a doubt, that you had sex in Bernard's car that evening. But that you were not actually with him at the time when Madeline was murdered?'

'That's what I said, didn't I?' Sue replied as she thanked DC Clarke for the tea. 'What's goanna to happen now?'

'If you're sure that's what happened then we will take a statement for you to sign. Are you happy with that?' asked Cadema.

'Suppose so. I won't get into trouble for my little-un, will I?'

'No, especially since it's a long time ago.'

'Don't suppose there's any reward is there?' She sipped at her tea.

'No, sorry. But you will be rewarded knowing that, if Bernard turns out to be innocent, he will be released.'

'Is that it then? I thought at least I'd get something see'in as I've helped you out. I suppose Bernard would have given me something, especially as I've helped to get him off. But I don't want him to find out where I am,' Sue snivelled, and then smiled. Later that day, she signed the statement.

'Thank you, I'll be in touch if I need to speak to you again.'

'If you do, then make it less obvious next time, it upsets me new neighbours when you lot shows up,' said Susan Tilly as she left the room with DC Clarke.

Cadema did not know why she nodded as Sue left, but for some reason she felt sorry for her. She was probably a nice-looking girl once, and had plans for her future. She reasoned that missed opportunities were to blame for her previous situation which had contributed to her looking ten years older than her twenty-five years. Now she had inherited some money, and her mother's old house, she had a new life.

Although Cadema knew Susan Tilly had had sex with Bernard in his car, it didn't mean that Bernard wasn't Madeline's killer. However, it could explain why Madeline's skirt had a small amount of Bernard's ejaculate on it; confirmed by DNA analysis.

Cadema's report on Susan Tilly's statement had the effect she expected. And, together with her report that DI Evans had written a false statement in the original police documents on the Belton case, it meant that Bernard Franklin was released from prison.

***

Given a safe house to protect him from people who believed he was guilty, Bernard began to look for Sue. After several fruitless searches, he realised that he would never find her. Now he had a plan, and after shopping for everything he needed, he returned to his safe house. Mumbling to himself, he filled his rucksack with the items he had bought, and then set off for the common.

Chapter 6

Detective Inspector James Pratt will never forget the event which occurred on his way to work on his first morning in a new job. Wanting to be early to impress Superintendent Sharma, he took the shortcut through the Hawkesbury housing estate. It turned out to be the most traumatic decision he had made since he joined the police service twelve years ago.

The woman just landed on the bonnet of his car, smashing the windscreen, and smashing her skull simultaneously. He didn't even have time to swerve, the body just landed there.

'She fell from that third floor window,' someone pointed and shouted.

Leaving the local police to deal with the incident, and the gathering crowd, DI Pratt headed for the station nearly two hours late. On reaching Cadema's office, he had managed to calm himself down and do up the buttons on his jacket.

'Sorry, Ma'am. Just bumped into something on my way here. You know how it is.'

'No, I don't know, but I've just heard about that poor young woman. Apparently, she was dead before she left the balcony. Well at least that's the preliminary findings. So don't treat anything like that as a joke again, and never on my team or you will be out. Is that understood? We treat all victims with respect here, and don't forget it,' said Cadema with anger in her dark eyes.

DI Pratt stood mesmerised for a moment. Had he heard correctly? Did she have the audacity to reprimand *him*? Or had he misinterpreted what she had said? Now he was standing to attention.

Cadema refused to ask him to sit. And as he stood there, with that indifferent look on his face, she had difficulty in restraining the urge to tell him to go back to his previous job. But she couldn't afford to lose such an experienced officer, and especially since she had pleaded with Andrew Long, Deputy Commissioner, to have him on her team which was depleted because of Evans. Besides Pratt had a good reputation for his tenacity, his hard work and most of all his probity, although a little blunt at times.

Now she had doubts about the man who was standing in front of her. He was too calm, too indifferent. His body too small for the size of his head and the paunch he carried, plus his greying blond hair, made him look at least ten years older than his thirty-five years.

'Sorry, Ma'am.' Pratt's voice interrupted her thoughts. 'It's just my way of coping with things. It won't happen again.'

'That's not the best coping strategy, so I think that some counselling would be appropriate for you,' said Cadema; her voice mellowing. 'Do sit down.'

'Thanks, Ma'am.' Pratt gingerly lowered himself into the chair. 'Just a bit of whiplash – nothing serious.' He laughed, and then lowered his head.

'Sorry to hear that, hopefully it's nothing too serious. Still you should get it checked over.'

Pratt grunted an affirmation. From today he would keep his head down and get on with the work. After all, he just wanted to do a good job, and then hopefully he would be able to apply for the next DCI post when one was available.

For now, Cadema decided to keep a close watch on Pratt, after all she didn't want a repeat of DI Paul Evans' behaviour.

***

Waiting noisily in the briefing room, the officers went quiet as Cadema entered, slammed a box file on the desk, and sat down.

'I know we're a bit sparse of officers now that DI Evans in no longer here, but I'm sure we can manage the workload.' She scanned the faces, and offering a smile she turned towards Joanna Johns. 'I would like to congratulate DI Johns on her new post as DCI.'

'Thank you, Ma'am, it's a pleasure to be back on the team,' said Johns as the rest of the team gave a quiet clap.

'Also joining us is Detective Inspector James Pratt. Poached from B-division and with a wealth of experience behind him. Welcome to the team.' Cadema nodded as Pratt nonchalantly brushed his hair from his forehead, and mouthed a 'thank you'.

'Now the introductions are over, I'm going to identify the work that needs to be done to find Madeline Belton's killer. This time we'll put a water tight case together for the CPS (Crown Prosecution Service). I don't want any mistakes, or omissions. All evidence and documentation is to be checked by two officers, one of which must be a rank above inspector. All this must then be signed by both officers before it's entered into HOLMES-2 (Home Office Large Major Enquiry System).' The team shuffled their feet as Cadema spoke. 'I'm not accusing anyone here of being involved with what happened before. But if you follow these procedures – everything should be acceptable. It will no doubt delay the investigation, but the quality of your work must be exemplary.' She turned to DCI Christine Ryan. 'DCI Ryan will not be with us much longer due to her pending promotion to superintendent, on which I congratulate her.'

'Here, here,' said the team.

'She is now going to remind you of the Madeline Belton case and then explain where we are now with the investigation.'

Ryan stood up, stretched her lean muscular body, and thanked Cadema.

'Since Bernard Franklin's release, all the files relating to the murders have been thoroughly examined. They include the murder of Jane Gaunt, Sophie Millburn, Francis Cole and Natalie Taylor. The evidence and documentation of these are sound. And as you know, Thomas, alias Philippa Gardner, was the perpetrator of these four crimes and will probably never be released from Broadmoor. That leaves victim five; Madeline Belton case, and it looks as if we are back to square one with this.' A couple of grunts were heard from the second row. 'Now then, don't be despondent, we'll just need to scrutinise every detail of the case again as we may have overlooked some vital evidence.' Ryan searched the faces of her audience. DC Galke raised his hand.

'I was just wondering, Ma'am. As there haven't been any similar murders since Bernard Franklin was convicted. Doesn't that mean he could still be guilty, but has now been released due to the lack of evidence?'

'That's a point we've considered. But no, due to further evidence he's been totally exonerated. However, we must also remember that there haven't been any multiple murders of women since Thomas was detained. But if further evidence links Thomas to the Belton case, he would be a suspect despite the different MO used on the first four victims.' The pitch of Ryan's voice was now raised. Her green eyes flashed as DS Marriott raised his hand.

'It appears to me that Thomas could have murdered Madeline, but some of us were so focused on Bernard that it was overlooked. Otherwise it means that someone else has waited a very long, and may kill again at any moment.'

'There is some logic there,' interjected Cadema. 'But it could have been a one off opportunistic murder, or even someone she knew. And that's where our second line of investigation is going to take us. So let's get on with the work and see what we can find.' She opened the box file and took out her notes, her ten-point plan, and a memory stick.

Why is it so important to do a ten-point plan? she thought. Why not eight or twelve? She did not have an answer. But reasoned that Chief Superintendent Jim Logan used this method in all his cases. And since his death at the hands of the sniper, and her subsequent promotion, she always used his method as it seemed to work for her, especially when she added the rationale for each activity. She looked at her team and coughed.

'As we are about to reinvestigate all the aspects of the Belton case, we need to revisit the case in detail so that we all start with the same knowledge.' Cadema nodded to Marriott to insert the memory stick into the computer. A couple of seconds later, her ten-point plan flashed onto the screen behind her. 'Good, so let's start shall we? No questions until I ask for them, or until I have completed the presentation.' She looked at her notes then to the audience.

'Madeline was nineteen years old when she decided to hitchhike to her grandmother's house. The night in question, the fourteenth of September, was very wet. We know she accepted a lift in Common Road from Bernard Franklin. But for some reason she asked him to drop her off before they had gone very far. He denies seeing her again.

'Madeline's body was discovered the next morning on Putney Heath. She had been hit over the head with a blunt instrument, probably an axe, which killed her. No ejaculate was found on or near her abdomen or genitalia, as it had been with the other victims. No sexual assault had taken place. When her clothes were examined in the laboratory, a small amount of white substance was found on the outside of her skirt. This was eventually identified as semen belonging to Bernard Franklin. And as you know he was subsequently arrested, charged and sentenced. Now I've finished this part, are there any questions before I move on?'

'I know this is going over old grounds. But didn't anyone think it was odd that the semen was on the outside of her skirt?' DI Pratt asked.

'Subsequently, yes, but at the time, no. We now know that the skirt was contaminated by the semen left on the car's seat after Bernard had sex with Sue. When Bernard gave Madeline a lift, she sat on the spot where the sample was. Does this answer your question?'

'Yes, Ma'am, and it just goes to show that we can all come to wrong conclusions.' Pratt gave a sardonic grin.

'You are right of course, but let's get on with my ten-point plan of actions. And as usual, please keep your questions or comments until I've finished.' The team nodded in unison.

'These are the areas we should investigate further.

1. Examine all the CCTV from the archives:

There could be something we've overlooked, or failed to notice before. So let's see what we can find this time.

2. Identify the witnesses, no matter how vague they seemed to be at the time, re-interview them again.

They may remember something that didn't appear important at the time.

3. Draw up a new list of suspects, add these to the existing list.

That includes everyone identified on the CCTV footage. It also includes relatives, friends and Thomas/Philippa Gardner.'

'But, Ma'am, Thomas' MO was so very different,' Marriott protested.

'I know, but he could still be involved. Don't forget that Madeline Belton had auburn hair, the same as Thomas' victims,' said Cadema, who then continued with her presentation.

4. Re-check all alibis.

5. Check on Madeline's relatives and acquaintances again. Have we missed anyone out? Check their alibis too.

As you know, we normally look at the immediate family first as many perpetrators come from within the family. We may not have scrutinised them as we should have done at the time, but we certainly will now.

6. Find the real reason why she was in the area at the time.

This is linked to number five above. She could have been running away from home; away from someone else, maybe?

7. Re-examine Madeline's clothing.

There may have been other fibres, or something that had been overlooked. I know how pedantic and thorough Doctor Lilly is in her work. And that Bagley did most of the forensics at the time, but something could have been missed. Now that Bagley had left the department, and a new person, Wilhelmina Cox, has just joined that team, something may be discovered.

8. Re-interview Bernard Franklin.

'But, Ma'am, I thought you'd finished with him now he's out of prison,' Marriott interrupted.

'I have interviewed him a couple of times since then. He doesn't remember seeing anything in the area. But we must jog his memory further. He was in the vicinity. He must have seen something, a car perhaps. Or someone loitering or acting suspiciously.' Cadema scratched her head and took a sip of cold coffee. 'So let's get on.'

9. Revisit the DNA analysis, there may have been something that was overlooked.

Doctor Lilly can follow that up.

10. *Re-enact the crime.*

'Although it's been well over two years since the crime, it may jog someone's memory.

'So there you have it. As you can see we have a lot to consider so let's not waste any more time. I'll leave the allocation of actions to the office manager, John Kasson. DCI Ryan will take the lead for the time being, DCI Johns will assist.'

Cadema scooped up the papers in front of her and left the room.

As she walked along the corridor, she thought about all the cutbacks that had taken place recently. The suspension of Paul Evans, the inevitable loss of Christine Ryan when she is posted elsewhere. And then there was DCI Joanna Johns, although she had been on her team before, and knew the case, she was a novice in her new role and needed to be supervised, at least while Ryan was still there. Now there's DI James Pratt. He had a similar reputation to Evans; she would have to watch him. The only stability was DS David Marriott, and she would no doubt lose him when he passed his pending promotion board. But at least Marriott would have time to investigate the trunk from the archives, that is, if he manages to procure funding.

That only left her with DCs Avrum Galke, and Richard Barry, plus Rosemary Clarke who was nearing the end of her current attachment. With all this going on, she would be left with fifty percent fewer officers then before. How was anyone supposed to solve crimes with no real team? They called it "efficiency improvement" but it was cuts, pure and simple. Not that she would admit it to the lower ranks. No, she had no choice but to support the current management strategy, whether she believed in it or not.

Reaching her office, Cadema sat in her chair and stared blankly at the list that would hopefully help her to find the killer. She was just about to reach for the telephone, when it rang. Picking it up she had difficulty in understanding what Chief Superintendent Norman Grimes was saying. Then, realising the urgency of his words she replaced the receiver and wiped a tear from her cheek. That's all I need, she thought to herself.

Chapter 7

Bernard Franklin's body had been cut down from the tree by the time Cadema arrived at the scene. Having discussed the situation with two of her officers, she left Doctor Lilly to continue her work and headed back to the police station. On her way there, she thought about the questions that the press would ask. They would need answers. Answers she could not give at this moment. Stepping out of the car, the cameras and microphone were at the ready.

'Yes of course I've heard the news,' said Cadema as she pushed past the group. 'No comment.' Under her breath she cursed them for jumping to conclusions. No, she had not inferred that Bernard Franklin was guilty of murder. Neither did she believe, what the newspapers inferred, that he must have been the accomplice in Madeline Belton's murder. Pushing passed the group, she entered the building and headed for Grimes' office.

'This is a real bloody mess.' Grimes snarled without any form of a greeting as Cadema entered his office. 'What I want to know is how you're going to handle this, and especially Bernard's family? What are you going to tell them?' he continued. 'Sit down will you? And stop that snivelling, you look a mess.' He looked at her with contempt, indifferent to how distraught she was. Women officers, regardless of rank, were an inconvenience to him.

Cadema remained standing erect – her eyes dry.

'I've already spoken to his sister. She is upset of course, and blames us for not giving him any support. But after I told her he had refused any help she calmed down. Now she's going to stay with her elderly mother. Her father died just over a year ago.'

'Well at least you've got something right. What about Bernard? Did he leave a note or indicate that he might top himself?'

'There was no indication. We've searched the safe house he was staying in. And no, there wasn't a suicide note.' Cadema remained standing, her face in contempt of the person sitting there. 'All we have are the things he left in his room. DC Galke and DC Clarke are examining these now. But I doubt if they'll find anything useful, or helpful to our enquiries. He was such a private man and of course obsessed with finding Sue. He must have gone over the edge when he couldn't find her. Doctor Lilly is getting ready to do the post mortem as we speak.'

'Well just let me know as soon as you've finished. I don't want to wait around forever on this one. Do you think he had something to do with the murder after all?'

'No, Sir. But...' Cadema bit her lip not knowing whether to tell him or not.

'But what...? Come on, woman, you know I must have everything. And I mean everything.' He raised his voice as he sat upright – his cheeks flushed. Cadema frowned believing that he would surely have a stroke. She took a seat and tried to relax in the chair, hoping that Grimes would follow her stance.

'I was just going to say – that when I asked Bernard if he had seen another car when he dropped Madeline off, he said he hadn't. But I believe he did see something but was reluctant to say so.'

'When did you question him?'

'Three days ago.'

'What the hell were you playing at?' He jumped from his seat. 'You should have seen him the next day. I know I wouldn't have even let him out of my sight, I can tell you. And when I was the SIO, if I suspected something, I certainly wouldn't have waited three days. You'd better have a good reason why you didn't see him earlier.' His face had now contorted so much that she thought he must be in pain. She refused to acknowledge it. Instead, she looked straight at his wire-faced features and his cold grey eyes; her voice calm and in control.

'All Bernard was interested in was finding Sue, whom he believed was his girlfriend.'

'But you interviewed Sue. She gave him an alibi, so why didn't you tell him where to find her. Then he may have cooperated better.'

'Sue's whereabouts were confidential. She didn't want to see him; he was just one of her clients, not her boyfriend. And she doesn't even live in that area now, and is no longer a prostitute.'

'I know all that, but you could have let it slip. Then he would still be alive. I hold you responsible for his death; you won't get away with this lightly.' Grimes spat out his words as he towered over Cadema.

'Excuse me, Sir, but I prefer to keep to the rules. And it's sheer speculation to think that he killed himself on my behalf. I know he was distressed, and refused counselling. He hadn't slept well since he left prison, he felt intimidated and still thought he was being accused…'

'That's a load of the old proverbial if you ask me. But nevertheless, you should have kept a close eye on him, and seen him the next day. Let that be a lesson to you.'

'Thank you, Sir, I'll keep you informed.' Cadema left his office with her head high. She had no intention of being bullied or intimidated by him, and hoped he understood this. Besides, he did not have all the information on the case as she had. Not that she deliberately held information from him; it was just that, with his obnoxious attitude towards her, she did not have the opportunity to tell him. Now Grimes would have to wait for the report she had from Galke and Clarke about the blind spots they had found on the CCTVs.

As she reached her office she decided to ask the two officers to check how many vehicles there were in the area at the time. And to make a note of how many disappeared, never to be seen again, and how many were seen in the area more than once on the night in question. And especially note if there were any cars travelling slower than the speed limit. They were to report back directly to her and no one else.

Sitting at her desk she thought of DI Paul Evans. And although she never fully trusted him in the past, he was a good officer in many ways. And she could certainly trust his tenacity to get on with the job and not to leave anything out. Since his suspension and pending conviction for perverting the course of justice, she had found other anomalies in the evidence he had accumulated on the Common Murders. Yes, Evans definitely had much to answer for especially with all the extra work he had caused.

Now she needed to put things right. Her officers were all busy, so she decided to take some of the Common Murder files home to examine them in more detail, without the usual distractions. Somewhere in there, she hoped to find a connection between the four murders and the murder of Madeline Belton. After all they all occurred in the same area of London.

Sitting at home, Cadema estimated that it would take her at least six months to go through all the files. There wasn't six months. She had to find the perpetrator before he killed again.

It was ten o'clock on Monday evening when Cadema opened the first file. Within minutes her eye lids began to close. She jumped with a start as two pages fell to the floor.

'That's it, no more tonight.' She reprimanded herself, yawned, then picked up the pages and replaced them in the file. The same scenario was repeated each evening, until Friday when she opened another file before going to bed. As she opened it she had that de'-ja' vu feeling. Something drew her attention to the middle of the file; the alibi section. Her fingers flipped over the pages. They came to the end of the section; a page was out of place. There it was. Everyone had overlooked it. The obvious. Thomas did not have an alibi for the night of Madeline's murder. She read it again. Turning the pages, there was no mention of his alibi. Did he have one but it had not been recorded? Had it been mis-filed? 'Paul again,' she tutted. But it was not like him to leave something out, especially something that important. No he was far too keen on making sure the evidence secured a conviction. So why it had been overlooked she did not know. But now, looking at the file, she realised, although Thomas was never a suspect in the Belton case, he would go to the top of her list as a suspect now.

Chapter 8

Cadema heard the telephone ring just as she opened her office door. The voice of DC Galke sounded so excited that she had difficulty in deciphering what he was saying.

'Just calm down, take a deep breath and talk slowly.'

'Sorry, Ma'am.' He paused and then took a deep breath. 'Well, Ma'am, we've found something, a car. We've both seen it three times on the night of Madeline's murder.'

'So what did you actually see, Galke?' She heard him inhale again, and imagined him swallowing as she waited for him to reply.

'A silver car, we've had the image enlarged. We can't quite see the registration but it begins with H. Ma'am.' He smiled at DC Clarke, who was standing next to him nodding as he spoke.

'Don't forget to tell her it's not a personal registration,' whispered Clarke, just loud enough for Cadema to hear.

'It's not...'

'I heard.'

'The main significant point to mention,' continued Galke, 'is this same car was driven by, what looks like a man in the first two videos, but looks like a woman is driving it in the last one.'

Cadema took a deep breath. 'Are you are both sure of this?'

'Quite sure, Ma'am, but of course there weren't any CCTV cameras near to where Franklin said he dropped Madeline off or where she could have been picked up. So we can't be sure if the person driving the car actually gave her a lift.'

Once Cadema heard the news she was sure that the only person who could have been driving the car was Thomas. He did not have an alibi, and he used several disguises, sometimes dressed as a man and sometimes as a woman, so it could have been him.

'No, we can't be totally sure that he gave her a lift,' said Cadema. 'But it's a high probability that he did. He may have been dressed as a man that night, seen Bernard drop her off, then changed to look like a woman. Madeline would have been more inclined to accept a lift if she thought it was a woman, especially as she had just been dropped off by Bernard Franklin. So thank you both for the work you've done on this.'

'Wait a minute, Ma'am, as we've been talking, DC Clarke has identified the reg and its current owner. I'll send you the details.'

**

With the details of the car's current owner in her hand, and its previous owner being Thomas, Cadema decided to visit Thomas in Broadmoor. Telephoning first, she was informed that he was currently quite lucid. She needed him to remain so, at least until she could speak to him. So, hopefully he would not retreat into that hollow of his mind where no one could reach him, not even his psychiatrist. Where he would sit, trance-like, his face contorted, then simultaneously smiling and frowning – his eyes oscillating – as if he were experiencing some inner turmoil. That is, until he would shout for them to stop, then lapse into a deep sleep for hours; exhausted.

No, it would be impossible to interview him encapsulated in his own world. But with all the circumstantial evidence – Cadema had to try, even if it were only to eliminate him.

Two hours later Cadema was sitting in an interview room in Broadmoor with DCI Johns, waiting for Thomas. In the distance, she heard the clatter of keys and the grating of metal doors opening. Feet shuffling along the corridor, then the door opposite to where she was sitting opened. In the recess she saw Thomas, shielded on both sides by two rounded figures as if they were guarding him from some unseen mob. Silhouetted by the light from the corridor, so she could not see their features. But after introducing themselves as Richard Kent and Mary Mackintosh, they guided Thomas to a chair.

Introductions over, Cadema sat upright in her chair and deliberately stared into Thomas' eyes as if she were searching for some recognition that there was someone there. But she knew, by the vacant faraway look on his face, that she would be wasting her time trying to talk to him. She confirmed this when she asked him how he was. There was no answer, only his pinpoint pupils and his sardonic grin, gave her any assurance that he was still alive.

'Sorry, I think we had better go.' Cadema's chair scraped the tiled floor as she stood. 'We'll come back tomorrow and see if things have improved.'

Richard and Mary nodded and said they were sorry but before they came to the room Thomas had been quite talkative. Cadema nodded in disappointment, but as she turned to leave she heard the unmistakable high pitched voice of Thomas, as a female.

'Thomas will talk to you now,' the voice said. 'Won't you Thomas?' The head nodded like a schoolchild who was being reprimanded by his teacher. 'Don't be rude, answer the question.' The head nodded again. Thomas smiled, flashed his eyes at Cadema, and sat back in the chair.

'Just call him Thomas. That's what he likes to be called. He doesn't want to be associated with any of us,' a second voice spoke in a whisper.

'Yes I will call him Thomas, but who are you? Are you Philippa Gardner?' asked Cadema with some hesitation, not being quite sure whether she had said the wrong thing. The voice began to answer.

'Don't be so impertinent. I wouldn't be seen dead with the likes of Thomas. He's too wayward, too much of a maverick; too difficult to control. He never listened; if he had he wouldn't be in this mess. And he won't speak about it, the other murder I mean. He thinks if he does he won't have anything to gloat over. But I've told him many times he'll feel better if he does.'

'There you are see, we are all on your side,' the first voice said. By this time Cadema and Johns were sitting in silence, facing Thomas. 'So tell them, Thomas, it's all over now. Do as we say.' The voice was almost shouting now. Thomas put his hands to his ears and began to rock backwards and forwards. The voiced stopped. Thomas resumed his previous position; the grin returned.

'What were you going to say, Thomas?' Cadema asked. But there was no reply. The two warders stood up, mouthed they were sorry and left the room with Thomas in their charge.

***

'Yes Ma'am, we've found the car. Forensics has it now. But with the condition it's in, I doubt they'll find anything useful,' DC Clarke said over the telephone.

'Why, what's the problem?' Cadema hoped it was not burned out, like so many cars, to destroy DNA.

'It's been crushed. I don't mean in an accident, but really crushed, as in a crusher. It's even difficult to tell the make of the car. Apparently, it was written off in an accident, and due to its age, it was crushed. It's waiting to go to be smelted down along with all the other cars there. I've asked the manger to hold onto it for us.'

When Cadema heard the news she doubted if it would be of any use. But hoped the forensic team would find something, especially as it was only recently crushed. Even if there was just a remote chance of finding some of Madeline's DNA there, at least it would show she had been in Thomas' car. No one else had had the car since it was bought by its current owner. So there was a slim chance... She lifted the phone and asked Johns to come to her office.

Briefing Johns about the car she asked her to take DC Clarke and interview Dora Miller, the last owner.

'Just make sure you ask her if she noticed anything unusual about the car or if there was anything left inside.'

'I've already thought of that, Ma'am. So I don't really need reminding.' Johns sounded a little annoyed. And I will make sure that Dora Miller doesn't feel as if she is being accused of anything.'

'That's good, you're learning my methods.' Cadema sounded patronising.

'No need, Ma'am, they've always been my methods too.' She smiled.

***

As Johns stood on the threshold of number 64 The Beacon, the blue paintwork gave the impression that the occupier had long given up on the DIY, and probably could not afford a painter. She lifted the rusted head of a Labrador dog and tapped it against its metal counterpart hoping the knocker would not disintegrate. She turned her head to listen, nothing. She knocked again. DC Clarke shuffled her feet in the light covering of snow and asked if she should go around the back. But, before Johns had time to answer, the door slowly opened and a woman in her late seventies stood in the doorway.

Dora Miller stood just over five feet tall, and wearing a yellow faded dirty jumper with two distinct holes in the upper sleeve. Her brown knitted skirt resembled the streaks in the threadbare carpet she was standing on. Standing upright; her alert eyes looked past the visitors as she moved her head from side to side.

'Can't be too careful these days. Knock my door all day they do. Now how can I help you?' Dora said as she gestured for them to enter after careful examination of their identification cards. Once the door was closed they followed her slender frame as she shuffled along the carpet to the living room.

'It's about the car you brought. Do you remember it.'

'I may be a lot older than you, but I can assure you that my faculties are as sharp as yours. So don't patronise me.'

'Sorry but...'

'Oh don't be. Just be seated and I'll get you both some tea.'

'We haven't come for tea; we just need to talk to you about...'

'Nonsense, I always serve tea when visitors come. So your questions will have to wait until I'm ready. It's only right you know.'

The two officers conformed to her request, sat on the edge of the couch and looked around the room.

Although it was daylight outside, the room was dark and smelled damp. The gas fire gave off some heat but other than that the room was as cold as a mausoleum. Somewhere in another room a clock struck the quarter hour. Johns felt as if she had gone back in time to her grandmother's house. Except that was clean, airy and light. But the smells were the same, of cabbage, of roast meat, and of course bleach.

'Here we are.' Dora's frail voice broke the silence as she wheeled a serving trolley into the room – cups and saucers rattling. 'This was my mother's best china. The house belonged to her too. And if she came back today, she wouldn't see any change since she left it twenty years ago. Milk and sugar?'

'Mrs Miller…'

'Oh no, don't call me that. It's Miss. Always has been and always will be. No nonsense mind, my students never called me anything else, that is to my face. What they called me behind my back, I don't care.' Dora began to pour the tea and then asked how they liked it.

Johns coughed. 'Sorry, Miss Miller. It's very kind of you of course. But neither of us take sugar, only milk please. But I must ask you…'

'In good time, let us drink our tea first. And do have a biscuit. I used to make cake, but as I have very few visitors these days, the cake used to end up as bird food. But fat birds cannot get away from the cats quickly enough. So now I stick to biscuits and do not feed the birds.'

Johns took a gulp of tea. As soon as she had finished she stood up and moved towards the window. In the garden she noticed the dilapidated shed and fence. Propped up against the fence was a small axe but there was no sign of any work that was taking place. She turned and faced Dora.

'Miss Miller, when you bought the car did you find anything in it? Anything at all? Please just think.'

Dora took the last sip of tea from her cup, placed it slowly on the trolley, and stood up facing Johns.

'Oh, so you have noticed it then; the axe I mean? That was all I found in there and that was by accident. It was tucked in under a piece of carpet in the boot. The carpet was dirty so I threw it away, but I kept the axe and put it where it is now. After all if I bought the car with it in, it officially belongs to me, doesn't it?'

'In theory yes, but we are investigating a serious matter, so I'm afraid it may be the evidence we've been looking for. Therefore I will have to take it away for analysis. Of course when we've finished with it, it will be returned to you.' Johns calm and assertive voice halted any reprisals from Dora.

'Oh, please take it and keep it if you want. It is no use to me.'

'And where did you throw the carpet?'

'You don't have to sound as if I've committed a murder or something. But I did not actually throw it away. I used it under the bushes in the garden to stop the weeds from growing. It's over there.' She pointed. 'And I can see from the expression on your face that you are going to ask for that too. Am I right?

'Sorry, but yes you are.'

'There you see, well you can have it. Help yourself when you're ready.' She smiled. 'But do come back and have tea with me again. Then you can let me know if my evidence was any use to you or not.' Dora winked.

Thanking her for the tea, the officers went into the back garden, donned latex gloves and retrieved the carpet and the axe. Placing the items into the evidence bags, they turned and waved to Dora.

***

After climbing the stairs to her office, Cadema could see Marriott waiting by her door, waving a piece of paper.

'I thought you would like to know first, Ma'am,' said Marriott with a smile. 'My application for procurement of funds to investigate the trunk from the archives, has been accepted.'

'That's great news. At least your research and hard work on that has paid off. And I knew, when I read your report, that you had a strong case.' Cadema said as she opened her door and gestured to him to enter.

'As you can imagine, Ma'am, I'd like to start on the investigation as soon as possible.'

'I gathered that, but you will have to wait a little longer. That is until the Belton case has been solved.'

'How long do you think that will be?' Marriott frowned as he took a seat.

'If all goes to plan, I think we will be able to solve the case by the end of this month. Except for all the paperwork of course. But the main investigation should be completed by then. I'll let you have some time to prepare for your presentation to the team as soon as I can.

'Thank you, Ma'am, that's great. It shouldn't take me too long to do that since most of the work has been done. Just needs to be more succinct.'

As Marriott left, Cadema wondered what Grimes would say about this. Had she gone too far this time?

Chapter 9

Cadema could hardly believe what DCI Johns had told her. How fortunate it was that Miss Miller had kept the axe and the carpet she had found in Thomas' car, and not thrown them away. She was not interested in why she had done this only that it was fortuitous that she had. If forensics could now find Madeline Belton's DNA on these items, that would be the tangible evidence she needed.

After speaking to Julia Lilly, the pathologist, on the telephone, Cadema emphasized the need for urgency. Julia said she would do her best, but warned that, as it had been exposed to the elements, it may be difficult.

The call ended and Cadema sat back in her chair, with her arms raised behind her head. She wanted to tell Grimes, but also wanted to savour the moment.

'That's it, Sir, the car on the CCTV, the axe, the carpet, and the lack of an alibi for Thomas at the time of the murder. All we have to do now is to wait for forensics, then interview him.' Cadema took a gasp of breath as she finished speaking.

'Just wait a moment.' Grimes assumed his usual military stance as the pitch of his voice raised several octaves. 'I understand Thomas had a relapse, so you won't be able to interview him. What's more, if he continues to deteriorate, as his doctor predicts, then we'll never be able to get anything tangible from him.'

'But, Sir, I must find out if Thomas actually murdered her. If he didn't then we'll have to keep looking for the perpetrator. No woman will be safe until we know.'

'Don't be so melodramatic, of course he killed her, all the evidence is there. You've just said so.'

'No, Sir, it's all circumstantial. We have to have proof and that will only come if there is a match with the DNA; or if Thomas confesses, or both. Whatever the case, I must get on with the investigation.' Cadema did not wait for his answer as she left his office with a tight feeling in her chest.

When she returned to her office there was a note waiting for her.

Urgent, please call Doctor Barns at Broadmoor. She read the message twice, and then picked up the telephone. As she dialled, she bit her lip and whispered, 'Please God, don't let it be bad news. Don't say Thomas has committed suicide or something.'

'Doctor Barns here, how can I help you?'

'It's Superintendent Sharma here. You wanted to speak to me.'

'Thank goodness you've called. Good news, Thomas wants to talk to you. But he wants you to come on your own, if you don't then he will not talk. I suggest you come immediately as he may relapse at any moment.'

'That's excellent news. I'll be there as quickly as I can.' After Cadema finished speaking she called Johns and asked her to accompany her to Broadmoor. Although she agreed to interview Thomas alone, she wanted company for the journey so she could discuss the case with Johns before and after seeing him.

***

Arriving outside the fortress of Broadmoor's Victorian edifice, Cadema waited for security to check her and DCI Johns into its outermost parameter. Flanked by two security staff, Gordon and Patrick, they entered the grounds which lead to the hospital. Walking up the ornate steps, Cadema shielded her eyes to admire the gothic architecture of a building that had housed some of the most notorious murderers since it was opened in 1864. The distinct clock face reminding patients of time they would no longer be able to cherish.

'Worrying isn't it, Ma'am, to think of spending the rest of your days locked up in such a place.'

'You have a point there, Joanna, but they don't just lock people away here, they also offer, and give them treatment.'

'That's right,' said Gordon, with his cockney accent. 'But the treatment doesn't work on everyone. And I can tell you some horror stories from when the place first opened. That's if you want to hear them?' he gloated.

'Certainly not,' Cadema retaliated.

'I do apologise for my colleague,' said Patrick in his well-educated Irish accent. 'He just likes to test out his historical knowledge, that's all.'

'Yes, sorry if I've offended you. But some people do like to hear the gory bits.'

'We see enough of them in our field of work, thank you,' Cadema replied as she, and Johns, increased their pace towards their destination.

Cadema had studied many cases while doing her degree in criminology. She recalled the case of Captain George Johnstone from 1864 who had murdered one of his ship's crew. Then there was Mather Bacon, who was sent to the hospital in 1863 after cutting the throats of her two children. Then of course there were the most recent ones, Reginald Kray, and then Peter Sutcliffe, the Yorkshire Ripper. They had all been there. Many more will no doubt arrive at the cost to the taxpayer of around £300,000 a year each for the privileged of keeping the public safe in their beds. She looked up at the CCTVs and pulled her coat collar close to her neck.

Forty minutes after they had arrived at the gates, Cadema was finally siting in an interview room while DCI Johns waited in another room.

Thomas arrived, escorted by four people; two were nurses. He sat grinding his teeth, and looked older than his thirty-seven years. His sunken eyes giving the impression that he was due for a good sleep. Once blond, his hair was now showing signs of grey. He certainly resembled a man, and was in a men's hospital. But even with this male persona, the woman within surfaced occasionally.

With permission to record the interview, the time, date and list of people present were spoken into the equipment; Cadema thanked Thomas for agreeing to see her. Thomas sat back in his chair and smiled. The two nurses sat at a distance, but although they appeared to be inconspicuous, it was impossible for Cadema to ignore them.

'As you can see I am alone, as you requested, but the warders have to stay here.'

'Yes I know, as long as they don't ask me any questions.'

'You have my word that the questions will only come from me.' As she spoke Thomas appeared to go into a trance. But after a couple of seconds he sat upright; his eyes bright. He began to talk before she could ask him any questions. Cadema decided not to interrupt him.

'I didn't tell them, I couldn't tell them; after all, Bernard Franklin had incriminated himself. When I discovered that Bernard had given Madeline a lift, and was stupid enough to drop her off, 'serves him right,' I thought. He should have done the job and not left it for someone else. He deserved to get a life sentence especially when they found out about the prostitutes. I've no sympathy for him.' Thomas said this in a calm voice as if he were telling a story he had written. Cadema remained silent – nodding a couple of times.

'Madeline was very much alive when I picked her up. Too alive for her own good. That constant talking she did nearly drove me mad. I just had to drop her off and leave her standing on the side of the road getting drenched. I couldn't cope with her; she was too much.'

Cadema wanted to know if Thomas picked Madeline up again and then murdered her. She hoped he would answer that without being asked. But when she heard what he said next, she felt devastated.

'Switching on the radio in the morning,' said Thomas. 'I was delighted to hear that Madeline had been murdered. At least she wouldn't have the opportunity to drive anyone else round the bend with her verbosity. I was even more ecstatic when I heard later that Bernard Franklin had been arrested. But decided not to tell anyone that I knew he hadn't done it.' Cadema wanted to clarify what he said, but before she could say anything, another male voice surfaced from Thomas.

'Tell her, Thomas. Tell her that when you left Madeline standing at the roadside on the edge of Wimbledon Common, you felt a tang of guilt. That you reasoned she would be okay, and would soon be picked up by someone else. Remember? Then I said, "What do you think you're doing leaving her there like that?" 'You just shrugged and headed for home. Remember?'

'That's not what happened,' a female voice interrupted. 'Thomas does not remember anything about it. But I do.'

'No,' Thomas shouted. 'I'll explain. You told me to go back. That it was my duty to do so, and that I couldn't ignore her auburn hair. "No," I protested. "I won't go back," I said as I swerved the car to avoid a guy who had just stepped off the pavement without looking. "Get out of my way, you bloody idiot," I mouthed. But as I drove on, I could still hear the voices.'

'No, Thomas wouldn't go back,' the female voice interrupted him. 'So when we reached the next lay-by I took off his disguise. He was no longer Thomas, it was me, Philippa.'

Philippa's voice disappeared as Thomas slumped in his chair. Then, as he sat upright again, Philippa continued.

'I was a woman again. Madeline would never recognize me. So, I drove the car back to where Thomas had dropped her off. As I pulled up alongside Madeline, I noticed how bedraggled she was; her long auburn hair sagged across her face like sodden spaghetti. I hoped she didn't recognize the car or me from before.

"Would you like a lift" I smiled.

"Oh, you startled me, for a moment there I thought you were someone else. It must have been the car," Madeline said.

"If you're waiting for someone else, I'll be going then."

"Oh no, don't go. I'm not waiting for anyone. It's just that you have a similar car to the guy that dropped me off about twenty minutes ago. Yes, I'd love a lift." She opened the door, mumbled her destination, and then got into the car.

"Now that's a coincidence, I'm heading in that direction too. You don't know who's around these days, do you?" I said, then revved the engine and drove off.

"No you don't, do you? But some weirdo picked me up earlier. I told him about me – you know – just polite conversation. He told me to get out of his car. Can you imagine just leaving me like that at the side of the road in this weather?"

"No I can't – that's awful," 'I said, trying to be concerned.

"I knew you'd understand. I thought he was a nice guy at first. So I told him about my boyfriend. Then he got all shirty and told me to get out of the car."

"Well that's a terrible thing to do. I would never do such a thing, especially on a night like this, it's awful. Men, you just can't trust them, can you?"

"No, and I never will again. When I got out of his car I was pretty angry, I can tell you. And, although I tried to get another lift, no one else stopped until you did. I was expecting to spend the night in the next bus shelter or something. And to top it all I've run out of tariff on my mobile. So thanks for the lift. You're a star. By the way I'm Madeline, what's your name?"

I hesitated before I answered, trying to decide what to call myself.

"Oh, just call me Amanda."

"That's a nice name." Madeline said as I handed her a bunch of tissues to help her dry herself.

"Thanks."

She took the tissues and wiped her face and hair. "Don't mention it. It's awful to be so wet. I'm sorry that's all I can give you."

"That's okay but I could do with some more as my hair is a frightful mess. And the tissues are too soggy now."

"Never mind, perhaps we can find somewhere to get some more from." I said, hoping Madeline wouldn't say any more as I needed to concentrate on driving.

"Oh don't worry; I'm sure I'll be okay. At least it's warm in here, I'll soon be dry."

"No bother, but if you're interested, I know where there's some toilets not too far from here. We could stop and get some paper hand towels. Beside I need a pee." I made my voice sound urgent.

"That's a great idea. Trust a woman to come up with that suggestion. The other guy couldn't have cared less about me. Men. You can't tell what they're at, can you?"

"No, I suppose not." I drove on. "Well here we are and it's stopped raining, thank goodness. The toilets are just down there but I'll need to get the torch out of the boot so we can see where we're going," I said light heartedly.

"Thanks, Amanda, you're a star."

As she spoke, I cringed and shrugged my shoulders. When I walked round to the back of the car, I noticed the clouds had gone and a full moon was visible; just right for the job. To prevent the light coming on, I only half-lifted the lid of the boot. In the dark I grabbed the axe and knife, stuffed them into my long pockets, and closed the car's boot.

"Good. I've got the torch." I angled the thin beam of light onto the path. It was just bright enough but not too bright to attract others.

"Okay let's go." I asked her to follow me along the path that I knew led to nowhere. Then, needing her to walk in front of me, I handed her the torch. The path was well defined and luckily there weren't any puddles. "Not much further now," I said, moving closer to her.

"Thanks Amanda," she said with a giggle.

"No problem."

I thought of letting Thomas take over at this stage. He would do the job with the skill of a warrior in battle with the enemy. Surprise is always the best method, as the enemy never know what's coming. But I could not trust him. So moving closer still, I thrust the axe at her head. When Madeline turned, I saw the horror in her eyes as she realized who I really was. And when I spoke again, she flinched and gave a muffled scream. The axe struck her again and she fell.

"There you see, I did come back for you after all, but not in the way you expected,' I said as she lay on the ground just before the last blow struck her. Then I took hold of the scarf around her neck and pulled it as tight as I could. Nevertheless, I suspect that she was dead well before that. I didn't mutilate her body, but just left her in a prominent place.

Cadema watched as Philippa's voice stopped. Thomas slumped in the chair for a couple of minutes, then Philippa began to speak again.

'As I drove home, I was pleased that Thomas was unaware of what I had done. At least that's what I believed, but now I'm not so sure. Anyway, by morning I had erased everything from my mind and began to imagine that Madeline was still there waiting for a lift – a lift that would never come. When Thomas heard the radio announcement, he was genuinely shocked. I didn't put him right.'

At this point, Philippa stopped speaking long enough for Cadema to ask a question.

'When did you remember killing Madeline, Thomas?'

He flinched and sat upright in his chair.

'I don't know. All I remember was being reprimanded for not doing the job when I picked her up the first time. And when I heard Bernard had been convicted of her murder, I thought, well, I couldn't have done it. But sometime, either just before or just after the trial I can't recall, I thought I may have killed her. Then realised I'd got away with it.' Thomas' voice was fading. He sipped at the remnants of the plastic cup of water from the desk and sat back in his chair. He began to grind his teeth again. His grin returned, his eyes rolled.

Cadema was about to respond but she could see that he had receded into his own world. Words would be useless. After thanking everyone, she left the building with Johns.

***

'You know, Joanna,' Cadema's voice was almost inaudible, 'he told me the whole story without any emotion or remorse. It was just as if he were telling a fictional story, as if his victims were not real people. At times I thought he was making it all up, but I know he wasn't. No, he really did kill Madeline.'

'It must have been awful for you to listen to him. And it makes me go cold to think he did all that and now he believes that his conscience is clear,' said Johns, her voice croaking. She swallowed.

'I know it's difficult, but don't let us forget that Thomas doesn't know who he really is. And as such he will never be released into society again. Anyway, the murder has been solved, so we can resume our other work. And of course Grimes will be pleased with the outcome of our visit. He was quite sceptical before.'

When Cadema reached her office, there were two messages on her desk. The first was from Julia saying that some of Madeline's DNA had been found on the axe. That the carpet was still being analysed, but the car had been taken away, by mistake, and smelted.

The second message was from Sergeant Marriott saying he had completed everything for the presentation and had agreement from the Cold Case Department to start the investigation on the murders from 1888.

With these messages in her hand, Cadema headed for Norman Grimes' office. After many deliberations, he reluctantly agreed for her to wait for the full report on the Belton case, before it was closed. In the meantime, he gave her permission to investigate the 1888 murders.

Chapter 10

Cadema examined the faces of the officers who had assembled in the briefing room waiting for information on the *Whitechapel Murders*. As DCI Ryan had now taken up her post as superintendent in another division, she was left with two senior officers, DCI Johns and DI Pratt. The remaining team members were DS Marriott, DCs Barry, Galke, and Clarke. Other officers in the room were there for interest. Now she needed three volunteers to investigate the murders, more would have been better, but there was only funding for three, plus Cadema as CIO.

'Thank you all for coming,' said Cadema. 'It's good to see so many of you interested in these cases.' She gave a twitch of a smile, and tossed her hair over her shoulder. 'As you know, Sergeant Marriott here,' she nodded at him, 'found a trunk in the archives room which we believe is connected to the so-called Whitechapel Murders of 1888.

'The trunk contains several pieces of clothing and other artefacts that, to our knowledge, had never been catalogued in any other archives. This includes, the National Archives at Kew. We have secured funding to do this and to investigate all the items in the trunk to ascertain their relationship, if any, to the murders of 1888.

'Chief Superintendent Grimes, together with the Cold Case Department, support these investigations. This is a real privilege for us. And hopefully it will lead to the discovery of the perpetrator.'

'With respect, Ma'am,' Pratt interjected. 'As these murders took place nearly 130 years ago, what is the use of spending taxpayers' money in this way? Surely it is not in the public interest to do that?' He sounded condescending and looked around the room for any reactions. There were a few nervous coughs and shuffling of bottoms on the seats from the group – no one spoke.

'You're right of course,' said Cadema. 'It's not in the public's best interest as such, but as we have obtained funding from the Home Office Pecuniary Edict department, or HOPE for short, there isn't any issue there.' As she spoke there were sniggers from two officers at the back of the room.

Cadema was used to such behaviour from younger officers, and would tolerate it for the moment. Later she would take them aside and let them know that, if they carried on that way, they would be off their CID attachment and back on the beat.

'Some of you may question this, but we don't just *hope* to solve the murders, we *will* solve them, is that clear?' The silence, and the look of embarrassment on the two officers' faces, answered Cadema's question. 'The details are in my business plan. But now I'm going to give you an outline of the cases, identify some questions and hopefully find the answers to these in due course.' She expected the presentation would stimulate discussion, and help with her ten-point plan on the cases.

As the first slide of the PowerPoint presentation flashed onto the screen, she reminded the officers that, despite the age of the cases, they were still real people who had been murdered. That some of their descendants were probably alive and that they should respect these people and the victims of the crimes.

1. How many women were considered to be murdered by the so called, Jack the Ripper? The consensus is five:

i. Mary Anne Nichols (known as Polly) in Bucks Row on Friday 31 August at 03.30 hours

ii. Annie Chapman at 29 Hanbury Street on Saturday 8 September at 06.00 hours

iii. Elizabeth Stride in Burner Street on Saturday 30 September at 01.00 hours

iv. Catherine Eddowes in Mitre Square on Saturday 30 September at 01.44 hours, the same day as Elizabeth Stride

v. Mary Jane Kelly at Millers Court on Friday 9 November between 01.00 and 02.00 hours, the precise time – unknown

'This is just the background; there will be more details later. But does anyone have any questions at the moment?' Cadema looked around the room – everyone seemed too engrossed in the subject to answer. There was some agitation in her voice as she introduced slide two.

2. Why were there varying gaps between the murders? Were they significant? The gaps were:

i. Seven days between the first and the second murders

ii. Twenty-one days between the second and the next two (third and fourth) murders

iii. Thirty-nine days between the fourth and the fifth murders.

'DCI Johns will now give you a short profile on serial killers.' Cadema looked at Joanna and nodded for her to start.

'Thank you, Ma'am,' Johns took a sip of water and coughed. 'Some of you may be aware of what I'm going to say. But if I tell you all together, there will be no misconceptions or speculations on the profile of serial killers. Is that clear?' The audience remained quiet.

'Serial killers do not always kill in close succession; this was the case with the Yorkshire Ripper, Peter Sutcliffe. Here is a photograph of him for those of you who were not around in the nineteen seventies.' As the third slide showed the face of the killer, the audience made incoherent noises. 'Peter murdered at least thirteen women and there were more than three months between the first and second murders, and over a year between the second and third ones. Any questions?' The slow shaking of heads gave the cue to continue.

'The next slide shows the face of Albert DeSalvo, the Boston strangler,' Johns continued. 'He is also reputed to have murdered thirteen women. He murdered four women in one month in 1962, it was over a month and a half later before he killed again. Then there was a four-month gap, from August until December, between this and the next murder. So gaps don't really tell us anything.'

'Then why are we concentrating on them in this case, Ma'am?' said Clarke, who then blushed as heads turned to look at the officer who had the audacity to ask a question when Johns was speaking.

'I'm not concentrating on them; I'm only identifying the facts. It's not helpful to speculate on things that are most probably irrelevant. Johns took a deep breath, hoping to calm herself. For a moment she was back in Antigua as a child, with all that questioning. The intimidation she felt then, was happening again. She couldn't have that, and especially from a DC. She took a sip of water and asked if there were any more comments.

DC Galke raised his hand.

'Good, so let's hear what you've got to say.' Johns sounded dismissive.

'I think there are some answers for the gaps that need to be considered, especially between the fourth and fifth murders. He could have been in jail or even abroad, or ill perhaps?' The room went quiet. His voice quivered, the same as it did when speaking in the Synagogue. But in front of so many officers…

'There is some logic in your surmises, but in those days people seldom travelled abroad. And I don't suppose you've considered that he may not have found the victim he was looking for?' Johns was now in her interrogation mode, nothing was going to stop her, especially Galke whom she gave no time to answer. 'Don't forget, as recent as the Common Murders, Thomas only targeted women with auburn hair. And it could have been that simple with this infamous killer.'

'Is there any evidence that these women had any other traits, in addition to prostitution, Ma'am?' Clarke sat upright now, her voice assertive.

'That's a good question,' interjected Cadema. 'No there isn't any evidence as yet, but we may find something. We just have to keep our minds open and ask as many questions as we think necessary.' Cadema did not look at Clarke, instead she focused on the contempt in Johns' dark eyes.

'Thank you, Ma'am,' replied Clarke, as she realised she had threatened the rank culture which prevailed in the organisation. But at least Superintendent Sharma had given her, and other members of the team, opportunities to question and give views. Johns, before her promotion had also been open and approachable. Now she upheld the culture amongst the higher ranks. It was not what Johns actually said to Clarke which disturbed her, it was the way she scowled, just as her own mother used to do before lashing out at her when she was a girl.

'So let's get on with the presentation,' said Cadema as the next slide came into view.

3. How did the murderer manage to carry out the first four murders, mutilate the bodies, and in three cases remove internal organs when the light was almost none existent?

'There was some light from the street gas lamps, and although he chose dark places to murder these poor women, there's no evidence of him having a lamp. Anyway too much light would, of course, have made him conspicuous.' Cadema paused as the team started murmuring – making suggestions and giving probable solutions.

'Quiet please. Before we speculate any further, Sergeant Marriott has some important background information.'

'Thank you, Ma'am.' Marriott stood facing his audience. 'I've done some research on lamps. Hopefully it will help to know what was available, and what was not at the time. Apparently, flashlights were not available until after 1902. Gas street lights gave some light, but not very much. Davy lamps had been available from 1815 but were dangerous due to their naked flame. Police were not issued with these. Bullseye lanterns were available but expensive, so may not have been available. Carbide lamps were not invented until the 1890s. Therefore, the police of 1888 were issued with a whistle, a long batten hidden in a concealed pocket, and a lantern if they were lucky. So lighting was inadequate at the time of these murders.' Marriott took a sip of water and looked around the room. As no one spoke, he decided to sit down.

'Thank you, Sergeant,' Cadema said reassuringly; the team shuffled in their seats. 'Okay.' She looked around. 'I get the message. Let's have a short break and resume in ten minutes.' She looked at her watch. 'Before you go – just keep in mind what Marriott has said, hopefully we will have more information in due course.' The scraping of chairs made her voice almost inaudible. Ten minutes later, the noise was repeated as the group reassembled and looked at the next slide.

4. As no one heard any noise from the victims, why didn't these women scream, or call out?

It was DCI Johns' turn to speculate now. With her newly acquired authority she added that the perpetrator was most probably local. That the victims had known him, so he was trusted. He obviously strangled them first; rendering them semi, or totally – unconscious; then cut their throats. Johns asked for a volunteer so she could demonstrate the procedure. None of the officers moved to oblige; she shrugged, and resumed her seat as Cadema stood, said thank you and turned to the next slide on the screen.

5.   'These are several questions on this slide to consider,' said Cadema.

i. How did he escape the scenes without detection?

ii. Did he have an accomplice?

'It is reputed, but I cannot find the evidence, that one witness mentioned someone had lit a pipe near the scene. Another said they heard someone whistling. This could have been a signal to the murderer that someone was coming. But there's no tangible evidence of an accomplice.

'However, if the perpetrator was local, as we suspect he was, then he would have blended in, so escape would have been easy.' Several heads nodded – no one spoke as the next slide appeared.

6.   Where did the perpetrator live?

'The murderer obviously knew the area very well,' said Cadema. 'Marriott will explain.'

Marriott stood again. 'I have done a rough geographical profile and decided that he could have lived at Aldgate East, the London Hospital, Brick Lane or Spitalfields; but it's impossible to be really sure. It does appear that he had some anatomical knowledge, so he could have worked in any one of the professions in these areas. Speculation was rife at the time, and included that he was a doctor, an orderly, a failed medical student, a slaughterhouse man, a policeman, a priest, a vicar and even a midwife.'

'You're right, Sergeant,' interjected Cadema. 'But all this speculation doesn't get us anywhere. Nevertheless, we have to eliminate as many people as possible.'

Marriott smiled and sat again.

'Excuse me, Ma'am.' Clarke raised her right arm. 'But has a motive for the murders been established?'

'As I said earlier, there have been many speculations in the press and in other media, including novels. These include: hatred of prostitutes, failing medical school due to catching syphilis from a prostitute, he was a misogynist, religious cleansing, or to stop prostitution – a moral conscience perhaps? And these are just a few. But we may never be able to say for certain what actually made him kill those women. There is some evidence that he stalked his victims, probably over several days. But still there's no proof of this.'

'Are there any other links between the victims other than prostitution?' DC Galke jumped up and then sat down quickly.

'We've touched on that before,' Clarke interrupted impertinently just as Cadema was about to answer.

'That brings us on nicely to the last slide,' said Cadema.

7.   Are there any links between the victims?

'The victims all lived in the vicinity, and must have known each other.' Cadema said as she felt a trickle of sweat run down her back. Asking for someone to open a window, she continued. 'Annie Chapman, the second victim, and Mary Kelly, the fifth victim, lived, from time to time in Dorset Street. Elizabeth Stride and Catherine Eddowes lived at different addresses in Flower and Dean Street; number 32 and 55 respectively. Annie Chapman, Elizabeth Stride, the third victim, and Mary Kelly were widows. In relation to their ages: the first four victims were all in their 40s but Mary Kelly was only about twenty-three years old.' Cadema coughed, took a drink of water and asked for the projector to be turned off.

'That's all we have at the moment. If you would like to volunteer to be on the investigation team, let DCI Johns know. As usual, if there are too many volunteers, then we'll instigate the selection process. But remember, I need officers who can be thorough in their work and not ones who are more interested in the sensationalism of these cases. I'll leave a copy of this presentation in the duty room, so you can re-examine the information whenever you want. And remember, my door is always open, just knock first.' Cadema scooped up her papers and left the room, hoping that someone else, in addition to Marriott, would volunteer.

Chapter 11

'Hi, Julia, how are you?' Cadema spoke into her mobile phone as she sat in her armchair watching the rain gouge out another track on her window.

'I'm fine. You?'

'Okay, I was just wondering if you're free, and since I've finished the Belton case and obviously got some time to spare, can we get together sometime?'

'Why not tonight, if you're free.' Julia never hesitated when it came to meeting Cadema socially. Although "socially" probably meant that she had something on her mind which she needed to discuss. And despite social events being infrequent, they were never immune from Cadema's busy work schedule. Invariably they would resort to discussing the fine details of a case Cadema was working on.

'Great,' said Cadema with some hesitation in her voice. 'I've been meaning to call, but with all the work, well you know how it is.'

'Not to worry. Anyway, I should also apologise – I could have… but with Bagley going, well I've been busier than ever.'

'I thought you'd found someone to replace him?' Cadema sounded concerned.

'I *have*, but she can't start for another three months. Something to do with her contract. But hey – she is, according to her references, fanatic when it comes to DNA profiling. So I'm expecting her to be much more on the ball than Bagley ever was. Don't get me wrong though, Bagley was good in his own way. But I'm sure Wilhelmina Cox will do better.

And of course, there's still Brown, despite his clumsiness, to assist me.'

'Well at least there's some good news,' said Cadema, who then agreed to meet Julia at her house in an hours' time, rather than go out for a meal.

As Julia turned off her phone she sat wondering why Cadema wanted to meet her so urgently. If it were that urgent, then she probably needed her in her professional capacity. So why not meet at her office, which would have been more appropriate? And why had she been abrupt on the phone when she was usually so polite? The only explanation Julia could think of was that something must be bothering her. Something she would have to find out when they met.

***

Cadema arrived in the Victorian street, where the terraced houses had once been dilapidated homes of the poor in London. Now, metamorphosed into to one of the most desirable residences in the area – prices had spiralled.

Half an hour earlier than expected, she managed to squeeze the car into a space almost opposite Julia's house instead of several doors away, as she had to before.

Standing at the new, light-brown front door, Cadema rang the bell, and waited. She rang again – no reply. Then, turning her head she noticed Julia peering out of the window. A minute later the door opened.

'Sorry, but the bell doesn't work yet. They're coming to do it tomorrow. Anyway, you're early. Just as well I saw your car.'

After the usual greeting, and the flattery Cadema gave over Julia's strawberry-pink dress, she hung up her coat on the hook and followed Julia to the lounge.

'What's all this, a brand-new suite and carpet. I thought you were thinking of moving when you found a new job?'

'I still am, but the old suite was uncomfortable, and the carpet... You know what I mean. When I put it on the market, it needs to look fresh, and neutral – no one likes a shabby carpet.'

'I wouldn't have called your last one shabby. But now you mention it, this one does give a lighter feeling to the room,' said Cadema as she perched herself on the oatmeal-coloured settee and surveyed the room.

'Before we start, I'll get you a drink. What would you like?'

'Coffee would be nice, thank you.'

'Coming up,' said Julia as she headed for the door, then stopped. 'I'm having wine, would you like to try a glass? After all, it's past six, so officially it's evening.'

Cadema frowned, thought for a moment, then spoke. 'I've had the odd glass or two of Merlot, so I'll try it. Just this once mind.'

Julia nodded and left the room. Moments later she returned with an open bottle of red and two glasses. 'Try this.' She began to pour. 'It's not the cheap variety, so it's nice and smooth and doesn't leave you feeling as if you've just swallowed sandpaper.' She handed Cadema a small sample. 'There, try it and let me know what you think.'

Cadema followed the protocol of wine tasting she had seen demonstrated on television shows, and then looked at Julia. 'Yes, it's very nice. But I'll just have a small one, as I'm driving.'

'Of course – wouldn't dream of jeopardising your career, nor my conscience for that matter.' Julia giggled as she poured a little more wine into Cadema's glass and then topped up her own one.

'I knew you'd like it,' Julia teased. 'But you seem a little tense; is something worrying you?' Julia scanned the lines on Cadema's face, some of which she hadn't noticed the last time they had met. Beneath her silky-black hair there were traces of grey. Her once well-fitting dark blue dress, now hung on her delicate frame as her gaunt face gave the impression that she wasn't eating as much as she should.

'I'm fine, but thanks for your concern. Just busy, that's all.' Cadema took a sip of wine, and threw a false smile.

'Are you sure, really sure? You seem to have… well lost about five kilograms, if I'm not mistaken?' Julia fidgeted.

'I may have lost some – not that much though. But you look great Julia. What's your secret?'

'Thanks, but I must tell you.' She leaned forward, her eyes sparkling. 'I have a new partner.'

'Not another one? I thought you were smitten with, what-his-name?'

'Never mind him. It didn't work out. His mother…' Julia raised her eyebrows and took a gulp of wine.

'So, tell me all about this one. Who is he and what's his name?'

'I will in time, but you go first – you've obviously got something on your mind.'

'That's true, but it can wait. You just tell me,' said Cadema in her interrogation voice.

'Hey – it's me here – Julia; not one of your suspects.'

'Sorry, but at least tell me a little bit about him, you can fill the details in later.'

'Okay.' Julia shuffled in her seat and then gave a physical description of Clive Stapleton, even down to the small mole he had just below his left ear lobe. 'He's nearly six feet tall, blond, and no grey. Apparently, he's good at his job at the Home Office, so one of my friends says, and he's very interested in pathology. He's good looking – and best of all – single.'

Cadema nodded and smiled occasionally as Julia concentrated on more of what Clive did in his work.

'Well, that's enough about me; what about you, Cadema?' Julia poured another glass of wine. She looked at Cadema, who shook her head at the bottle.

'There's nothing much to tell, except we have a new case,' said Cadema, who then give a full account of the Whitechapel Murders and what Sergeant Marriott had discovered in the archives. 'I expect you realize that your expertise, and those of your new colleague, will be invaluable to this case.'

'That may be the ideal, and I'm very interested.' Julia sat upright and took a deep breath. 'But, as you are aware, I will be busy for a while with Wilhelmina's induction programme.'

'I understand that,' said Cadema, then explained about the work the police had done in 1888, the possible suspects at that time, and what she intended to do now. Once she had finished speaking, Julia put down her drink and looked Cadema full in the face.

'It all sounds very interesting, and when I have the time, I may be able to help. In the meantime, I expect you'll do your usual ten-point plan.' Julia gave a coy smile.

'I have thought about a plan of course, but not in any detail. But whatever happens, it must include you. I need to have your support, otherwise the work cannot be realized.'

'Now you're sounding like an MBA graduate,' Julia giggled and fanned her face with her hand. 'But do go on, I need to know exactly what you're planning – and perhaps scheming too?'

'That's not fair, I never scheme.' Cadema smiled as she spoke, knowing that Julia was on the tease again. 'It's like this, Julia.' She leaned forward, as if someone was eavesdropping. Julia mirrored her actions. 'I told you about the trunk Marriott found, and the contents. Well I haven't actually seen them, but from what Marriott said, there are several garments, some old papers, but most importantly, an old stained dress that probably belonged to one of the victims. I've arranged to have the trunk delivered to the station for safekeeping, it's due tomorrow. What I would like you to do, when you have time of course, is to take samples from the clothing and the dress to see what the stains are. I suspect some to be blood, some semen or other body fluids, it's hard to tell.' Cadema leaned back in her chair watching the frown on Julia's face. 'What's wrong with that, Julia?'

'Nothing, that is of course if I had the time, which I don't. Anyway, it's not just the time, it's also the cost. We just don't have the funds in our department, what with the Government cutbacks. And I expect the next thing you'll want me to arrange is the DNA analysis?'

'Yes, that's right. But don't fret about the cost. I've procured funding from HOPE: the Home Office Pecuniary Edict, so there'll be enough to cover forensics.'

'That's great but what time frame are you working towards? I know how important it is to you, so I expect it's going to be a short lead time?'

'You're wrong there, Julia. It's been nearly 130 years since the murders took place, and the garments are from that era. So a little wait won't make any difference.'

'As usual, you appear to have thought of everything, so I'm happy to help. But it will not be until after Wilhelmina starts, if that's okay with you?

'Perfect. There's just one more thing I'm concerned about. If we manage to find DNA and carry out profiles, will we be able to trace the descendants and the perpetrator?' Cadema watched Julia's pupils dilate. But she wasn't sure whether she had seen a smile, or a grimace, lurking below the surface of Julia's pink lips.

'I'm not too sure about that. That may be a step too far.' said Julia.

'I realise that, but it's all conjecture at the moment. And of course, if we do trace descendants, then we'll have to be sensitive to their needs, and of course, discreet.'

After further discussion, and then some social exchanges, they agreed to meet the following afternoon to discuss the case in much more detail; and in works' time too.

Chapter 12:

Preparing for work the next morning, Cadema sipped at her coffee and thought of Jim Logan, her predecessor. Killed by a sniper, he was her internal mentor now. Jim would know what to do, she reasoned. He would use his famous helicopter approach to look down on the situation. Then he would map out the scenes of the crimes around Whitechapel. See a man stalking his victims, and organise a geographical, and a psychological profile. Then, within a radius of a kilometre or so, he would identify where the murderer lived, and discover who he was.

Perhaps Jim would tap into her thoughts, and be happy with the plan she had developed. After all, the cases were relatively straightforward. There were the five murders, several suspects, and of course the newly found trunk. All she had to do was to make sense of it all.

Sitting there she felt her heart flutter. Some tightness in her chest made her think of an impending heart attack. But when Cameo, her rescue cat, meowed, purred and began entwining herself around her ankles, she dismissed the idea.

The day she first encountered Cameo – the cat was so well camouflaged against the grey and white carpet in Thomas' sitting room, that she almost missed her. It was only the rustle of the tail, and the strange growl, that encouraged Cadema to look closer. When she did, two green eyes stared back at her with the intensity of a tiger waiting to pounce. As it did, Cadema felt its claws latch onto her trouser leg. The cat screamed and screeched, its back legs furiously scrabbling at the kill. By the time one of her officers, who said she was a cat lover, had encouraged the cat to let go, Cadema felt the trickle of blood through her clothes. But after the Cats' Rescue Service (CRS) had taken Cameo away, and Cadema had been to Casualty for the statutory "jab", she remembered what the women, with grey hair, from the CRS, had said:

'She's such a beautiful cat, just got scared that's all. 'I expect you'd have been scared if you were cornered like that.' She scowled.

Cadema had looked at the woman as she nursed her own injuries. It was that evening, when Cadema tried to sleep, that the cat snuggled into her conscience and stayed there. Next morning she was standing outside the CRS building waiting for them to open. Preliminary checks on Cadema's suitability to adopt the cat were satisfactory, so a week later Cameo was entrenched with her new owner. Now Cameo purred at every opportunity and followed her from room to room, as if saying 'sorry.' Today was no exception.

At least Cameo was company, especially as Cadema's mother was still away.'

Buttering her toast, the thought of the ten-point plan gnawed at her conscience. It had to be done. But for the first time since Jim's death nearly three years ago, she was having difficulty. But now her meeting with Julia was imminent, she couldn't procrastinate any longer. So after taking nibbles at her toast she opened her laptop and started typing.

The ten-point plan.

She looked at the words on the page. What good would that do? Things had changed beyond recognition since the 1880s. She sat back, drained her cup, and then started typing again.

1. Examine the documents relating to all the victims. There may be none to examine, only the ones from the trunk. But surely most would have survived from the original investigations? she thought.

2. *Examine the content of the trunk and make sure that nothing is overlooked.* This sounded straightforward enough. At least there *is* some tangible evidence which hopefully comes from the scene of these crimes.

3. *List all the suspects, their trades, their idiosyncrasies, and their alibis.* "A little list", she smiled, thinking of a Gilbert and Sullivan opera. Over the years, she had read some details on the suspects, but knew there were many other details on them in the public literature. How feasible it would be to compare them with the police files, she would have to see.

4. *Ensure that forensic analysis is carried out on everything, including the inside of the trunk, on all the papers and the clothing therein.* There was definitely dried blood on some of the garments, there may be semen, and even fingerprints there. Not that fingerprints would have been used until 1901 at the earliest. But at least there was a chance that the fingerprint database, collected after this time, may contain a match with a perpetrator of a crime. That is, if by chance, his fingerprints were taken after that date.

5. *Take samples for DNA analysis from all the items in the trunk.* Julia would surely be able to do this and perhaps forensics could find a match with descendants of the victims and the perpetrator using the current VIVA; the Virtually Instant Verification Apparatus and the DNA database.

6. *Exhume the remains, where possible, of the murdered victims and obtain samples that may be available for DNA analysis.* Again, Julia would be involved in this. Of course, there would be many ethical issues to consider. But without this, it would be impossible to identify to whom the dress in the trunk belonged.

7. *Identify and interview living relatives of victims.* They may have information or relics that were handed down through the generations, which may be useful to the investigation.

8. Obtain DNA samples from relatives of the victims. This will help to verify the links and may even identify links to the perpetrator if he were a member of the family.

9. Construct a geographic and psychological profile of the killer. This may help to identify where he lived, and examine records of residents from that time, however transient they may have been.

10. Ensure samples are taken for DNA analysis. If male DNA is discovered from the trunk items: Identify who this belongs to using VIVA. Julia's baby again. Possible relatives of the perpetrator may be found.

Finishing her plan, she saved it on her laptop and memory-stick. Printing a copy, she began to read her plan. There was too much reliance on DNA. And what would she do if no DNA were found, what then? However, this was her first draft, no doubt she would alter it. In general, she thought it was realistic enough and just needed to have a few tweaks here and there.

After showering and dressing, Cadema left for work with more enthusiasm than she had the day before. Julia, dressed in her usual casual style, was waiting for her.

Cadema ushered her into the cluttered office, closed the door, and hung their coats on the hook.

'Sorry about the cramped conditions, and as you can see by these boxes, we're still in the throes of moving offices. What they expect me to do with all these filing cabinets, a great big desk, all these coffee tables and chairs, I cannot imagine. I'll have to get them moved soon. But at least we have some privacy.' Cadema gestured at the furniture. Then offered a chair for Julia to sit on.

'Don't worry, this is perfect for me and it's quiet too,' said Julia. 'I know you like everything neat and tidy, and even too organised at times,' she giggled. 'But at least it's only temporary and suits us both to be hidden from view.'

'Thanks for your cynicisms. I suppose you'll be wanting tea now?' Cadema smiled and looked more relaxed.

'For once, no I don't, I've just had breakfast. So if you don't mind let's get on. I don't want to sound snappy, but I've only got an hour to spare. And I'd like to discuss a few things with you before we look at your plan.'

'That's fine, I'm just pleased you've come at such short notice. I'll be as succinct as possible.'

'Good. You mentioned about DNA profiling,' said Julia as she sat on the edge of her chair, her eyes attentive, her thin lips slightly grimacing.

'Yes, the DNA, is that a problem?'

'It could be, we mentioned this last night if you remember.'

'Of course I remember. And I think we agreed that once the DNA profiling has been done, it needs to be matched against our national database. Then we can see if there are any living relatives of both the victim and the probable perpetrator.'

'But wait a minute, Cadema, there's something else you need to consider first. You mentioned the stains on the dress. Well, they may be blood, as you said. But don't forget the woman was most likely a prostitute, so we'd expect to find other body fluids, especially semen. And there could be several samples of that, all from different men. So how can we possibly tell which, if any, belonged to the murderer?'

'I didn't say it would be easy, but with the DNA and other evidence, plus good detective work, I'm sure it'll lead us to the killer. And with the vast amount of brown staining, on the neckline and bodice of the dress, which is no doubt the victim's blood, this can be eliminated. If there's blood from a male that doesn't match with any semen, then we can surmise that the killer may have cut himself, and didn't have sex with the woman. That means his motives were not sexual. I know I'm speculating, but that's all I can do at the moment.

Besides, we've found a piece of apron, torn from Elizabeth Stride, in our main archives from the case. The detectives at the time suspected that the murderer used it to dry his hands on as he fled towards Mitre Square where he murdered Catherine Eddowes. There may be two samples of blood on the piece of apron – one the victim's and the other the murderer's.' Cadema relaxed back in her chair, smiled, and took a sip of water.

'I must admit you have some good points there, but there is something else you need to know.' Julia's eyes strained to scan the corridor outside the office, no one was there. Cadema sat upright and folded her arms before speaking.

'So what's that, Julia?'

'As you know we've had the VIVA test and database for over two years now, but there's a new system being introduced next month. The database will remain but it's going to be replaced by the new IVD; that is the Instant Verification Database. This will support our work tremendously and I'm really looking forward to its implementation as we are one of the pilot sites.' Julia's voice raced, her arms gesticulating at every word.

'That's fantastic, but why didn't you tell me all this before?'

'It was being kept secret until it was properly tested. Anyway, as the current UK database is incomplete, this one will be much larger and will eventually cover the whole population. So it needs to be managed well and not used inappropriately.'

'What do you mean by inappropriately? Do you think that my investigations come under that category?' Cadema's voice raised several octaves, but her posture remained calm.

'I'm not saying... it's just that… have you thought of the families you may upset with these enquiries?'

'Yes, and we discussed that,' said Cadema defensively.

'We did, but I've thought about it a lot since then. It is a very delicate subject for the families and needs a diplomatic approach. And of course, there are ethical considerations. Not to mention the shock they will have if they find out that a long dead relative may be a murderer, and the most infamous murder of all; Jack the Ripper. They may need counselling.'

'You're right, and I guarantee that all living relatives will be protected from the media.'

'Can you really be sure of that?'

'I intend to be. And in the longer-term, it will be worth finding the perpetrator and solving the crime of a lifetime.'

Julia began to see something in Cadema that she had never seen before. The wide eyes, the flaring of her nostrils and the keenness of her features, portraying some kind of mania. That was something she didn't expect. Cadema was always so calm and professional. She took a deep breath before she spoke. 'Sorry, Cadema, but it sounds more like sensationalism to me rather than just trying to solve the murders. So let's take one step at a time, and see how we get on with the evidence.'

'That's certainly not what it's about.' Cadema sounded defensive. 'I'm just anxious to get the job done and bring an end to all the speculations on these cases.'

Julia began to realise that she may have over-reacted. Now if she were as objective as possible, she hoped Cadema would follow suit and become less obsessed with the case.

'Well you know I'm here to help you, Cadema, and will be happy to examine the clothes and the other items from the trunk. I'll arrange for it to be taken to the lab and everything will be carried out as if it were a new scene of crime. In the meantime I would like to discuss your ten-point plan when I have more time.' Julia bit her lip, realising that she sounded as if she were talking to one of her students, rather than an experienced police officer. She hoped Cadema was not offended.

'I know you don't really have the time just now, so I'll work on it, then we can meet up as soon as possible.' Cadema tried to hide the disappointment in her voice. Nevertheless, she didn't like the way Julia behaved today, but reasoned that it was because she was overworked and stressed. Hopefully it was nothing to do with her enthusiasm, but deep inside she believed it was.

From her office window she watched Julia get into her car and drive off, just as a removal van entered the car park. Hopefully there would be space in her office again.

Chapter 13

Cadema followed Marriott as he entered the disused prisoner cell underneath the police station, where the trunk was now stored. The place certainly deserved its name, *Dungeon* – with its vacant cobwebs, and the dank metallic air of ancient blood. She gave a shudder, pulled her jacket tighter around her neck, and squinted as she looked at the trunk.

Marriott moved forward, undid the two new padlocks, and lifted the trunk's lid. Cadema peered inside and saw the brown-stained dress.

'I can certainly see why you're excited about this.' As Cadema spoke she took a pair of latex gloves from the box on a nearby table and slid them on. Gingerly she extracted a little of the brown-stained dress by its shoulders – as if it were about to disintegrate. She shook her head slowly. 'It's a great pity this is in such a disgusting state.' She examined it from side to side. 'Yes, I can see it's Victorian, similar to ones I've seen in the V and A museum.' She lowered it back into the trunk.

'I thought it was old the moment I saw it,' said Marriott. 'But it wasn't until I read the date on *The Illustrated Police News,* in the glazed wooden frame, that I realized the significance of what I'd found.'

'I'm pleased you did. Now we need to send the trunk off to Doctor Lilly for her to examine. Before that, let's get photographers down here so it can be preserved as it is.'

'Yes, but, Ma'am, you know I've taken photographs, you saw them and said they were good.' Marriott gave a little tut.

'I know how capable you are with your hobby. And although they *were* good, and *were* useful in helping to procure funding for the project, they still need to be photographed forensically. So organise that will you?'

'Yes, Ma'am,' Marriott sounded despondent as he closed the lid on the trunk and secured it.

When Sergeant Marriott told Edward Cummings, head of forensic photography, about the trunk he said he would be there within the hour. Half an hour later he stood, panting and sweating, in front of Marriott in the reception area of the police station. Cumming's bloodshot eyes matched the redness of his hair. He looked bedraggled in his half-opened checked shirt, and carried more equipment than his body seemed to be able to accommodate. He tried to speak, but only managed a few hoarse words, then gasped to take in as much oxygen as he could. Carefully placing the equipment on the floor, he gasped again, pattered his chest, and then took out a handkerchief from his grey jacket and proceeded to wipe his cropped beard with it.

'Must give up the fags. Call me Edward.' Cummings's voice was just audible.

'Sergeant Marriott. We spoke on the phone earlier.' Marriott offered his hand – it was taken with a weak shake.

'Pleased to meet you…' Cummings stopped to cough, then stood upright. 'Do you have a first name, Sergeant? I can't work with someone of my own age without a first name.' He coughed again.

'It's David. Here let me help you.' Marriott took hold of the tripod and lifted one of the bags from the floor.

'Be very careful with that one, David. It's got the lighting equipment in. And the bulbs – well they cost a bomb.'

'Don't worry I'll be very careful. Follow me through the security barrier. The trunk's down in the basement.' Marriott gestured with his head. Cummings, picking up the remaining equipment, followed as a puppy would when the word *biscuit* is uttered by its owner.

'Watch your head,' Marriott shouted as they entered the cell housing the trunk.

'No problem, I'm at least ten centimetres shorter than you. So there's no need...' Cummings carefully placed the equipment on the floor and walked over to the trunk. 'My goodness, I didn't expect it to be in such a poor condition. Looks as if it's been on the battlefield of two world wars.' He gave a shudder, then began to unpack.

'I suppose it could have been for all we know,' Marriott retorted as he placed the bag and tripod on the floor next to the trunk. Helping Cummings assemble the items, he wondered how detailed each photograph would be, and whether Cummings knew how internationally important the work was going to be.

Cummings, now dressed in his forensic attire, began to photograph the outside of the trunk. Hand-holding the camera, rather than using the tripod, Marriott noticed how methodical he was. Every angle was covered as he leaned over, bent down, or lay prostrate on the floor photographing every crack, every chip, every stain, and every line on the covering. Opening the lid, he photographed its inside with the same vigour, then turned his attention to the content of the trunk. Standing upright, he stretched his back and then stared at the dress. Mesmerised for longer than he had ever been before, he leaned forward to touch it.

'Hey, be very careful with that, it's fragile.' Marriott lunged forward.

'Don't fret, David.' He turned and gave a taunting laugh. 'I *will* be careful – that's my job.' He grinned again. Marriott, eager to help, trod on Cummings's foot.

'Be careful,' Cummings snarled.

'Sorry,' Marriott mouthed as he struggled with his Latex gloves.

Standing together alongside the trunk, they examined where to take hold of the dress. It was nearly a minute before Marriott spoke.

'It's quite heavy, so if you take hold of the shoulders, I'll take the waist and gather up the skirt. Then we can lay it on this table.' Marriott pointed.

Cummings agreed and manoeuvred his body into the appropriate position. In unison they held their breath, and managed to carry out the procedure without the garment touching the floor.

The lighting adjusted to avoid any shadows, Cummings instructed Marriott to hold a small-gauged rule, and began to photograph the dress, sometimes using a standard lens and while at other times, a macro one. Taking shots from every angle. He missed nothing, not even the smallest of threads, or spots.

Having finished, what seemed to be more than a thousand photographs, he turned to Marriott and sighed.

'There, that should do it. Don't think I've overlooked anything. What do you think, David?'

Marriott coughed, and looked at his watch. 'You've been very thorough Edward, but I didn't realise how long it would take to do just one item.'

'Long, what do you mean long? I was very pedantic I know, but I did it as quick as possible under the circumstances. And it'll take me the best part of the day to finish, so don't be so impatient.'

'I didn't mean to imply that it was taking too long, only an observation, that's all. Anyway, it's fascinating to see what you're doing.'

'Good. Then I'll get on with the other things in the trunk. But before that, I'm parched. So is there any chance of at least a drink? A biscuit would also be nice; that is if the station can afford it.' Cummings smiled.

'Of course, and I'll get some sandwiches for lunch if you like.'

'Splendid, cheese and some salad will be great. No mayo. Tea, milk, no sugar.' He gave his culinary order. 'While you're doing that, I'll just nip out, be back in a jiff.'

Cummings removed his protective clothing and disappeared along the corridor in opposite direction to Marriott. Returning a few minutes later, Cummings re-clad and then continued with his work.

The framed newspaper, the warrant books and other garments were photographed with the same enthusiasm as the dress. Once finished, they returned everything to the trunk in reverse order. Tucking the dress's skirt well away from the lid, Marriott closed the trunk and pushed home the new padlocks.

'I'll have all these ready in a couple of days,' Cummings said as he and Marriott gathered up the equipment. As they left the room, Marriott locked the door.

***

'Hi, Julia. How are you?' Cadema asked as she sat in her office the next morning, holding the telephone receiver.

'I'm okay. I suppose you are calling to let me know when I can have the trunk. Well the lab's ready, and Cox, my new assistant, is anxious to get started – especially on such an highly emotive subject. As a matter-of-fact, so am I.'

'You never stop surprising me,' Cadema giggled, hoping that Julia wouldn't be offended. 'So Cox has already started work with you? So you didn't have to wait the statutory months?'

'No, they let her go early, so I've been lucky. And I'm sure she'll do a good job.' Julia sounded much more cheerful than Cadema had heard in a long time. 'Anyway, I'm anxious to get on with the work before the media find out. It's difficult as it is, to keep these things secret. And I've told the rest of my team that they're not to breathe a word of it until everything is done. I expect it to be like Bletchley Park in here.'

'You're right, Julia, I'm in a similar boat, but if anything leaks out from my team there'll be disciplinary action. Hopefully I'll contain it, at least for the time being.'

'Yes, hope so.'

'Anyway, I'm sending the trunk to you this afternoon. Marriott and the courier are expected to arrive there at around two-thirty. Just let me know what you think about it.' After saying goodbye, Cadema closed her eyes.

***

The trunk was now secured in the vehicle. Marriott took one last look around the car park. Someone that he did not recognise was standing in a doorway speaking into his mobile phone. *A likely suspect for an ambush*, he thought as he reached the passenger seat, jumped inside, closed the van's door and pushed his seat belt home. As the automatic police car park barrier lifted, Marriott jumped as if expecting armed robbers when a nearby driver sounded his horn.

Without any further disturbances, apart from the traffic hold-ups, they finally reached the building – Doctor Lilly was waiting at the door.

'That's great, and on time too,' said Julia, then smiled at Marriott.

'It still took longer than necessary. But at least there were no real incidents.' Marriott looked over his shoulder. Was there a movement or not? He turned around. Seeing nothing out of the ordinary, he picked up a folder and handed it to Julia. 'I need you to sign those and then I'll officially hand over the trunk to you for safe keeping.' He handed Julia a pen.

'Thank you, Sergeant,' said Julia as she walked over to the back of the van and peered inside. 'It all looks okay to me, but I didn't realise how big it was going to be. How on earth did it lay hidden all those years without anyone noticing it?'

Marriott coughed. 'Beats me. But at least it's in good hands now.'

'Yes, and hopefully I'll be able to find out what secrets have been hidden all that time.' Signing the papers, she closed the folder and handed it, together with the pen, back to Marriott.

Once the courier had manoeuvred the trunk into the laboratory and Marriott was happy to leave it there, he said goodbye.

In the fifteen years that Julia had been a senior pathologist, she had developed her own methods of making inanimate objects release their secrets. She would be receptive, alert and vigilant in order to discover everything there was about the trunk and its content. As a child, she had always been inquisitive. Much more than her classmates, and certainly more than any other girl in the school. So she got into trouble.

It started with the dead bird she had found in the garden. Saying a little prayer she placed it into a shoe box and buried it in the garden. After a few days, she exhumed it. "To see what it looked like," she had told her mother. This was Julia's first reprisal.

Next came the dead cat she had dragged home. This time she buried it at the bottom of the garden. Then exhumed it three weeks later, examined it, and reburied it without being discovered. It was only the smell of the corpse, and the numerous flies, that alerted her mother. She had to swear, on the bible, that she would not do such a "wicked thing" again. Next time, on the instruction of her biology teacher, and with the blessing of her mother, she acquired an ox's eye from the butcher. Crudely dissecting the eye to examine the lens in front of a candle, she decided, there and then, to study pathology when she grew up. Now, although there was no body involved, she would realise her full potential and Cox would be there to help.

Wilhelmina Cox was not as experienced as Bagley had been, but Julia expected her to be as thorough, if not more so, than Bagley. Not only that, but Cox didn't have any family to distract her. She could work late. The only downside Julia could see, was that Cox had to attend her local church, and that sometimes it wouldn't be convenient to her department. Julia, at Cox's interview, had agreed to work around this, as long as it did not delay any work. Since starting work, Cox was as keen as a lion who had managed its first kill.

'Haven't you got a home to go to, Doctor Lilly?' Cox asked as she was about to turn off the lights and go home for the evening.

'Hi, sorry, is that the time, nearly seven? I intended to get all this paperwork out of the way tonight so we can start promptly in the morning. Anyway, as I told you before, you can call me Julia.' She yawned and stretched her arms above her head. 'And yes, *I'm going* as soon as this trunk has been stowed away. It's really too heavy for me, so I'd appreciate your help with it, then we can both go.'

As Julia and Cox started to move the trunk into a cupboard, they heard footsteps in the hallway. The head of a man around fifty, appeared around the door.

'Want a hand with that?' George, the night watchman, asked. 'It looks too heavy for you two skinny ones.'

'No thanks, we can manage.' Julia tried to control her anger at such a comment.

'Bet you've got a dead body in there?' George gave a guttural laugh. 'Sure you don't want any help?'

'Quite sure, thank you.' Julia stood with her hands on her hips and watched as he returned to the corridor, then walked off, whistling.

'Typical chauvinistic…'

'Don't say it, Wilhelmina. Let's just get on with it.' Together, they managed to lock the trunk inside the cupboard. But, on leaving the building, Julia had a feeling that George, with his dark-grey eyes, was watching them.

***

Arriving at seven o'clock the next morning, Julia arranged for the trunk to be taken into the laboratory again. When it had been positioned just as she had requested, Cox arrived. Both suitably dressed, Julia began her examination.

Leaning over the trunk, Julia scrutinised every scuff, scratch, and tear on the leather covering. Taking swabs, fibre samples, and fingerprints from the exterior, she opened the lid and took more samples. Systematically, she began to inspect the contents and, as Cox took more samples, Julia dictated her report.

'This is all very interesting,' Cox said. 'But one thing is puzzling me.'

'Go on, don't hesitate, Wilhelmina, just ask. I'm happy to answer if I can.'

'I can understand why you are taking all these samples, but why fingerprints?' Cox sounded as if she were clarifying something in her mind.

'You're right to question that, as it doesn't appear to be a useful thing to do, especially as anyone involved in the crime is dead. But it will tell us how many people handled the trunk and its content. We can also eliminate anyone who had recently been through the trunk, Sergeant Marriott, for example. Besides, research is currently being carried out to identify fingerprints on materials such as clothing. And in future, who knows, we may be able to detect DNA from these, depending on how the research goes,' Julia explained.

'Yes, I've heard something about it. But I expect it'll be quite a number of years until it's been approved.

'You're right, but the theory has to be tested somewhere. And once I've finished with these samples, I'm going to talk to the professor organising the research. And maybe, depending on how things are progressing, we will be involved in it.'

'Wow that will be great if we can.'

'It's just conjecture at the moment, so don't get too excited as we may not be able to find the fingerprints we need for the research. So let's continue with the work in hand.'

Cox nodded and turned towards the trunk again.

Once they had lifted the dress from the trunk and carefully placed it on the stainless steel worktop, Julia began her autopsy-style inspection. Periodically she asked Cox to take samples as she continued with the dictation:

The dress has been cut at the neck, probably to make it easier to grip before it was torn. The knife must have been very sharp, probably a scalpel but with a much longer blade. It suggests that it was done with a single cut, and then ripped apart. The neckline is impregnated with a dark brown substance which has also soaked into the bodice.

Julia looked up and asked Cox to take a sample. Under the microscope they could see pieces of tissue and some fibres.

'What do you think these are, Wilhelmina?' Julia asked as if she were addressing a student.

'I know what it is. It's tissue from the victim and there's no doubt in my mind that the fibres are silk, most probably from a scarf that may have been used to strangle the woman. It's a pity we don't have the cadaver.' Cox sounded despondent.

'Yes it is, but at least we have the dress. And I agree, the wearer of the dress was probably strangled with a silk scarf, and then had her throat cut.' Julia looked up and slowly shook her head. 'So we've discovered nothing that we couldn't have read about in the press reports from that time, or from the internet now. We must discover something new, something more tangible that has never been found before.'

'They didn't have the forensics in the 1880s as we have now. So we're bound to find something unique, aren't we?' boasted Cox.

'Not necessarily. Anyway, we may be jumping to conclusions. We're not entirely sure whether or not, the wearer of this dress, was murdered in the 1880s. What's more, just because these is a copy of *The Illustrated Police News* in the trunk referring to the Whitechapel murders, it doesn't mean that the clothing belongs to one of the victims. So we have to bear this in mind as we do our work.'

'Yes, of course,' said Cox.

Julia turned towards the dress again. 'This brown substance is definitely blood. And these splatters of blood across the bodice and skirt, which are no doubt arterial, indicate that the woman was still alive when her throat was cut. But this blood, which has seeped into the bodice and into the back of the dress, is definitely venous. So what do you think happened?' Julia asked.

Cox cleared her throat. 'Well, once the woman was unconscious, her throat was cut as she lay on her back, and her blood pooled there.'

'Exactly, so we have plenty of tangible evidence. Hopefully the samples of blood and tissue we've taken will provide us with her DNA profile. And I know this is sheer conjecture, but if the murderer cut himself, we might have his DNA profile too,' Julia added.

'Let's hope so. But what about these stains on the skirt? They don't look like blood to me?'

'They're probably dried semen. Take some samples and make sure they're labelled correctly.'

Cox raised her eyebrows and gave a quiet tut at being told what to do. One day, when the time was right, she would tell Julia what she thought.

'Of course, but do you mean to say that you can tell that it's semen just by looking at it, and from all those years ago? That is surreal, wow,' Cox exclaimed as she cut minute pieces of cloth from the dress. Taking swabs from the rest of the dress, she added them to the mountain of work for the laboratory.

'Not really, it's just an educated guess. If she was a prostitute then they are likely to be semen stains, but from different sources,' said Julia.

Finishing with the dress, the undergarments and the shawl, they both extracted the wooden, medium-oak frame with a copy of the newspaper clearly visible. After measuring it, they took swabs and one fingerprint. Then, Julia placed the frame on the worktop with the other items, and picked up the police pocketbooks from the bottom of the trunk. Clutching them she noticed there was a gap in the string they were tied up with; *one of the books was missing*. She looked carefully around the trunk. Nothing. Opening one of them, she gasped as she read the police officer's name on the first page: Detective Constable Marriott.

A coincidence perhaps? She would have to find out if he was related to Sergeant Marriott.

Six hours and over one hundred samples later, they had finished. Julia asked Cox to pack everything away, secure the padlocks and arrange for the trunk to be locked in the cupboard again.

Two weeks later Julia telephoned Cadema and arranged a meeting with her.

Chapter 14

It was just before one in the afternoon. Cadema's meeting with Julia was scheduled for one thirty, so she had enough time to finish reorganising her office. Dragging a chair into position nearer to her desk, she looked up to see Sergeant Marriott hovering in the corridor. He knocked and opened her door.

'Can I help, or get you anything, Ma'am?' said Marriott , popping his head around the gap in the door. Then smiling, he took two steps into her office.

She wondered what he really wanted. Help her, perhaps?. But pester her again, hopefully not. Especially since the report from forensics was imminent. She wasn't in the mood to answer anything, at least not until she had spoken to Julia.

'I'm perfectly okay as I am, thank you. Just get on with the work I've given you. When I've seen Doctor Lilly, I'll brief you along with the rest of the team.' Cadema didn't look up from her work.

Marriott grimaced and with some sarcasm and anger in his voice, asked, 'Haven't you heard anything *yet,* Ma'am. Not even a whisper?' His voice was harsh, almost anxious.

'I've just answered you, haven't I? Anyway you know I would if I had. You must be patient.' Cadema looked up as he shuffled his feet and coughed. It wasn't like him to be impatient, he was usually calm; placid even. *Was there something else on his mind?* She decided not to ask. *Hopefully there was nothing in the trunk to make him so anxious?*

'I'm trying to be patient. But I feel like an expectant father, waiting… And, after all this is my baby.' He turned to leave.

'I know how you must be feeling, but this is teamwork now. You'll just have to be patient. You'll find out soon enough.'

'Yes, Ma'am, I will,' he said despondently as he retreated back into the corridor.

Cadema continued organising her office and hoped she had given Marriott enough work to distract him. Ten minutes later she looked out the window and saw him walking towards an unmarked police car. Then, getting in, she watched him drive off.

Good, she thought, then smiled as she watched Julia drive into the car park. But her heart quickened and skipped a beat when she saw Marriott returning. Getting out of his car, he walked swiftly towards Julia's car. The driver's window down, he mouthed something to her.

Cadema opened her window a little and manged to catch snippets of the conversation. Marriott asked if there was any news. Julia shook her head. Marriott mouthed something else, Cadema assumed it was an apology, especially as he lowered his head and stood scraping the gravel with his foot. She knew Julia was always careful not to divulge anything to the lower ranks before speaking to her. *Quite a diplomat*, she thought as Marriott walked slowly towards his car, got in and then drove off again.

Julia looked up at the window where Cadema was standing. Her hands full, she nodded an acknowledgement – Cadema waved. A few minutes later, Julia was in Cadema's office.

'It's good to see you. Here let me help you with that,' said Cadema as she rushed forward to take hold of the briefcase

Julia had almost dropped, as she struggled with her handbag and laptop case.

'Thanks, I suppose I should get one of those trollies on wheels for this lot.' She giggled as Cadema relieved her of some of the burden. Julia looked around the room. 'You're on your own then, I thought the rest of the team were going to be here?'

'They were going to be, but I thought we could have a chat first. And as you saw, Marriott has just left. DI Pratt is going to be late. That leaves DC Galke who is in the next office,' Cadema explained as she ordered tea.

'I thought you said that DCI Johns would also be involved.'

'She is, but it's not that simple. As I mentioned before, I only have funding for five to investigate these cases, that includes me.' Julia nodded. 'With Pratt, it will be six. As he's new to the division, Johns is going to shadow him until she's happy with his work. Then she'll move onto other duties. That leaves Pratt, Marriott, Galke and Clarke with me acting as SIO. Chief-superintendent Grimes will still be the boss and I will also have other work to do. So you see it's all working out well, and will be in budget.'

Although this was a feasible answer, she wanted to be alone with Julia. She could then hear all the results first, and ask difficult questions without her team being present. Understanding everything would put her in control. Then she could brief Grimes with confidence before speaking to her team.

'How are things going with you, Julia?'

'Not had a body for two days now. This is unprecedented, but no one seems to need my services these days.' She smiled. 'I suppose that's good – no bodies I mean. That's the nature of what I do – sometimes I'm rushed off my feet, while there are other times... well you know what I mean.'

'That's true. Anyway, I can see you haven't come empty handed.' Cadema smiled. 'I suppose you've got the results in there?' Cadema gestured as Julia foraged in the briefcase. They both looked up as the tea was delivered by a PC, who quickly departed.

'I've got some good news, but I've also discovered something that you will not be too happy with as it may concern Sergeant Marriott,' said Julia, whose hair hung limply across her pallid face as she searched Cadema's eyes. Frowns appeared for microseconds then disappeared. *What would she say?*

Cadema grimaced and sat upright with her hands in her lap like someone waiting for examination results. Her eyes narrowed.

'I'd prefer to hear the good news, but go on, tell me what you have discovered that might involve Marriott first.'

'As always in these situations, I examined the trunk as if it were a crime scene. Knowing it must have been handled by numerous people over the time frame, I decided to take fingerprints. There were twenty-two different ones. Some were quite preserved, while others were too smudged to be of any value. This is remarkable in itself, but with the new research that's taking place, these fingerprints may be even more useful to us than expected. Especially if we can extract some DNA from them.'

'That's great, Julia. Do you think some of them will be identifiable?' said Cadema moving closer to Julia.

'Some may well be, however, I found several sets belonging to your sergeant. They were found on the lid, inside the trunk and on several items within the trunk including on the glass picture frame and pocketbooks. That's not unusual since he was the one who found it. But it's the pocketbooks I think you will find interesting.' Julia looked around the room then fumbled with one of her files.

'Hold on a minute, I thought Marriott was wearing gloves when he handled the things in the trunk. That's what I expected him to do. Sounds as if he's been careless,' said Cadema frowning. 'But what about the pocketbooks?'

'Marriott must have handled them without gloves on,' said Julia in a concerned voice. 'However, the pocketbooks I have are not a problem. But one is missing – that's the issue.'

'Missing? Are you suggesting that Sergeant Marriott took some of them?'

'*One* is missing, to be precise. Someone has taken it. They run in sequence, and the one from October 1888 is missing.' Julia explained about the gap in the string which had been tied around the bundle.

'That's appalling. You could be wrong of course. Anyone could have taken it. And it may have been missing for decades. Besides, Marriott is the most trusted of my staff – full of integrity and probity. No I can't believe he's taken it.'

'That's your prerogative. I'm keeping an open mind – you're the detective. I'm just giving you the facts.'

'Thanks anyway, Julia, I'll certainly look into it and let you know what transpires. Hopefully he hasn't got anything to do with it.'

'I hope so too,' said Julia who was still shaking her head as the telephone rang.

'Excuse me, I must take this call.' She looked at Julia and lifted the receiver to her ear. 'Yes, Doctor Lilly is here, Sir. She's giving me some of the details from the forensic analysis. No, she hasn't been here long. We'll be at least half an hour.' She paused, listening to the voice. 'If it's okay with you, Sir, I'd prefer to assimilate the information first, then come to your office.' She paused again. 'That's good, I'll see you later then.'

Placing the telephone on its stand she apologized for the interruption saying that Norman Grimes always telephoned when he heard she had someone in her office, just in case he was needed. Cadema didn't tell Julia that he always knew exactly what was going on, and suspected someone in her team was the informant.

'Not to worry, it's all here in my report,' Julia coughed.

Cadema leaned back in her chair and shook her head doubting that Marriott would take anything without her consent. Surely he would realise…

'One thing I found quite amazing.' Julia broke into Cadema's thoughts. 'The name of the police officer who wrote in the pocketbooks was a DC Marriott, now that's a coincidence, and a fact.'

'Good grief, you're right, it is. I've never been in favour of coincidences. Off the record, and as friends, do you think that there is any connection, family wise, between the Marriott then and now?' Cadema leaned forward and whispered. Her brow furrowed. 'If Marriott had taken it, that may well account for his behaviour earlier.'

'Yes I suppose it would. It's impossible to know at the moment. But sure, I've considered a family connection,' said Julia.

'I could follow it up through ancestral archives,' said Cadema. 'But for what purpose? Anyway, there's probably no connection. And if there were, and Marriott knew, he would most probably have told me. The same as he told me about the trunk.

'No, I don't think he took the pocketbook, but I wouldn't have put it past Paul Evans to have done so; although he didn't know about the trunk until after his suspension. No, it must have been someone else, even DC Marriott back in 1888,' suggested Cadema.

Julia nodded as she began searching her briefcase, finally extracting her most important – purple file.

'That's an interesting colour.'

'I always have a colour coded system, and my DNA results are always kept in purple files. You'll be interested in these results, they are from all the samples of body fluids taken from the dress and other garments. A couple of separate semen samples were from the skirt, and several blood samples from the bodice. These are the most important ones.' Julia's voice raced on. 'I'll give a brief description of them but won't go into the technical details if that's okay with you?'

'Perfect,' said Cadema, and then asked if Julia wanted a drink of water from the bottle she had just taken out of her small fridge.

'No thanks, I'm fine since having the tea. Now to the semen stains.'

'Does that mean that the murderer had a sexual motive for his murders?' Cadema was pleased she was alone with Julia so she could ask that question. At the time the perpetrator, according to police accounts then, would not have had the time for sexual activity as he killed and mutilated his victims. Except for Mary Kelly, the last murder victim, where he had ample time, hidden from view, in her room. Therefore, DNA from the semen, must have come from male acquaintances or from clients. Cadema shuddered at the thought of those poor women having to make a living out of prostitution, and then being murdered in such a brutal way.

'I don't know what his motive was. What do you think Cadema?'

'It could have been sexual, who knows. He may have had sex with them earlier that evening. Seeing him again, would not arouse any suspicion until it was too late. And of course, there was a theory that all the victims knew their killer.' Cadema took a sip of water from the plastic beaker, and sat back in her chair.

'I suppose so.' Julia's face blushed and her mouth went dry. 'I think I'll take up the offer of some water please.'

Cadema nodded, stood up and walked over to the window where the fridge was kept. Glancing out, she noticed that Marriott was in the car park again. *Damn,* she thought while pouring the a drink. Surely he wouldn't have the audacity to bother her, especially as it was obvious that Julia was still with her? She watched as he disappeared into the entrance of the building, then returned to her chair.

The knock on the door was no surprise; she ignored it. Without another knock, the door burst open – Grimes thundered in. His wiry frame looked as if he were about to crack in half as he stood, red-faced, and oscillating in the doorway. His glasses, twisted across his crooked nose.

'Oh so you *ladies* have all the time in the world to drink tea, I see.' He glanced at the empty cups – addressing no one in particular. 'Marriott's bemoaning in my office. To top this, I expected you to be there ten minutes ago. And what about briefing the team? Well I don't know what's going on, but I intend to sit in and find out for myself.'

Cadema, determined not to retaliate, took a calm, deep breath and a sip of water.

'You're welcome, Sir. Here, have my chair I'll get another one.' She slowly vacated the chair – Grimes lunged his body into it. Cadema dragged another one towards her desk.

Was he about to use his power of authority and humiliate her in front of Julia? If so, she wasn't going to let him do that.

Grimes shuffled in his seat, his back upright, his eyes alert, his chest expanded as if waiting for information that would make him feel important. Cadema sat back, took a deep breath, and began the briefing.

On reaching the part concerning the semen DNA, Grimes inhaled loudly, held his breath, then let it thunder into the room. 'That's bloody bullshit. Of course his motives were sexual. It doesn't take a detective to work that out.'

'You may be right, Sir. Nevertheless, he wouldn't have had time to have sex with them and simultaneously carry out the murder.'

'How do you know that? Were you bloody there? No. And what about the last one? He had the time. I'm a man, I know how they think. And by God I've seen many sex offenders and murderers to know how they tick. You can't possibly understand that kind of motivation,' Grime snarled.

Cadema decided to say nothing – Julia would see what he was really like. What she had put up with so long. As she listened, she postulated on what Grimes would have done as a detective in 1888. How would he have handled the crimes? If he knew men so well, he may have murdered the women himself. He was most probably capable of it, if only to prove a point.

'So what else have you got, Doctor Lilly?' asked Grimes, portraying a cynical, condescending concern.

'With the DNA profiles I have, the next thing to do is to find out who they belong to by using the new IVD (Instant Verification Database).'

Grimes face contorted, then grimaced. He had never been sure about VIVA (Virtual Instant Verification Apparatus), since it was introduced. And he was even more sceptical about IVD, which sounded like a venereal disease; especially as it hadn't been properly tested. These could never replace real detective work. So why was Cadema going to use them to solve these crimes? Besides, he had no time for Bills that were passed through Parliament quicker than any of King Henry VIII's had done over 450 years before. Guillotined Bills were abhorrent to him, and that included VIVA and IVD.

Now, he'd been told, there are millions of DNA profiles on the database, and he believed it was about to get worse especially if doctors and midwives had to take samples from newborn babies as part of their statutory duties. The only thing Grimes did agree with, was that DNA had to be obtained from everyone entering the United Kingdom so no one would escape to become an illegal immigrant or terrorist.

Grimes was even more surprised when other countries followed the United Kingdom. Of course there had been opposition from human rights protesters. Nevertheless, murder, rape and other serious sexual crimes, robbery and violent crimes had reduced. But he still believed that his police officers were losing their skills. Relying far too much on IT systems, and will do the same with IVD.

'Well you know my views on all of that,' Grimes sneered. Then, pushing his chair from under him, he began to leave. 'Excuse me but I've got much more pressing work to do than sit here all day.' His flushed face turned towards Cadema. 'And when you've finished I want to see you in my office before you brief anyone. Is that understood?' He banged the door shut behind him and his heavy footfall could be heard stomping along the corridor.

'Is he always like that,' asked Julia who then noticed that Cadema's eyes were watering.'

'Not usually that obnoxious,' Cadema replied.

'I know he isn't my boss. But if he were – he has no right to talk to us like that. He is abusing his rank, and to my mind has crossed the bullying line, not to mention the sex discrimination one. No, it just won't do. I don't know how you put up with him. You are usually so assertive. Always so sure of yourself, and proud of what you do. And your recent diversity training should have given you the means to act on what is happening. So blow the whistle on him and his misogynistic and bulling behaviour. If you don't, I will,' Julia threatened.

'You're right, but he's not going to change. Anyway, now he's near retirement – people tend to ignore him – as I do.' Cadema dabbed at her eyes with a tissue, moved her chair closer to the desk, then sat down, facing Julia.

'Look, Cadema, Grimes has become that irritating grit that gets in your shoes from time to time. No matter how much you search for it, it can never be found. To help ease the pain from the grit, you walk with a limp whilst moving the foot from side to side to dislodge it, but it never goes away. After time, your whole leg begins to ache, then your back, and eventually your whole body. If only you had got rid of the grit when you first noticed it, you would not be in such pain.'

Julia's voice hovered in the space between them, like fairy mist oozing into Cadema's thoughts. She nodded. 'That's a profound statement, and I understand what you are saying. But there's not much I can do.' She shook her head slowly.

'I realise it's difficult for you.' Julia took hold of Cadema's hands. 'But I'm not going to let the situation continue any longer. I know it might sound harsh.' Julia looked at Cadema's gaunt face. 'Are you okay? Come on, just take a deep breath and let's talk about it.'

'I'm fine, really.' She gave an artificial smile. Julia was right, but letting her sort out the problems with Grimes was abhorrent to her. She would never let that happen. His abuse had been, up to this point, covert. But now, and in front of Julia – that was a different matter. Once her briefing with Julia was over, she would definitely write a report on the incident, and make an official complaint. It was no use talking to Grimes first – he would never listen to her. Instead he would reflect it back to her, tell her she was paranoid and had to stop for her own sanity. She took a deep breath.

'Sorry about his behaviour, he can be such a pain at times, but that's the worst I've ever seen him.'

'Don't you dare be sorry for *his* behaviour – never make excuses for *him*. It's not you who should be sorry, he should apologise. That kind of behaviour should *never* be tolerated.' She released her hands.

'You're right. So I'm definitely going to do something about it. But I was wondering if there was something wrong with him, mentally or physically, I mean.' Cadema sounded calmer.

Julia sat upright in her chair, her voice angry. 'There you go again, defending him; he's not worth the trouble – he must be stopped.' Her words tapered off, almost to a whisper.

Cadema had never seen Julia like this before. Usually, she was always calm, kept her head down, and worked all hours to get jobs done. Now she was self-assured, militant even.

'I know he has to be stopped, Julia. I've decided to do just that. I'll handle it in my own way. Then put you down as witness, if that's okay with you?'

'That's the spirit, yes of course you can, no need to ask. So let's forget it for now and concentrate on this work,' Julia said as she opened her purple folder again. Then, after discussing the semen samples, she resumed the briefing.

'The next ones are samples of blood taken from the dress. The majority were female – from the woman who was wearing the dress. Two of the other blood samples were from one male. There is no correlation between these and the samples of semen. To my mind, it suggests that they come from the murderer who may have accidently cut himself while perpetrating the crime.'

'Just as I thought might be the case – that's excellent, Julia. Hopefully it will help the search on VIVA and find a match with the DNA from there. If we can find a living relative of his, we can trace the family back over the generations and identify the killer.' Cadema eyes widened – her voice quickened. 'How exciting if we can. But of course, we can also trace the victim's family through this.' She stood up, walked over to the window, opened it and took a deep breath. 'That's better, I felt a bit hot and clammy before.'

'You look better now. And don't forget, if you need any help or advice, I'm only a glass of wine away.' They both smiled.

'I'll remember that. You know I can't thank you enough for all the work you have done, it's remarkable.'

'No need for thanks, but let's meet up again for an update on this and your progress on the Grimes issue.' Julia reached for her iPhone, and after agreeing dates, she left.

***

The assembled officers sounded like a Sunday market in Petticoat Lane. The more someone raised their voice, the more other voices were raised until it was impossible to decipher what was being said.

'Right, let's have your attention,' Cadema said quietly as she entered the room holding a couple of files. But her voice was lost in the mayhem. 'Quiet.' She raised her voice an octave. Still no response. Undignified as she thought it was to shout, but as rank did not always assure acknowledgement of her presence, she banged a heavy book on the table. 'That's enough.' There were a few nudges, and coughs in response as the officers went quiet. 'Why are there so many of you here. There's five on this team, so all those who are not directly involved with these cases, leave the room *now*.' After a few moans, a 'Yes Ma'am', and the plodding of feet, she turned to the three remaining officers.

'So where's DI Pratt?' All she heard was a few 'erms'…
but no one really spoke. She tutted, placed the flies on the
table, and stood wondering why, after giving Pratt specific
instruction to be on time, he wasn't there.

'I'm not going to wait.' She cleared her throat. 'I'll just
give the facts as they are.' After explaining about the male
blood samples and the semen samples she asked if there were
any questions.

'I have one, Ma'am?' said DC Galke, timidly.

'Go ahead,' replied Cadema.

'Well, Ma'am, no disrespect meant but…' He cleared his
throat and looked around the room. His eyes bulged. He tried
to swallow; no saliva. 'If we find out from VIVA the name of
the current relatives, and we manage to locate them, there are
two questions to consider. The first one you might think
trivial…

'If we do locate the relatives, won't it upset them to find
out that one of their ancestors was a victim of the
Whitechapel murderer?'

'I've thought of…' Cadema was interrupted.

'Sorry, but there's something else. If we manage to
identify the family of the murderer as well, do you think it
will cause anger between the two families?'

'You have asked two very intelligent questions there,
well done. I'll do my best to answer them.' Galke seemed to
grow in size as he smiled. Despite this, Cadema noticed his
neck had reddened.

'Before you do, Ma'am, I have a question,' said Marriott.

'Go ahead.' Cadema had seen competition between
fellow officers before. The lower ranks would start the ball
rolling, and then the upper ranks would feel they had to say
something to assert their standing, irrespective of what was
said; the battle of rank had begun.

'If we find relatives of both the victim and the perpetrator, what do we do next?'

'Another good question. What do *you* think we should do next, Marriott?' By turning the question to Marriott, Cadema hoped to avoid rhetorical questions, and encourage discussion instead. Besides that, she may get some sensible answers, some that she hadn't even thought of herself.

Marriott hesitated as he looked at the ceiling. 'I don't know if there is anything we *can* do, is there?'

'You have a point. There are things that are *nice* to know, such as which of the five women owned the dress we have. And it might be *nice* to identify the victim's relatives. But nice for whom? Certainly not for the relatives. Nevertheless, there are things that we *need* to know. For instance, who was the actual killer? Our aim is to discover the name of the perpetrator. To achieve this, we definitely *need* to know the names of the relatives of the murderer. The perpetrator is obviously dead, so finding some living relative is our first step. Once we have a suspect, we must find some tangible evidence that links directly to the victim. What that evidence will be is open to conjecture.' The officers sat quietly listening to Cadema. She was just about to continue when DI Pratt burst into the room.

'Sorry I'm late, Ma'am. A spot of bother with the car.' Cadema nodded to him to take a seat, and then continued with the questions.

'In answer to Marriott's question, what will we do once we've discovered relatives of the victim? Of course we will have to share our evidence with them. I know this will be a very delicate matter, but with sensitivity and probity, we will be able to support them through the ordeal. And, who knows, it may turn out that they know something about an ancestor that they had not considered before.

'Conversely, if we find the relatives of the proposed perpetrator, that is a different matter. We will not be able to identify him until we find evidence that will stand up to scrutiny. Doctor Lilly will help with this. Again it will be difficult for the living relatives, so they need to be treated as I said before. And keep it in mind that they may also have some evidence that has been handed down from their ancestors.'

'Excuse me, Ma'am, but what about IVD...' said Pratt leaning against the wall.

'As you missed the main part of the briefing I'll meet with you in my office in ten minutes' time and go through everything with you.'

'That's difficult as I've got another meeting after this.'

'You'll have to put it on hold. I need to see you first.' Cadema frowned as she picked up her files. Entering the corridor, she met DCI Johns and asked her to accompany her.

Reaching her office, Cadema explained to Johns what Doctor Lilly had said about the missing pocketbook. She asked her not to mention it until she had spoken to Marriott.

'So tell me,' said Cadema, 'what is DI Pratt up to? Do you know why he was late?'

'Not sure there, he seems quite elusive at times, so I'll have to keep an eye on him.'

'Good, just let me know what happens. Right now I've got something else that's important. I can't tell you any more as it is confidential, but will let you know in due course.'

Johns said she understood, and would keep the conversation confidential. At that moment, Pratt knocked at the door. As he entered, Johns left.

Chapter 15

Sergeant Marriott sat at his desk in the sanctuary of his own home fumbling with the police pocketbook. He had procrastinated too long – now it was time to read it properly. Although alone, he looked around, listened for any anything unfamiliar – then took a deep breath.

On the first page he read the dates – August to December 1888. He turned over to the next page.

'*This pocket book belongs to...*' He blinked, then sat gazing at the handwritten name. Brushing his hand through his brown hair, he read the name again, shut the book and closed his eyes.

His hands began to shake – the feeling of faintness – overwhelming. Was he going to be sick? A distant bell rang somewhere in his mind – last night's meal simmered in his throat. He opened his eyes, looked around again, and then swallowed.

Opening the notebook again, there was no mistake, the writing was clear. The book had been written by a DC Marriott – City of London Police. It was real. *Could this be my doppelganger? A coincidence.* He shook his head. *Coincidences like this just don't happen. A dream perhaps?* He thought, and then pinched himself – he was wide awake.

How could it belong to someone with the same name? he reasoned. Someone in the same job. If he were family, why didn't they find out and tell him? He clasped it tightly in his hand – afraid to let go.

He wondered why he had it. *It was waiting for him. He was compelled to have it – to read it. There was no choice – greater powers saw to that*, he looked upwards, wondering if someone could hear him. This relative perhaps? He needed to search his family history. He shrugged, opened the pocketbook, and turned to the third page.

The writing had changed, no longer was it printed and precise as on the previous page. In some places it was merely scribble. The spelling made it indecipherable – as if it were written in a hurry. He slammed it onto the table and sighed. Then, leaning back into his chair, he closed his eyes. 'Relax,' he said, then began to take shallow breaths in and out, in and out. He relaxed his shoulders, his arms, his legs and his toes with the rhythm of his breathing. His body now calm, but his mind raced on.

Alert again, he had supper and he went to bed at nine, much earlier than his usual eleven o' clock. Head on his pillow, he closed his eyes. In his shadowy sleep, his mind was walking the beat, back in 1888. He was standing on the corner of Aldgate High Street and Fenchurch Street. The smell of gas lamps and stench from the nearby abattoir, stung at his nostrils. Blinking in the half-light he saw the lone figure of a woman slowly walking on the opposite side of the street. Her dress, one he remembered seeing before but didn't know where, swept the pavement. She tugged at her coat collar and hung onto her hat. She stopped, turned and faced a man who had approached her. She moved closer to him. They exchanged words he was unable to hear. Then stood for a couple of minutes under the lamp, until, arm in arm, they walked away.

Marriott had seen the killer. He could describe him perfectly but was paralyzed to do anything about it. The man was about five feet ten inches tall, and of medium built. He wore a thick dark grey or black overcoat, that, had the man chosen, could have been buttoned up to his chin. Instead, he had left the first two buttons undone despite the cold weather. His face was long, his forehead, partially covered with a small hat, was high. Marriott could not determine the type of hat – but it wasn't a deerstalker, as some people had supposed. His low thick-black eyebrows failed to hide the man's dark penetrating eyes. The beard and moustache were well cropped and there were no sideburns, or at least he couldn't see any. He could not tell how old he was, but he stood erect, in command, and walked unhindered and unaided. There was no sign of a bag or anything else to carry instruments in, such as knives. The man seemed polite enough, gesturing the way to go, as if the woman were a lady. Yes, he seemed to be a perfectly ordinary gentleman of his generation. *Perhaps a little too ordinary to be caught*, Marriott thought. There was something odd about the man – he was trusted. The woman happily chuckled when they walked off together, despite the recent murders.

The scene vanished in a microsecond. Marriott turned on his bedside light, sat up, reached for the pocketbook, turned to the third page, and began to read. After deciphering the first two sentences, he found a description of a man seen with Annie Chapman just before she was murdered. The description matched the man he had just seen in his half-sleep. Turning his light off again, he tried to go back to sleep.

Tossing his head from side to side, and punching at his pillow, he wished he had returned the pocketbook to the archives when he had the chance; now it was too late. All he could think of was Doctor Lilly and her vigilant reputation. She would definitely notice a pocketbook was missing, and would tell Cadema. He turned the light on again, got out of bed, and started to pace the floor.

What would Superintendent Sharma do if she found out? Would she suspend him like she had Evans, or just give him a verbal warning? He hoped she would see his point of view, especially as he took it inadvertently. Surely she would see the mitigating circumstances when she found out that it belonged to a Marriott? He climbed into bed again and switched off the light.

Waking up from a nightmare, Marriott looked at his bedside clock; three a.m. He reasoned that, if he ignored the pocketbook, it would continue to burn a hole in his brain that he would never recover from. Sighing, he got out of bed again and wrapping himself in his dressing gown. He picked up the pocketbook, sat in his chair, and began to read. Three lines in, he slammed it on the table and went back to bed.

It was eight o'clock the next morning when Marriott stood outside Cadema's office – the pocketbook concealed in his pocket – burning his brain. It wasn't like her to be late; *bad omen*, he thought. Cadema arrived at nine o'clock, dishevelled and with her eyes full of anger.

'Good morning, Ma'am,' his voice croaked out.

'It's not as good as it could be Marriott.' She took a sip of her Starbucks coffee. 'The traffic's appalling, a broken-down lorry again,' she grumbled. Walking into her office, she tore off her coat and rammed it on a hook behind the door. Then, raising her eyebrows, she held the door open and faced him. 'Well, don't just stand there, come in.'

Marriott nodded – eyes averted, he entered her office. Cadema walked over to her desk, she took another sip of coffee and gestured for him to sit down on the chair in front of her. He coughed, and sat with his shoulders hunched.

'I've come to…'

'Don't say anything else. Just be quiet, I've got something to say to you first.' She coughed and took another sip.

'But, Ma'am…'

'Not another word, Sergeant.' Cadema sounded officious as she noticed his dishevelled appearance. 'You look as if you haven't slept much lately, your eyes are sunken. Are you ill?'

'No, Ma'am, well…'

'If that's the case, I'll continue, so keep quiet and let me finish what I have to say.' Marriott coughed. 'I suspect that the reason for your disquiet is the pocketbook you took from the trunk.' Cadema looked at him – waiting for his reaction at being accused without much evidence. She waited for him to say something – to give him the opportunity to return it. She hoped he would be honest and not deny it. But if he lied, then she would instantly suspend him from duty. She sat back in her chair, folded her arms and remained deliberately mute.

He couldn't speak, but coughed and turned his head away. Slowly he reached inside his jacket and eased out the pocketbook.

'Sorry, Ma'am, but I intended to study it and then give it to you some time ago. But for some reason it took me ages to gain enough courage to even open it, let alone read it.' He reached over the desk and handed it to her. 'I know I shouldn't have taken it, and I'm ready to face the consequences, whatever they are.'

'I could suspend you for this. And I emphasise the word *could*. Do you understand, Sergeant?' He nodded his head. 'But I don't think that will be necessary as you have at least been honest in bringing it back. You know you shouldn't have taken it in the first place, but I think your intentions were sound, just misguided. Am I right?' He nodded again.

'I just wanted to…' She suppressed his words with a hand gesture.

'Never mind what you wanted to do. This time I'm giving you a verbal warning, but if anything like this ever happens again, then you'll know what to expect?' Again he started to speak but she stopped him with a traffic hand signal. 'It won't go on your records this time. But if you do anything like this again. I'll suspend you. Is that clear?' She waited for him to respond.

'Yes, Ma'am, but I'd like to explain,' he said in a muffled voice.

'There's no need to explain.' Her voice quivered a little. She had never spoken to an officer with such mixed feelings before. In one way, she was reprimanding him for something that was beyond his control. But in another way, it was as if he had actually committed a crime against her; that she was the victim. After all she had trusted him, he was one of her team, and to take something without asking was a violation of her trust, her authority, and of course the whole police service. She coughed and began to speak in her usual controlled way. 'You've disappointed me, Marriott. But now you've handed in the pocketbook, you need to concentrate on showing me that you can be trusted again.' She gave a twitch of a smile, but Marriott's eyes were on the pocketbook on her desk.

'Yes, Ma'am, and I'm so...'

'Don't say it. It will only mean one thing to me, that you are sorry for being caught out and not sorry for what you've done...'

'I want to assure you that I'll never be tempted again,' said Marriott as he began to rise from his chair.'

'Sit down, I've not finished yet. Tell me what you found in the pocketbook.' He cleared his throat as he resumed his seat.

'I've only got as far as page three, and it's written by a PC Marriott in 1888. I couldn't read any more. For some reason, I felt guilty. As if I were raiding a grave or something; as if someone was watching me.'

Cadema frowned, reminded him that honesty and loyalty were paramount to the job, and then told him to leave. She would have liked to give him all the other pocketbooks to read, but thought better of it. After all, she reasoned, it would be like catching a child stealing sweets, and then saying it could eat them. And what lesson would that be to the child, or to one of her team? No, she had to be strict. She had been lenient with Evans, and that had backfired.

Chapter 16

Chief Superintendent Norman Grimes sat in his leather reclining chair in the most palatial office in the police station. He was sampling his newly acquired vintage single malt whisky, a rare brand. With only a thousand bottles sold – he was privileged to drink it.

'What's this all about, Norman?' Duncan Mander, the Commissioner, burst into Grimes' office, a three page document in his hand.

'Oh I expect it's from Superintendent Sharma, she's always wittering on about something. Now she's a bee in her bonnet about me. Something about me being rude to her when she was having tea with that Doctor Lilly, I suppose. I'll speak to her about it. It's all a misunderstanding I expect, and no doubt taken out of context. Fancy a drink, Sir? Oh sorry I forgot you don't drink.' Grimes took a deep breath and then exhaled as slowly as he could. His face remained emotionless as he gave a slight shrug to his shoulders, hoping Mander would think he was indifferent to the issue. But inside he was angry with Cadema. *The little bitch, how dare she do this? I'll make sure she doesn't step out of line again.* He grimaced at Mander, who was now sitting down and undoing the top button of his jacket.

'How come it's so hot in here when all the other offices are much colder?' he asked.

'It's the central heating, Sir, hasn't been working very well lately. But at least it will be fixed soon. And a good job too, since we haven't had the bad weather they promised yet.' The idiot, thought Grimes; *if you can't take the heat…*

'Good, let's hope it's fixed soon. January's not the best time to have the boiler up the spout.'

Mander was one of those fast-trackers with a degree in economics. Grimes believed that he had been promoted to comply with the ethnic quotas, even though he was not quite sure which ethnic group he belonged to. Nevertheless, he could never understand why they chose Mander above him. The only consolation Grimes had was that he would be retiring soon. He smiled at the thought of putting his feet up and doing absolutely nothing. Taking a sip of his single malt, his daydreams were interrupted by Mander.

'Are you with me, Norman? Seems to me as if you're in another world.'

'Sorry, Sir, I was just thinking.'

'Well don't. Anyway there's no need for the sir. Duncan will do as we're alone. Anyway, this complaint from Cadema Sharma, why didn't you tell me about it?' Mander stood up and was pacing the floor.

Grimes couldn't see what all the fuss was about. It was just a report and he could handle it. He shrugged his shoulders again and gave a twitch of a smile as Mander walked past him again.

'I didn't think it was such a big deal. I mean, I didn't think she would take things this far.'

Mander swung round, his red face dripping, his arms gesticulating as he held the paper a couple of centimetres away from Grimes' face. *Like a bird trying to take flight,* Grimes thought, hoping he would.

'This far, this far. What were you thinking of? Do you realise Sharma's sent a copy of this to Fredrick, the Mayor of London, and no doubt one to the Home Office as well?' He leaned across the desk and brushed the papers in front of Grimes' face so fiercely this time that it caused a draught.

Grimes pushed back in his seat fearing that Mander would actually have a fit.

'Sorry, Sir, I mean Duncan. But I didn't think she would do such a thing.' He turned, poured himself another single malt, and took a gulp. It didn't calm him as he hoped it would but at least it would do him good. *Anyway, what the heck. I'm too old for this sort of thing. The younger ones should get on with their jobs as I've had to do since joining the Met thirty-odd years ago. That's how I've managed to get where I am now. So I had to step on a few toes now and again, but if it helped with promotions, so be it. I don't have any regrets.*

'There you go, Norman, far away, again.' Mander breathed slowly as he pushed his fingers together to form an arch, then tapped them near his own lips. 'It seems to me that you don't always think. I hope you realise that, *now* this is an official complaint, I'll have to treat it as such. Nevertheless, before I take any action, I'm going to speak to Fredrick. In the meantime, make yourself scarce, go on garden leave or something. But don't you dare go anywhere near Sharma, is that understood?' Mander screeched.

'Yes, Duncan, but she's on her way to brief me about these cases she's working on.'

'Well send her to me instead. I'll let her know where she stands. In the meantime, you'd better have this and write your report.' He placed the copy of the file on Grimes' desk.

As the commissioner left the office, Grimes couldn't help wondering what all the fuss was about. Surely Sharma wouldn't make a meal of it? After all it was just a bit of fun, nothing at all like harassment or bullying. He poured himself another drink and thought of how hard he had worked over the years. How he was always respected and the number of crime he had solved. Now everyone was against him. He couldn't do anything right. Yes, he was going to write his report, but not what Duncan would expect. He was going to say how everyone was ignoring him. How Sharma and the others had laughed at him. He was the one who was being bullied. He was the one who had not been promoted, when others, whom in his opinion, didn't deserve to be. People were obviously against him. He was surrounded by them, especially the women – they were discriminating against him. He had to put a stop to that.

When I retire, he thought, *I want to go with dignity and with my good reputation intact. I might even get a knighthood; something I truly deserve for services to the country.*

Another glass of the malt warmed his body, and, sitting in his chair he looked out of the window – watching the sun beginning to set. He could see most of his London patch from here. And sipping his drink, he remembered every crime he had detected over the years. He recalled joining the force just after the arrest of the Yorkshire Ripper, Peter Sutcliffe. As he moved up the ranks he had been involved in many other high profile cases. The embassy sieges, riots in Brixton and Tottenham, and the six murders, including last year's Common Murders. *Thank goodness for the introduction of DNA analysis – used initially in the Pitchfork murders in Leicestershire,'* he muttered. Then he recalled the introduction of computers, and HOLMS-2 that helped to coordinate intelligence in major crimes.

Yes, detection of crime was much easier now than it had ever been when he joined. But conversely, criminals were getting smarter; *they'll never outsmart me though*, he reasoned. Smiling, he sat upright in his chair and straightened his tie, as if he were on parade.

'Yes, I can at least say I'm proud of the work I've done in my service, and especially as Chief Superintendent,' he saluted his own photograph on the desk, and then raised his glass to it. 'And now that my work's nearly over, I can retire with a clear conscience despite Sharma's bloody grievance.'

He filled his glass with the remnants of the single malt, and then drifted off to sleep.

***

When the cleaner went into Grimes' office at six the next morning, she could see he was asleep as usual. So, instead of opening the blinds and cleaning his office, she quietly slipped out of the room and closed the door.

It was not until Duncan Mander went to see Grimes about his report at ten in the morning that the alarm was raised. Later, it could not be established if Grimes had died of natural causes or not. But under the circumstances, a post mortem examination was ordered to establish the cause of death.

When Cadema heard the news, she managed to hold back her tears of frustration. Not because Grimes was dead, but because she hoped that her grievance with him, and the subsequent investigation, may reveal the undertones of institutional sexism in the division. And, with her Asian ancestry, probable racism, although she would have difficulty proving the latter even though there was a deficit of ethnic minority women in the higher ranks.

Chapter 17

Cadema wondered if working for the police service was worth the effort she, and no doubt Grimes, had put into it over the years. After all, since Superintendent Jim Logan's death, Grimes had been a constant in her life. Not the constant she would have liked, but now, since he drank himself to death, she felt overwhelmingly guilty.

Returning from his funeral, she sat at her desk just looking at the pile of files from the current investigation. She couldn't touch them. Instead, she wondered if her grievance with Grimes had somehow contributed to his death. Perhaps she shouldn't have been so vociferous in the wording of her report. Perhaps she should have listened to him. Perhaps he had real problems and needed someone to talk to or at least someone to realise that something was wrong. But she had been adamant in her pursuit of justice. The report on him had been the means for her to sort everything out – for good.

But today, during the funeral, she had looked into his widow's tearful bloodshot eyes and realised she had made a mistake. She had robbed Grimes of his retirement, of the plans he had undoubtedly made with Jane, his wife. The happy years they would have spent together, no longer interrupted by the pressure of work.

'Over thirty years, all lost, and for what?' she muttered. The tissue in her hand was all she had now. Perhaps she shouldn't have listened to Julia, although she wasn't blaming her; she should have been more assertive and rational? Then she would have done what Jim Logan had said when he was alive:

'When you are distressed or angry about something, you should write it down in a letter or a document. Lock it away in a drawer or somewhere safe so that no one can inadvertently see it. Leave it for twenty-four hours to think it over. Then, with your rational head on, you can revise it, shred it, or send it.'

If she had done this, she would never have sent such a raw and insensitive report. She was too headstrong at the time, it would never happen again. Next time, if there would ever be one, she would do what Jim suggested.

She had just finished wiping her eyes with a tissue, when the phone rang. Her hand hovered over it – her fingers hesitated. She cleared her throat, brushed a strand of hair from her face – waiting for the answerphone to start. After the sixth ring, she picked it up but didn't speak.

'Hello, is anyone there? I'm trying to contact Superintendent Sharma.' Julia's voice echoed in her ear. Still she did not speak. 'Hello is anyone there?' Cadema silently replaced the receiver onto its station and sat looking at the unopened files on her desk. She didn't want to work. She couldn't work. The devastation she was feeling right now – she may never work again. She spoke to no one as she put on her coat and left.

The flash of the lights and the sound of menacing voices confronted her as she stepped out of the station and into the street. The Press followed as she ran along the pavement. As she reached the taxi they stopped – watched as she hurled herself inside, and then screech away.

'Blimey, that was close. Paparazzi after you, hey? Well I'm the cavalry. Where can I take you?' The driver's head turned sideways for less than a second, his cockney accent sharp and clear. Turning his face to his windscreen again she noticed his eager dark blue eyes watching her in the rear-view mirror. He stroked his grey beard, then flipped back his thinly tapering ponytail. 'Where do you want to go, Miss?' he shouted above the noise of the engine.

'Home, I want to go home.' She felt the tears fill her eyes, her voice choking. 'I want to go home,' she repeated. Her voice began to fade away – she wished she would too. 'Oh no, not there. Take me to the Raven Hotel in Bloomsbury.'

'Right-t-oh Miss.' He took a quick U-turn which started a cacophony of car horns as he manoeuvred the vehicle and sped off in the opposite direction. 'Don't worry, I knows these shortcuts. Just hold on and we'll be there in a jiffy.'

Trust a London cabbie to know even the shortest route, she thought then blew her nose on another tissue.

'Terrible business that. Don't you think? Can't trust anyone these days can ya, terrorists and all that?' The driver craned his neck as he looked at her again. Cadema didn't answer. She didn't want to talk to anyone right now. She nodded a couple of times, hopefully at the right moments. The driver took the hint and was quiet for the rest of the journey. 'There ya are, safe and sound. That'll be...'

Fumbling in her handbag, she found her purse and extracted an appropriate amount. 'Thank you, and please keep the change.' She handed him the money and alighted from the taxi.

'Good on ya, Miss,' he said, and without a second glance, drove off. Sighing, she slowly turned, straightened her shoulders, and then walked towards the hotel. Its automatic doors opened as she reached them. As she walked into the hotel lobby it seemed as if she had just stepped into another century. She moved on, her shoes sinking into the deep-pile red and green carpet. The whole room, with its dark wood panelling, was in congruent with her mood. But as she looked up, she managed a smile at seeing the elaborate plasterwork of the ceiling that might have been done by one of Michelangelo's pupils.

A young man with red hair stood at the counter. Computer in front of him, he smiled a welcome, and began to ask her questions about her booking.

'No, I don't have a reservation. Nor do I have any luggage. Yes, for two nights if you have a room.'

'Yes, we have a vacant room, but for security reasons we need a credit card, or bank card please,' said the young man – offering a smile. She hesitated for a moment and looked around the empty lobby. Slowly she opened her handbag, took out her purse, and handed him the cash for her stay.

'I don't have a card on me right now. But as I'll be paying cash, is my driving licence acceptable as ID?' She considered showing him her warrant card but decided the driving licence would be better. Nevertheless, any trouble – she would use it as a last resort. Most irregular, but after all, she could be on police business.

'It's not our usual policy, Madam, so I'll have to check with the manager.' He smiled again, and then disappeared through a door behind the desk. Moments later he returned, took Cadema's details and pointed to the lifts.

The room was furnished with opulent decorations. Some had obviously been there since Victorian times; everything was clean and well preserved. The king-sized bed with its white lace coverings, added to the brightness of the room. A swivel television stood on a small chest of draws in the corner. On a table, she found a remote control that served, not only the television but also controlled the opening and closing of the curtains. Dropping her handbag and coat onto a chair, she removed her shoes and entered the bathroom. It reminded her of a Roman bathhouse she had once seen on a documentary programme. The marbled tiles covered the floor, the walls and around the bath matching perfectly with the hand basin. On the heated towel rail were two fluffy-white towels. Choosing the *muscle-relaxant* foam bath liquid, she poured a generous amount into the bath. Then turned on the tap, and checked the water temperature. As the bubbles surged upwards she undressed and slowly slid into the foam.

She didn't know where the last forty-five minutes had gone as she stepped out of the bath and swathed herself into an enormous gratuitous dressing gown. Decamping to the bedroom again, she walked to the minibar and poured herself a small glass of red wine. It was time to switch off the world. Two sips of wine later, she began to nod. Then, secured under the bedclothes, fell into an agitated asleep.

'No, don't do that.' She squirmed as cold calloused hands touched her naked body. She tried to push Paul's hands away but she was powerless. 'No, Paul, I don't want you. I'm your boss not your lover.' Paul's hands didn't move away, she knew they wouldn't. Then she heard his menacing voice, the voice she had heard before. The voice of someone who was guilty.

'Come on, I know you mean yes. They all do.' He sniggered and then laughed. His hot body pressed against hers.

'I mean NO. No. No. No.' She tried to scream – no sound came from her lips. She kicked out with paralysed legs. Angry and sweating now, she clawed at whatever was in front of her. Her heart pounded. She struggled to breathe. She tried to scream again, but the rattle from her throat alerted her senses. She moved her head towards the sound. She opened one eye, then the other eye. Her eyes wide open now, they oscillated in unison, searching the room. Nothing. She was in bed – alone.

The nightmare was over. In the chaos, she found herself wrapped in the hotel's white sheets like a mummy. Untangling one arm, she stretched it out and turned on the bedside light. Two pillows were over by the door. The other bedside lamp was knocked over, as was the chair where her clothes had been neatly laid earlier that night. But there was no intruder. Unravelling her body, she ventured to the fridge. Taking out a bottle of water, she drained it and then returned to bed where sleep was waiting for her.

***

'Where's Superintendent Sharma?' asked Duncan Mander when he looked into Cadema's office and discovered it was empty – the blinds still closed.

'Sorry, Sir, I don't know,' said Marriott, standing to attention.

'At ease, no sense in ceremony.'

'No, Sir,' Marriott remained standing in the doorway. A frown appeared on his face; he shrugged. 'I haven't seen her since the funeral, Sir.'

'When she comes in tell her I want to see her in my office immediately.' Mander brushed his bald head with his right hand, stroked his greying trimmed beard and straightened his jacket. Then turned and marched down the corridor.

Marriott stood for a while as other officers arrived at their desks. The cacophony of voices worked up to a crescendo as officers postulated on what could have happened to her. Some said she had probably got drunk and was at home sleeping it off. Others thought she had taken a prayer break. While others agreed that it was out of character for her to go missing.

After speaking to Doctor Lilly, who said she had no idea where Cadema was, DCI Johns organised a search for her. She would go to Cadema's address, Marriott was to telephone hospital accident and emergency departments. And Galke was to enquire if the press had followed her the previous evening. Uniformed officers were deployed in the search, while DI Pratt was supposedly on another case.

By two in the afternoon, every enquiry was fruitless. No one had seen or heard from Cadema. Her car was still parked where it had been the day before. Her mobile phone was switched off. And further investigations revealed that she had not used her credit card.

'Sorry to inform you, Sir, but Superintendent Sharma has not been found and therefore, with your permission, can we assume that she is missing and may be in danger?' Johns sounded anxious as she spoke to Mander.

'Yes of course. You've done a good job so far in treating her as a missing person. Now we need to push the search up a peg or two. I'll let the press know. So what is DI Pratt doing in all of this? As Mander spoke, Johns' eyes searched his face looking for some hidden message.

'Sorry, Sir, but I haven't seen Pratt today. I heard he was investigating the stabbing of a man from last night. I'll give you the details as soon as they become available, Sir.'

'Well when *he* does materialise, I need to see him. By the way, how are the other officers coping since the death of Chief Superintendent Grimes? It's never easy when one loses a colleague, especially in such exceptionally tragic circumstances. And it's all been such a rush, what with the funeral and everything. But I'm assured that the counsellors will be with them all later today, and hopefully by then, we'll have found Superintendent Sharma.'

***

It was six o'clock the following evening when Cadema woke up and made herself a cup of tea. For the first time since Norman's death, she smiled at her own actions. Why had she been so threatened by the press? They couldn't harm her. She had acted like a child, but would have to face them at some stage. Sitting in bed with her knees almost touching her chin, and sipping at her tea, it all seemed such a long time ago. She would have to face everyone sooner than later, but not yet.

Julia was the only person she wanted to talk to now. She had telephoned her three times using the hotel phone, but there was no answer. Perhaps Julia hadn't answered because she didn't recognise the phone number?

Finishing her tea, she reached for the hotel phone again and dialled Julia's number. She would definitely leave her a message this time. But instead of the answerphone she heard Julia's voice.

'Hello, this is Cad...'

'Hi, where are you, Cadema? I've been so worried. And half of Scotland Yard are looking for you. Where are you?' Julia's voice raced on.

Cadema sighed, then put the phone down. Standing by the bedside, she bit her lip. She could tell Julia was worried about her, by her quivering voice. Why hadn't she spoken to her, put her mind at rest, she didn't know. Now she just couldn't.

'Maybe tomorrow morning,' she mumbled, 'but not tonight, not now.' Instead, she decided to have another glass of wine and watch TV. To help her forget the realities of life, at least for now.

But what life did she have? It had all become one boring routine. Up early, feed the cat, empty the cat litter, and go to work. Reprimand some of her officers, and solve the latest case a member of the public had committed. Go to the hairdressers once a month for a colour and blow dry. The colour was important to her, no streaks or greys would be allowed. And what about Julia? She was also part of her routine now. The Merlot, the curries, the talks, the planning, her ten-point plans...

She needed to get control of her life. But now she realised that life, and the death of Grimes, were controlling her. The reality was that she had never really been in control, it was all an elusion. Everything was lost; her father, her husband, the baby, Jim Logan and now Grimes. Her mother had left her and returned to India. And Julia would be next to leave?

Julia, so in control, so casual, so knowledgeable and so professional. Nothing worried her; there was always a solution somewhere. Everything seemed black and white; there was no room for other colours, except perhaps purple. There were only a few lines on her face despite nearing forty-one. Cadema had many, and looked much older, despite being a few years younger. Julia was radiant, her bobbed hair casual with shades of brown and blonde – nothing seemed to bother her.

As these thoughts were escalating in Cadema's mind, another thought occurred to her. Why was she thinking of these things now? Something had changed. She turned and looked closely at her image in the mirror, searching for something tangible. Nothing was evident. She looked away – thinking of the things she had done in her life. How she had climbed the ranks. How proud she and her parents had been. Was she true to her faith? Was all this "God's will"? Was everything in His hands? She didn't know any more.

And what was the nightmare telling her? Perhaps it was something she had not faced in a long time. That she was too busy in her life to find another partner. Perhaps she should have complied with her mother's wishes, and got married again. Then given up her job, settled down and had the family she should have had all those years ago, when her husband was alive. But she had loved – no one would ever take his place.

All she had now was her career. 'Well at least for the next day or two,' she said as she sipped her wine. Grimes' death was her fault. Unintentionally or not, she was guilty. And even if she did manage to keep her job, and her rank, she wondered if she could ever be in control again.

After showering, she got into bed; this time she kept the light on, just in case. At three o'clock in the morning she woke, and lay in bed listening to the creaking building. In the distance, probably just a couple of room away from hers, she could hear someone snoring. A door banged somewhere up the corridor. There were faint voices next door, then the unmistakable sound of a squeaking bed.

She pulled the covers up over her head and tried not to listen. The extraneous noises vanished – replaced by her own heart pounding. Her mind active – still analysing – alert and ready for action.

Flinging the covers off, she sat upright – *Cameo the cat*. She must go home and feed her and change the cat litter. She imagined Cameo trying to devour the most inedible morsel of something to stay alive. She would be emaciated and dehydrated; clawing at the cat flap to get out. The neighbours would hear her pathetic calls and send for the RSPCA. She would be charged with animal cruelty. But she couldn't go back; the cat would be all right. The cat flap would be open. Cameo would go next door to be fed as she always did when she was working late. *Clever cat*, she thought, then drifted off to sleep.

The chiming of the church bells woke her with a start, Was it seven, eight, or nine o' clock in the morning? She had counted five – had she missed any? Lying in bed and listening to the purring of the traffic, the occasional beep of a car's horn, and seeing daylight around the edge of the curtains, she surmised it was around eight o'clock. The knock on the door confirmed it.

Donning the hotel's dressing gown, she tied the belt tightly around her waist and headed for the door. Following a quick peep through the security hole, she opened it and took the breakfast tray, mouthed 'Thank you' to the young woman, and shut the door. Sitting at the only desk in the room, she began to eat as if she were a dormouse who had just awoken from hibernation. Spooning the cornflakes, she glanced at the headline in the complementary newspaper.

'Missing... Superintendent Sharma of the Metropolitan Police ... last seen two days ago fleeing from the paparazzi. Police believe that there is no connection between the death of Chief Superintendent Norman Grimes, her boss, from *natural causes*, and her disappearance...'

She stopped reading and swallowed the last mouthful of breakfast cereal. Then, sat staring at the photograph of a twenty-five-year-old woman from India. How the years had changed her. No one would ever recognise her now. She wouldn't be identified at the hotel as the missing person.

Picking up the hotel phone again, she stood for a moment rehearsing what she was going to say to Julia. She pressed the numbers and listened; no answer. Wiping a tear from her eye with a tissue, she placed the phone back on its station and headed for the bathroom.

Showered and dressed, she was ready, if only for a walk around the block. Being cooped up wasn't her forte – fresh air was on the agenda again.

With light steps she walked towards the lift humming a tune from a happier time in her life. Entering the lift alone, she pressed the button for the lobby. As it stopped at the first floor, a mother with a child in a stroller, struggled in. Cadema nodded a 'Good morning' and turned to read an advertisement on the wall. She helped the mother alight from the lift, followed her into the lobby, then stopped.

The mêlée of people seemed to stop too. She sensed them looking directly at her; watching her as she gasped for breath. She began to sweat, her heart thumped against the inside of her ribs. A thousand needles seemed to fire at her muscles.

She stood firm and alert. She wanted to go; to get away from them all and never look back. But something was keeping her there; paralysed.

A glance at the security camera. A look at the faces. Everyone and everything were watching her. Her mind scrambled. Were all these people undercover officers from other divisions? They looked menacing. She took a deep breath; *mustn't panic, mustn't run*. She slowly turned. Her body was heading towards the lift. Trancelike she entered and ascended. The key opened the door. She exhaled. Her body toppled onto the bed and fell asleep.

'Jim is that you, is it really you? Are you all right? I've been hit, but I don't think it's serious; I'll be okay.' She grimaced in her pain.

'Be brave, you're a fighter, you'll survive. I'll look after you till the ambulance comes,' she heard him say as his voice, and his image began to fade away. She tried to speak to him again, to say goodbye. She clawed at the space between them – trying to hold on to something tangible; nothing.

The ringing of the telephone jolted her from her torment. Wrapped even tighter in the bedclothes, she struggled to reach it. Gingerly she picked up the receiver.

'Hello, is that Miss Sharma?

'No, sorry. I mean yes.'

'Good. Sorry to disturb, Ma'am, but...' She sat upright her eyes surveyed the room – searching every corner – fearing she was being watched. Fearing that, at any moment someone would burst into the room. She listened again. 'According to our records, you've only booked in for two days. Therefore you should have vacated your room at ten o'clock this morning. It's now one-thirty.'

'Oh yes, so it is. I must have drifted off to sleep. Is the room available for another day?'

'Yes, Ma'am, it is. But after that it's booked. So you can have the room until ten tomorrow morning.'

'That's good, thank you.' She replaced the phone. Seconds later she dialled for room service and asked for the lunch to be brought up to her room. Ten minutes later it had arrived and five minutes after that, the plate stood empty. Drinking the tepid tea she picked up the phone and tapped Julia's number. She was just about to replace the phone after it had rung several times, when she heard a voice.

'Julia...'

'Cadema. Please don't hang up on me. Where are you?' There was no answer. 'I know it's you, so speak to me please. Where are you?'

Cadema heard a faint weary voice give the name of the hotel and the room number. She didn't know whose voice it was but it didn't sound like her own. It sounded like a child's voice, lonely and in desperation.

'Try not to worry.' Julia sounded sympathetic. 'I'll be there as soon as I can, probably in half an hour.'

'Okay.' She could hear the echo of a child's voice again, half sobbing, as she buried herself in the bedclothes.

Julia arrived in fifteen minutes followed by the ambulance, and a police car.

'This is a delicate situation,' Julia said to the senior personnel from both services. 'It's not life-threatening though, so I will see Superintendent Sharma on my own. Once I've spoken to her, I'll call you.'

Julia had no intention of asking for their permission to do this. She preferred to tell them first, and then wait for protests. With both parties in agreement, she left them in the lobby and entered the lift.

When Julia entered the room, all she could see in the partial darkness was the outline of a still body wrapped in sheets. She shuddered, held her breath and walked slowly towards the bed. She whispered, as one might do when someone has died:

'Cadema, it's Julia.' She forced a swallow against the dryness in her mouth and then stopped in the middle of the room. Clearing her throat, she edged closer – stepping over several items of clothing as she went. Taking care not to touch or disturb anything. 'Cadema, are you all right?' She took another step forward and reached the bed. 'How are you?' She touched the sheets. The body was hot. 'Cadema, its Julia.' The body moved. Julia sighed and began to unravel the sheets. 'I know you're not well. I sent for an ambulance; it's waiting outside. Will you go with them? I'll come with you if you would like me to.'

'Where's Jim Logan. Is he okay?' Cadema whimpered.

'He's not okay, but you are going to be all right.' She didn't want to tell her that Jim had been dead for years. She was obviously reliving the day when he was killed by a sniper and she was also shot. 'I'll get the ambulance men to come up if that's okay with you?'

Cadema did not speak as she was wheeled out of the hotel on a stretcher and taken in the ambulance to the nearest hospital. Julia paid the hotel bill and then headed to the A&E department.

Happy that Cadema had been admitted and then sedated, Julia left for home. Sitting in her living room she suppressed several yawns, but rather than go to bed, she turned on the television and heard the news:

'Superintendent Sharma, has been found alive and well. She was admitted to hospital suffering from mental exhaustion, but is expected to be discharged home in a couple of days.'

A typical press statement, Julia thought. *When they can't find anything to say – and not wanting to say that she was in a psychiatric unit; they always called it exhaustion.* Julia hoped it was only that, and Cadema would soon be better.

Chapter 18

Cadema was discharged from hospital the following day. After having an additional week off, she was ready for work.

The usual, *Glad to see you back, Ma'ams,* over, Johns asked Marriott to give a brief update on the progress he had made on the cases. Opening his mouth to speak, he was interrupted with a message from the station PC saying that Doctor Lilly was waiting to see Superintendent Sharma. Cadema turned to ask Johns to accompany her, then had second thoughts – Julia would no doubt want to discuss some personal things in addition to professional ones. So giving her apologies, she left. Arriving at her office, Julia was waiting for her.

'It's good to see you,' said Cadema as Julia walked towards her. Both giving a gestured kiss on the cheek, they sat facing each other.

'How are you feeling now?' Her voice sounded concerned.

'Not too bad, but I'm itching to get started on the investigation again.' Cadema surreptitiously wiped moisture from her eye with her finger.

'Good to hear. But do take care of yourself, and don't overdo it.'

'I'll try. Anyway I'm much better now.' She sounded as if she were trying to convince herself.

Julia nodded and cleared her throat. 'We've discovered some new evidence since you've been away. I would have told you earlier, but didn't want to burden you. Besides I was busy with the rail disaster with which I'm still involved.'

'I heard about that. It must have been pretty awful. Twenty dead, that's a lot to be doing.' Cadema shook her head slowly and grimaced.

'It *was* awful, but that's my job.' Julia shrugged as she handed Cadema a purple file. 'I think you will find this very interesting. As you can see,' Cadema sat flicking through the pages as Julia spoke, 'the samples I took from the dress for DNA analysis were analysed by the forensic scientists' team. After agreement with the authorities, including data protection, the data was entered into the IVD (Instant Verification Database). You remember Wilhelmina Cox our new pathologist?' Cadema nodded. 'She identified several potential matches for the perpetrator's descendants. Further scrutiny eliminated most of these except two. One of these families is called Forrest, the other one is Ribley. Hopefully further research may eliminate one of them.'

'That's excellent work, Julia. I'll follow those two families up and find out if they had relatives who lived in the East End of London around the time in question. I'll get my team onto it tomorrow.'

'There's just one other thing, I've also got data on the female DNA and intend to identify the person who was wearing the dress found in the trunk. I'll let you know what transpires,' said Julia as she stood up and headed for the door. Saying goodbye, she left – knowing she would have further work to do once Cadema had spoken to the two families.

***

When Cadema explained about the progress Doctor Lilly had made on the DNA samples at the team briefing, they awoke from hibernation. There was no mistake on their faces – they had won the lottery.

'That's all well and good, Ma'am,' said Johns, 'but we still have to wait for data on the victim. Then find some tangible evidence linking her to the killer. All this work will take months, and our timescale is fast coming to an end.'

'I realise your concerns, so I've already spoken to the department. The assistant commissioner is happy for an extension especially when I explained that the investigation had, in reality, only just begun. That the funding was still virtually untouched. So now we have extra time to complete the work, and still have the ring-fenced funding to do it,' said Cadema. 'By the time DI Pratt returns tomorrow, I expect to have a new time schedule, and the actions for the project.' She scooped up her papers and headed for the door. Johns followed.

***

Through DNA analysis, and then IVD, Julia identified the probable family of the woman whose dress was in the trunk. She believed the woman was Ethel Redberry – murdered on the twelfth of November. And, although this woman was not considered to be a victim of the notorious murderer by the police at the time, she believed there was a link to her and the other victims. That was especially because of all the other evidence in the trunk, together with the police pocketbooks. But to be absolutely sure of the woman's identity, she needed DNA samples from a living relative. Cadema decided to begin that line of enquiry as soon as she could. In the meantime, her officers had traced a relative of the Forest family and was about to interview him. Marriott was still trying to trace the Ribley family.

It all sounded a bit too easy to Cadema. What if it wasn't the killer's blood on the dress? It could have been someone else's; another client perhaps, even a police officer? All this work could lead to nothing. And if one family was a perfect match, how easy would it be to trace the family back to 1888, especially, as she suspected, that the killer had most probably hidden any trace of being found. If he eluded the police then, how on earth was she going to solve the murders now?

Despite her doubts, Cadema was determined to be receptive. Especially as this was the only opportunity any police service might ever have to solve the murders. She had to stay positive, focused and have the tenacity to continue regardless of dead ends that may obstruct the progress. After all, her team were eager to succeed.

The next team briefing would be short; no presentation or ten-point plan. There was only one plan now – to identify the perpetrator and find out what happened to him. Entering the briefing room, she faced her officers – DI Pratt among them.

'I know you're anxious to get on with the work and see this through, so let's get started. There has been some speculation in the press, so from this point onwards I want you to treat these cases in the strictest of confidence. We're in a very sensitive and emotive situation and don't want any mistakes. Or upset any family that may be involved.' Cadema looked at the officers – no one spoke.

'Good, so let me bring you all up to date. Since our last meeting, Doctor Lilly obtained samples for DNA analysis from the Forest family. But there was no match with our sample DNA from the dress. So we can now eliminate this family and concentrate instead on the Ribley family.'

DC Galke waved his fingers. 'Excuse me, Ma'am, but does that mean I have to drop everything I was doing with the Forest family?'

'I wasn't aware you were doing anything.' Cadema stared at him – her hands on her hips. 'Explain.'

'I was working on the family's genealogy and managed to trace them back to the nineteen thirties. Does that mean I've been wasting my time?' Galke grunted, DI Pratt raised his eyebrows.

'Time is *never* wasted, especially if you've learned something from the experience. So remember that. Anyway I suspect you've learned a lot about the process of genealogy. Now I suggest you focus your newly acquired skills on the Ribley family if they turn out to be the descendants of the perpetrator.' Galke nodded, so did Marriott.

'Anyway, we have found the address of the current Ribley family. DCI Johns and I are going to visit them this evening. If they proved to be the descendants, then hopefully they may be able to name the probable murderer.'

DC Galke waved his fingers. 'Excuse me again, but why is he being referred to as the probably one, and not the actual one?'

'DNA is not the panacea you may think. Although there was blood from a male on the dress, it didn't mean that this blood was from the murderer. It could have come from any male, at any time over the years, and through contamination. It's up to us, which includes Doctor Lilly, to eliminate as many probable ones as possible, leaving the most likely one.

'But there's something much more relevant to consider, continued Cadema. 'It's the tangible evidence we need so we can link the person to the actual crime. There has to be no shadow of doubt about this, otherwise our sponsors, the world-wide media, and other interested parties, will never accept that the murderer of the five women, and now probably six, has been found and the case closed.' She smiled, then thanked them as Johns began to give the next set of actions for DI Pratt to oversee, and left the room.

***

Cadema didn't know if she were doing the right thing in not telephoning the Ribley family before her visit. She had thought of this. Twice she had picked up the telephone – but what would she say if anyone answered? She didn't dial. The personal approach would be much better. The personal touch always worked. Put people at ease. Johns had agreed. They had arranged to meet at six o'clock that evening: smart casuals – less threatening. By six, people would be home and getting ready for the evening meal.

Waiting for Johns to meet her in the car park, Cadema began to sweat, her mouth dry as if she were about to be interviewed by a promotion board.

She thought of the questions she needed to ask the Ribley family. She needed to be knowledgeable, succinct and above all, sensitive. She had to get it right – set up a rapport – win their trust. She hoped the family would be receptive and helpful.

'Sorry to keep you waiting, Ma'am, last minute phone call,' said Johns, sliding into the car seat next to Cadema, closing the door and applying the seatbelt.

'No problem. There's another fifteen minutes yet – we'll be fine.' Cadema answered as she drove the unmarked car out of the car park and headed for the main road. 'Not the best of times, rush hour, but at least the traffic's moving.'

'That's good. But I'm a bit anxious about this. Much more than I thought I would be,' said Johns.

'Tell me about it. But we must remember we have a job to do. An obligation to fulfil. If we approach it from that angle, we'll be fine,' said Cadema – hoping to convince herself.

'You're right,' Johns answered as the car swerved to miss a wobbling cyclist. 'Christ that was close.'

'Yes, and thank goodness the lorry driver spotted him in time otherwise there'd be another cyclist fatality to add to the list.' At that moment Cadema realised that her heart was beating much faster than she would have liked. She took a deep breath. 'Just around the bend and we'll be there.'

Leaving the parking permit on the dashboard, they both got out of the car. A couple of minutes later, they stood outside the gate of number eighteen Showfish Gardens.

The quiet cul-de-sac was tucked away in a tree line street. Every house looked as if it had recently been painted. Remnants of once blooming climbing roses, canopied the pergolas with skeletal branches, dead leaves and rose-hips. The once manicured lawns were now covered with winter debris. The garden gate squeaked when Cadema lifted the latch and stepped onto the herringbone block paving. Johns jumped as a blackbird flew from a rhododendron bush across their path – just missing her head.

Standing at the door now, Cadema waited for a micro-second, and then rang the doorbell.

No one answered, she tried again. No answer. 'Maybe there're out of range,' said Cadema. She knocked louder this time and looked around. No neighbours peering through curtains at them. She took her keys from her pocket and knocked with them. *A typical police officer's knock.*

In the bowels of the building came a shuffling noise – footsteps from the other side of the door. A jingle of keys. In the distance, a dog barked. A muffled voice spoke:

'Just a minute.' It was female. A grating noise, as if a key were being forced into a lock, was audible. When the door finally opened as far as the chain would allow, a tall woman of about thirty, with black hair, appeared in the gap.

'Sorry for the delay – couldn't find the keys. If you are selling anything we're not interested, thank you.' She began to close the door.

'Please madam, don't be alarmed, I'm Superintendent Sharma and this is my colleague DCI Johns, we are here on a routine police visit. Are you Mrs Ribley?' Cadema pushed her identity card through the gap in the door.

'Yes, Mrs Sarah Ribley.' She opened the door to the end of the chain again. *Why such high-ranking officers for a routine visit? Must be important.* 'Hang on a minute and I'll open the door.' She sounded anxious but also annoyed as she closed the door. The grating of steel on steel could be heard as the chain was removed – the door fully opened.

'Don't use this entrance much, we prefer the side one; much more convenient. Do come in.' Sarah gestured as she rubbed her spindly fingers through her black hair, and peered at the officers over her dark-rimmed glasses. Entering the house, Sarah closed the door behind them.

Cadema could see that the hallway was far from the usual bland entrance she was used to. She estimated that it was about four-foot wide and fifteen-foot long. Its arched ornate celling was lit by two chandeliers in the Art Deco style – emphasising the grandeur of the William-Morris wallpaper, and the mosaic tiled floor. Escorted into an over-stocked lounge, dotted with relics from earlier generations, gave the impression that no one dare discard it. Incongruous, and some threadbare armchairs, smelling musty, were scattered around. Heavy brocaded curtains hung from dark-wooden rings on bent poles, looking as if they would fall at any minute. The wood burning stove spluttered into life at the same time as the clock on the mantelpiece chimed the half-hour.

'Do sit down. So what's this all about?' Sarah fell into one of the armchairs as the two officers took an upright chair each facing Sarah.

'It's quite a delicate situation.' Cadema shuffled in the chair. 'We need to speak to you and your husband, so I can explain everything to you both at the same time.'

'He'll be here soon. Can I get you some tea while we wait?' asked Sarah with a half-smile.

'Tea would be nice, thank you,' answered Cadema. Accepting tea was one way to be welcomed into a household. To refuse was sign of rejection. This was the last thing she wanted when she was about to question the couple.

Returning from the kitchen with mugs and a plate of biscuits on a tray, Sarah placed them on the nest of tables.

'Hope you like custard creams, that's all I have at the moment.'

Cadema nodded. 'That will be fine, thank you.'

'My husband, Ashley, will be with us when he's finished feeding the dog.' Sarah moved two coffee tables into place by each officer, put place mats on the tables, and then handed them the mugs of tea.

Cadema cleared her throat. 'Thank you for this and for the opportunity to speak to you. I hope our visit is not inconvenient.'

'It depends what you've come for. But at the moment it's good to have visitors now and again. Don't see many people since we moved here from the East End.' Cadema looked at Johns and took a sip of tea.

'We've only been here two years, that's when we had a small win on the lottery. But of course we're not ready for retirement yet. So Ashley managed to get a much bigger chemist shop and is now doing better than he ever was before. But the people are not very friendly here, not as down to earth as they were in Whitechapel,' said Sarah leaning forward, almost too close to the edge of her seat. Her voice was heavy with the excitement of a child at Christmas. But as soon as Ashley entered the room, she became quiet – subdued.

'What's this then? Been up to your old tricks with the car again, have you Sarah?' Ashley grinned, then frowned as Cadema stood up and introduced herself and Johns.

Sarah did not answer, but looked away as Ashley moved forward. Cadema searched his gaunt face and dark dubious eyes – framed by ill-fitting glasses. He was about five feet eight tall. His small black and well-trimmed goatee beard emphasised the long features of his face. He peered at Cadema – almost encroaching on her personal space. Any other woman might be intimidated, but he would respect her, not as a woman though, but for what she stood for.

When Cadema shook Ashley's firm businesslike hand, his eyes remained fixed on her – his body tensed, as if facing a hurricane. Finally releasing his grip, he pushed his shoulder-length black hair, away from his face and rubbed his beard. His well-tailored suit giving the impression that he had just returned from work. His attire was in complete contrast to his wife's who had obviously been walking the dog before he came home. Somewhere in the house Cadema could hear a dog moaning, and a radio playing classical music.

'Do have a biscuit,' said Sarah who then stood up and offered a small plate of custard creams to Cadema. But both officers politely declined the offer. Cadema coughed as Sarah placed the plate back onto the table and sat down.

'Don't mind if I do,' said Ashley as he marched up to the table, took a biscuit, bit into it, and then sat in one of the spare chairs. 'So what's all this about?' He looked at Cadema.

The couple listened with interest as Cadema explained about the trunk found in the archives. Ashely frowned occasionally, Sarah nodded.

It was when Cadema mentioned the probable link to the Whitechapel murders, the evidence that had been collected, and that Ashley Ribley could be a relative of the perpetrator, that Ashley exploded.

'I can't believe that you would go to such depths of depravity and do such a despicable thing as that. You dare to sit there, all calm and quietly talking, sharing our hospitality, and accusing me and my family of being related to such a monster.' He was almost screaming, his face flushed and contorted. He stood up. 'How do you know? How certain are you?' Cadema tried to answer, but was cut off.

'I know about DNA, mitochondrial DNA, databases and all that. I know you could be wrong. And if there is a match to my family, which I very much doubt, how can you be so sure that you have the murderer's DNA? Answer that will you?' Ashley was sweating now, his eyes staring. He took a gulp of tea and sat again.

'As you no doubt know, it's not a simple as that Mr Ribley. And of course you are correct in your surmise.' Cadema looked into his cold black eyes – determined to be calm and professional despite his manner. 'The DNA *was* obtained from the dress of a victim who had no doubt had her throat cut. So it is tangible evidence to a point. But, as you say, the male sample of blood, and therefore the DNA from this, may not belong to the perpetrator. We need much more evidence than that to know, beyond any doubt, that it was from him and no one else.'

'So why are you bothering me and my family about this when you've no chance in hell of finding any other tangible evidence? What else do you expect to find – the spoils of war? Trophies from his victims concealed in our family archives. A signed confession from a madman?' Ashley gesticulated. Cadema expected to see sparks flying across the arch from one of his hands to the other. She twitched a smile at the thought.

'Mr Ribley, we're not expecting anything of the sort. But there is always a possibility...' She knew she'd said the wrong thing the moment Ashley jumped up again.

'How dare you. What are you suggesting? That my family have concealed this fact for all these years? Have hidden the truth? That we have the evidence? We may have lived in the East End, and it's a fact that my ancestors were there at the time, but you are wrong. No one knew anything. If they had, they would have gone to the police. They would never have lived with such a secret and neither would I.' He coughed, loosened his tie and sat back into the chair. 'And although we have moved away, the rest of the family still live there. One of my cousins lives over my chemist shop, and will be appalled at your suggestion.'

'I understand how upsetting this is for you all, and appreciate your concerns. But I'd like to find a solution to this dilemma if possible.'

'Dilemma, what do you mean, dilemma?'

'Please, Mr Ribley, let me explain.'

'Okay, but it had better not involve searching this house or the chemist shop where I once lived, and now have a part-ownership in with my cousin.'

'Nothing like that, Sir, I assure you. And as you rightfully said, there's only the DNA as tangible evidence. And there's no way of knowing if this *did* belong to the perpetrator, or was contaminated by someone else either at the crime scene, such as a doctor or police officer, later in the morgue, or at any other time afterwards.'

'I agree, so what are you expecting me to do about it?'

'I would like you to consent to a DNA test. At least it would be useful, if only to eliminate your family.'

'I might consider it. But what if it does match with the sample you have?' Ashley sounded much calmer now.

'We can only discuss that point once we have the analysis. But of course you can refuse and nothing will come of it.'

'Well to help put the records straight, I will consider it and let you know.'

'That is very good of you, Sir,' said Cadema. 'As you know, everything will remain confidential. And there will be no publicity. And if you don't mind, I would prefer you not to tell anyone otherwise you may be inundated by the media.'

'Strictest confidence,' said Ashley. Sarah nodded.

They both agreed to meet in Cadema's office at eleven o'clock the next morning. After a few minutes making the final arrangements, Cadema and Johns left.

***

The next morning Sarah and Ashley arrived at the police station promptly. It was Sarah who was well dressed this time. She wore a black jacket and skirt with a red blouse that reflected the colour up to her face, giving it a glow that wasn't evident before. Her short black hair was neatly pushed back behind her ears. Ashley had dressed down, his formal suit from yesterday replaced by grey trousers, a tee shirt, and jacket. After a congenial greeting, Cadema, together with Johns and Marriot, went with the couple to a ground floor interview room.

Five chairs were strategically placed in the room so that they all faced each other. Sarah wriggled her bottom into the chair which faced the door. She perched herself upright, like a bird ready for flight. The hint of her Chenille perfume in sharp contrast to the smell of the dog from before. Ashley flung his light-framed body on the chair, stretched out his legs, and folded his arms as if he had grown impatient at waiting for a late train in some dimly-lit railway station.

'Thank you very much for coming, said Cadema. 'I hope you don't mind Sergeant Marriott joining us. He's been involved in the investigation from the start. In fact, it was he who found the trunk in the first place, so if it wasn't for him, none of us would be here.' Cadema searched the two faces for any sign of disapproval but the couple said they were now resigned to help.

'Coffee will be here in a moment,' said Marriott.

'So while we're waiting, I'll make a start,' Cadema continued.

The couple nodded. Ashley uncrossed his arms – his dark eyes now alert.

'Good. Well as we said last night, we believe we have traced the male DNA from the dress to your family.' Cadema turned to look directly at Ashely. 'Mr Ribley, have you had time to consider giving us a sample for DNA testing?'

'I've thought about it overnight, and have decided that you can take samples, hopefully it will eliminate my family of all suspicion.'

'Thank you. Once we have the results, and if they do indicate that your family were in some way connected to the crimes, with your permission, we would like to trace your family tree back to the eighteen eighties.'

Ashely shuffled in his chair and coughed. 'I suppose that will be the best thing to do. Anyway, I've been wanting to do it before my father died a couple of years back. I think he believed there was some hidden scandal in the family, a bastard child of a noble, or something of that sort. But I just didn't have the time. Since your visit yesterday, I searched for some letters and family photographs I have never looked at before, so they may be helpful.'

As he was speaking, Sarah opened a blue zipper bag and took out a yellow A4 ring binder containing plastic pockets with various pieces of family memorabilia. Ashley took the folder.

'My father, who was a doctor in the East End, compiled this. He had started on the family tree when he had his first MI, sorry I mean a heart attack. He was only fifty-six when he died,' Ashley spoke in a whisper – as if he was still grieving.

Sometimes people never get over the death of someone close, thought Cadema – remembering her own family.

'That's very helpful, Mr Ribley, and I appreciate all the effort you must have put into this in such a short time. However, we will not be doing any research on this until we have the results of your DNA samples.'

'Good, that makes sense to me. No point in wasting funds on this unless it's necessary. So now I've agreed to the DNA test, I would like to know what the process is.'

'As you are aware, we don't want to make any mistakes. So we ruled out thousands of other near matches. Yours is the only one that we are ninety-nine per cent sure of.'

'Not one hundred?'

'I though you realised it wasn't. But before we go any further, I think you may benefit by talking to Doctor Lilly, our pathologist. She will be able to give you the statistics and the logistics of the DNA testing.'

'That sounds good to me, I look forward to meeting her.'

'If that's the case, she will be here at twelve fifteen, I can arrange for her to speak to you then.'

'Yes, as we're here, we might as well see her. Anyway I've got my business to run and need to get home and change before going to work this afternoon.'

Cadema thanked him and said that, as it would be a little while before Doctor Lilly arrives, Marriott would order some lunch while she and Johns left the room.

Marriott took the lunch orders. Later, he made sure the couple were happy and left them tucking into the selection of sandwiches and drinking coffee.

Having completed some correspondence in her office, Cadema heard a knock at the door. Without any hesitation, she shouted 'Come in.'

'I knew it was you, Julia, do take a seat.'

'So what's this all about?' asked Julia as she sipped her cardboard container of cappuccino and sat facing Cadema.

'I hope I haven't put you in a spot. But I have the couple, Mr and Mrs Ribley. He's a chemist – so he knows about DNA. They're okay at the moment as I've left them having lunch.' Cadema explained about his reluctance for DNA testing, but that he had now agreed to it but needed more information.

Five minutes after agreeing to talk to the couple, Cadema and Julia sat in the interview room – facing the couple. Following the usual introductions, Julia clarified a few areas with Ashley.

'I understand that you are a chemist, Mr Ribley?' asked Julia.

'Yes that's right, but do call me Ashley, this is my wife, Sarah. I know a bit about DNA, but my knowledge is a little rusty on the technicalities.'

'So just let me know what you are already aware of, so I don't have to go into those areas. Or would you prefer to start from the beginning, most of which I suspect you already know?'

'The former would be best.' Ashley leaned forward in his chair but shuffled a little giving the impression that he was not as confident as he had been when talking to Cadema. 'I obviously know about DNA and the Y-chromosome that carries the specific markers down the male ancestry line. I'm familiar with PCR and the amplification of DNA. But if you could explain about sequencing and the loci of peaks for ancestral markers and their significance to the specification of data analysis, I would be very grateful.' Ashley sat back in his chair and crossed his arms.

Cadema was lost at this point – the technical issues and language was far from her repertoire. She waited for Julia to simplify it for her sake as well as Sarah's. But she was bewildered as Julia began to speak again.

'You certainly do know your genetics, Ashley. I don't think there's much more I can tell you.' Julia continued on about what happened when the test was performed, what happened in the laboratory and how long it would take before the results were ready. She explained about sequencing of DNA and the fact that nothing was one-hundred per cent reliable. That mutations could occur along the line, but these don't usually cause any problems to the specificity of the analysis.

'Is this making sense to you, Ashley?' He nodded. 'Good, and as you've agreed to the DNA test. I can guarantee that we can either, rule out a connection with the samples we have, or conversely confirm that we have an exact match. You can always look this up in the latest science journal if you want to know more.'

'No thank you, you've cleared my mind on the subject. I think it would be quite interesting to see if I am related to the person whose blood was found,' said Ashley as his wife nodded in agreement.

After swabs were taken, Cadema said she would let him know the results as soon as possible. She thanked him for the photographs of the family and other memorabilia and asked if she could keep them for the time being. Ashley was reluctant to leave them at first, but after some persuasion, and with Cadema agreeing to keep them locked away, and to give them back to him personally when she had finished with them, he agreed to her request.

Chapter 19

Cadema was reading the report from forensics, when her office telephone rang. It was Julia. The usual greeting over, she spoke.

'I suppose you're standing there with the report in your hand?' Julia said.

'How did you know...?'

'Intuition. Anyway, as we thought, there is a match between samples of blood taken from the victim's dress and Mr Ashley Ribley's family.'

'Yes, I see,' said Cadema excitedly. 'At least it indicates that one of Ashley's ancestor had direct contact with a murder victim. I'll tell Mr Ribley immediately. Hopefully he will continue to cooperate.'

'I'm sure he will, especially after the chat I had with him. Underneath that steel facade, I believe he's as interested as we are. But we need to keep in mind that his ancestor may not have been the murderer.'

'Yes, and I'm fully aware that we need tangible evidence to directly link anyone to the murders.'

'Good.' Julia sounded a little condescending – Cadema ignored her.

'Now we've got the appropriate information I intend to construct the family tree. And working backwards from Mr Ribley to the eighteen eighties, that's about six generations in all.'

'That'll be an enormous task, so good luck with it,' said Julia as they ended the call.

Cadema was relying on everything going to plan. And with Ashley's cooperation, she expected to discover the name of his ancestor. Then she could find out what he had done for a living, when he died, and hopefully, where he was buried.

As Cadema began the search on the family tree, she realised what an enormous task it was – she needed expert advice. But there was no one in her team who had the expertise to do this work. Mulling this over in her mind, she decided to discuss it with Andrew Long, the new deputy commissioner. Besides, when she had discussed the case with him earlier, he was eager to support the *project*, as he called it, no matter how long it took.

Would he still be as eager? Especially now, as it would take much longer than anticipated if she brought someone new into the team?

She had worked with Andrew when he was chief superintendent in another division. He was approachable then, so why not now? Despite his six foot six inches slim build, she never felt intimidated by him. Probably because he was quietly spoken, never raised his voice, and was respected by officers of all ranks, she reasoned. He hadn't changed much since then, except his thick wavy brown hair, had been replaced by scanty grey threads, and his stoop was more pronounced. Still his smiling blue eyes and dimpled cheeks seemed to put everyone at ease – including her.

Meeting Andrew in his office this time, Cadema asked if he knew a genealogist who could work on the family tree. He suggested someone with the appropriate expertise who had worked in the police headquarters in Sunderland. That person would be the best option, as he was reliable and it would cut out the tendering process, which normally delayed things. Andrew scratched his head and frowned – the name of the person blank. Cadema, sat quietly opposite him – unable think of anything to prompt him. A couple of minutes later, with many mmms, and buts in-between, he frowned and began to speak:

'If I recall correctly.' He rubbed his chin. 'The person I'm thinking of...' He stopped again. 'Mmm, his name is How... Howard, or was it Harrold? Anyway something like that. Yes, that's it, Harrold. But I'm sure when you meet him you'll find out.' He scratched his head again, took a sip of water, and then sat back in his chair. Cadema believed that he was evading something, as if he knew much more than he was telling her. She decided not say anything, but to wait and see what this Harrold was really like.

'I don't suppose you know Harrold's contact details, do you?'

'No, it's too long ago. But if you contact Superintendent Jim Short at Sunderland, I'm sure he'll find the details on file. Pity I can't recall his last name. Just say hello to Jim, we go back a long way.'

'Will do, thank you.' Cadema stood to leave.

He nodded, and smiled at her as she left, but he failed to mention the business case he needed relating to the genealogist, before seeing the commander in a couple of days' time.

***

It was easier than expected for Cadema to track down Harrold, or Haady Dawoud, as he turned out to be. Now, two days later he was expected in her office.

Arriving promptly at eleven, he smiled. At that moment, Cadema felt a burning sensation throughout her whole body as if someone had lit a furnace there – it refused to go out. She was speechless – mouth dry. What could she say? It was like seeing a long-lost friend.

He held out his hand and took hers.

'Haady Dawoud.' He smiled again – friendly, but firmly holding onto her hand. Cadema frowned and then returned his smile – he let go. 'Don't worry everyone seems to translate my name as Harrold, so they expect an older, white male. Not a young Asian one. So I usually put up with it. You can call me Harrold if you feel more comfortable with that.' He smiled into her eyes this time. She averted hers, nodded to a vacant chair, cleared her throat, and then asked him to sit.

Both now seated, the heat Cadema had experienced earlier – gone, her heart – calm. But her body was tense. She cleared her throat.

'I've no intention of calling you anything but your real name,' said Cadema assertively. 'That is if you don't mind'? She picked up the phone and ordered tea.

'Thank you, and for the tea when it comes. It's good of you to be respectful about my name. Perhaps, when others hear you use it, they may do the same. But what shall I call you, Superintendent?' He shuffled in his chair.

'Please call me Cadema when none of my team are around; then if you don't mind, call me Ma'am, as they do.'

Agreeing to do this, they sat talking about the project and the problems she was having with the family tree. During several exchanges of information, she discovered that he was a couple of years older than she was. Sipping his tea, she estimated that he was about five foot eight inches tall. Slim with an angled face – half-hidden by his well-trimmed beard. His thick black hair pushed back enough to reveal thick eyebrows and dark smiling eyes. The fine-cut blue suit he wore, together with his burgundy leather briefcase, matching shoes and cover on his iPhone, gave the impression that he was pedantic in his personal life. Cadema hoped this would extend into his professional life too. When he revealed that he had once been a serving police officer, and risen to the rank of detective sergeant, she was surprised and asked him why he had left the service. He shuffled in his seat again and brushed his hand through his hair.

'I was doing very well until I became involved in genealogy. This took over until I hardly had any time to do real police work. That's when I decided to change career and do genealogy full time.' He shrugged.

Although Cadema could understand this, she had a feeling there was something else, but was reluctant to tell her. She decided not to ask.

'How easy was it for you to do that?' She spoke softly, as if she were counselling him.

'What, to change career?'

'No, to make the decision I mean.'

'It wasn't difficult, especially when I'd decided to apply for university and get a degree on the subject. It proved to be a good choice and beneficial, as it not only gave me the credibility that clients expected, but it opened a whole network I wouldn't have been able to tap into otherwise. Most of my business has come through those networks.'

'So how long have you been doing the work?' Cadema noticed he was avoiding eye contact with her and wondered what the issue was.

'Five years. And in that time I've accumulated clients from all over the world including Australia and New Zealand, Canada and South Africa. I've even managed to trace a family from New South Wales in Australia to their relatives during the Great Fire of London in 1666.' He sounded like a salesman – boasting.

'It all sounds very similar to police work to me. As if you haven't really left – just moved sideways.'

'I'd never thought of it like that before. I suppose you're right. But I've been my own boss – something that I could never have been before.'

'I suppose that's a bonus.' Cadema smiled.

'In a way, it is, but it's also hard work to keep clients satisfied and bring in the funds for new projects. This project sounds exciting as I can utilise all my skills to get the job done effectively. And, as they're such high-profile cases, I intend to waive my fee.' He sat back in the chair, made an arch with his fingers and moved them towards his face.

'That sounds commendable, but what's your motive?' She shook her head slowly.

'I can see you're sceptical. And you're right to be so. It *is* a high profile case, and no doubt worldwide. Therefore, if I do a good job, which I assure you I will, it'll save me much more in marketing fees than you could pay me from your budget. All I'll need are my expenses, and I'm happy to have them at the same rate as your police officers.'

Cadema agreed to this, even though she had to verify it with Andrew Long. Agreeing on a date for Haady to meet her team, he said he would have an outline of the family tree by then. He smiled into her eyes as he left her office.

***

A week later Haady was back – briefcase bulging with files, his face perspiring after running up the stairs to Cadema's office.

'It's good to see you again,' said Haady as he took off his wet coat and hung it on a hook, then shook hands with her. 'Sorry they're a bit cold – just dried them on a paper towel.' He extracted an A4 ring folder from his briefcase and opened it. Taking out several pages he placed them across the desk.

Cadema began to study them. 'These look very impressive.' – The furnace inside her returned. This time with more intensity than before.

Haady cleared his throat. 'It's only the skeleton of the family tree, seven generations in all. As you can see, it's not complete, but I've done my best with the information I currently have.'

'I can see you have done well in such a short time,' said Cadema as she stood, then leaned across the desk and traced her fingers across the landscaped pages of an obviously complex family tree.

'It's always the same when you get to the Victorian era. Too many children, some of whom died before reaching five years of age; mostly from diphtheria.' He pointed to the chart. 'And when the plague happened, a few centuries earlier, well you can imagine how difficult that is.' Cadema nodded. 'And of course, most of them didn't have proper burials or papers to say who they were. But it's much easier now with DNA from the time in question. It makes researching more of a pleasure rather than a chore.'

'I suppose it must be, don't know what we would do without it now? That reminds me, you must meet Doctor Lilly, our pathologist, and a friend of mine. I know she would be fascinated in the work you're doing.' Cadema glanced at Haady, not as a colleague, but as a woman looking at a man. For a microsecond, their eyes met. At this, Cadema shook her head, gave a cough, looked down, and moved her hand to another page. 'This bit here' She pointed to the first page. 'I can see that there's a George Riberly who married Annie Baker in 1850.' She felt cooler now. (The family tree, reference 1)

Haady lowered his eyes and shook his head. 'Yes, that's right.'

'But the name is different from the one we're looking for.'

'It is. Nevertheless when studying documents from those days, you often come across different spelling of names, but from then on, the name is Ribley. Their first child is called George.' Haady pointed.

'I see. So now you've done all this, I think it's time I took you to meet my team. I'm sure they will be fascinated with this work. Then later, we'll meet up with Julia.'

Haady scooped up the papers from the desk and followed her along the corridor.

Cadema listened for the sounds of her team, nothing. She looked at her watch. Yes, the time was right, but all remained quiet as they approached the briefing room. She listened again, but all she could hear were the extraneous noises of any occupied office building. The slow clanging of the lift doors, footsteps of people moving above, the occasional muffled voices, a shout here and there, and the buzzing and bleeps of electrical devices in the vain hope of being answered. But nothing like an assembly of officers.

'I hope they received the message that you were coming Haady.' Cadema sounded apologetic.

'Sure, everything will be okay. But if they are too busy I'm happy to meet them when I see Doctor Lilly,' Haady glanced sideways at Cadema as she began to open the door of the briefing room.

'We'll see.' As the door swung open, her team were sitting there – silent – hostile. 'Here you all are.' Cadema sighed and looked around the room. 'I thought the place was empty. Let me introduce Haady, the genealogist I mentioned to you before. He's already started on the family profile, and I'm sure you'll be as impressed as I am when you see it.' Two of the officers nodded but no one spoke.

'Now let me introduce my team to you.' Cadema spoke quietly as she nodded to each member in turn: 'DCI Johns, DI Pratt, DS Marriott and DC Galke.'

All politely smiled, in sequence, at their name. 'Thank you. I'm sure Haady will be happy to be part of our team while he is searching the family tree. Anything you need to know about genealogy – just ask him, he'll be delighted to help.' Cadema turned to Haady.

Haady began to sweat. There had been some animosity towards him when he was introduced. What could that be? Perhaps he was being hypersensitive, especially since he had never met anyone from this team before today.

Cadema sensed there was something was wrong but decided not to say anything. She would find out later if there was a problem or not.

Haady stiffened, drew in his stomach and stood – military style, giving no indication of how he was feeling. After he had explained about the work he had done on the family tree, the team seemed to relax a little. But still there was a covert atmosphere in the room. When he said goodbye, he sensed their relief – Cadema did too.

As Cadema and Haady walked along the corridor together Cadema spoke after a silent interlude. 'Sorry about the atmosphere in there, they're normally quite articulate and verbose. There must be some explanation. I'll find out what it is.' Cadema tried to be reassuring.

'There's no need really. I'm sure it's nothing.' He looked at her with sorrowful eyes.

She looked at him – there was something there, but what? Haady was reluctant to say. And the more reluctant he became, the more determined she was to find out.

Perhaps, in some way he had threatened the team by his enthusiasm and the amount of work he had done? No, she thought, the hostility was there as they entered the room. So it had to be something related to his past. Probably while he was a police officer?

Further discussions with Haady on the subject were fruitless. Instead, she would discuss it with her team and find out what the problem really was.

***

Returning to her office, Cadema picked up the telephone and pressed Julia's number.

'Julia, it's Cadema here,' she spoke to the answerphone. 'When you have a moment please phone me, there's someone I would like you to meet.' She hung up.

A couple of minutes later, just as Haady was about to leave, the telephone rang. Picking it up, Cadema was delighted to hear Julia's voice.

After explaining about Haady, they all agreed to meet the following afternoon at two o'clock. Haady was particularly happy with this as he had a lot of questions on his mind, and thought Julia would be the best person to answer them.

As Haady said goodbye his handshake lingered again. In those few seconds, he portrayed his feelings towards her. Cadema accepted them with a smile, but no more. It was too early...

Leaving, he took a backwards glance at her – she looked away – hoping he could not feel the furnace.

If he did feel it, what would he expect? she asked herself. Anyway, they had only met twice, and only in a professional capacity. If he were interested in her, he would have to wait.

Haady began to think too. In his mind, she was beautiful, but like a dream when you reach out to touch it in the night – it fades away. She was real – with a mind of her own. A woman who commanded respect from her colleagues, and got it. He had no chance. But he had sensed something, a warmth, a sensuous smell – something was there – tenderness – affection perhaps?

Then he thought about Sergeant Marriott. Haady noticed the way he looked at Cadema. The admiration, the willingness to do everything in his power to please her. As if she were the Snow Queen and he would be denied the

Turkish Delight if he didn't do as she asked. Marriott couldn't hide his feelings from Haady, even though he kept his distance from Cadema. They showed in his blue sorrowful eyes – like a dejected puppy. Haady had witnessed these signs before, but reasoned that Marriott was not foolish enough to think that his love would ever be reciprocated.

Haady was different, he tried not to show his feelings, even though, when Cadema looked at him, he had goose bumps – his heart raced. Was she covertly telling him something? That she liked him, as a man – maybe as a potential suitor? If so, he didn't think Sergeant Marriott would have the audacity to interfere in any relationship he may have with Cadema. No, Marriott would know his place in the scheme of things.

***

Cadema decided not to invite any of her team to the meeting she had arranged with Julia and Haady. She wanted a cordial meeting – without them creating an atmosphere, and asking inappropriate questions.

The interview room was as informal as possible, with three comfortable chairs being brought in especially. And then arranged, circle-like, around a small coffee table. Despite the current cutbacks, tea and biscuits were available. By two o'clock, the usual greetings and introductions were complete.

Settled in, Haady turned to face Julia: 'I've heard quite a lot about the work you've done on DNA, Doctor Lilly. It sounds fascinating to me.' Haady croaked as he picked up his mug of tea.

'Oh please call me Julia.' She brushed away a strand of blonde hair from her face and tucked it behind her ear, as she examined his features.

'Thank you, Julia. It seems to me that the work you've done is outstanding,' exclaimed Haady.

Julia felt the heat rise in her face but she didn't understand why. 'It's all just routine to me.' She offered a frown, then she sat upright, as if she were on guard for his next comment.

He remained silent.

'Anyway, that's my job. It's not that difficult when you know what you're doing, and I've been doing it for around fifteen years now.'

'Sorry, I didn't mean to be offensive. It's good to have the opportunity to talk to someone with your experience about my research into genealogy,' said Haady. His saliva had disappeared – his hands sweating. Fidgeting in his chair, he hoped they wouldn't notice he was out of his cognitive temperate zone, and annoyed with himself at not making a good first impression with Julia.

'Don't worry, Haady, I've not been offended. But I'm curious to see what you have achieved.'

As Julia spoke, Haady began handing out the papers he had printed that morning, after spending several hours the night before editing them.

'This is the copy of the Ribley family tree. I've colour coded it so it's easy to follow the lineage. As you can see there are some gaps, many of which are probably insignificant. And until I know otherwise, I'll not waste time and money pursuing them. But of course, if it becomes evident that further research is necessary, and then I'll do it.'

'This looks very impressive,' said Julia as she traced her fingers over the seven generations portrayed across the two A4 pages.

'Thank's Julia. I did do a rough sketch before, and no doubt Cadema will agree, this one is much more succinct and easier to follow than the previous one.' Cadema nodded.

'That's all well and good, but this one isn't perfect. There are still many gaps to be filled in.' Haady smiled at Cadema – she didn't reciprocate. His eyes moved back to the papers. 'I'll just explain it in a bit more detail, hopefully you can follow the pathway I've identified to the proposed perpetrator. As you can see I started off with Ashley Ribley.

'Good,' said Julia. 'And with the DNA we've found, we've also taken into account that some mutations will have happened along the generations. Nevertheless, there's no doubt in my mind, that Ashley is related to the male person whose blood was found on the dress.'

'So do you think that Ashley Ribley is a direct decedent of the killer?' asked Haady.

'No.' Cadema answered this time. 'It means we have matched DNA to the blood on the dress. It doesn't mean it belongs to the murderer.'

'This is all very confusing, but are you saying that all this work I've done may turn out to be irrelevant to the case?' Haady looked at Cadema for an answer.

'It could be, then again, possibly not. However, this is the only lead we have at present. Hopefully it will turn out to be the right one. If it's not, then at least we can rule him out.' Cadema chose her words carefully as she didn't want to give the impression that she would be reckless in her pursuit and come to false conclusions along the way. Neither did she want to curtail anyone's enthusiasm.

'Thank you,' said Haady. 'I can appreciate this is all speculative. Nevertheless, I'll continue with this work. So let me explain what else I have done on the family tree.' He shuffled the papers on the desk, took a sip of tea, and sat upright in his chair.

'First of all I'm very grateful to the British Parliament for their foresight in passing the Census Act in 1800, known as the Population Act 1800. If it wasn't for that, and the subsequent census commencing in 1801, my job, in compiling this family tree, would have been impossible.' Haady looked at Cadema and then to Julia as if expecting some response to his didactic presentation. All he received was a nod and two mmms... He coughed, loosened his tie, then leaned forward and pointed to the top of the first page of the family tree. (Appendix 1)

'A quick glance of the tree, spanning over 170 years, shows that the family has always been connected with the medical profession. Ashley Ribley is a pharmacist, his father, John (1958), was a doctor as was George (1931), John's father. But John (1902), the father of George, is listed as a physician.' Haady's voice raced on hardly pausing for a breath.

'Then we come to another George (1875), a physician. His father, Ernest (1852), is a surgeon. From then on it becomes a little confusing, as the surname seems to have changed from Ribley to Riberly. But this is not unusual, so Ernest's father is called George Riberly (1828), who was an apothecary. Well I think I'd better stop there, as it's difficult to concentrate for too long,' said Haady when he noticed that Cadema and Julia were trying to suppress yawns.

'Thank you. You've done a good job, and your illustration of the family tree will be invaluable to our work. Without it, we would have had difficulty in following what you were saying,' said Cadema as she studied the papers, stretched her arms above her head and took a deep breath. 'I think it's time we took a short break to clear our heads before you go any further. I'll order some more tea.' Haady and Julia agreed, as they both stood up and walked across the room several times – neither spoke. Minutes later Cadema and Julia were heading towards the ladies toilets.

Making sure the booths were empty, Julia turned to Cadema. 'What do you think?'

'As I said in there, I think he's done a good job so far.'

'I agree, but I didn't mean that. I want to know what you think about the way he looked at you and smiled?' Julia stood with her hands on her hips – almost confrontation if Cadema didn't know otherwise. Nevertheless, Cadema felt uncomfortable with the gesture, gave a nonchalant cough, then turned away.

'If he did, I didn't notice. Anyway I'm sure it was quite harmless,' said Cadema dismissively.

'No, I think he genuinely likes you, but if you're not interested in him you need to say something to him – the sooner the better.'

'But I hadn't even given him a thought,' Cadema lied.

'Well I've given you my advice, it's up to you to act on it. I know how sensitive you are. I'd hate for you to get hurt in any way.'

'Don't even go down that route, Julia. I know I've had counselling before. What do you expect after the death of my husband in the car crash and then me losing the baby,' she snuffled. Julia went to comfort her. 'No don't.' Cadema backed away. 'Then after Jim Logan…'

'I know and I'm sorry. I shouldn't have brought it up, I'm just concerned about your welfare, that's all.'

'Look, Julia, I know you mean well. But you should know by now that I can handle myself. So please don't interfere. If Haady likes me, that's okay. I'll do nothing unless *I* want to.' Cadema's voice was almost at a whisper now.

In silence, they stood for a few seconds listening to a dripping tap and the footsteps walking up the corridor – nothing threatening.

'As long as you're sure.' Julia returned the whisper as the door began to open. 'Just let me know if I can help in any way.'

Cadema nodded as they exited the room and saw Haady standing at the bottom of the corridor.

He smiled as they approached. 'Hope everything's okay, Cadema?' He sounded concerned as they returned to the interview room and resumed their discussion.

'Looking at the family tree from the top of page one,' said Haady pointing, 'you can see that George Riberly- born 1828, is the first person there. He married Annie Baker in 1850. Somewhere along the line, and I don't know where, the spelling of the surname became Ribley. George and Annie had five children together. It's probable one of their off spring may be the person we are looking for.'

'That's a possibility, but do go on,' said Cadema.

'Exciting, isn't it?' Haady looked up, noticed a nod from each woman, and continued his narrative. 'The first child was George, born in 1851. He became soldier and died in the Zulu war in 1879. The next was Ernest, he was born in 1852. He became a surgeon and married a Francis Day in 1873. The next two children were female. Mary born in 1854 and Elizabeth born in 1855. They both died during the diphtheria outbreak in 1857. The last child, John, was born in 1856.'

'This is very interesting,' said Cadema. 'And as the father was an apothecary, it's feasible that this John was in the profession, and may have practiced alongside his father. And could be the person we are looking for. But we shouldn't dismiss the fact that the father could be involved, or even perpetrated the crimes, with or without his son. But as he was too old by then, it's unlikely.'

'That's a good point, Cadema,' said Haady smiling. Julia frowned.

'So let me sum up,' said Cadema. 'What we need to do now is focus on the remaining males. George Riberly, as we've said, was probably too old. As the George Ribley was dead by then, he can be eliminated. That leaves Ernest, aged 36, who was a surgeon. And John, aged 32, whom we appear to know nothing about.' Cadema gave a questioning look to Haady, who nodded his head in affirmation.

'That's all I could find in the 1881 census,' said Haady. And when I examined the census of 1891, Ernest was still practicing as a surgeon, while John had vanished. That surely fits into our assumptions. What do you think?'

'It's feasible, but we don't want to be too hasty. We need much more evidence than that.'

'I know, but I've searched all I can at the moment. Anyway, a lot of documents were destroyed during the Blitz of 1940, so we may never know.' Haady sounded a little defensive, as if Cadema was cross-examining him. But when she smiled and nodded for him to continue, he relaxed.

'So did you find any evidence that John was married?' asked Cadema.

'None at all.' Haady pulled out more papers from his briefcase and placed them on the table as he spoke. Julia and Cadema bent over to examine them. 'These are copies of the census. John is staying with his brother Ernest on the 1881 census, but that's all.'

'Did the male children have any middle names?' asked Cadema.

'Only John had a middle name as far as I know. It was Temple, so he was John Temple Ribley, the initials of Jack the Ripper. A coincidence – yes?' Haady smiled, his dark eyes shining as he raised his eyebrows. But seeing that Cadema and Julia were not reciprocating, he apologised and continued with his narrative. 'What I intend to do now is to find out more about the two brothers.'

'You could, but don't forget, I'm SIO here,' said Cadema authoritatively. 'I shouldn't have to remind you – you're no longer a serving police officer, so it's my job to continue with this investigation...'

Realising she sounded as if she were reprimanding a subordinate officer and not someone external to the police service, she stopped. Then looked at the two people in front of her. She smiled, hoping to ease the tension – it didn't.

'Sorry if I've offended you, Haady?' He shuffled but said nothing. 'It wasn't intentional. Of course your work, and the work of the team, is invaluable. And without your expertise, we wouldn't have got this far so soon.'

'I agree with Cadema,' said Julia. 'But there are just a couple of other things that would be helpful to know. That is, when did Ernest and John die and where are they buried?

'If we can discover this, then we may be able to exhume their remains and obtain samples for DNA analysis. This would give us primary research sources, which is paramount in any investigation, especially this one. Besides, it will help to eliminate one, so we can then focus on the other.'

'That's true,' said Cadema with an air of relief in her voice as if she had been wondering what to do next. 'I'll speak to my team about it, hopefully they can find out what we need.'

Haady cleared his throat at this suggestion. 'Excuse me, but most of the initial work that needs doing here lies in my neck of the woods. Through my expertise at genealogy, I can find the answers to your questions much quicker than anyone in your team. All I need is your say-so to do it.'

'That's very sensible, and of course you have my support. I'll let my team know.'

'Thank you,' said Haady 'I'll get on with it then.' He smiled at Cadema and left.

Cadema and Julia discussed the next stage of the investigation. Cadema would get her team to do more research. She would re-interview Ashley Ribley to find out more about his family history. Whether he was aware of any archives that may have been forgotten. Julia, before she left, agreed to examine any items relating to the case, should they be discovered.

***

Cadema could hear her telephone ringing even before she reached her office. Racing in, she picked it up.

'Yes, we've finished the meeting. Yes, you can come straight away.' As the conversation ended, she sat wondering what DCI Johns wanted to discuss with her. Two minutes later, Johns was explaining why the team were so hostile when Haady met them.

She explained that when Haady was a police officer, he had been sent to a job that turned out to be a double murder. Instead of reporting it as such, he left the scene and went home. Six hours later, when other officers were called to the scene, they discovered the bodies of a mother and child. Haady went missing for three days. When he returned to work, he handed in his notice and never said a word about the murders. It was rumoured that he may have been involved with the crime, but no physical evidence materialised. He was lucky not to have been charged with perverting the course of justice.

As Cadema listened, she felt a little pity for Haady, but still it didn't fully explain why her team were so hostile towards him.

'Is that the whole story or is there something else?'

Johns frowned. 'No, there's nothing else that I know, except that no officer should abandon his post. After that, he was labelled as a coward, ostracised by his division, and left in disgrace.'

'And was he involved in the murder?'

'No, it turned out that it was a domestic. The husband had gone berserk, stabbed his wife and then his daughter.'

Johns authoritative and emotionless voice echoed around the room, as if she were giving evidence in court.

'Well I appreciate you letting me know. And if that's all, I have to finish this report. So will you tell the rest of the team that I intend to brief them in an hours' time?' she looked at her watch.

'Yes, will do,' said Johns as she left the office.

Chapter 20

When Haady telephoned Cadema a week later, she tried her best to be as cordial as possible, and hoped he would eventually confide in her and tell her his side of the story.

'Hello, I have found something I think you'll find useful. Do you have a couple of hours for me to go over it with you?' said Haady – his voice excited.

Cadema flipped through her paper diary. Of course she had an electronic one, but preferred paper. Especially at meetings, when her colleagues spent several minutes accessing dates, while all she had to do was to turn a page or two. Yes, her version was much more convenient.

'I've no time tomorrow, or the following day, but hold on a minute. I've a couple of hours free this afternoon from around two o'clock.'

Haady did not answer. He had already rehearsed what he was going to say before calling her. He had expected her to be busy. Now she had changed all that by her quick response, he didn't know what to say. One thing he was certain about was that he didn't want to meet her in her office. He wanted to see her on neutral territory, more as a friend than a colleague.

He imagined her now – pen in hand, waiting for his reply. Those luminous ebony eyes – shining on the page. Passionate eyes that warmed his heart when she last looked at him. Then, without a second thought, she would flip her black lustrous hair away from her shoulders – forming a shawl across her back. She would then give a coy smile, and, if he were there to see, would send magnets of fire down his back and into his loins.

'Are you still there?' said Cadema, listening into the void. She tutted. 'I suppose they've cut me off again.'

Haady's mind woke with a start – he cleared his throat. 'Hello, no they haven't, I'm still here.'

'Good, I thought I'd lost your call. What do you think about two p.m. today?'

'Oh yes, sorry.' He shuffled in his chair. 'I was just wondering...' He sounded more like a school boy as opposed to a grown man of thirty-five years.

'Just wondering what?' Cadema said sharply.

'Can we meet earlier and combine the meeting with a little lunch.' *There I've said it – no going back...*

'I don't usually have lunch. Just a sandwich and a cup of tea at my desk. And to tell you the truth I don't usually mix business with pleasure.'

Was she implying that meeting him for lunch would be a pleasure? – He didn't really know if his interpretation was correct or not. He wanted to say it would be pure pleasure, not business. But that would be presumptuous.

He bit his lip, then spoke softly. 'Neither do I, but on this one occasion would you like to have lunch with me, so we can discuss what I have found?' Haady hoped he'd expressed himself in a sensitive way and not been too forthright.

'So in a subtle way, you *are* asking me out on a lunch date? I expected you to be more assertive than that. In asking me out, I mean. So I'm not so sure if you are the type of person I would want to have lunch with,' she teased.

'Okay, I take the hint. I would like to take you out for lunch. So what is your answer?'

'That's better. And my answer is yes. But remember, I only have two hours to spare, so nothing elaborate.'

Haady felt the fever in his face again. 'That's great, I'll meet you at thirteen forty-five by the entrance to New Scotland Yard. I know a great Italian restaurant near there.'

'That sounds good. But what makes you think I like Italian food?'

'I meant to add; that is if you don't mind Italian food for lunch. I know it's a bit garlically, but it's a nice place with good food.'

'Great – see you then.' Cadema smiled as the call ended. It had been a long time since she went out for lunch, and even longer since she had a date with the opposite sex. At least she knew him. And despite the derogative reports about him, she was determined to give him the benefit of the doubt. But she couldn't help wondering if the incident Johns had mentioned, had affected him in some way. However, she didn't want to spoil the date by applying her usual detective methods, she would just have to wait and see.

Now there were other things to consider – what to wear. All she had to hand were her blue business suit and flat black shoes. And, although her office was cluttered with boxes for the impending move, somewhere amongst them were a pair of navy higher-healed ones. A short search and they were found. Tying her hair into a neat bun, and then applying a subtle amount of make-up and perfume, she was ready.

Cadema, always early, was waiting for him under the sign that most of the populous of London, if not the world, would recognise.

'It's good to see you, Cadema. You look a little different somehow.' *Should I give her a kiss or not?*

'It's nothing, just a little make-up and a better pair of shoes. I thought I'd make the effort even though it's just a working lunch.'

'Well if you put it like that. I suppose it is.' He sounded disappointed. 'Looks like rain, and I haven't got an umbrella.' He smiled.

'Don't think we'll need one, according to the forecast it's going to be fine and dry, but I'll leave it to your better judgement,' said Cadema.

As they headed off down the road talking trivia they swerved at times, just to miss bumping into other pedestrians. Then, turning into Rogues Barn Road, Haady became serious. 'This is where the highway men held up the last stagecoach. They killed all the occupants but were never caught. Now that's one for your cold-case department, don't you think?' He smiled, Cadema nodded. But now, with all this rhetoric, Haady was lost. The restaurant was somewhere near, but he couldn't quite remember as it was dark when he visited it before. *Not a good way to start a relationship.* Just as he was about to ask someone, he saw the building on the opposite corner. Quickly crossing the road, avoiding the traffic, the aroma of garlic, mixed with oregano and other herbs, steadily increased as they neared the restaurant. Once inside, they stopped and simultaneously took a deep breath.

'Wonderful,' said Haady. 'And on time too. I booked a table, just in case. I hope you don't mind.

Assertive again, Cadema thought as the waiter began to escort them to a table in the window.

'Sorry,' said Haady, 'but can we have a table near the back.' He pointed.

The waiter tutted. Cadema realised it would be the restaurant's strategy to put customers in the window seats first to encourage other potential customer into the premises. But despite this, the waiter turned and escorted them to a secluded table.

Cadema looked around. The place was nice enough with its subtle lighting and soothing music. But the tables and chairs were devoid of any soft furnishing – incongruous with comfort.

Once seated and the meal ordered, Haady looked at Cadema and gave a warm smile. 'It's good to see you out of the office. And the clothes you're wearing suit you.' He sniffed. 'Coco Chanel, if I'm not mistaken?'

Cadema shuffled. 'How on earth...?'

'Always liked it, ever since... well you don't want to hear that...'

'No, I mean yes, do go on.'

'It's embarrassing and rather sad, but...'

'Sorry, I didn't mean to pry.'

'That's okay. There was this young woman I knew, Sarah. She developed leukaemia.' He leaned forward. 'Her mother tried to cheer her up many times. But one day she brought her a bottle of Coco Chanel. She loved it, wore it every day. It reminds me of Sarah even now.'

'I'm sorry, if I'd have known...'

'No, don't be. She loved it, made her happy, it lit up her whole face. And when she succumbed to the illness, her mother had a bottle of it placed in her coffin.'

'How touching,' Cadema leaned forward and looked into Haady's sad eyes. She wanted to comfort him – tell him it would all be okay, but...

'A long time ago. Anyway, I think we should move on. I'll go over what I've discovered about the two brothers as we eat lunch.' Cadema agreed as they both sat upright.

He then explained that Ernest Ribley, who was born in 1852, had died in April 1888, leaving Francis to bring up eight children on her own. As the family were relatively wealthy, the older children were sent to boarding schools. George, the eldest, went to Eaton and then on to Cambridge. The younger ones went elsewhere, while the girls remained with their mother at home.

'That's very interesting,' said Cadema. 'I just wonder how families managed in those days as some boarding schools were not very good, I understand.'

'No I don't suppose they were. But they had little choice,' said Haady. Then he explained that he was unable to find any more information about John who was born in 1856. But said he would hopefully find out more when he visited the Apothecary Society the next day.

Moments later, the two pizzas, together with the side salad they'd ordered, arrived.

Eating lunch, Cadema relaxed her posture, and looked at Haady in a way she had never done before. She noticed how his features and his mannerisms, were similar to her late father's. Haady had the same square chin and a similar small neatly-cut beard. Where her father's one had been grey, Haady's was black. His high cheek bones and thin features were exaggerated as he leaned his head sideways. Those dark eyes, almost hidden by long black eyelashes, flickered continuously as he spoke, giving her the impression that he was anxious, but his voice and body posture said otherwise. *Just like Father.*

'Well, this is an excellent meal.' Cadema leaned forward.

'Glad you like it.'

'Anyway, looking at the Ribley family again. It looks as if your research puts John Temple Ribley centre stage.' She took a bite of pizza and then sipped at her glass of water. Looking up she noticed Haady looking at her – admiringly. She looked away – her face hot.

Julia was right, and she wondered why her friend was so tuned into these things, when she had never noticed. But what should she do now? Popping another piece of pizza into her mouth gave her the opportunity to think. She had to remove the barriers towards Haady that she had assembled in her mind. After all, he was friendly enough, and they

202

seemed to get on well together, as professionals, that is. She hoped that they could become real friends, but only platonically, at least for the time being. Anything further, and she didn't think she could handle it.

Cadema swallowed, leaned forward, and smiled. Haady reciprocated. She explained that she liked Chinese food. That she often went out with Julia to an Indian restaurant which served excellent food. When he said, he liked most types of food, she was delighted, but admitted that her work sometimes prevented her from socialising.

'When I do have time, I like to go to the theatre,' said Cadema.

'Me too. What do you like?

'Musicals and some ballet.'

'Me too,' answered Haady.

Then, for some reason Cadema changed the subject. Instead she began to explain about Jim Logan and how he had been killed by a sniper right next to her. That she had some counselling, and now Jim was her internal mentor.

Haady sat upright when she mentioned counselling – nodding as if he understood. 'I appreciate you being so open with me – you didn't have to.' He gave her a coy smile. 'God only knows how difficult it is to find someone you can trust and confide in, especially where counselling is concerned. It seems that we're in the same boat with this.' His eyes were now firmly fixed on Cadema's. 'I think it's time for me to explain to you why I left the police service, but it's quite complex.'

'You don't have to if…'

'But I do need to. Anyway you've probably heard something quite different. So please, let me put my side of the events.'

'Okay, go ahead I'm listening.'

'Thank you,' he sighed. 'This is what happened. When I arrived at the scene of a job I was sent to, I discovered the bodies of a seven-year old girl and her grandmother. They had both been stabbed. It was the death of the little girl that upset me the most. So I left the scene, and didn't call in. In fact, I didn't go to work for three days. And then only to hand in my resignation after that. All I could see after that was the little girl's body lying in a pool of blood and urine.

'It didn't take my colleagues long to identify the killer, Paul Daring. He had murdered his own mother, who lived next door to the girl and her grandmother, before killing them. In an effort to cover up the murders, Daring staged both scenes to make them look like burglaries that had gone wrong. He was arrested soon after and later charged with the triple murders.

'But I couldn't get over the death of that little girl – her body just lying there. The counselling I received, helped a little.'

Up to this moment Cadema had remained silent, apart from a nod and a mmm… a couple of times. Now it was time to speak. 'I understand how you must have felt during that time. And I know that counselling isn't the panacea it's meant to be, well at least it wasn't for me. It doesn't seem it was for you either?' There was concern in her voice, but she felt helpless at not knowing what to say or how to really comfort him.

'It probably wasn't the panacea, as you put it.' Haady took a sip of water – the tension in his facial muscles relaxed – he gave a twitch of a smile. 'But the counselling did help to some degree. And don't think I'm dismissing it altogether, as it seems to help others.' He fidgeted.

'Anyway, back to my decision. As you know, I'd been dabbling in genealogy as a hobby during my police work. So, after leaving, I did a degree in the subject... and it made my career.'

As Cadema listened she realised that, if they became real friends, they could support one another if events came flooding back, as they inevitably did with her. And although Julia had listened to her during these times, Julia would never really understand.

Haady was different. She felt closer to him in a way that she had never felt with anyone since her husband's death. But she would have to apply the brakes a little, until she got to know him better. Hopefully, if a real friendship did develop over time, he would eventually become the only therapy she would need.

Nevertheless, sitting there, facing Haady, she recalled what Johns had said to her about the murders, but wondered why Haady was so ostracised by his peers. Had he told her everything, or was he holding something back. Somehow, she had to find out. But her thoughts were interrupted.

'How's your pizza?' Haady asked as he filled the glasses with water for the second time.

'Hot but good. Of course the salad helps to cool the situation – the chilli I mean.'

'I'm glad you like it. And thanks for listening, you're the first person...'

'You don't need to say it, I understand.'

'Thanks anyway,' said Haady. Putting down his knife and fork he smiled at Cadema as the waiter approached their table.

'Anything from the sweet menu?' They both politely declined the offer.

After Haady had paid for the meal, which he insisted on doing this time, they left the restaurant and stood outside for a moment. As they said goodbye, Haady fought back the urge to give Cadema a kiss, but decided that it would have been inappropriate this time. Next time he would have more courage, and he hoped they would meet up for lunch again soon.

***

'Hi, Cadema, I'm pleased to see you back. Enjoyed lunch?' said Johns as she hovered next to Cadema's office door.

'Yes thank you, but I'm sure you're not here to ask me that.' Cadema opened the door and entered her office. It was the longest lunch break she had ever taken, and at that moment she felt elated.

'Right as usual. But I'm pleased to hear you enjoyed yourself. But I'm not sure what the team will think about you and Haady having lunch together. On my part, I hope it works out for you, one way or another,' said Johns who wasn't sure if she had overstepped the mark for speaking out, and being presumptuous.

'Don't assume anything, we only had a working lunch- that's all. And I'm not sure whether the rumours are true about him. You know how they can be distorted. Anyway I'm not prepared to discuss it right now.'

'Sorry, I was just being concerned about you.'

'Well don't be. Anyway Haady has found some very useful information which we need to follow up. And in addition to this, I've examined the content of the file which Ashley Ribley left about his ancestors. There are a few papers in the file relating to burials of some of his family members. The papers are very old, and it's difficult to decipher the writing in places. But there appears to be a reference to one in 1889, but I can't be sure.' Cadema picked up the file, opened it, and showed Johns the content she was referring to.

'I agree, it isn't easy to read. If you want me to, I can follow up the reference, take a copy and then return the file to Ashley on your behalf.'

'That won't be necessary. I promised to return it to him myself. Although I don't think there's any more useful information there. I just want to find out if he knows any more about the burial.'

'I can do that, and return the file at the same time – save you the trouble.'

'On refection, that's a good idea as I've got an Everest of paperwork to get through,' said Cadema. Johns suppressed a smile.

'Fine, I've just got a couple of things to do myself and then I'll go once DI Pratt arrives.'

'Good, and when you've finished, I need an update on how he is settling in. If you're happy with Pratt, then we need to identify a date for your departure to pastures new,' said Cadema, smiling.

Johns returned the gesture, but wasn't about to tell her the truth.

***

It was nearly dark when DCI Johns and DI Pratt reached the Ribley's house – hoping they hadn't started their evening meal.

Ringing the doorbell twice, it was Mrs Ribley who answered. Giving a grimace of a smile, she grunted, and then asked them to come in. Without saying another word, she ushered the two officers into the lounge.

Johns couldn't help noticing the change in Mrs Ribley. Instead of smiling eyes, they were fixed on something, invisible to Johns, on the floor. Her shoulders were bent forwards, making her look as if she had aged ten years over the past two weeks. Even her clothes hung like a shroud from her shoulders, giving the impression that Mrs Ribley had lost weight.

'Sorry to disturb you, but we need to speak to Mr Ribley.' Johns was as apologetic as any other police officer would be in the circumstances. Pratt gave a cough and stood with his feet together, his hands at his sides, and his head held high; *as if on parade*, Johns thought. After giving him a disparaging look, she whispered something to him. Immediately after this, he changed to a little less formal posture. Mrs Ribley didn't seem to have noticed, and said, in a monotonous voice, that she would get her husband, then left the room.

Johns took the opportunity to ask Pratt to keep quiet and try not to interrogate the couple when they appeared. It had never been his nature to do either, however he agreed and would question Johns' orders, later.

Mr Ribley entered the room first, followed by his wife. He was dressed casually in a blue T-shirt and matching jogging pants. His wife in a casual floral dress – evading eye contact.

'It's good to meet you again Mr Ribley. Superintendent Sharma sends her regards and asked me to give you this.' She handed him the file. Ashley gestured for them to sit down again as his wife left the room to make some tea.

'Good,' said Ashley as he looked furtively around the room, as if there were unseen eyes looking at him. 'I don't want her to hear this.' He nodded towards the closed door where his wife had been. 'But I've something to show you. It's an old medical book, dated 1890. I found it in the attic with some other books.' He pulled out a scruffy looking, leather-bound book. 'It's called; *A Treatise on the Theory and Practice of Medicine* by John Syer Bristowe M.D. London, L.I.D. EDIN; F.R.S. 'The thing is.' He looked around the room again. 'I found this cutting inside.' Ashley held up the piece of paper. 'It's from a newspaper, most probably from *The Times*, announcing the death of John T Ribley in 1888, he began to read it:

'John T Ribley, died of a Rupture of the heart on the third of December 1888. His funeral took place at Bow Cemetery on the twelfth of December 1888.' Ashley's voice sounded hoarse – his hands shook as he handed the cutting to Johns.

'On the surface, it sounds feasible. But I'm a bit confused about the dates.' Johns took hold of the book and skimmed the pages. 'You are right about the date, 1890. But why the cutting from 1888 – more than a year before the book was published?'

'Obviously the cutting was placed there well after the deceased, John T Ribley, was buried,' Ashley added. 'But I've no idea why. Perhaps one of my relatives had it and decided to keep it safe after he had purchased the book.'

'That's reasonable, I suppose. Do you mind if I take the book and the cutting away for further analysis?' Johns asked, hoping he wouldn't refuse.

'Only if you swear to be careful and return it to me in the condition it is in now, then I'll lend it to you. It's a bit battered, I know, and the spine is broken, but all the 1285 pages are intact. The person who owned the book, I believe, was George. He was born about 1875, married in 1901 when he was a physician. He probably made the notes we see here in the book. And I think he was the one who underlined several parts of the text. He's my great-great-great grandfather. But he was only fifteen when the book was published, and after he qualified, the book would have been out of date for his practice. The only explanation I can offer, is that the book was handed down to him, and he later found the cutting, and concealed it among the pages.'

'That's a feasible explanation,' said Johns. 'Perhaps the person who handed it down was an uncle. But not John – the deceased person referred to in the cutting – the one we're trying to find. But don't worry Mr Ribley, we will be discreet. And of course, everything will be treated as confidential.'

'Thank you. But there's also something else. I found this in the attic as well.' He handed Johns an A4 size brown envelope full of photographs. 'No idea who they are though. But looking at some of the faces, I suppose most are my ancestors. Some as you can see are sepia and mottled. One, I think, could be my grandmother, but she must have been very young then, probably four or five. As to the others, well there anyone's guess.'

By now, Pratt was itching to speak. At a gap in the conversation, he interjected. 'My goodness,' he said, looking at some of the photographs. 'We've something very similar at home. These people could be anyone. It's useless to us when relatives write 'Mother' or 'Aunt' on the back.'

'But it shows that this happens all the time,' said Johns. 'The older ones – the ones that appear to be taken in a studio, do at least have the mark of the photographer on the back.' Johns noticed as she flipped some over. 'Would you mind if we took these away with us together with the book and clipping?'

'That's fine by me, as long as you can assure me that they will all be returned to me safe and sound.' As Ashley spoke the rattle of cups and saucers could be heard coming down the corridor. 'Shush, don't answer that. Just take them.' He thrust them into a plastic shopping bag and handed it to Johns. 'I'll expect it to be…'

'Sorry it's taken so long – couldn't find any biscuits I thought we had. But when I looked in the jar, it was empty. And there were no spare packets in the cupboards,' said Sarah as she pushed open the door and then put down the tray. 'Have I missed anything?'

'No, not at all dear. We were just clarifying a few things. The officers will be leaving once they've had their tea.'

'Oh, so soon, I was hoping to find out more about...' Sarah glanced at her husband who scowled back at her.

'Don't worry, said Ashley. 'I'll fill you in on the detail later so stop wittering, will you?' Sarah did not answer but looked sorrowfully at Johns and Pratt. It was then that Johns saw the bruise on Sarah's wrist. Looking up, Johns noticed that Ashley had seen her reaction to the bruise; no one spoke.

Johns and Pratt downed their tea, then stood up. 'Well we'd better be off. Thank you for the information you've provided which I'm sure will be very useful,' said Johns who then turned towards Sarah. 'And thank you for the tea.' As they began to leave, Sarah turned to her husband:

'What do you mean by *information*?' she asked, then stopped speaking as Ashley reminded her about the file.

Johns coughed and took a deep breath – hoping to control her anger about the situation. *It isn't my problem*, she thought.

'We must be going now. But we'll be in touch with you soon.' Johns smiled as Sarah stood and lead them to the door.

***

Returning to the station to get their own cars, Pratt said he would return to work the following afternoon, once he'd completed what he had to do. Johns, seeing that Cadema's office light was still on, decided to forfeit her yoga class, and instead, speak to Cadema.

After positioning herself in front of Cadema's desk, Johns began to give an account of Pratt's behaviour. Saying that he kept to the script, didn't speak out of turn, and when he did speak he was courteous.

Cadema frowned. 'Are we talking about the same person, because that's not what I've heard about him?'

'Well, that's what I've observed. But of course, he could be on his good behaviour while I'm about,' said Johns bewildered. 'There is just one thing, and I don't want to trivialise it, but he is elusive at times. Take this evening for instance. I've no idea where he's going tomorrow morning, but I'll expect him when you see him.

'Anyway, after all this time, I've received my papers to go and join my new division. They want me to start as soon as possible. But I know you expect one months' notice.'

'That's the usual case, but as you've waited such a long time for the vacancy I'm happy for you to go sooner. Besides, as you are aware, my funds are being stretched as it is. And if you can do Pratt's appraisal before you go, I can see no reason to protract your leaving any further. When would you like to go?'

'I'm doing the appraisal in a couple of days' time. So, I intend to leave at the end of next week, if that's okay with you.'

'Perfect on both accounts. And I know it's late in the evening now, but how did you get on with the Ribleys?'

'You'll never believe this, but after Mr Ribley was so set against all of this at the beginning, he's now over cooperative – as if he is hiding something,' said Johns as she placed the items Ashley had given to her on Cadema's desk. 'What's more, we didn't need to ask him anything – he just volunteered. Apparently, after our interview with him here, he returned home, went straight to his loft and found a box that had once belonged to his late father. He said his father knew it contained some old books which he inherited from his own father. Opening this book,' Johns pointed, 'he found this cutting. Searching further, he was surprised when he came across this envelope with photographs inside. He thought all these would be interesting to us, especially the newspaper cutting with the obituary of a John T Ribley.'

'This is excellent news, and the cutting, no doubt, is a very significant piece – the best piece of information we've found in this case so far, apart from the familial DNA, that is.'

Cadema sat examining the outside of the book and read the newspaper cutting again. Johns mentioned Ashley's attitude towards his wife, Sarah.

'I can understand him keeping the cutting a secret. And of course the photographs, as one of them may contain our suspect. But I can't dismiss his attitude towards his wife, and his obvious physical abuse towards her.' Johns sounded angry.

'Maybe he's thinking that there's a family trait of violence towards women. And there could be other family secrets that he doesn't want us, or his wife, to find out about,' said Cadema. 'Therefore I think we should dig a little deeper into Mr Ashley Ribley's past too.'

'That's a good point, but if he didn't want us to find anything out, why do you think he volunteered to give me all these things?'

'I believe he realised we would find out sooner or later, and he didn't want the investigation to be more protracted than it already is. And another thing, at least he knows what information we have, that gives him some control of the situation.'

Johns agreed, and said she would send Marriott to *The Times* newspaper office to find out when the article was published.

'Don't be too disappointed if Marriott doesn't find it, as it may not have been published in *The Times*, but in a local paper that may have gone out of business.' Cadema smiled.

'Yes, I've thought about that, but we will just have to see...'

'Tell Marriott to search from November 1888. And of course he needs to verify the death with the General Registry

Office and make sure he gets the death certificate. If this John Ribley died before the ninth of November, then we need to think again. But let's hope this isn't the case, and Marriott finds what we're looking for.'

'What do we do if he turns out to be the right person?' Johns asked.

'In that case, we should be able to identify exactly where he is buried. Get an exhumation order, and take samples for DNA analysis, and if possible, find some physical evidence.'

'What physical evidence do you think there may be?'

'I haven't the faintest.' Cadema shook her head slowly. 'But if there is any, Doctor Lilly will certainly find it.'

Johns, nodded in agreement, said goodbye and left.

Chapter 21

After Johns had briefed Marriott the next morning, he eagerly left with a copy of the cutting – excited to be doing something useful.

Johns had kept the original cutting, the book, and the photographs until Cadema could speak to Julia to see what she could do. Hopefully, she would find some fingerprints, if there were any, from the book and the photographs. Then, if possible, extract DNA from them. If the DNA from the fingerprints, matched the ones found on the book in 1889, then the person, supposedly John T Ripley, could be eliminated if he died in 1888.

However, if Cadema could locate his grave, take samples for DNA analysis and match it with DNA from the dress, then John T Ribley was most probably the perpetrator. But of course, physical evidence was needed to link him to the murders.

***

The day before Johns was about to leave, she was concerned after receiving Marriott's message, and the DNA results from forensics. Arriving back at the station, she ran up the stairs – two at a time. Stopping for breath a couple of times, she eventually made the top. Entering Cadema's office she tried to speak as she tapped her chest with her hand. At every word, she took another deep breath until she was composed enough to form a whole sentence.

'Spell it out.' Cadema looked into Johns' anxious face.

'Well it's like this,' she coughed.

'Go on I'm listening.'

Johns took a gulp of air as if she were about to take a plunge into the local swimming pool, or even a leap off Beachy Head. She had been determined to give up the cigarettes on her promotion. Months later, she was still smoking, as, each time she stopped, she put on weight. So, what was the worst – lung cancer or diabetes – a stroke perhaps? A conundrum she couldn't resolve.

Slowly releasing the air from her lungs, she managed to speak clearly and precisely.

'We have a match with the DNA from the fingerprints on the book.' She paused for breath and sat down – facing Cadema. 'It's from a relative of Ashley Ribley, not sure who yet. But the most important thing is the newspaper cutting. Marriott couldn't find any reference to the death of John T Ribley from any of the newspapers of the time. Furthermore, there is no record of his death in the public records. So, after 1888, it appears that he just vanished.'

'That's impossible. The cutting must have come from some newspaper.' Cadema sat behind her desk studying the script. She was no specialist, but she needed one right now. Someone who would tell her how old the cutting was, the type script used, and more importantly, the newspaper from which it came.

'We'll have to see,' replied Johns. 'But you need to know that I took the cutting at face value, did some research and found the cemetery where the supposed burial took place.'

'What do you mean, took place? We haven't verified that yet,' said Cadema her face contorted with anger.

'No, but I thought it was just a matter of time. So to speed things up – well I made an appointment to visit the church and examine their archives.'

'But you're supposed to be leaving tomorrow?'

'I was, but I've a couple of days off first. And as I'd like to see this through, I made the appointment.'

'Look Joanna, I know how anxious you are to get this sorted, indeed we all are. But we're supposed to be working together. Besides, you need time to get yourself ready for your new responsibilities.'

'With respect, I think you're overreacting.' Johns wiped the perspiration from her face. Cadema sat upright, her dark eyes fixed on John's face. 'Anyway, as I haven't been to the cemetery yet, I'll cancel the appointment, if that's what you want?'

'Now you're being melodramatic. I just want to be kept informed, and deploy my officers appropriately.' Cadema's voice began to mellow – her look softened.

'I know how enthusiastic you are,' Cadema continued, 'and that you've done a great job here. But at your rank, you should have let Marriott sort out the church. However, as you've already made the appointment – see what you can find out. But after that, you must let go.' Cadema smiled and pushed her hair back across her shoulders. Johns nodded, returned the smile and left the office.

***

It was ten in the morning when Johns arrived at the church just as the church warden, Vera, was unlocking the gates. Opening them, they groaned as they scraped along the ground as if their crumbling metal joints were being torn apart. Johns stepped over a couple of puddles stained a reddish-brown: *the colour of old blood,* she thought, *that has dripped like tears from the gates – screeching out to be oiled.*

'You must be Chief Inspector Johns. Pleased to meet you?' Vera grimaced a false smile as she looked over her half-rimmed glasses and held out her hand. Johns took it firmly but there was no reciprocal grip, just a cold – dead appendage. But as they touched, it seemed that Vera grew from a crouching five foot nothing, to a five-foot four- inch slim woman of about sixty years old – fading hair severely plastered against her head. Straightening her tailored dark-blue dress and matching jacket, she pushed her glasses further onto her nose.

'Yes, and I'm pleased to meet you. And I appreciate you opening up for me, especially since seeing the notice on the gate saying that you don't open until eleven.' Johns smiled.

'That's right, but as you said it was important police work, I decided to open up. But the vicar won't be here for at least another hour.

'No problem, I'll have a walk around the grounds first and come to the vestry afterwards,' said Johns assertively.

Vera nodded in response, grumbled quietly, and said she had work to do and would see her sometime in the next hour.

Johns watched as Vera sauntered up the gravel path, picking up pieces of paper, and other rubbish on the journey, then rammed them into a plastic bag which materialised from one of her pockets. Then, stopping by a bin, she mumbled, emptied the bag and replaced it into her pocket. Johns shuddered at the thought, and continued on.

Entering the cemetery, she could see flowers on newly dug graves. The smell of freshly dug earth met her senses as she walked along the gravel path. She noticed how majestically the church stood, as if guarding the occupants in the graves below. The skeletal outline of a once blooming wisteria spread out like a black sheet on the south-facing wall of the church, as her shoes crunched on; like the grinding of corn in a mill. There were the usual standpipes and jugs left in neat rows for the visitors to use. A couple of squirrels startled her as they darted across the grass a few feet away, and then ran up the lone oak tree. Blackbirds and jackdaws foraged in the leaves of last autumn – scattering debris. A cat stalked.

Johns moved on. Row-upon-row of regimented clean gravestones, the short-cropped grass, and the lack of faded or dead flowers – a cemetery well kept. Not just by the grounds people, but by visitors who tended their loved ones' final abode. On occasions, she stopped to read a headstone, many were illegible. When the sun switched on its beam at another, she caught a glimpse of an insignificant date and moved on again. The musty aroma of January, mingled with the spice of an early snowdrop was no comfort to her – the rustle of the cigarette packet in her pocket was. But what would Vera think if she succumbed to temptation? 'Damn it,' she cursed.

The gravel path terminated abruptly. In its place was a corrugated grass pathway, made by the wheels of some farm machinery. Now she was moving towards the back of the church. Here the scene changed. It was dark, and the dank dead air stung at her nostrils. Regimented graves had disappeared, replaced by chipped, leaning, and fallen headstones. The long moss-patched grass was full of pot holes. Skeletal leaves from previous winters still littered the ground under the overgrown hedge and around the two oak trees. A few bent and broken watering cans waited at the dripping tap where algae and moss forged a narrow green slimy looking rivulet. The only sounds here were Johns' own footsteps, and a wheeze now and again. *The dead part of the cemetery.* She pulled up her coat collar around her neck, and shivered – dead eyes watching her?

There were no flowers here. *Probably no one living to bring them.* Then she stopped to examine the faded outline of a date on a headstone. A sudden breeze lifted a few dead leaves, as if warning her that she was unwelcome. Now even the sun had disappeared, and she tugged at her collar again. Her own breath wheezed again, just like it had done when she was a child.

She moved on, her eyes oscillating from side to side – terrified.

Several of the headstone were of crumbling grey slate – words obliterated over time. She stopped to trace her fingers across a couple of them, but the dates were illegible. Further on, she bent down to examine another headstone. Tracing her fingers across it she found the date; 1910. 'Not significant,' she whispered, and walked on.

Several headstones were off the main path. She looked across the unkempt grass, and noticed one that looked interesting to her; why it looked interesting she didn't know. Perhaps menacing in some way. She began to walk towards it – her foot hesitated, she hesitated. If she went on she would have to step over the depressions. Depressions that were the size of bodies. She stood, her heart raced as the words of her mother echoed in her mind.

'*Never* walk on anyone's grave.' No, she could never do that. Instead she tried to estimate where the head of each person was in their grave; then, on tiptoe she circumnavigated it. After several excursions, and grave-hopping – she reached the headstone that had drawn her across the minefield of death.

Crouching, she traced her fingers over the letters on the damp slate; 188…, were the only numbers she could decipher, no name – nothing. *Damn it*, she thought. *It could be anyone*. Standing again, she arched her aching back, let out a deep sigh, and then looked around. There were hundreds of headstones from that era.

She froze. Was someone watching her? No one was there, but she had the uneasy feeling of someone standing behind her. Gingerly she turned her head and looked over her shoulder. She exhaled a deep sigh when she saw Vera standing there.

Facing Vera now, the woman's mouth smiled, but her cold steel eyes looked past Johns, as if they were focusing on something, or someone else.

'I've opened the vestry if you care follow me,' said Vera who looked at Johns for the first time. 'Perhaps you will be able to find the papers you're looking for there. At least it's warmer, and I can make you some tea if you like.'

'That will be very welcome, thank you.' She smiled and followed Vera – relieved to be getting away from the eerie graveyard. 'I didn't realise there would be so many headstones for me to examine. And the inscriptions are very difficult, if not impossible, to read in that part of the cemetery.' She nodded back to where she had been standing when Vera arrived.

'I know. And we've tried to contact the living relatives, but when the graves are over a hundred years old, what can you expect. It's only when the grave is big enough to be handed down to the next generation, we have some success. But even then, people just don't want to know. And of course cremations are common now. Back in 1888 they were almost non-existent. If that trend continues, we'll have no option but to clear the site of the old headstones, especially as many of them breach health and safety regulations.'

Johns shook her head. 'It would be such a pity to lose that history of the church, and how would people, researching their family history, find their ancestors?'

Vera grunted, but did not answer. Instead she began to grumble at the rubbish people had left, even though most of it must have been there for several weeks. Vera picked it up – *justifying her diligence and tenacity to keep the place tidy*, Johns reasoned.

Entering the church, Johns stood in the nave and instantly recognised the musty damp smell that always emanated from such premises. She had been in many churches before, but preferred her own Methodist church where she used to sing in the choir until she went to university. Now all she had time for was the weekly service, but this was never as good as the ones she attended in Antigua when she visited there with her mother. Reminiscing over, she could hear Vera's voice prattling on about the church's history.

'Built in the fourteenth century, almost demolished by Henry the VIII. The stained glass was replaced in parts after the bombing in 1942.' Vera spoke as if she were reading from a crib sheet – her voice – monotonous and emotionless. Leaving Johns looking around the church, she began to busy herself behind a large wooden door that separated the church from the kitchen. From within, she heard Vera's high-pitched voice.

'Kettle's on. How do you like your tea? I don't do this for any old visitor, but seeing as it's you, I'll make an exception.' The voice sounded acidic.

Johns gave her tea preferences then, as her eyes adjusted to the church's interior, she moved from one stained glass window to another. She glanced at the one with Jesus on the cross. A pulse of light penetrated the glass and lit the ring of thorns on the head of Christ. She stopped – mesmerised. Perspiration began to form on her forehead. Wiping it with a tissue, it seemed as if the season had suddenly turned to summer; the solstice sprang to her mind. Now she began to shiver – a threatening presence spread over her; a warning perhaps? Shrugging – she gained her upright posture and told herself not to be so stupid. This wasn't like her, she was always so composed, so professional and controlled.

'It's a lovely church, isn't it?' Vera's voice snapped at the silence – ricocheting around the church walls. Johns turned. She expected to see the tea cups. Instead Vera was holding an enormous brown and faded ledger. 'The kettle takes ages, so while you're waiting I thought you'd like to take a look at this.' She held out the ledger with some difficulty.

'Good grief, let me help,' said Johns taking hold of one side, then realised it must be at least three kilograms in weight. 'I don't know how you managed to carry this so far.' She smiled as they both held the ledger, then walked sideways towards an old round oak table that wobbled as they dropped the ledger onto it.

'Thank you,' said Vera, stretching and rubbing her back as she handed Johns a pair of white cotton gloves. 'You'll need these before you start reading.' She gave a wry smile and for the first time showed her uneven yellow-stained teeth.

Johns obliged without question, knowing that all archives must be handled with respect and preserved for future generations. She discovered this when she was studying for her degree and had to visit the National Archives at Kew. They were, *quite rightly*, she thought, pedantic about such things.

With gloved hands, Vera opened the ledger and turned to the first page. 'As you can see,' said Vera, 'it has been compiled in date order. So instead of looking for a name, you'll need to find the date first. By the side of the date, you will find the name and a reference number to the grave itself. Then you should be able to find where the grave is located on this map of the graveyard.'

'Thank you. That sounds easy enough,' said Johns as she looked at the date coverage on the page. '1768 to 1899. Turning to the first full page, the ledger now resembled two-A3 size pages. With difficulty – her hands trembling, she turned over a bulk of pages until reaching 1888. Tracing her fingers over the names down the page, she could not find any reference to a John T. Ribley. She moved closer to the page, but despite it being legible, as if it had been typewritten, there was no mention of that name for that year. With anxious eyes, she looked at Vera – no response. She turned the page to 1889 – still no one with that name. Frantically turning the pages backwards and forwards, she finally settled on 1888 and took mental notes of the names.

Everything seemed in order. She turned to Vera. 'I suppose it's going to be very difficult to find anyone unless we have the actual burial date.'

'That's right,' said Vera.

'This cutting,' Johns took it out of her pocket, 'mentioned the funeral in 1888, so he must have been buried then. So why isn't his name in this ledger? There isn't another ledger in your archives, is there?' She tried her best not to sound accusing.

Vera raised her pencilled eye-brows. 'Not that I know of, besides why should there be. This is the only ledger covering the date you are looking for. And if it's not there, then he couldn't have been buried here. You must have the wrong church,' she said indignantly. *Typical police – never get their fact right*, she muttered.

'But despite what you say, the cutting definitely mentions this church by name. So no, we haven't made a mistake. He must be here somewhere.' Johns turned to the ledger again and began to examine each name and reference numbers after October 1888.

Reading out the sixteen names, with concurrent grave references, she noticed that between Benjamin Smyth and Russell Hargrove, there was a gap in the numbers. The former had grave number 1443 and was buried on the first of November. The latter was grave number 1445 and was buried on the twenty-ninth of November 1888. Number 1444 was missing from the list. She checked again, but there was no mistake. According to the ledger reference number 1444 was unaccounted for. Turning back the pages again, she checked the others – they were all in sequence. Was there a genuine error at the time? She did not think so. Was it done by someone deliberately? She imagined that that would be very difficult to do. Especially as everything in the ledger appeared to be complete.

She stood for a while contemplating the scenario. Could someone had been bribed to keep quiet about a burial? If this were the case, it meant that the person who paid must have known who the dead man *really* was. If there is a grave, then it could be occupied by John T. Ribley.

Using her smart phone, she took a photograph of the page, then closed the ledger. Thanking Vera for her help, and saying she couldn't stop for tea, she left. As she walked back down the gravel path, she had the same feeling of someone watching her. She did not think it was Vera.

***

Sitting in Cadema's office, Johns could see that she was unhappy about something. And after Cadema had told her that Marriott was unable to find the actual newspaper where the cutting came from, she was not surprised. Explaining about the ledger seemed to be the last straw. Both agreed that further investigation was necessary.

'The first thing I need to do,' said Cadema, 'is to contact someone who can discover which newspaper the cutting came from.'

'You're right,' said Johns, 'and I think I know the right person. His name is Peter Hurd, he's a graphologist. If I remember correctly, he started a PhD in the origins of printing but never completed it. I only met him once, when I was at uni. But he was somewhat of an expert in identifying old printing. And I'm sure he'll be able to tell us which newspaper the cutting came from.' Johns sounded enthusiastic again.

'That's the same person I was thinking of too. Great minds and all that… So can you find his contact details and we'll see if he can help.' Cadema's face glowed – the monotone of her voice replaced by her usual high-pitched tone that reverberated off the walls. She leaned forward, as if to deliver a secret. Johns mimicked her posture. 'You know what I think?' she said rhetorically. 'I think that, for some reason, the cutting was deliberately planted in the book. As if someone hoped it would be found. On first glance it looked genuine enough, even to me. Hopefully, Peter can help, and establish whether it is genuine or not. As for the missing number in the graveyard, well, that's another conundrum.'

Johns nodded. 'I think the only way forward is to see if there is an actual grave between reference number 1443 and 1445.'

'You're right, but you are about to leave this investigation. I'll take over now. But before you go, I've bought a little something. It's not much, but hopefully you'll put it on your new desk upstairs.' Cadema handed her a small wrapped package. 'I know you wanted to leave without ceremony, but if you change your mind, I'm sure the team will be pleased to celebrate with you.'

After thanking Cadema for the gift, she placed Pratt's appraisal on the desk. 'Just keep the reins on him a little, and I'm sure he'll be okay,' she said, and then left.

***

Two days later, and another small team briefing over, DI Pratt was assigned to visit the church along with Marriott.

Instead of seeing Vera, Cadema had arranged for them to meet the vicar, Fredrick Coombe. As they approached him, they could see his large bulky frame almost filling the entrance to the church. He moved towards them, his left arm outstretched, he right hand in a sling. His firm handshake surprised both officers, as did his Scottish colloquialisms as they introduced themselves to him.

'Sorry for this, but broke my arm a couple of weeks ago – fell off the ladder.'

Pratt nodded. 'No problem, hope it gets better soon.' He gave a frown at the thought of his over six-foot large frame balancing on a step ladder, let alone falling off.

Composing himself again, Pratt began to examine the vicar more closely. His greying hair and beard were long and a little shabby. But his ocean blue eyes mellowed his face, giving the impression that his congregation would be able to confide in him as his whole persona, and his slight stoop were comforting. *Like a father to his son.*

'Don't just stand there, come in. And please call me Fred, all my parishioners do, except the older ones of course.' Leading the way in, they sat in one of the pews.

'Needs a bit of work done, but as you can see from our thermometer,' he pointed to the cardboard cut-out which showed the target amount, halfway up, was the horizontal line identifying where they had currently reached, 'we'll soon be there.' He tried to convince himself, but didn't fool anyone.

'How long did it take to reach where you are now with your target?' Marriott asked, as if they had plenty of time to talk.

Fred lowered his head. 'Two years I'm afraid. But one never knows when a substantial donation might come in.' He raised his head and looked towards the altar.

'We can all live in hope,' said Pratt who began to explain what Johns had said about the ledger. When he asked if Fred could show them the part of the churchyard that corresponded with the reference numbers 1443 to 1445, he looked puzzled.

'We just want to see if there is space for another grave which could account for number 1444, which is missing from the ledger,' Pratt added, hoping he would understand since he had explained it better.

'I don't think that will be easy as the grave numbers in that part of the churchyard are difficult to determine, especially the date you are looking for. But I'll do my best. I expect the best person to show you around is our groundsman, Barry Bates. He also manages the graves, gets new ones dug, and liaises with the stone masons.'

'If he can help us, we'll be grateful,' said Marriott.

'I am sure he'll be able to give you the information you need. Besides, I've only been here a couple of years. And couldn't possibly know where every grave is. But Barry will definitely know,' said Fred – his body swaying forward and backwards – as if his feet were too small to balance him. Closing his eyes at each word, Marriot wondered if he might fall over, but decided not to say anything. 'Yes, Barry's the person. Been here for ever, so they say. But certainly, for the last thirty years. And before him, the Bates family had managed the grounds for a century or more. So yes he'll be the one.'

'Thank you, you've been very helpful, Fred,' said Pratt, grimacing. As they precariously shook hands again, Pratt wondered if one of his ancestors might have given Barry the answer to the mystery.

As Fred introduced Barry Bates to the officers, Barry looked suspiciously at them. His leathery skin stretched over the contours of his face, outlining every bone, especially when he frowned. His flat cap – failing to hide his shoulder-length greasy-grey grisly hair, hung at the back in a ponytail as he rammed his earthy hands into the pockets of his tweed jacket.

'So you've come about the graves. Well you've come to the right person. I'll show ya where to look. Know these graves like the back of me hand I do. I'll show ya the number of rows and then we can find the one you're looking for. It won't be easy though.' As Barry spat out his words, the officers moved sideways to avoid being sprayed.

Barry rushed to the area in the graveyard where Johns had stood when she had visited. Now the two officers were watching Barry bending down at a gravestone. He pushed away some thistles and grass from its corner, then looked up. 'If you start here, you'll probably find it.' He looked at the officers – his sideways smile revealing his stained teeth.

Pratt thanked him for his help and said they would look along the rows and if they needed him again, he would call him. He shuddered as Barry moved away, not because of his breath, but the eerie feeling Pratt now had.

Examining the headstones, their fears were realised – there would be no early retreat. Despite what Barry had said, the graves were not in distinctive rows like they were in the newer part of the cemetery, but were scattered about. They could see remnants of some, but others were completely obliterated, some being infiltrated with long grass. Even when they compared the layout with the sketch of the graveyard, they could only identify the odd one or two. Finally reaching the reference point for grave number 1443, Marriott found a distinctive gap between it and 1445. The latter was a stone rectangular-shaped grave, filled with green stones. Keeping watch over this was a three-foot high headstone of chipped slate, which tilted at a strange angle.

The nearly obliterated words were difficult to decipher, but just visible was the date, 1888. Marriott called to Pratt, who moved to grave number 1443, next to the gap – no headstone. Stepping sideways, he surreptitiously scraped the wet grass with his heel where grave 1444 should be. There was something hard underfoot. Reaching for his mobile phone, he pressed a number; Cadema answered on the second ring.

'I think we've located it, hidden near one of the oak trees, and between the two graves,' Pratt whispered. 'There is definitely a depression here.' He scraped his foot across the surface again. 'The grave next to it is definitely 1445 and is dated 1888. So if we dig where 1444 should be, I'm sure we'll find what we're looking for. Sorry, Ma'am, must go now,' said Pratt as he saw Barry appear from a water hub.

***

Cadema would normally have applied for an exhumation once she heard Pratt's news. But on this occasion, she had doubts. What if there has been a genuine mistake with the numberings? What if the grave was found and it was empty; all those police hours and other resources – wasted? The press would surely find out and the media would then ruin any further investigations.' She ruminated, then picked up the telephone.

'Sir, it could be the grave we are looking for. But we'll not be sure unless we open it.' She listened to crackling on the line, but the deputy commissioner, Andrew Long, was still thinking. Then she heard his forceful voice.

'Convince me,' he said.

How could she convince him, when she couldn't even convince herself? She shook her head and took a deep breath.

'I think we've reached a hiatus. If we don't open the grave, we will never know. This is probably the only way we can find out one way or another.' Her rationale was weak, but that was all she could think of saying.

'Okay, just this once. But you'll need all the information you have for the coroner even to consider it. So emphasise the DNA data, and the current position with the proposed relative, Ashley Ribley. You could even ask him to give a signed letter supporting your theory. And remember, you will also need to convince the diocese.' He took a tissue from a box on his desk and wiped the sweat from his forehead. 'I hope I'm not making a mistake in supporting you. But I know what you're like from working with you some eight years ago. Like a dog with a bone,' he chuckled. 'By the way, you'll not be reporting to me for much longer, as we have a replacement for the chief-super's job. Can't tell you who it is, but she starts next month.' There was a sharp intake of breath as he put down the telephone.

Receiving the exhumation documents, Cadema decided to allocate Pratt to oversee the task along with Marriott. She would visit Mr Ribley and thank him personally for the supporting letter he had sent.

Meeting him the following day, she explained that the grave would be opened at night to avoid anxiety or distress, and to prevent the press from knowing about it. She also mentioned that, as the grave was unmarked, there was a possibility that there was nothing inside.

***

Marriott, with two uniformed officers accompanied Pratt to the cemetery. By the time they arrived, the vicar, Fredrick

Coomb, had already seen where the grave might be. He left instructions with Barry Bates, saying that he was only to be called if an actual grave was found.

Pratt thanked Barry for his message and walked towards the site where two gravediggers were already working and ordered the officers to erect the tent.

'You were not supposed to start until we arrived,' said Pratt in an exasperated voice as he watched the gravediggers down their tools, take a gulp of water from a dirty bottle and move away from the dig site.

'Look, we've only just scraped the surface – can't go no further.' The heavy-framed man spoke directly to Barry – ignoring the officers.

'What d'ya mean, Andy, it aint that difficult to shift a bit of soil,' said Barry as he looked towards the spades.

'That may be, but there's concrete, not even a couple of inches below the grass. And me and young Ray here aint shifting that lot.'

Barry walked across, took hold of a spade and thrust it into the ground – clang…g, then simultaneously a grating sound echoed around the graveyard like a tuning fork. Barry turned to the officers;

'It could even be a blooming concrete sarcoph… or whatever – it'll take ages to shift it. We're going to need a pneumatic drill before we can do owt else.' Barry's words spat at Pratt as he wiped his mouth on the sleeve of his jacket.

Pratt kept his distance, as did all the others present.

'It's obviously not a sarcophagus. I think you will find it's just a layer of concrete. Anyway, whatever it is, we can't drill at night,' said Pratt to the officers.

Barry stood, his face half smirking. 'You're right there – the noise a'l weaken the dead,' he chuckled. 'Then it won't be a secret no more. But I suppose, we can't keep this a secret for long,' said Barry as he took off his cap. 'Anyway, if we take your tent down and put everything else away, then no one will be any the wiser. And I knows a bloke who can do the pneumatising job for a Bertie.'

'A Bertie?' Pratt frowned as Marriott stepped beside him and whispered.

'Thirty pounds.'

'We can do the tidying up, but I don't know about the money. I'll have to speak to my boss first. Is this friend of yours reliable?' Pratt asked.

'I can put me money on him. And he'll not blab either.'

Pratt nodded, then walked some distance from the others, took out his mobile phone, and called Cadema to explain the situation, and the offer of assistance from Barry's friend. After some deliberation, Cadema agreed the plan saying there was enough petty cash for the work, but reminded Pratt to get a receipt.

Returning, Pratt said everything had been agreed and that he would return the next day.

Barry turned towards the two gravediggers, who were sitting on a broken slab smoking. 'That's it, mates, let's go home. There's nothing we can do until the concrete's been moved.'

Just before Pratt and his team were getting ready to leave, he turned to Barry.

'This is my phone number.' He handed him his card. 'I want you to call me once the concrete had been removed, and before any more work is carried out at the site. And don't forget to tell, what ever his name is, to keep quiet about all this or he'll not get paid.'

Barry gave a cough and kicked at a small piece of gravel, like a bull waiting to charge. 'He'll not do it 'till he sees the money – up front mind.' He shuffled his feet again.

'You want me to give you thirty pounds *now*? But we don't keep petty cash with us.'

Barry stood perfectly still as he looked into Pratt's eyes. 'He'll not do owt unless he sees it first.'

Pratt released an exasperated sigh and turned to his officers. 'Anyone got any money on them?' he asked.

Having put their hands in their pockets, they managed to raise the money – reassured that they would be reimbursed at the station. Handing the money to Barry and telling him to make sure he got a receipt, he mumbled quietly so no one could hear him, 'You'll be lucky,' then disappeared down the path.

The pneumatic drill, along with its operator, arrived at four thirty the following afternoon. The concrete layer removed and the job completed - with no sign of a receipt.

With the same team of officers from the previous day, and everything in place, the gravediggers started work at ten p.m. They had only dug out about a half metre of soil and clay when everyone heard a grating sound of metal against metal. Prodding further, Andy, the gravedigger, asked for more light. As he scraped away the debris with his fingers, he could see a metal plaque fixed to what appeared to be a coffin lid. The words etched onto the plaque were illegible. Digging further into the ground, the rotted wood of the coffin began to disintegrate.

Pratt looked in. 'Don't dig any further. We'll need to be careful with this, especially as the coffin is too fragile to move. Beside I'll also need to call the vicar, and speak to the pathologist.'

It was nearly midnight by the time everything, including the wooden planks to secure the walls of the grave, were ready for the gravediggers to continue. The vicar now in attendance, decided to wait at the site "just in case,". Doctor Lilly was out on another case, and was unable to contact Wilhelmina, her assistant. She told Pratt to continue, and she would see what she could do in the morning.

The space between the graves was narrow. Everyone agreed that the only way to view the whole coffin, without totally destroying it, was to dig a trench around it. This needed to done without the risk of disturbing the graves on either side. Then the planks could be secured, and the coffin preserved.

'This is taking far too long, Sir,' said Marriot as they stood at the site, which was becoming misty by the minute. An owl tooted in the background as the men dug deeper and wider – but not too wide.

'Yes I know, but we have to be patient. These men know what they are doing and know the risks. When everything is secure, we can have access. It shouldn't be too long now,' said Pratt despite feeling impatient himself.

'It's all yours now,' said Barry, as Andy and Ray emerged from the grave. The three of them shared a drink of water from the same dirty plastic bottle that Pratt had seen the night before. Then the two gravediggers walked off together saying goodnight.

Nodding to them, Pratt turned to his team as the vicar and Barry waited. 'I'm sorry to say that it's much too late to do anything else tonight, so now everything's safe and secure, we'll resume in the morning.'

The vicar, Fred, moved closer to Pratt. 'It looks as if you're going to find someone or something in the grave after all. In that case I will be here when you arrive tomorrow, just let me know when,' he whispered.

'Certainly, Fred, and if you're delayed for any reason, we will wait for you before starting.' He stifled a yawn.

Fred thanked him and then walked off through the churchyard as if he were blessing the deceased.

Leaving the two uniformed officers to guard the site until they were relieved, Pratt said goodnight to Barry and began to leave with Marriott.

Marriott hesitated – a frown on his face: 'Sorry, Sir, but I thought we had to do everything at night so no one would be any the wiser?'

'That *was* the plan,' said Pratt condescendingly. 'But we didn't expect the coffin to be in such a state. We've been at it for hours now, and the weather's closing in. So it's time to call it a day. We'll come back in the morning.'

Sergeant Marriott nodded, thinking of his bed, but realising he also had other work to do before he reached it.

***

Pratt arrived the following morning. The two uniformed officers guarding the site the previous evening had been replaced by two new ones. Fred was waiting. Marriott – absent.

When the remnants of the wooden coffin lid were finally removed, Pratt, and Fred, were not surprised that there were no human remains. Instead, all Pratt could see was an oblong metal box about forty centimetres long, thirty centimetres wide and twenty deep. The metal was a puzzle to him – no sign of rust except on the padlock. It reminded him of his grandfather's old cash box in Stoke. Fred looked at the box. Could it be a cremation? He doubted it. Nevertheless, he said a prayer. On leaving, he asked to be informed, if, when it was opened, it contained any ashes. Pratt nodded in agreement. Turning to the metal box again, he tried to lift it, but even with help, it was much too heavy. Defeated, he instructed the officers to guard the area, saying he would return later.

Cadema was in her office when Pratt arrived at eleven. Marriott, he assumed, was still in bed after his late night organising replacement officers for the graveyard.

There were no signs of surprise on Cadema's face when she heard about the metal box. Somewhere in her mind she knew it had all been too easy – life just isn't like that. She turned to Pratt who was sitting opposite her.

'I don't believe in coincidences; they just don't happen. First the old wooden trunk Marriott found. Then the dress with the blood stains. Then the DNA, identifying possible ancestors. Next, finding Ashley Ribley, and the cutting from the newspaper leading us to the graveyard. And now this metal box. Someone must have planted it all. Someone is trying to control us, but who?' She sounded angry.

'Well they are the facts, Ma'am. We can't ignore them,' said Pratt as his heart quickened, more from annoyance than any chest problem.

'Of course we can't ignore them,' said Cadema. 'But I do feel we're being manipulated. All the evidence points to that. And as far as I'm concerned, the whole scenario is a potential hoax. And the metal box in the grave – that could be another wild goose chase.'

Pratt took a deep breath. 'So are you saying that we should give up – throw all the work we've all done down the drain and walk away?' He was almost shouting now.

'No need for that tone. I've no intention of giving up. We have a duty, and not to mention the ring-fenced funding, to find the *truth*. So let's start with this box you've uncovered. Find out what's inside, and how old the concrete is, and what the significance is to our investigation. I'll speak to Doctor Lilly about this,' said Cadema as controlled as she could be.

'Good, at least that's a start,' Pratt sat back in the chair. 'So what now?

Cadema didn't answer but trance-like she looked around the room – perhaps for answers? Then, as if just waking from unconsciousness, she smiled, stifled a yawn and with menacing dark eyes looked at Pratt. Still she didn't speak. What could she say? What would Jim Logan say, what would *he* do? He certainly would not have put himself in this position in the first place. But here she was – now she had to get on with it. To come up with answers – Julia, yes Julia…

'Are you okay, Ma'am?' asked Pratt, sounding worried.

'No I'm fine. I think Doctor Lilly is our answer. I'll contact her to see what she can do.'

Happy with the answer, Pratt left her office and headed for the graveyard, a little bewildered at Cadema's reactions. He'd heard rumours about her "little turns". Was that one of them he had just witnessed?

***

Alone in her office, Cadema sat looking at the telephone – debating whether to call Julia or not. Having reached for the phone on three occasions, she pressed the button.

'Hi, Julia, I know how busy you are, but I've another problem I need your help with.' Cadema rubbed her fingers through her hair and tossed it back over her shoulders, then cleared her throat. 'Are you free to come over to my office so I we can discuss the issues.'

'Sorry, Cadema, that's a problem as I'm due in court in an hour and have papers to read before then. Will tomorrow do?'

'No, sorry, but could you possibly find some time this afternoon,' said Cadema with hope and anxiety in her voice in equal measures. She then explained further about the church, the coffin and the metal box. 'I'm sure it's what we've been looking for. Obviously I don't want to disturb the grave any further until you've seen it. And besides that, we need to keep things from the public and media. The sooner we can remove the tell-tail signs of our presence, the better.'

'I realise your dilemma, Cadema, and know how important this is to you and your investigation, but I simply don't have the time today. I could, as I said to DI Pratt, send my assistant, Wilhelmina Cox, I know how keen she is, and she'll be very thorough. I'll ask her to arrange photographs and take samples. Your metal box can be removed and brought back here. She'll report back to me much better than Bagley would have done.'

'I'd appreciate that.' Cadema sounded despondent. 'Can you tell her to meet DI Pratt at the churchyard by twelve thirty?' Julia agreed to do this, said goodbye, and put the phone down.

Having explained to Pratt about Wilhelmina, Cadema asked him to report back as soon as the metal box had been removed and the site returned to its original state.

When Wilhelmina reached the entrance to the churchyard, Pratt was some distance away, looking at her inquisitively. He surmised that she, or her ancestors, came from the Caribbean. About ten years younger than the now decamped DCI Johns, Wilhelmina had similar features and figure, but with wild hair, and probably a temperament to match – someone to take on perhaps? But her high forehead, long facial features, displayed intelligence. She would probably rebuff him. He shrugged and then smiled at her. But, although her bright eyes smiled back at him, they failed to hide the anxiety on her face. As she approached Pratt, he held out his hand and greeted her.

The briefing Wilhelmina received from Pratt only lasted about five minutes, barely giving her time to complete the copious notes she needed when dealing with crime scenes. Then, having to run behind Pratt carrying her forensic cases and gripping her pocketbook firmly in her other hand, she arrived at the dig site – panting.

The two police officers Pratt had left guarding the site earlier had been replaced by one other. His slender frame stood sentry-like just inside the tent as pools of muddy water gathered at his feet. Inside, Pratt noticed the grave had been considerably extended along with the tent which obscured the publics' view.

Pratt nodded a greeting to the officer, he reciprocated. Moving into the tent with Wilhelmina, Pratt noticed a ladder, he assumed the gravediggers had left for easy access.

Wilhelmina gave a nervous giggle, but stopped when she saw the mud. As she began to change into her forensic clothing, she slipped over.

'Not my best day,' she mumbled. Changing into another suit she gingerly climbed down the ladder.

'You'd never believe it's daylight down here, I'll need much more light. Can you arrange some please?'

'No problem,' said Pratt as she called for the officer to help.

The light improved – Pratt and Wilhelmina stood for a moment looking down at the debris of rotted wood and sodden earth.

'Where's the lid?' asked Wilhelmina as she turned to face Pratt.

'I thought I'd explained that, but I'll go over it again if you like.' Wilhelmina nodded, as it would be impossible for her to consult her notes in such an inhospitable place. So this time she listened for a change.

After Pratt had repeated the information about the grave numbers, the concrete slab, the disintegrating wooden lid of the coffin where no corpse was found, and the metal box, Wilhelmina said she was happy to have the whole scenario put into context.

Pratt's feet slushed forwards, to where the head of the coffin should have been. 'This is the plaque I told you about, but the words were obliterated. I don't suppose...'

Wilhelmina nodded and began to examine the remnants of coffin lid. Stopping to take photographs, she almost lost her balance again. It was then she noticed that the wood had rotted away much quicker than she would have expected. It certainly wasn't the type of coffin lid that was used in the 1888s. They were usually made of oak and could last centuries, especially in acid soil. And it wasn't in the water table, so she presumed it must have been used for a pauper's grave. Taking samples of it, she saw the metal box inside the coffin area.

'Instead of opening it here,' she pointed out to Pratt, 'I'm going to take it away and examine it in the laboratory, if that's okay with you?' Prodding with a metal probe there was a distinct sound of dulled metal, giving her the impression that there was something inside.

'No problem. I'll organise it. In the meantime, don't try to lift it, it's much too heavy for a scrap like you. I'll ask Barry Bates, the groundsman, to have it lifted out. Then it can be transported away, and hopefully reach you later this afternoon.'

When Pratt explained what he wanted Barry to do, he agreed to organise it but said it would cost "thirty quid", and "up front", he emphasised.

***

Once the box had been lifted from the grave, placed in a police van and was heading for the laboratory, Pratt arranged for the site to be cleared. Leaving the graveyard with Wilhelmina he said he would meet her in the laboratory.

Arriving at the police station, Pratt rushed into Cadema's office. 'It's all finished, Ma'am. So when you're ready, we can go and see what's inside the box.' He waited for an answer, wishing he could have a drink. After all it had been an exhausting day.

'Excellent, and you're just in time as Marriott has now arrived. He's been at the records office, but there's still no

241

registration of the death being recorded. And now that you've discovered the empty grave, I'm not surprised,' said Cadema as she quickly lifted her coat from the door and followed Pratt to the car park, picking Marriott up on the way.

When they arrived at the laboratory Cadema was surprised to see both Julia and Wilhelmina there. Julia explained that the judge at the morning session had an adjournment until the next morning. She was now free to work on the metal box which had been placed on a stainless-steel trolley.

Soil and other debris removed, its surface was no longer dull but reflected the light coming from the overhead lamps. Wilhelmina made a note of this and said there was an integral lock, but no key, so she had sent for a locksmith.

Julia walked around, examining the box from every angle. 'This is very odd – not a sign of rust. That suggests that it must be made of rustless steel. That type of metal was developed in the late nineteenth century, but was not a commercially viable success until it was refined further and became known as stainless steel in the twentieth century.'

'Is that's why it's so heavy?' Cadema asked as she bent down to take a closer look.

'I don't think so. When it's opened, no doubt we'll discover why that is,' said Julia who turned to see the locksmith, Philip Smith, standing in the doorway with his tool bag. He took a couple of goes at the lock and then opened it.

'Well, no wonder none of you could carry it, it's lined with lead,' said Philip rubbing his hand across his smooth head as everyone stepped forward.

'It certainly is,' said Cadema excitedly and then thanked Philip for his work. As he left the room he put a key on a table saying that it could be used to lock the box again.

Julia, with gloved hands, lifted the inner lid then frowned at the content – it was full of, what looked like, notebooks.

'Now, I'd like you all to stand back while we take swabs. Then we'll lift them out as carefully as possibly. Hopefully they won't fall apart,' said Julia as she gestured to Wilhelmina to help.

One by one, each of the six notebooks were carefully lifted out and arranged, in date order according to their cover, onto the stainless steel bench. Inside the first notebook there was an index written in English.

'It seems as if we have some sort of diary,' said Pratt, who was trying to imagine why someone had gone to so much trouble to preserve them. 'They must have been very important to someone.'

'They *are* diaries,' Julia confirmed. Removing the last notebook, she realised that there were other items hidden there. As the others watched, she began to remove them. They included one brass ring, a piece of folded soiled cloth, and a piece of an old hair comb. Wrapped in six silk handkerchiefs were, what appeared to be, small fragments of mummified tissue. The final item was a once white but now mottled-stained envelope. Squinting, she manged to read the addressee: "Inspector Aberline, Scotland Yard". Her hands shaking, she turned to Cadema, and gingerly opened the envelope. 'There's a piece of paper inside, but I don't think I'll take it out until I've examined the envelope microscopically and taken swabs for DNA analysis.'

Marriott peered over the items on the bench. 'It certainly looks as if we've found the tangible evidence we've been looking for,' he said excitedly.

Cadema, having inspected the items, turned to him. 'No, we cannot make assumptions. We need evidence that links these to the murders. That will come from further analysis by

Doctor Lilly, and then much more work from us.' She looked towards Julia who was still examining the items.

'That's right, Sergeant. And as we've taken as many samples as we can it'll take several days to analyse them. Then I'll have to write my report before any of these can be handled,' said Julia. Wilhelmina nodded in affirmation.

'We've waited a long time for this,' said Cadema. 'A few more days won't cause us a problem.' Although she sounded calm, she was angry at not being allowed to take the notebooks away to read them. Or at least to discover what the letter inside the envelope revealed. But everything had to be done according to protocols.

Now Cadema's mind raced on, there were so many things to do. But where to start? Although reading the notebooks was important, there were other issues to address while she waited for the results.

By the time she had thanked Julia, and left her to her work, Cadema had already developed an action plan in her mind. Leaving for the police station with the two officers, Marriott took the driver's seat. Pratt – quiet.

'I know. It's very frustrating,' said Cadema as she fastened her seatbelt loudly. 'But we must be patient.'

'I know,' Pratt interjected, 'but at the very least we should be allowed to see inside the notebooks – damn it. We all had gloved hands, so what harm would it have done?'

'I agree with Pratt,' said Marriott. 'And with all the work I've done, to be denied access at this time, leaves me fuming.'

'Listen, both of you. I've had enough of your moaning. There's nothing I can do, so you'll just have to accept it – a few more days then we'll have the answers.' Cadema took a deep breath and waited. No one spoke for a while, until Cadema began to share her thoughts with them.

'Once we've got the notebooks I'm sure they will be useful to the investigation. The ring is certainly significant. If

I recall correctly, there were many items missing from the victims. And among those, were three brass rings from the second victim, Annie Chapman. That ring we saw could be hers.'

'But there's only *one* ring, so *two* are unaccounted for?' said Marriott.

'So that's another mystery, what's happened to the other rings? We'll know more when I find the list of the other items which were missing from the victims.'

Pratt kept quiet, lost in thought. Why was everyone going on about the victims when they earned their living in such a disgusting way? They do the same today – it's a wonder more are not murdered. And searching for a killer, over a hundred years later, was pure sensationalism. Why not let the perpetrator rest? But of course, they couldn't, no one could, neither could he, but he didn't know why.

Cadema's voice interrupted him as they reached their destination.

'Now for the real work. I'll explain when you both come to my office.' She looked at her watch. 'Shall we say half an hour?' The officers nodded as they stepped out of the car.

After freshening up in her office, Cadema opened the drawer to a filing cabinet, removed a file, took out a list, sat down, and began to read.

What seemed like a few minutes later, the two officers were standing at the door.

'Come in and sit down.' She watched them do as she asked. 'This is the list of items. And I was right. There were other things missing.' She began to read the list to them:

'The uterus and some of the bladder were taken from Annie Chapman. The left kidney and the uterus were missing from Catherine Eddowes, the fourth victim. And the heart was missing from Mary Kelly, his last known victim. And as there are six handkerchiefs, they probably contain this tissue and no doubt some from the other two victims.'

'Well, Ma'am,' said Pratt. 'I think we have found all we need to solve the cases.'

'It certainly seems that way, but let's wait for the forensics. However, there's nothing here to lead us to the killer.'

'I suppose not, but I'm itching to read the notebooks,' said Pratt.

Cadema decided not to respond. Her mind was far too busy thinking of the samples and wondering if they would be suitable to trace living descendants of the victims. And when Julia had finished with the notebooks, she decided to read them first.

As Pratt and Marriott were leaving, Cadema said she would brief the rest of the team and asked Pratt to arrange this. She told Marriott to go to the churchyard, clear things up there and return for the briefing.

***

Having finished at the dig site as instructed, Marriott decided to pay a courtesy visit to the vicar. Thanking him for his help, Marriott was about the leave when Fred began to talk:

'It's a pity we had to go through all that. And no matter how careful you were, it will certainly have upset some of our parishioners. But I'm amazed why someone would go to so much trouble to mimic a burial, have a grave dug, and then hide a box in it. Besides that, I don't know how he managed to organise it in the first place, and then lay a concrete slab without anyone noticing.' Fred sounded angry – accusing. His face flushed as his body swayed forwards and backwards as if his feet were made of dumplings. And, if he leaned too far backwards he would fall over.

'There must have been someone or other who could keep it quiet,' Marriott mumbled, just audible enough for Fred to hear.

'Yes, of course,' Fred exclaimed. 'The only person who would have been in that position was the groundsman at the time.'

'You're right, that's it,' said Marriott's excited voice. 'It must have been one of the current Bates' ancestors.'

'It could have been I suppose.' Fred scratched his head. 'I'll look into it if you like. Better me than you. It's a delicate subject and I don't want to upset Barry if it can be avoided.'

Fred had always wanted to be a sleuth. Now he had something worthy of his talents, he was eager to get started.

As they were parting, Fred smiled for the first time and said he would make some undercover enquiries, then he would let Marriott know as soon as he could. Marriott gave an acknowledging nod, knowing that Cadema would not agree to Fred's meddling in police work.

Chapter 22

Cadema searched the faces of the five officers as they sat waiting in the briefing room. DC Avrom Galke was sitting on the edge of his seat, obviously waiting for the opportunity to say something as usual. DI James Pratt sat with his hands behind his head and his legs stretched out under the table. To his left, was DS David Marriott, his brown hair much less formal than it used to be. He smiled at her, then looked away. DC Rosemary Clarke, still to remain in the team for a while, sat next to Marriott. Cadema noticed the slight blush on Clarke's face as she smiled at Marriott – he didn't reciprocate. DC Richard Barry, on secondment, sat upright and alert.

'I know we are a small team, but there's just as much work to do as ever. And I'm sure we will appreciate Clarke staying for a bit longer. And Barry who is leaving soon. So let's get down to business. Since our last briefing a lot has happened. I'll tell you where we are up to, and then I want you to contribute to the action plan.' After explaining the progress the team had made, and that there were still more questions than she had answers to, she noticed a raised hand.

'I've got a question, Ma'am,' said Galke. Cadema raised her eyebrows, but hoped he had not heard the sigh she gave as he spoke.

'Go on, we're listening.'

'Well, Ma'am, how could anyone dig a grave without someone noticing?'

'That's a question we are about to pursue. Hopefully we'll have an answer soon.'

'Yes, that's right,' said Marriott. 'Fred, the vicar at the church in question, is about to look into this, and with our help, it shouldn't take too long to solve the mystery.'

'Thank you, Sergeant,' said Cadema, somewhat dismissively as another hand was raised.

'Excuse me, Ma'am,' said Clarke, 'but what's happening about the notebooks you've discovered in the grave?' She blushed and lowered her head.

'We intend to read them as soon as forensics have finished with them. That will probably be tomorrow,' said Pratt curtly.

'So now we've found the empty coffin, what happens next?' Galke interrupted.

'We intend to find out who put it there. And discover what happened to John Temple Ribley, who was supposed to be buried there. He couldn't just vanish,' said Cadema. 'We will most probably find out when we've read the notebooks.'

'But you said,' Galke interrupted, 'we need to find tangible evidence that links him directly to the murders. Are the items in the box tangible enough or do we have to keep on looking?' Galke sat upright and looked straight at Cadema.

'It's all circumstantial at the moment, but as Pratt said, we will know more when we've read the notebooks.'

'I'd like to go back further,' said Pratt, 'and revisit the set of police pocketbooks we found in the archives.'

'With what relevance?' Cadema asked.

'Not sure; but at least we could cross reference them with the notebooks from the metal box. Who knows, there may be some relevance,' said Pratt assertively.

Cadema looked down, shuffled her feet, and sighed. 'I suppose you're right, but let's see what the notebooks reveal. Then, if necessary, we can revisit the old police pocketbooks.' Pratt nodded with a disparaging look on his face.

There were a few rumblings in the room, but as no one had anything else to add, Cadema ended the session. She asked Marriott to see if the vicar had found the name of the person who could have dug the grave. Or who may have known about it.

'I think it's, as you said, one of Barry Bates' ancestors,' said Cadema. 'The current Bates probably knows something. See if his relatives left anything, either in a will, or if something was handed down informally. Take DC Clarke with you, she'll benefit from some hands-on experience.'

Marriott left the room much happier than he had been in a long time. At least he was in control of something where he could utilise his detective skills. Something he had not been able to do, since finding the trunk in the archives. But as he was about to take his inspector's exam soon, he needed as much experience as possible. Being in charge of Clarke was a bonus.

With the exception of Pratt, the remainder of the team had been deployed so Cadema asked him to collect the notebooks as soon as Julia finished with them. In the meantime, Cadema would try to find out what happened to John Temple Ribley. She had the feeling that he had somehow left the country, and probably had been hanged in another part of the world. She decided not to share her assumption with Pratt.

***

When Marriott had finished speaking to the vicar again, he asked Clarke to go to back to the station, and he would catch up with her later. He said he was eager to tell Cadema what he had found, but before that, he needed to check something out. Protesting about him being evasive, Clarke agreed to meet him as requested.

Two hours later, Marriott parked the car in the police station car park, ran into the building, and up the stairs. Without knocking, he opened the door to Cadema's office, and stood gasping for breath.

'When you're ready, Marriott,' said Cadema smiling, 'take a seat and tell me what you have discovered.' She handed him a glass of water.

'Ma'am, after the grave had been completed, at the end of November 1888, Reggie Bates, the ancestor of Barry Bates, was found with his throat cut in the graveyard. Apparently they found his body near grave number 1445.' He paused to take a sip of water. 'I think, and this is purely speculation, that Reggie was killed by the Whitechapel murderer to silence him once he'd finished the grave. This meant there would be no one alive who knew about the grave, or could identify the perpetrator.'

'That's interesting, but don't get too carried away with your assumptions, Sergeant, just give me the facts,' said Cadema, a little flushed at being curt with him.

'Yes, the facts.' He coughed and drained his glass. 'Barry Bates said he couldn't add anything else, except that, when Reggie was murdered he had over two hundred and fifty pounds in savings. No one could find out where such an amount came from. It could not have been his wages, as the pay for a gravedigger then, according to the church records, was sixty-two pounds a year. It would have taken him a lifetime to save up such an amount. So he must have obtained the money from illegal payments or other underhand work.' He looked at Cadema's expressionless face, wondering if he should continue with his theories; she did not interrupt him.

'I believe Reggie had a lot of information on people who paid him to do their work, so he was probably a blackmailer. Or he had at least gained a reputation of helping people out, for payment, that is.' He cleared his throat.

'You've got some good points there, so do continue.'

'I don't think Reggie would have had much time to blackmail the killer because I think he was murdered just after completing the grave.

'Once I'd discovered this, I left the church, and went straight to the archives to examine the file on the murder of Reggie Bates. All I could find was a newspaper article. It said that Reggie's throat had been cut. The coroner stated that he had been killed by a person or persons unknown. The paper reported that he left a widow and six children and they all attended his funeral at the church where Reggie had worked. He was buried next to a grave that he had just completed. That was grave 1446. Apparently, Reggie's wife never remarried but died three years later in a horse-drawn coach accident. The driver of which had never been prosecuted, but I could not find out why. If you like I can make some enquiries...'

'We haven't got time for that now, but I know what you're saying,' said Cadema. 'You've done excellent work so far, despite your speculation on some of the facts.'

Marriott shrugged. 'All in a day's work.' His smile lingering longer than was professionally acceptable. Cadema pretended not to notice but felt a flutter in her chest.

'Don't be too dismissive, Sergeant. I am genuinely pleased with your initiative and the tenacity, to find out what you did. Well done.' At this remark the sergeant seemed to grow in size, but he only gave a grimace of a smile.

'Thank you, Ma'am, but I wish I could do more.'

'Well let's see what the notebooks tell us. I'm sure they'll augment more work. By the way, you were with DC Clarke, where is she now?'

'Probably engrossed in computer work. Did you want to see her?'

'No. But you should have kept her with you, not abandoned her. Anyway, I want you to take some time off to prepare for your inspector's examination.'

Marriott, with a little protest, agreed to do that. As he left the room, Cadema's telephone rang.

'Hi Julia, it's good to hear from you. Good news I hope?' Cadema sounded eager, but tried to relax and listen.

'Yes, there is.' Julia was placid and almost indifferent.

'You don't sound very good to me. Are you all right?' There was concern in Cadema's voice.

'Oh, don't worry about that. I'm just tired that's all. Have been extremely busy but I need to meet up with you rather than talk over the phone. Are you free this afternoon?'

'Sorry to hear that, perhaps you've picked up something. Yes, I'm okay from four o'clock. Just come straight to my office, Julia.'

'Will do.' Julia put down the phone. Later, she gathered up the papers for the meeting and took a throat lozenge.

Reaching Cadema's office, Julia felt better as she draped her wet coat over a chair, then sat facing Cadema.

'This is all fascinating to me.' Julia took a deep breath, her voice racing. 'And the most significant items, in the metal box, are the one brass ring, and the mummified samples of tissue. I remember you saying that the ring could have come from one of the victims? I think you're right. It was obviously removed roughly from someone's finger as I found skin, together with a small amount of blood on it.' Cadema opened her mouth to speak, but Julia spoke too quickly. 'I took samples of the tissue but they didn't match the stains found on the dress.' Julia paused for breath.

'That's really not what I expected to hear.' Cadema shook her head slowly her voice despondent.

'But there is something else you *will* want to hear. When I took DNA from the tissue found in the silk handkerchiefs, one of them matched the DNA found on the dress.' Julia smiled as Cadema's face lifted up and she let out a deep sigh.

'You're a star Julia. A wonderful star. What excellent news. Now we have tangible evidence linking the metal box directly to one of the murders. That means, all the items in the box could be trophies taken by the killer.' Cadema leaned forward, her eyes bulging.

Julia agreed, but said there was something else. 'When I examined all the pieces of tissue from the handkerchiefs, one of them turned out to be a piece of human kidney.

'I've taken samples of this for DNA analysis, but I don't expect to be able to match it up with any victims, unless we can discover relatives of the murdered woman. The other four samples were tissues from different women. One was a small piece of skin. The second was a small piece of uterus, the third was part of a vagina, and the fourth was a portion of a heart. All samples had been sent for analysis.'

Cadema stood up, took a deep breath and walked to her filing cabinet where she took out a folder from the top drawer labelled "Murder Victims". She fingered through the file and extracted five clear plastic wallets, each containing two sheets of paper.

'I made these tabulated notes for easy reference on each victim.' Cadema took out the notes in date order. 'The first one was Mary Anne Nichols, known as Polly. There was no mention of anything missing from her body, but a bit of skin could have been missed at the post mortem examination. So the skin you've found could have come from this victim.' Julia nodded in response.

'It could well be.' Julia sounded unconvinced as Cadema opened another plastic wallet.

'This is the second victim, Annie Chapman. When Annie's body was examined, the doctor noted that the uterus and part of the bladder were missing.' Cadema's hands were slightly shaking as she realised that everything seemed to be falling into place. She felt like a child that had just found the missing pieces of a jigsaw after a mishap on Christmas Day.

Julia moved closer – scrutinising the notes. 'You're right. So what's in the next wallet?'

'This one is Elizabeth Stride, the third victim. It was supposed at the time, that the murderer had been disturbed, as he cut her throat but didn't mutilate the body.

'The fourth victim, murdered on the same night as Elizabeth Stride, was Catherine Eddowes. After cutting her throat, he took her left kidney and uterus.' Cadema was holding the file in one hand while taking a sip of water with the other. Her hands were still shaking, as was her voice.

'Are you all right?' asked Julia, 'you look a little pale.'

'I'm fine, thank you. It's just that all this is very overwhelming.' Cadema sat as she recalled reading that half of a kidney was sent to Scotland Yard in 1888. There was a letter bragging that he, Jack the Ripper, had eaten the other half of the kidney. She shuddered as she thought, and began to open the final plastic wallet.

'But of course nothing was as awful as the fate of the last victim.' Cadema brushed a tear from her eye, then picked up the faded photograph of the mutilated body of Mary Jane Kelly. 'It was almost as if the murderer had been totally out of control as he slaughtered her. Cutting flesh off her bones, tearing out her organs, then taking away her heart. Some speculated that she may have been pregnant. But no fetal remains were mentioned, only the parts of the uterus.' Cadema, although still pale, said she was feeling much better, despite the notes she was reading. Julia mentioned that she had a sore throat and thought there was something going around.

'Fascinating as it has been for me,' said Julia. 'when I think of the actual human suffering at the hands of that monster, I too feel sick – despite it being my job. Sometimes I find it difficult to disassociate myself from these sorts of horrors.' She swallowed.

'I always thought that murderers used the same MO.' Cadema coughed as she spoke.' 'So I wonder why he took the heart and not the uterus? And I'm surprised that, if she were pregnant, it was not mentioned in the post mortem report.'

'I expect, as everything was in such a mess, it would have been difficult for them to determine whether or not she was pregnant, especially if she was in early pregnancy. Besides you said that a lot of things have gone missing from the original files. But if they had noticed she was pregnant, it would surely have been mentioned in the press,' said Julia.

'There was a sentence in one of the tabloids from that time, but nothing came of it, so I suppose you're right, Julia. But at least I now know that the person who left the box in the grave was no doubt the murderer, or knew the murderer very well.'

While speaking, Cadema realised she only had five sets of notes on the murders. There were six handkerchiefs with remnants of human tissue in them. Could the sixth victim be Ethel Redberry who was murdered on the twelfth of November? She knew there was no reference to this murder being attributed to the killer. More work for the team to do, she thought. Sharing these thoughts with Julia, they agreed to see what other evidence there might be to identify a sixth victim. It meant that, if all six samples were from six different women, then there would be no doubt there were six victims.

'And there's something else,' Julia continued, 'I've found male DNA on the notebooks. And, this too matches the DNA found on the dress.'

'That's great, Julia, so we can say for definite that the dress is directly linked to my suspect. And the suspect I have in mind is this John Temple Ribley,' said Cadema, her excitement escalating at every word.

While Cadema was still speaking, Julia leaned over and took out the six notebooks from her briefcase.

'I think you're going to find all the evidence you need about the murders in these books, including your sixth one,' said Julia solemnly, with emphasis on every word as she deliberately placed each book, one by one, onto Cadema's desk, in date order.

Julia left, saying she would send her a full report once she had all the results from the samples she had taken.

Fifteen minutes later, Cadema had flipped through the six notebooks. Each page contained around two hundred words, written on both sides of the paper. There were twenty sheets of paper in each book, but only ten of the sheets were written on. So Cadema estimated that there were four thousand words in each book and as such there were twenty-four thousand words to read. Almost a novelette, she thought.

It was not the number of words that were important to her, or the amount of time it would take to read them, but it was the amount of time it would take to make notes of the most important information contained in the notebooks. She thought it would take about four days to read them and make notes. The information, she hoped, would help her to develop her final plan. Before anything else was done, she asked the computer technician to scan every page into the computer.

***

Cadema had never been an ardent reader, in fact when she took up a book to read, she would invariably fall asleep at the first page. She now regretted not giving Marriott some of the notebooks to read. But she had made the choice to read them first.

At home, and alone with Cameo, she made herself a cup of tea, took a yogurt out of the fridge, sat on the couch, lifted the first notebook, and turned to the first page.

Chapter 23

***Reflection on the murder of Mary Anne Nichols (Polly): The
first of my six murders. It was the 31 August 1888, at 03.30.***

Cadema turned the page.

*So you have found my memoirs, well done whoever you are;
perhaps even Inspector Abberline? Now you will instantly realise
that I am the Whitechapel Murderer, the infamous JTR, my initials,
not the pseudonym they have given me. But do not expect to find
my name here as I will only leave that on the last page of the last
book. This is a safeguard measure, for if you found any of my
notebooks before I had time to complete the last one, then you would
never find out who I am. But if you are holding all six books from
the box in the grave, then you know my name and will be able to
trace me to my final resting place. Before you do that, I hope you
will read my books in chronological order, as I have left the best one
till last.*

*Only a killer knows how difficult it is to murder someone,
especially in less than perfect illuminated conditions. It is even more
difficult to dispatch them in the open when the fear of being caught
is forever forefront in the mind. But fear can be an incentive in itself,
a form of cat and mouse with one's nerves.*

*Before embarking on such a mission as murder, I had to
thoroughly know and understand the topography of my chosen area.
Not just in geographical terms, but in human terms too.*

*I had to know every street and road, every alleyway, every dark
corner, every strategic spot where a lamplight was placed, every
gate and where it would lead to, and every wall and fence. All this
knowledge would facilitate my means of escape should the
circumstance of my presence be suspected.*

As for the human condition, their work, their leisure, their circumstances were paramount. My cognition had to be precise, I had to know the course each policeman followed every night on his rounds and know exactly how long it took for him to complete them. I had to know where people worked, when they had a break, the hour in which they finished work, and the route of their journey as they walked home. The most difficult ones to determine a pattern of domicile were the vagrants, and of course those unfortunate women who would ultimately be my victims.

The latter, of which, I had to know everything there was to know about them. Their names, who they were, what their habits were, the places they frequented, the common lodging houses they stayed in, and every movement they were capable of making. For without such extensive intelligence, my plan would not come to fruition, or I would be caught before it did so. However, you will see, that there were, on occasions, sometimes when my actions were interrupted, and I was nearly discovered, despite my pedantic rehearsals.

Having already decided to slit the throats of my victims, I realised that it would be difficult to undertake such a task without previous practice in the art of doing so. Thus my first experiment was with a rabbit. This proved to be a disaster due to me becoming covered in blood when I drew the knife across the animal's neck, and with difficulty slit its throat. So I postulated, that this would surely be the case when dispatching my human victim in a similar manner. I thus tried a different posture. Holding another rabbit from behind, I held the jaw of the animal with one hand while I slit its throat with the knife in my other hand. Again the blood spurted from the artery, spraying my arms and hands. This would never do. The only alternative method, without a premature sanguineous outcome, was to throttle the person first, to ensure death, then take up the knife and cut their throats. Yes, strangulation had to be my method of choice. It would prevent them from wriggling or screaming. And *once life was extinct, there would be no spurting of blood upon my person.*

Again I turned to the rabbit. Thus I found the best method was to sedate it first, and while it was stupefied, strangle it, and only after this, cut its throat. It worked well, but how was I going to sedate a human and then strangle them?

I had already chosen unfortunate loose women as my ideal victims. They were generally in a state of intoxication most of the time, so in effect, they were unwittingly sedating themselves. Thus rendering my job so much easier to do. And if their addictive state induced alcoholic insanity in them, so much the better. There would be no noise and no spurting blood. Then I could do whatever employment there was to do on their dead bodies. The only sound I would make then was the sound of ripping flesh.

So to do some practice on humans first. Thus, I perfected a criterion. I would choose only women who were intoxicated enough to walk, but who were also on the verge of alcoholic insanity. On my person I would carry a silk scarf, a very sharp knife, and a pouch to carry away my spoils. The grip of my hands on her throat had to be just right, as not to induce any sound. I allocated enough time, fifteen minutes in total, to render the woman lifeless, open the abdomen, and then extract the organs I was searching for.

Having decided what to do, I took myself away from the streets of Whitechapel, and onto the streets of Leeds, where I could perfect my technique. I did not want to practise in my local area, for if I were to be seen there, I may be found out before I had time to perfect my art. But once I was happy with my results, I would return to Whitechapel and induce my plan.

Cadema stretched, picked up her pen and notepaper, and started to write. Yes, that's it, she said to herself, the killer was definitely living in London at the time and was probably well known in Whitechapel. She put the pen down just as her cat, Cameo, jumped onto her lap and began to nudge at her chin.

'Okay, you win.' The cat meowed then jumped off as she stood to go to the kitchen for the cat food. Leaving the satisfied cat munching away, she made herself a cup of tea and returned to her notes.

'Yes', she said out loud, and then made a note to find out where the perpetrator lived. She resumed reading the notebook.

The women in Leeds were most obliging. During sexual encounters, they allowed me to mimic strangulation almost to the point of death without either resisting or calling out. In fact, they seemed to enjoy it. Mind you, I was determined to never let myself have sexual intercourse with any of them. I did not want my penis entering a woman, any woman for that matter. And I certainly had no intention of mixing my seed with another man's or catching the pox. And I had to pay them more than the standard fee for the privileged of half-throttling them. But at least I had achieved my objective. All I had to do then was to find the right women from the crucible of those unfortunate loose women who frequented my streets in London's Whitechapel area.

I chose them because people who mistreat their bodies disgust me. It appalled me to see vagrants, unkempt and unwashed, begging in London's streets. I even detest people who sell their hair to the wig maker. Do not misunderstand me though; I do respect hygiene. So the mixing of one person's flesh with another, revolts me. But most of all I abhor people who sell their bodies either during life or after death. Therefore, these unfortunate loose women, who indulge in want, neglect and debauchery, who, through inoculation of their diseases into other specimens of degraded human life, cause untold suffering, are there for the taking.

Thus with my plan perfected, and my justification for it rationalised, I stepped out onto the pavement in Commercial Street and knew what I was about to do.

Cadema made a note of the location he had mentioned, and wondered if she would be able to find out exactly where he had lived. And if the place were found, and then searched, there may be some tangible evidence there. But she knew this would be doubtful, especially with the slum clearance that had taken place over the years in that area of London. Nevertheless, she would follow it up.

Finally refreshed after another cup of tea, she took up the notebook again.

They were there, their kind always were. And I knew them all; their habits, their idiosyncrasies, their families. Their eager eyes would always be there, searching into the darkness, looking for their next customer. And I knew the men whose whoremongering kept these women on the streets. The women who, for a few pence, would willingly oblige him by standing up against some filthy damp wall as he thrust his manhood into the cesspit of her body and transfer some vile and pestilent malady between the two.

The disgusting and degrading way these unfortunate loose women earn their keep had to stop. I had to make it stop. And the only way I could do that was to show them, and society, that their sins would be punished. Not by their God, or any other god, but by me. I would become their judge, their jury, and finally their executioner.

I am cunning, daring, alert, and most of all, dangerous. I see everything, and miss nothing. I work among them. I blend in. I am the unseen face in this decadent metropolis of a city. They will never know who I really am, but they'll surely find out exactly what I am capable of doing.

In carrying out these deeds, I aim to arrest others from leading such licentious lives. For, once people realise what I am capable of; once they see what I can do to them, then they will be filled with terror. And that terror, I live in hopefulness, will send them fleeing from the streets and into a better life. And if these women disappeared from the streets, then the men would too.

Cadema leaned back in her chair, stretched her arms above her head, and yawned. She had read enough to induce nightmares, if she really knew what nightmares were. Her job was difficult as it was without such things. Bringing the notebooks home to read was definitely a mistake – she had brought the killer into her home. She felt him sitting there in the armchair her mother always used when she wasn't in India searching for a husband for her. He was watching every reaction she made as she read his words. She blinked, where was he now? Her eyes darted to every corner of the room in anticipation of seeing him. Even Cameo, restless as she had been ever since Cadema had started to read, darted from her bed and hid under a cushion on the settee. Does that mean I'll never be able to get rid of him? she asked herself as she gingerly walked towards the window, looking over her shoulder once or twice, just in case. Would Jim Logan have been so stupid? She doubted it. He was always so sensible, so rational. She looked around the room again, hoping for some guidance from Jim. Nothing. She shook her head, and twitched a smile.

As the clock in the distance struck eleven, she closed the curtains and turned. The room looked different now, cosy with the glow from the pseudo-logged gas fire. This time her smile was genuine. All she needed now was a normal human to talk to instead of reading the ramblings of a psychopath. Knowing that sleep was out of the question, she made another cup of tea and snuggled into her chair again. Tomorrow she would contact the police profiler – maybe he would have some answers? She rubbed at her eyes and picked up the notebook.

***

On the 31st August 1888, I chose my first victim, knowing that she would soon make headlines in the daily newspapers. As she stopped and waved at some other female underclass she knew, I held back, making sure I wasn't seen. They exchanged words I could not hear, then the other woman hobbled away. Standing for a minute I could see there were a few people about, for I had left it a little later than I should have done. But as I felt for my concealed knife in my long, improvised pocket, I knew that I had no choice but to use it on her that very night.

Polly was about forty, thin, ill dressed and the worse for drink. So I followed her as she went in and out of every public house. Not that I went in any of those places of course, for they were not the sort of establishments where any respectable gentlemen would ever consider entering. The noise emitted from those places filled me with disgust. The smell of gin, beer and tobacco, mingled with the sweat of rancid unclean bodies as it oozed from every orifice that the buildings were endowed with. These were the places where the great social evil was generated.

Each time Polly emerged from one of these places, she staggered more and more, and on a couple of occasions she began to sing to herself. Then arm in arm with some half-sober scoundrel of a man, they found some dark recess in which to copulate. A public house, and a few pennies later, another encounter with a whoremongerer ensued, and the previous scenario was repeated.

As the couple emerged from an alleyway and stood near to where I was hiding, I heard her say, 'Thanks Gov, that'll do for my doss.' She then turned and hobbled away, humming a tune to herself until she reached her next drinking post. Only to emerge some five minutes later and then stagger towards someone standing near the light.

'Hello, Mister, care for a good time?' Her words belched out through the gap in her teeth, her body oscillated like a bunch of rags hanging from a washing line.

'Don't mind if I do,' I heard him reply. The thought of even touching that creature filled me with disgust. 'Will this be enough?' Some coin glistened in his hand and she did not resist his temptation.

'Oh you is generous aint you, Mister? It's here when you're ready,' said she in a reassuring way. As I listened to their conversation, I almost thought of abandoning my mission there and then. And I would have done had it not been for my plan – the pleasure of which, I could not inflict any further delay. He held her arm as they sped to the nearest convenient place to carry out the deed.

The moment she emerged without her male companion, was the moment I was waiting for. My patience would soon be rewarded. The street was silent except for the faint hum of industry hidden away in those dark recesses of alleyways.

I waved to her, she acknowledged with a nod of her head. Words were unnecessary at such encounters. Anyway PC Neil had just strolled by on his rounds and I didn't want to alert him with any noise. I crossed the road towards her giving the impression that I was a willing customer, eager to taste her wares. The coin in my hand would show her that I meant business.

With a reassuring smile, I walked towards her. And then I gave her a touch of my hand in places where it would mean business to her, I told her of the shilling she would receive. She smiled, burped, and said she was satisfied. So arm-in-arm we strolled, as lovers might, down the Whitechapel Road and into Bakers Row. At that precise moment she pulled me towards her. I resisted her advances of course, until I saw the form of a policeman pass closely by. It was then that I realised that she had unwittingly protected me from detection. The officer continued on his rounds oblivious to our presence as we made our way towards Bucks Row.

'Aint got much to say for yourself, have ya Mister? Cat got your tongue has it?' she said mockingly and with the drawl of a person who had lived for many years among the unfortunates of Whitechapel.

I instinctively, and without showing any disdain, whispered, 'Good to see you, Polly.'

The minute I mentioned her name, a pair of ferocious eyes turned on me.

'Hey what's you game, I've never seen you before? And you're dressed as a gentleman, so what's with this knowing me name? How comes you know the likes o' me?'

'A gentleman that I am, but I am still a man. And I heard someone call you Polly. Such a nice name, and when I saw you with your nice hat, well I thought…' My voice was barely audible, which made her come closer to me; so close that I could almost hear her breathing. I could smell her unkempt clothing, and her foul breath as it whistled through that gap between one tooth and its distant neighbour. She took the sweet violet cashew from my fingers, eager to freshen her breath.

'Thank you, Sir,' she whispered. 'Just follow me; I knows just the place where we won't be disturbed.' It took her barely a minute to find Bucks Row. She chose the perfect darkest spot for her own murder. Not too dark though, for I needed the dim light emanating from the street lamp some distance away. She was eager to please, I was eager for other reasons. When I touched her, she relaxed – she trusted me.

'Oh what a lovely scarf.' She whispered as she took it from my hand and began to throw it across her shoulders with the eagerness of a young woman on her first date without a chaperone. I helped her to secure it in the position that would be most favourable to me. She looked happy, too happy I thought for a person who was about to die. And the gaiety that the scarf had brought would help me in my work. So naïve was she, that I knew she would not struggle or call out. When I asked her to turn around to face the wall, she did so without hesitation; for all positions were natural to her. As I lifted her skirts and pressed my knee between her legs, she sighed. It was at that very moment that I pulled on both ends of the scarf until her body became limp. Quickly removing the scarf, I then thrust my hand around her neck and squeezed until her life drained from her body. As I lowered it to the ground, I detected a slight shudder – the aftershocks of a dead body.

Two thrusts of my knife across her throat nearly decapitated her – exsanguination had begun. But there was no time to dwell on this. Instead I lifted her skirt, tore at her stays, and then began to slice at her abdomen. Deeper and lower went my knife, almost nicking her pubic bone, as I foraged inside. But my endeavours were arrested by the sound of approaching workmen. I no longer had the privilege of time. I had taken too long; my knife too blunt – next time it would be sharper, and I would also carry a scalpel. But this time I reluctantly pulled down her dress, and casually walked away.

Two workmen passed me, but they were in too much of a hurry to notice me. But they did stop and bend down to look at, what appeared to be a bundle of rags in the corner of Bucks Row, and discovered Polly's body. Nonchalantly, I walked on in the opposite direction. When I reached my rooms, I had made up my mind that the next one would be better. For now I had done the ultimate rehearsal. Now I knew which parts I had to improve on. But one thing I had learned, that was I could kill someone in only five minutes. My next murder would be much quicker. That would give me more time to spend on my anatomical pursuits. Carrying out the murder in the dim light was tricky, so much so that I nipped my finger a couple of times. I would have to be much more careful in future.

Why I pulled down her dress I will never know. Later I read in the newspapers that they did not discover my real work, on her abdomen, until she was in the mortuary.

***

Cadema put the notebook down on her coffee table, and began to rub her stiff neck. After doing some exercises and making yet another cup of tea, she was ready for bed. After a long night tossing and turning, she was not really ready for work as she dressed and headed for the station.

Chapter 24

Sergeant Marriott's hands began to sweat as he picked up the telephone and dialled Cadema's direct number. The information he had gained was certainly the key to the whole investigation – the key now burning in his hand. He had stayed in the library until ten the night before, searching the stacks until he found exactly what he was looking for. The information he now had was almost as exciting as the time he found the trunk in the archive room. He could hardly compose himself, but hoped he would be able to control his voice when he spoke to Cadema. To be certain of this, he made sure he had all the facts, and in the right order, so that nothing would be confused. He knew exactly what he would say to her from the script he had rehearsed. There would be no errors, it was that simple. But something in the back of his mind told him that it would not be easy. When he heard the dialling tone, he took a deep breath – waiting. The tone changed to a crackle – he waited for Cadema to speak, then cleared his throat.

'Hello, can I speak to Superintendent Sharma please?'

'It's Marriott, isn't it?' said Cadema angrily. 'I thought you were on study leave? And why go to such trouble, when you know perfectly well I would be on the other end of the phone?' She heard an intake of breath but gave him no time to speak. 'Anyway,' she continued, 'you know I don't want to be disturbed unless it's urgent. I've had a very busy night reading the first notebook. Now I need to finish my office work here and get back to that task. So your interruption had better be good.'

'Sorry Ma'am, I was on study leave, but couldn't study. So I…'

'Don't tell me.'

'Okay, but I think what I *have* found *is* urgent. If you're going to be in your office in about an hour's time,' he looked at his watch, 'then I'd like to see you to explain about the ship I've discovered?' Marriott wasn't adhering to his script – the words just blurted out as if they belonged to someone else.

'What ship?' said Cadema somewhat sceptical. 'Go on Marriott, elucidate,' Cadema hesitated. 'On second thoughts, you had better come to my office and give me the details.'

Marriott agreed, and was in her office within the hour.

'Take a seat, Marriott and give me the facts as succinctly as you can,' said Cadema, gesturing him to a chair.

'Thank you, Ma'am,' Marriott coughed, the papers in his hands rustling as he began to read his notes. 'In relation to this Reggie Bates. I've also found the coroner's report. And there definitely was speculation, that his murder was linked to the Whitechapel ones. This was never fully investigated. But as we are aware, there were only five murders attributed to him, and these were on women not men.'

'Yes I know. So what's this about a ship?'

Marriott shuffled his notes. 'I've discovered that a ship called *Bairnsdale*, may have set sail for Australia soon after the body of Reggie Bates, the groundsman, was discovered.

'It sounds as if we may have something there. Well done, Marriott. But as I'm very busy today, and you're supposed to be studying, we'll put it on hold for the time being. That will also give me time to finish reading the notebooks. Then we can brief the rest of the team and decide on what further investigations we need to do to verify everything.'

'So it will all have to wait?' said Marriott, despondently.

'On second thoughts.' She looked up and smiled. 'I don't suppose you'll study anyway, so you can talk to PC Clarke.

Put her in the picture, and continue with your investigation. Find out about the ship and see if there's a passenger list.'

'Yes, Ma'am.' Marriott resisted the urge to salute. 'But can we meet and discuss this again soon?'

'Look Marriott, I'll do what I can, but just give me some space to get on with my own work. You have shown good initiative here, so don't start whingeing. Anyway, as you'll be moving up the ranks, hopefully soon, use your initiative. Develop an actions plan, then we can discuss it later. It'll be a good exercise for you. Now please go.' Cadema flushed – her voice angry.

'Yes of course, thank you.' As Marriott left the room, the phone rang.

'Yes, I'll be there in a few minutes, Sir,' said Cadema as she gathered up the papers from her desk, and then headed towards Andrew Long's office.

Chapter 25

The meeting with Andrew had gone well, especially when she mentioned the work Marriott had done. Now, back in her own home, a little later than Cadema would have liked, she settled down at three o'clock in the afternoon and began reading the next notebook.

***

Reflection on the murder of Annie Chapman, my second victim; the eighth September 1888 just after five thirty in the morning.

It was time to do my next murder. My knife was much sharper than it had been with Polly. And now, with the scalpel and dissecting forceps adding to my medical instruments, I did not want to wait any longer. I had to continue with the momentum to emphasise my message. This time I would make it clearer; that unfortunate loose women will die at the hands of the most capable killer the East End of London has ever seen. My crusade was going to be easy. Especially as women had seen my previous work, and had the audacity to ignore it. They were still there. I expected that, once the news was abroad about Polly, and the way she had been murdered and mutilated, they would stop their licentious work; but no, they kept on and on, defying my objective and the skills I was using. So my work had to continue.

But something much more sinister had happened inside me. I felt the unmistakable thrill of that electrifying power as it sped through my body when I squeezed the life out of Polly. Such was the thrill; I had to experience it again – soon. For it felt as if my whole body was burning like the fire of a tinderbox. And that fire inside me seduced my loins until I thought they would burst from the anguish of my unfulfilled passion.

Eight days after my last murder, I stepped out into Commercial Street. I was carrying my instruments hidden in the elongated pocket I had created in my overcoat. Accompanied with a brand new silk scarf I had the fortune to purchase from Wiry Bill in the Lane. The scarf was not the best quality, nothing ever was from the Lane, but it would do the intended job perfectly. Besides, after the last one, I needed to give the police something else to think about as I always had to be ahead of those two detectives, Spratling and Abberline. They were baffled by my first one. My next one would be even more baffling.

Annie saw me as I passed the lamp post in Hanbury Street. She waved as I crossed the road to meet her. I could see that she was worse for the drink she had consumed, by the way she staggered. This suited me perfectly.

'Hello, Sir. Do you see anything that takes your fancy?' She looked at the coin in my hand. 'My, that looks good,' she whispered. I drew closer to her and then had to hold my breath, for hers was as sour as a neglected cesspit. 'Is that for me?' Her words burped from her cracked lips. It was then that I caught sight of the bruise on her left eye. She, aware of my insight, tried to hide it with her left hand which was donned with three brass rings.

'Could be,' I whispered in return, mindful of the inhabitants asleep in their beds who hated whores on their doorsteps. As she looked closer the coin seemed to light up the contours of her face, which may have once been considered angelic. But now, in a woman of around forty odd, her face, gaunt and her skin sagging, resembled someone for the want of nourishment. I was just about to speak again when I heard the faint steps of a woman cross the street towards us.

Determined not to be seen by this second woman, I turned my back and stood facing Annie; much too close than I would have liked, for the stench of her unkempt body almost made me retch. But

I had to remain close, at least until the other woman passed by us. Annie obliged admirably. That was no doubt because she would not want to lose a potential customer. And certainly not one with a shilling in his hand. Once the other woman had walked passed, I took a couple of steps backwards, away from Annie, but still facing her. Then, extracting the scarf from my pocket, I held it up.

'What do you think of this? If I give it to you, will you?'

'Yes, oh yes. I know the perfect place to go where we won't be disturbed,' said Annie excitedly as she walked arm in arm with me. Passing through the arched entry between the buildings, she opened the gate at the end of the passageway and we stepped into the backyard of number twenty-nine. Both of us hoping we wouldn't be seen but for very different reasons. Once or twice she put a grubby finger to her lips and uttered 'Shush.' That was the only noise she made. I followed, ghost-like, my senses alert for any morsel of movement, any sound or even a smell that might have been out of place. The dart of some rodent across my path made my heart pound. Loud enough to wake everyone, I thought. But all remained calm after that. All I could hear then were distance human voices, horses neighing, and the dragging of cart wheels over uneven streets.

The advancing day light was an advantage in one way, for at least I would be able to see what I was going to do. But it was a disadvantage in another, as I could have easily been seen. In less than an hour the whole place would be vibrant with people trudging their wares to markets.

When we reached the back steps of number twenty-nine, Annie was happy for me to drape the scarf around her neck – sighing like a queen receiving her crown.

'Oh it's just lovely, but let's get down to business,' she whispered as I took hold of both ends of the scarf and pulled her towards me. The smile soon disappeared from her face when I pulled the scarf tighter and tighter, so tight that she could not let out the scream that was gurgling up in her throat. As her body fell against the fence, I throttled her. Holding my breath, I looked about but I could not detect the presence of anyone. Although my knife was sharp, I didn't cut her throat deep enough the first time. At the second attempt, I almost decapitated her as her blood ran like a pig at slaughter.

I worked quickly. Having put my knife away I took out my scalpel. Then pulled up her clothing and used it to cut open her abdomen. Using the scalpel, with its short handle and blade, was an excellent idea. I was much more dextrous and precise than I had ever been before, and thus apt in the delicate operation of finding the organ I was searching for. Although there was only a modicum of blood, I found the intestines difficult to contain within my hands. Notwithstanding this, I did not linger long, and despite the poor lighting, I quickly found her uterus. And, although I was as careful as I could possibly be under the circumstances, when I removed it, I accidentally nipped her bladder. At that precise moment, I heard people stir within the house. So removing the organ and placing it in my pocket, I quickly displayed her intestines on her shoulder. Then, before leaving her there half-finished, I ripped the three rings from her fingers. I had not done the best of jobs. Next time I would be more meticulous and make sure I had ample time to do the necessary work.

As the voices of the people in the house became more coherent, I retreated. In doing so, I did not have the time to avail myself with the use of the tap to swill my bloody hands, in the yard. Stealthily, but with impeded agility due to my heavy coat, I fled the scene by clearing three walls from one backyard to another. By the time I had reached the last backyard the outer portion of my pocket containing the uterus was wet. So I took the organ out of my pocket, cleaned it on some old newspapers I had found, and then wrapped it up and replaced it whence it came. When I had dusted off my coat, it again looked presentable. Finally, I emerged from my hiding place and out onto Hanbury Street in front of house number twenty-five. In the distance I heard the distinct cry of "Murder". As people ran towards number twenty-nine, I joined them. But instead of *loitering in the vicinity, I carried on past as if I were late for work, while others trampled into the narrow passageway I had visited earlier with Annie Chapman.*

I suppose you will check with the police reports and the coroner's report on the death of Annie Chapman. When you do so, you will see that what I have written is the truth. I was there, I did it. But you will also have read the reports in the press. I can assure you now that I do not possess a leather apron and never have had. So you need to put that line of enquiry to rest.

Cadema rubbed her eyes – she needed a break before starting the next notebook. And, after opening the window, she went into the kitchen to have a snack and to make yet another cup of tea. Was it really five o'clock? Until that moment she had not realised how long it had taken her to read the notebooks and jot down the salient points in her own notes. I expect Julia will still be at work, she thought as she pressed her number.

'Hi, Julia. I don't suppose you've got any spare time this evening, have you?' She tried not to sound presumptive, but was disappointed when Julia said she was going out with some old friends of hers from her university days. But after a moment's pause said she would cancel, if it was urgent.

'No, that's okay,' said Cadema, wishing she hadn't asked her in the first place. She knew what Julia was like when she had to make choices. And she knew what her choice would be tonight. She took a deep breath. 'Really, Julia, it's not a problem and it's certainly not urgent. It can wait. I just wanted to take a break, that's all. Anyway, I wasn't thinking of an evening out, just a chat, that's all.'

'Well, if you need a break you can always come out with us, you'll be most welcome. Besides, they're all practicing pathologists, so you won't feel out of place,' Julia giggled.

'No, I couldn't do that. I know what it means to you to catch up on things in your sphere of practice. Besides I must get on and read the next notebook.'

'If you're sure?' said Julia.

Cadema began to give her a brief outline of the information that Marriott had found and said she would bring her up to date once he'd done more research.

Then, finishing the call, Cadema returned to the kitchen, hungrier than ever. Realising that she had consumed all the snacks she had, she raided the fridge for cheese. Now, back in her chair, she was just about to pick up the third notebook when the door bell rang. What now, she thought as she replaced it on the coffee table and walked slowly to the front door muttering to herself. Looking through the spy-hole, all she could see was a bottle of Merlot. Julia, she tutted as she opened the door.

'I decided to cancel. You are more important. And your voice said it all. So let's have a drink. I don't suppose you've eaten yet?' Julia's high pitched jovial voice was like a whirlwind that swept away the cobwebs as soon as it entered the house. 'Don't answer that, the pizza will be here in no time. Now let's talk. You look awful.'

'Thanks for your observation. In fact, I feel fine. Just a bit tired reading all the time, especially those.' She nodded toward the notebooks.

'Let's forget them for now. No talking shop,' said Julia as she smiled and opened the screw top on the wine bottle. By then, two glasses had materialised from Cadema's cupboard and were waiting to be filled on the table. Julia poured the wine with the dexterity of a waiter from Claridges. 'Cheers.'

'You know I hardly drink. But on this occasion, cheers.' Cadema frowned as the doorbell rang again.

'Don't look so worried, it's only the pizza,' said Julia, heading towards the door. But as she opened it, money in hand, she was confronted by Andrew Long.

'Oh, I'm terribly sorry, I didn't know you had company,' said Andrew stepping into the hallway as Cadema walked up to greet him. 'I was just passing and as you seemed preoccupied today, I thought I'd call in to see how you were getting on.'

'You are very welcome, Sir,' said Cadema as Julia stood facing him; for once – silent.

'Sorry, Sir, let me introduce you. This is Doctor Julia Lilly, our pathologist; our Deputy Commissioner, Andrew Long.'

The two nodded a response as Andrew spoke.

'Pleased to meet you, but I'd prefer Andrew, especially when I'm, off duty, in inverted commas.' He smiled. 'And as you've got company, I won't stay.' Andrew turned towards the door. But when Cadema offered to take his coat, and asked him if he would like some wine, he decided to stay just as the doorbell rang again.

'Pizza!' said Julia as she handed the money over to a young man and took the goods.

Finishing his wine and eating a morsel of pizza, Andrew began to reminisce about the work he and Cadema had done together some years before.

Julia, although she thought he was arrogant when he first arrived, now wasn't sure where to place him in her category file. She discovered that he had lived alone since his wife was killed in a car crash. That made her look at him as a man. She liked the way his dimples showed when he smiled. And his sense of humour mirrored hers to some degree. He was tall and handsome – distinguished looking and about fifty-five. But Julia felt a little humbled when she learned of the tragedy in his life that had left him with a permanent limp.

She moved closer to him and leaned forward. Pushing a strand of her blonde hair away from her eyes, she giggled as a teenager might on her first date, but for some reason, she could not imagine why she felt so hot. It wasn't the wine, but she did feel comfortable with Andrew. Was she flirting? She didn't think so. A couple of minutes later, she decided to check herself, so she took on a more professional stance. After all she had given up the internet dating, and had promised herself to focus only on her work from now on. But looking at Andrew now, she began to describe him in her mind as if she were carrying out an autopsy. She noticed every blemish, every line in his face, the blue of his eyes, his dimples, his long eyelashes, his greying hair. But she failed to notice the compassion in his voice and the passionate look he gave. When she felt a flutter in her chest, she put it down to the anomalies in her own body that would be investigated when she had the time. She felt a little uneasy at the silent discourse that travelled between them. Yes, there was some attraction between them, but she failed to find a slot that it would neatly fit into. So she filed it in her mind where it became lost in the mêlée of her emotions.

'Are you all right Julia?' said Cadema, interrupting her thoughts and making her jump.

'Yes, of course.' She giggled; thinking of the wonderful atmosphere she was in – better than her stuffy friends.

After finishing the wine and the pizza, and chatting about work, hobbies and other interests, which Cadema labelled as trivia in her mind, she offered her guests coffee.

'No thank you,' said Julia, 'I must be going now. I've an early start in the morning.' Suppressing a yawn, she stood up and headed for her coat on the hook. Andrew coughed and stood formally. Stretched his back as if on parade, and, thanking Cadema for her hospitality, said he had to go, too.

Saying goodbye to them both at the same time, Cadema watched as they walked along the pavement together to their respective cars, and wondered…

Retiring to bed soon after they had left at eleven, Cadema lay awake churning over the day's events in her mind.

Chapter 26

Fifteen minutes after going to bed, Cadema was wide away and ready for the next penned pernicious autobiography from a serial killer. Getting up, she picked up the notebook and began to read.

***

Reflection on the murder of Elizabeth Stride, my third victim: one o'clock in the morning of the 30 September 1888.

Little did I know that, when I stepped out into Commercial Street just after midnight, I would have the most harrowing time of my whole career.

I did not have to wait long until I saw Liz waiting on the corner of Burner Street not far from the Working Men's Club. She noticed me, and then she hobbled with a slight limp in her gait, across the road to where I was standing.

'Hello, fancy a little tonight, do we?' Her words seemed to whistle through, what remained of her teeth. Despite the chill in the air, she wore no jacket. The parched flower pinned to her bodice looked as if it were about to dislodge itself to join the rest of the detritus on the ground. And the bonnet she had on would afford her no protection from the weather.

She was a little taller than I would have liked, but not too tall for my stature, so I knew I would be able to handle her. I offered her a cashew, she took one out of the packet I held towards her, she smiled and said. 'Thank's.'

'So what have you to offer,' said I, nonchalantly, so as not to give her the impression that I was eager.

'Go on, you know what I'm offering,' she tormented.

'Of course. But it is quiet back there so let's go,' said I pointing towards the open club gates that were clear to see from the lamps in Burner Street. I politely took hold of her arm and began to walk briskly towards the gates.

'Hey, what's your hurry, Mister?' She whispered accusingly as she pulled slightly away from me.

'No hurry whatsoever. I just thought, as there is no one about, we could take advantage of that.' She seemed to be happy with my answer as we walked arm in arm into Duffield's Yard and found a dark corner there. As we entered I offered her another cashew to sweeten her breath. She took it with pleasure.

'Go on, have another, I've got plenty more,' I whispered even softer then before. She took them and said she needed to get on with the business in hand. It was then that I took the scarf out of my pocket knowing that she would just be able to see it.

'What's that for?' she asked as I draped it across her shoulders.

'Well I bought it earlier and I think it goes well with the flower you are wearing. And will help to keep the rain off.' She became relaxed and smiled. As I drew the scarf around her neck, she put her knee between my legs.

'No not that way. Please turn around, I like it better that way.' When she turned I quickly tightened the scarf. She went limp. My knife was as swift as it had ever been. It didn't even give her time to call out. As I lowered her to the ground I knew I had to be quick. It was not the place to linger. Besides I could hear the faint tapping of horse's hooves somewhere in Burner Street. Quickly I slashed at the throat again as the hooves came closer and closer. I was about to lift her skirts and inflict the usual trauma to her abdomen, when I heard the voice of the driver as a cart turned into the very yard I was in.

I kept my posture as low as I possibly could, and hunchbacked, I crept into the darkest corner of the yard, near the water-closets, in the hope that he would not observe me there. The horse reared, instinctively knowing that someone was close. The driver of the cart *dismounted. He lit a match, and then walked to the front of his cart. The match was soon extinguished by the keen wind, but he must have known that someone or something was there. He obviously noticed something on the ground that, to him, probably looked like a bundle of rags, for he turned and ran into the Working Men's club. As he did so, I sprinted out of the yard, into Burner Street where I heard the faint cry of 'Horrible murder'. It was lucky for I knew my way around as I had lived in Whitechapel for many a year. I kept walking, as if I had a purpose to reach my destination.*

Safely out of the area, I slowed my pace and headed for Aldgate. As I continued on, I ruminated over the fact that I did not have the time to finish my work on Liz. So, washing my hands in the first water-trough I came to, I decided to continue with my pursuit for another unfortunate. I did not have to search for long.

***

Cadema put the notebook down. So he *was* interrupted and didn't have time mutilate the body. She added this to her notes, together with the fact that he had lived in the area for several years. And that he was taller than Elizabeth Stride, although it is thought that she was only five-foot-five. She wondered if he had actually lived at the same address during this time, or had he been peripatetic in order to avoid detection? How did he remain unknown, especially in those days when neighbours knew each other, where doors of houses were left open, and people looked out for one another; and especially with a sadistic killer around? She didn't have the answers, but if he were, what they called "a gentleman," then she supposed that he would live among them and be regarded as respectable. She remembered Doctor Jekyll and Mr Hyde, although a fictitious character, she understood that anyone could appear to be respectable one minute and a killer the next. There had been many "respectable" killers since 1888, and recalled Doctor Crippen, John Christie a supposed war hero, and of course Doctor Harold Shipman. She sighed as she picked up the next notebook, then, deciding not to read it, she replaced it onto the coffee table and went to feed Cameo. Mission accomplished, and her own hunger satisfied, she was now wide awake. So, returning to her previous seat, she picked up the notebook and began to read.

***

Reflection on my fourth murder; Catherine Eddowes: 30 September 1888 whose body was found at one forty-four on that morning

Never run, that was always my philosophy. Never run – even though my heart was running the race of its life and my body was geared for flight. I had to walk for running would be fatal. I would be caught, charged, and hanged if I ran.

So after all the murders I had committed so far, I always walked quietly away. Never to be seen, as people barely noticed I was there. I did get the occasional 'Morning Gov.' in some acknowledgement of my presence and status. But they never really looked at me; if they did they wouldn't be able to describe the real me. The stance I took would give them the impression that I was an older man, not one to really bother about. So I would go on my nocturnal pursuits, protected from detection. Only when I reached the sanctuary of my abode could I really become myself, and relax.

After narrowly being discovered at the scene of Elizabeth Stride's murder in Duffield's Yard, I hid in the shadows until the driver of the cart went into the clubhouse there. The horse was still uneasy as I erected my posture, replaced my hat and then I slid fast and silently out of the yard and into Burner Street. I was going to head for home. But I sensed that someone unknown was following me so I decided to change my plan and lead, whoever it was, and whoever had the audacity to do so, on a merry path; perhaps the path to Hell.

I couldn't turn around to see who was in pursuit, so nearing the crossroads at Fairclough Street, I stood holding my breath and listening for any noise, any footsteps or the rustle of clothing. Apart from some far-off voices, which I assumed were from the people who had discovered my work in the yard, I heard nothing. As home was further from my mind I took up my pace again, travelling along Fairclough Street. I eventually reached Back Church Lane, and thus avoided the area in Commercial Road, where I would have expected any one of the witnesses to go in pursuit of a police constable. At the end of the lane I turned the corner and continued on. After some treacherous manoeuvres, some over brick walls, I eventually reached Great Alie Street and then turned towards Whitechapel. I looked about, no one, I thought at that time, was following me. So I stopped to wash my hands, and then continued my journey. Still vigilant, I kept close to the shadows with my collar well up and my hat pulled down. And if I really needed to, I could have slipped into one of these shadows and be lost. My plan was then to double back and head for home. But something, I didn't know what at the time, was driving me on.

On reaching Aldgate, I could hardly believe my luck, for standing on the opposite corner to me, near Mitre Street, was a woman. A gift – just waiting for me to open her up. I smiled and I headed towards her, hoping she would be able to see me in the meagre light from the lamp post. She didn't move as I approached and asked her if she were waiting for someone.

'Well, I could be waiting for you, if you can spare the time. Anyway, anything's better than the cell I've just come from.' She spoke in a tone that made me believe she was intoxicated. And I had the distinct impression that she came from some other part of the country, Birmingham perhaps, though I could not be sure. I thus assumed that she could be lost, or, at the very least, be unfamiliar with the topography of the place. And thus, not know her way around as well as other unfortunates would do in the area. Her array of garments, ill-suited for the time of the year, swayed on her body as if they were trying to seduce me. But with my lack of response, she tutted, tugged at her bonnet and pulled her cloak tightly across her shoulders. I smiled, not directly at her but at the thought of the scarf she wore being pulled tightly around her neck by my hands. She would unwittingly be supplying me with the means to help me with her own murder.

'Where have you come from then?' I enquired indifferently. She smiled.

'It aint really your business, nor mine either. But if you've fou'p'nce, I'll show you what my business is.'

'How about a shilling?' At this the woman smiled again, took my arm and guided me down a passageway into Mitre Square. It took me a while to adjust to the dark, but I did manage to see a little by the light from the lamppost in the nearby street.

When we had reached a dark corner, she began to touch me. I made the expected moans at the right time and then said she should turn towards the wall. She obeyed without question. I caressed her neck, and traced the contours of her jaw and face, as if I were fondling her. She relaxed and sighed, but I knew she was feigning enjoyment, they all did. But the thought of a shilling worked magic in those situations. After loosening the scarf she had around her neck I caressed her neck and chin with my left hand, and pushed my knee between her legs. She responded with a swaying motion of her hips. Then suddenly I took hold of the scarf, pulling it as tight as I could. When she had stopped struggling, I wrenched her neck backwards, and with the knife in my right hand I slit her throat before she could make a sound. It was difficult to hold her there as she slumped, but I didn't want to get too much blood on me.

Lowering her body to the ground, I got on with the job. I blamed her for the work I had to do. If she hadn't been there, blatantly selling her body, she would still be alive. I quickly took the scalpel I had used earlier that evening, on my last victim, out of my pocket and lashed out at her face. Then, ripping her dress and undergarments, and exposing her despicable flesh, I cut open her abdomen from the sternum to her pubis. When I removed her entrails, they slipped in my hands as I placed them on her shoulder. As I foraged inside her abdomen, I eventually found what I had been searching for; her uterus and left kidney. Removing these, I tore a piece of her apron and wrapped the organs in this before putting them into my coat pocket.

The whole procedure had taken me far too long, so being mindful of the police presence in the area, I arranged her body so that everyone could see the work I had done, and then hurriedly left the area. Again, avoiding the main streets, I found my way out of the square and into Duke Street, across Hounsditch, through Gravel Lane and on until reaching Goulston Street. Here, a stray dog began to follow me. I could not get rid of him; even after I had kicked him, his pursuit of me was relentless. I knew what he was after, he could smell the blood. It would be food for him. So when I reached a water trough I removed the piece of apron from my pocket, took out the organs, and threw the empty piece of blood-stained apron at the dog. Then after returning the organs into my pocket, I cleaned my hands as best as I could and walked off leaving the dog with the blood-soaked cloth. As I walked away from the area and towards my abode in Whitechapel, I heard people saying that another 'Orrible murder had taken place.' I did not stop to talk as I was too exhausted and busy with my thoughts on such a successful finish to one day and to the start of another.

But I must get the records straight on my activities. Contrary to popular belief from the police and also the press, I assure you that I did not linger anywhere as I fled the scene. And I certainly did not stop to write the "Jewes" message on the wall. If I had written the message, I would certainly have spelt Jews correctly. Why should I have written it, for if I had lingered I would certainly have been caught. Besides, I had no malice for the Jews, and have no idea how the message came to be there. And I did not even notice it as I threw the bit of apron at the dog. I can assure you that I fled as quickly as possible from there.

You may be wondering why I put the organs in my pocket and not in the bag that I was reputed to be carrying. Well that is simple. I did not carry a bag, as this would have aroused suspicion, both with my victim and with the constabulary. But I always wore my overcoat, and who would not have done so at night in the East End at that time of the year? And the pockets I had were no ordinary pockets. They were longer and bigger than any others, and thus copious enough for what I needed them for. But they had to be waterproof, so I lined my pockets with the very best Mackintosh material that I could find. And by the way, I have never written to the press in any form, and why should I? The fellow who addressed his letter; "Dear Boss", and called himself "Jack the Ripper", is a fraud. But you can see that I am genuine. My actions certainly speak much more than his words will ever do.

***

Cadema yawned, put the script on the coffee table and decided it was time for bed again. But she knew that if she were to go to bed that instant, it would be difficult for her to go to sleep. So after making herself a cup of cocoa, she snuggled on the sofa and began to make some notes.

A few words in, she put the paper and pen down, and then sat thinking about the poor women of Whitechapel in those days. She imagined the intense cold they must have felt. The lack of a few pennies to pay for a bed for the night or for any other night. She had read that these women, with no money for the common lodging house, would be desperate enough to spend the night in a shed, no bigger than ten-feet square, with at least twenty other poor destitute souls. What clothes they owned, would have to be worn layer upon layer, one to keep them as warm as possible and the other so that they would not be stolen. Perhaps in the summer they could even pawn some of them, so at least they would have some money. But come winter, they may not have had enough money to buy them back, and so were colder than ever.

There was no health care, their teeth were either missing or decaying, for want of a dentist. Many were half-starved. They were rejected by society, and some even by their own family. There was little pleasure in their lives, so many took to drinking, giving them some consolation on the lives they had to live.

The only way they could survive in that harsh environment was to prostitute their bodies to any man who had sufficient funds. They could not be choosey. Even when they realised that there was a serial killer in Whitechapel, they still had to survive. And no doubt they hoped that they would not be his next victim.

Cadema scribbled some notes, then, as her eyes closed, she believed he was being followed by what he had written earlier. Perhaps she would find out in another notebook?

Cadema was awoken with a start, as Cameo jumped onto the couch and nudged at her chin. A ray of sunlight stung at her eyes as she realised that the curtains were still open from the previous day. Showered, and both she, and Cameo fed, she dressed and headed for work.

Chapter 27

The station was much quieter than Cadema had expected as she headed for her office. Opening her diary, she found the answer; Sunday. Sitting at her desk yawning and shuffling papers, the ring of the telephone startled her.

'Superin…'

'Sorry to trouble you, Ma'am, but I've got Doctor Lilly on the line. She tried your home number but didn't get a reply,' said the duty officer.

'It's okay, just put her though.' Cadema listened for the usual click, then heard Julia's voice.

'Just catching up,' said Julia. 'I was worried that I hadn't heard from you since last night. I tried your mobile, but there was no answer.' She sounded concerned.

'That's because I forgot to charge it. I've been too engrossed in reading the notebooks. And there's still two more to do.' Cadema stifled another yawn.

'So why are you at work, and especially today?'

'You know me; I can't keep away forever. Besides I needed a break from that gruesome work. A change of scenery and all that…' she chuckled. 'But why have you *really* phoned, Julia?'

'As I said, it was just to find out if you were okay, and to tell you that I'm going to meet Andrew Long for lunch and wondered if you would like to join us.' Julia hesitated, as if she hoped the answer would be *no* – she really wanted to see Andrew alone. But of course, if she *did* see him on her own, and Cadema found out…

'Surely you don't want me there. I saw the way you two were getting on. No, I think you should go ahead without me.

Besides I'm not staying here for long as I need to get back and finish the notebooks. Just let me know how you get on with him. I'm sure you'll be fine.'

'If your quite sure, then I will. When you've finished the notebooks, we must have another curry together, or it'll be too long again.'

Cadema agreed, and after saying goodbye she continued to aimlessly shuffle the papers on her desk. An hour later, with no productivity visible for her efforts, she left the office and headed for home.

On opening her front door, she shuddered, recalling the feeling she had as a child when she was taken into the dungeons of Warwick Castle. There had obviously been many tortures there, and now she felt as if she were about to suffer that same fate.

After making tea, and positioning herself on the chair again, she opened the fifth notebook.

***

Reflection on my fifth murder in Whitechapel: Mary Jane (Jeanette) Kelly on the ninth November 1888 about 1.30 am.

I could smell her even before I could see her. I had experienced that smell before; this time I could not place it. But I would find out what it really was once I had completed my work on her. And that would haunt me for the rest of my life.

There she was, waiting on the corner of Dorset Street for her next customer. Mary was not a stranger to me. I had seen her before, but not in her current capacity.

As I approached, her head acknowledged me in the usual way. This time she knew business was on my mind. They can always tell a man on heat, even when they are worse for drink. Well, at least that was what she was supposed to think. Anyway, I had my usual work to do, and I knew she would be an easy target because of the state she was in.

'Come on, love, I'll take you to my place, 'tis just around this corner. It's too cold to hang about here tonight,' said Mary in a subtle mix of Welsh and Irish. She pulled her shawl across her shoulders, and lifted her skirts above her ankles. Turning around she staggered on towards the alleyway. I followed her tall, and somewhat slender form, as it swayed from side to side. When I caught up with her she had nearly reached the alleyway, which was situated between numbers twenty-six and twenty-eight Dorset Street, and led to Millers Court. At that very moment I saw a woman walking towards us who obviously knew Mary. So I took hold of Mary's arm and we both moved, with promptitude, hoping to reach the alleyway before the woman. For I could not have anyone recognise me, that would not do. And Mary, sensing my urgency for anonymity, and she, most probably wishing to avoid dialogue with the woman, eagerly disappeared with me into the alleyway, just as the woman went by.

As there was no other soul around, Mary went to a window and pushed her arm in through a broken pane. Reaching in, she flipped a latch, so that the door could then be opened to number thirteen Millers Court. I followed Mary into the room. It was about fourteen-foot square and smelt fetid, as if something had died in a corner somewhere. This was mixed with the smoke from the fire which gave the whole room a brown tainted hue that penetrated my clothing, and stung at my eyes and throat. In this atmosphere, we staggered towards the bed. The wooden floor creaked, as if it would succumb to our weight and we would fall into the bloody hell that lay beneath it.

Mary turned towards the fire. 'Just as I thought,' she said, 'it's still alight so at least we'll be nice and warm. So come, let me help take off your coat.' Mary swayed from side to side as she sprayed her slurred words. 'Not much to say for yourself now, have you? Is this your first time? Don't worry, you'll be okay with me.'

I nodded and grunted as she pulled at my coat. She shrugged when I refused, and instead, began to undo her own clothing.

'Here, let me do that,' I said in a whisper. 'Just turn around and I will undo it for you.' I was surprised when she turned with the composure of a ballerina and giggled. Then, by the glow of the fire and the one candle, I undid her top clothing.

'I knew you were a gentleman, thanks,' said she, then turned to face me. I smiled, she exhaled as if relieved of some tension. 'Can't trust many men these days, what with that Jack on the loose as well. Suppose the Runners will find him soon?'

'Yes, I suspect they will, but let's forget about Jack. Anyway, I have a little present for you. Close your eyes and I will show you.'

'Why do I have to close my eyes?'

'Well it will not be a surprise if you see it before I have it ready.' I felt for the new silk scarf in my pocket and spoke to her as a father might do to a sleepy child. Then I wondered what she would say when she saw it. Would she be alarmed and fearful for her life, and scream murder? Or would she like it and be pleased with such a gift?

'Oh, you're just teasing me, I can tell. But I'll close them just as you please.' As I drew out the scarf, I sensed a shudder from Mary's body. She then sighed and opened up her eyes.

'My, what a lovely scarf, is it silk?'

'Yes, of course it is. And it will look lovely on you,' said I, as I draped it across her shoulders. The scarf had the desired effect. I could do almost anything to her. And I knew, when she danced around the room and sang, that she trusted me. Her voice was soft and homely, the kind of voice that would lull any baby to sleep. But when it got louder, she shushed herself to be quiet and giggled again.

She looked serene, angelic even, in the twilight created by the fire and the candle. And too young to be a woman of the streets; my youngest yet. She was almost desirable, that is if I were drawn to such a creature. But I had to put a stop to her ways. Perhaps the government would take notice this time; a young woman in her prime at the hands of that notorious Jack the Ripper.

'Now let's take off your coat.' This time her voice was assertive, as if I would be compelled to obey her.

'No,' said I, adamant that it should stay on for it contained the tools I needed for my work. And I was sure she would be horrified if she had seen them.

'No,' I repeated.

She gave me an indignant look, but she smiled as I pulled her towards me by the two ends of the scarf. Closer and closer she came, her face glowed, and her blue green eyes smiled as she looked at me. But the magic of the moment disappeared when she burped and began to sing again.

I released my grip on the scarf, and as she danced around the room, I joined her as a lover might do. She began to undress, placing her outer garments on a chair as she did so. Still wearing the scarf, she looked into my eyes, barely noticing the second gentle pull I gave on it as she moved closer to me. She sang softly, I smiled. She was lost in her own world and had forgotten that I was her customer. If she were someone else, I would have wanted the moment to last forever.

She was not anyone else. She had stirred feelings in me, taunted me, making me question my own motives. Her debauched body was invading my loins until I could hardly maintain my composure. But I had a job to do; after all she **was** a whore. I could not give myself the privilege of holding back any longer. It had to be done, so I pulled the scarf across her throat.

'Hey what's your game?' Her words were harsh – rasping as she struggled to free herself.

'Do not worry so, Mary, it's just may little game.' I hoped my quiet voice would reassure her that she was in no danger.

'Stop it, it's too tight.' I saw her eyes in panic as they began to bulge, her face livid, she clawed at the scarf and then began to lash out at me. 'Murder…,' she tried to shout as much as the scarf would *allow. I pulled it tighter and tighter, until she no longer made a sound.*

She grabbed at the scarf again in her futile attempt to release it. But I held tight, the scarf didn't relent, silk never does. As I lowered her limp body onto the bed, I quickly knelt across her chest, put my hands on her throat and strangled the life out of her. Not daring to move any fragment of my body, not even my lungs, I listened for any noises that may be in the yard outside or from the adjoining rooms. The only sound I could hear was the crackling of wood still burning in Mary's fireplace.

Now it was time for my real work. I heard the faint chimes of clock striking two. For the very first time I was happy in my work, knowing that I had the privilege of time, and could carry out my work undisturbed. I didn't have to wear my coat, nor any other garments that restricted what I needed to do. I could keep clean and therefore my clothes would not be covered with blood when I walked home.

***

Cadema had just turned to the next page when her telephone rang; it was Sergeant Marriott

'Sorry to trouble you, Ma'am, but there's something I need to tell you.'

'You're not troubling me, Sergeant, I needed an excuse to have a break. But what's so urgent?'

Marriott bit his lip, there wasn't any urgency, he just wanted to see if she was okay. And to find what she had discovered. There were, of course, more details of the ship he could tell her about, but that could wait. He took a deep breath.

'So you're still reading them, Ma'am. I'm surprised it's taking so long to do.' His voice sounded concerned, but also accusing.

'It's not an easy task to read such graphic details about murders even though they happened such a long time ago. Victims are still victims...' She stopped, wondering why she was trying to justify the time it was taking. 'Anyway,' she continued, 'I have to take a break from them from time to time, just to clear my thoughts and...' Again she paused. 'Anyway, what's this all about, Marriott, why have you *really* phoned me?'

'Do you think that the notebooks are written by the perpetrator?' Marriott was hesitant, as if he was fishing inside his brain for something intelligent to say.

'Look, Marriott, while I'm talking to you, I'm not doing the work I should be doing right now. So if you haven't got anything else to tell me. I'm going to hang up. I'll brief you with the others when I've finished.'

'Sorry, Ma'am, but I was going to tell you about the progress I had made in identifying the ship called the *Bairnsdale*. I think the miscreant travelled abroad to evade justice.'

'You told me that already, and I thought I asked you to discuss that possibility with Pratt,' said Cadema accusingly.

'I did, but he's been busy with other enquiries.'

'So you're wasting my time?'

'No, Ma'am, I think the ship went to Australia. Sydney to be precise,' said Marriott as he waited for a reply.

'As you say, he *may* have travelled on it, but may is not good enough. We have to be one hundred percent sure. So keep searching. In the meantime, do that written report and we will discuss it at our next briefing with the team. And you never know, when I've finished reading, I may find something else that will help with this conundrum.'

After saying goodbye to Marriott, Cadema rubbed at her eyes and took up the notebook again, this time with more enthusiasm than she had recently. Marriott, despite his faults, had lit a fuse somewhere in her mind. Now it was time for her to light the gunpowder and send the investigation into another dimension. And as she sat there she thought of the helicopter approach that Jim Logan had always insisted upon. She would do better than that now.

She began to read…

Taking the knife and scalpel from my coat pocket and laying them down on the table next to the bed, the scene resembled that of an operating theatre: I, the surgeon.

Removing my overcoat and other garments, I then took hold of the knife and with every care and precision, I quietly slid it across her throat. My unassuming action almost decapitated her. I watched as the blood trickled out of the orifice I had created and collected, first on the mattress, then onto the floor.

'There ,Mary, there, they won't think you are pretty now, will they?' I said in a quiet sneer as I replaced the knife on the table and took up the scalpel. After slashing at her face several times, I opened her undergarments to expose her torso. There was not too much blood around to hinder my next task. Then, for some reason I cannot explain, the scalpel took over, and instead of being methodical and opening her abdomen as I had intended, it ripped open her bodice. I could see her white flesh and her full breasts. She had such a beautiful body.

I took hold of her right breast, and in a more controlled fashion than I had used on her face, I removed it. Then I held the piece of warm flesh close to me for a couple of seconds, before placing it on the table next to the bed. Holding the scalpel again, I did the same to the other breast. And when I held it, dripping with blood, I felt sick – my heart pounding in my chest. I waited a couple of seconds before hanging it on a spare nail on the wall next to the bed, then I continued with my work.

Her abdomen was easy to open but I was careful when I lifted out her entrails and stomach. With two cupped hands, I supported them and placed them with the first breast on the table.

The remnant of the lighted candle wick made it almost too dark to see now, so I gathered up some clothing and threw it into the fire. I had worked well in the near dark with my other victims I know, but this time I wanted to be more thorough, more precise and did not want to miss anything.

My scalpel moved down her body slicing at the abdomen as it travelled from the sternum to the pubic bone. Pushing my fingers over the pubis, and into the lower pelvic cavity, I foraged for her uterus. It was much easier to find than I had expected; too easy.

At that moment, my blood ran cold as a shiver travelled down my spine. I knew what the cause of a larger than expected uterus might mean. And if my instincts and knowledge were correct, then I would be appalled at what I had done.

Examining the uterus, I found what I expected to find; a swelling, smaller than an inch, between the layers of the uterus. My suspicions were realized; she was with child. I had killed the little mite. Had I committed the ultimate sin in the eyes of God? I was devastated at taking an innocent life. I took a deep breath, intending to be more meticulous and in control. I began to cut at the fallopian tubes and part of the cervix, then carefully lifted the uterus from its resting place. Placing it on the table, I made a small incision and then removed the rudimentary embryo. I was unsure of the gestation, but I realised what I had to do with it. So I took the silk scarf from its would-be mother, wrapped the little mite into it, and carefully placed it in my overcoat pocket. Later I would give it a decent burial, something it would never have had, had it been born alive.

I turned to her body again with anger in my heart. The scalpel took over and lashed out in all directions until I could not tell if the body on the bed was human or that of a newly slaughtered animal. When my anger subsided I meticulously removed flaps of skin from the abdomen and some off her leg. I wanted to tear her very flesh from the bone to make her suffer for what she made me do. So I lashed out again and again, cutting and cutting as her flesh peeled off her like a carcass in an abattoir. The hate inside me was pure, I had to do it. I was not going to stop unit I had totally denuded her.

Although time had been favourable to me up to that moment, I was devastated when I saw the faint light of dawn seeping under the door and through the curtained windows. I had to leave. Before doing so, I reached up into her thorax and quickly cut out her heart. I wanted to throw it on the fire, then hesitated. The smell of burning flesh would surely wake the sleeping populous around me. So after I had squeezed all the blood out of it, I wrapped it up in some cloth and deposited it in the same pocket as the embryo. Then, moving her body towards the edge of the bed, near to the door, I thrust one of her breasts and viscera under her head to steady it. After hurriedly tidying up, I left tissue and organs in distinct neat piles. Leaving her legs apart, with one bent at right-angles to her body, I put her liver and the other breast at the foot of the bed while the rest of her organs I deliberately place where they would be easily identified. Having already burned some of my clothes, I made do with the ones I had left, knowing that my overcoat would cover any stains.

Then, after wiping my shoes and then my hands on a cloth, I threw it into the fire. Opening the door, I turned to see Mary's face again, knowing that whoever found her body would stare into that mutilated face of death.

***

Reflections on my night with Mary Kelly:

I should have recognised the smell I noticed when I first encountered Mary, for it was the unmistakable smell of a woman with child. But I was negligent, and failed to notice the glow on Mary's face that could have warned me of her condition. She hid it well; unfortunate women, such as Mary, always hid their condition for fear of losing customers, and in consequence, their livelihoods. But later, if the gin did not suffice to augment abortion, and when it inevitably showed, there were always the odd clients who liked women in that most delicate condition, just before birth. I could never condone such a debauched practice. A murderer still has his principles. Notwithstanding this, if I had known of her condition before I throttled the life out of her, Mary would still be alive. And later, as I heard the news of my work, there was no mention of her pregnancy, an oversight on the pathologist perhaps?

Nevertheless, I was appalled by my lack of self control. And from that day I decided the murders had to stop. There were a couple of ways out of my dilemma, to either kill myself and rid the world of an evil monster, or to disappear. I chose both, metaphorically that is.

On that last night, having arrived home, I bathed and then slipped into my smoking jacket. Taking up my seat in front of the fireplace, warm and contented, I began to nod off to sleep. The knock on my front door startled me from my slumber. It was Ethel, my neighbour from the lodging house across the street.

***

Cadema closed the notebook, collected a drink from the kitchen and picked up the final notebook.

Reflections after the death of Mary Kelly. Notwithstanding this, my sixth murder, Ethel Redberry. And furthermore, notes to Inspector Abberline, or whoever reads my deliberations.

The following day, I stepped out of my abode in Commercial Street with a tiny wooden box I had made, hidden in my bag. On reaching the nearby churchyard I saw the mourners of a funeral that was taking place. As they entered the church, I hastily went to the newly dug graveside. Standing there alone for a moment with the box in my hand, I said a silent prayer for the little mite. Then let the box slowly fall from my fingers into the depth below. A handful of earth was all it took to cover the box. After donning my hat, I walked sadly out of the churchyard, knowing that no one would ever suspect what I had done.

Then there was Ethel. Ethel Redberry had hidden herself well as she always did when she followed me on my nocturnal sojourns. I thought this was innocent enough as she had never rendered the opportunity to intervene or to make a visit to the police. But when she had the audacity to knock on my door, the morning after my work with Mary Kelly, and asked me for money, well that was a very different matter. So I arranged to meet her discreetly on the following Monday after I had the opportunity to procure the advance she had requested.

The alleyway was quiet. The only gaslight was some distance away but sufficed to illuminate our rendezvous. She stepped out as I approached her. Such a young thing. About fifteen, with such a virgin body never to be ravished by the unscrupulous. It would be difficult to annihilate such a creature, but even if she were not already involved in vice, she would no doubt be in the future. And blackmail, well despite her age, this was her current vice.

I had no choice. She had seen me. She knew where I lived. So, as she emerged from the alleyway, I intimated that I had the money and asked her to return to the alleyway with me so as not to be seen. On seeing the small package covered with brown paper in my hand, she obliged without question. It was then that I decided not to give her the money. So, catching her off guard further into the alleyway, I strangled her then slid the knife across her throat. With no intention of mutilating her, I tore the brass ring she had off her finger, and walked away from Ethel's crumpled bloodied body. Her murder was not attributed to that miscreant, Jack the Ripper! Notwithstanding this, and with some remorse for my last two victims, the little mite and Ethel Redberry, it was time for me to disappear from the decadent streets of Whitechapel forever.

So now that you have found the metal box full of my memoirs, you can rest assured that you have found the murderer who terrorised Whitechapel in 1888. But I can hear you say that these *pages could have been written by anyone who was involved in the detection of the murders at the time. A policeman, a mortuary assistant, a pathologist, or even a member of the press perhaps?*

I do not have a crystal ball, so I do not know when you will find these documents, I cannot give you any other clues than the ones you already have from the box you found. So, in addition to these memoirs, you now have pieces of human tissue. No doubt they are mummified by now, each one wrapped separately in a silk handkerchief. But you also have the brass ring I wrenched off the finger of Annie Chapman. The other two rings Annie wore, plus the one I took from Ethel Redberry, you will find in my real grave, wherever that may be. But until then, good luck for I must be off to where the wind takes me.

But of course, there is just one thing missing in my memoirs, and that is my real name. They called me Jack the Ripper. And, although I am sceptical of coincidences, they are the initials of my real name.

Signed: JTR. Alias Jack the Ripper.

Chapter 28

While Cadema had been reading the notebooks, and making notes over the last three days, she had lost count on how many times she needed to put them down and have a break. The dreadful accounts of the murders by the perpetrator, sounded more like fiction; as if he were writing a, "How To", book on murder.

At times, she felt nauseated. At other times, she almost fell asleep. Walking had given her some distraction as she watched people pursuing various leisurely activities, but in her mind, she was still reading – analysing. Even listening to Radio Three only gave her a little respite, as did yoga. She could not remember cooking anything but never felt hungry. However, the occasional soft drink and copious amounts of tea had somehow managed to sustain her.

Since joining the police service some fifteen years ago, she had read many documents. But none were ever as chilling, or so calculated, or so indifferent to the suffering of victims, as those words written by the perpetrator. They were so vividly imprinted on her mind that she could recite them verbatim if asked. When she had managed to sleep, she dreamt she was standing facing the killer; his frozen words forming horizontal icicles as they travelled, in slow motion, through the space towards her. Her body immobile, her eyes transfixed, fearing that when those frozen daggers reached her, they would cut into her throat and she would become another of his victims.

When awake, she was more determined than ever to catch him, despite him being dead. And, from what he had written, he intimated that he had left the country to settle somewhere else in the world, and never return; or did he? Did he cease killing? There were no records of similar murders around the world, so many believed he had stopped. But she knew he would never be able to stop. He would only stop when it was impossible for him to perpetuate his crimes. Through illness, death, or from being incarcerated in some institution. She assumed the latter was most probable.

Now she had finished précising the notebooks, she planned to discover what progress her team had made while she had been absent and then to brief them on her findings.

The noise of the assembled officers at police headquarters continued as she entered the room and placed the notebooks and her own notes on the table. Standing in front of them, her arms folded, she coughed. The noise continued. Why so many here? For interest again, she reasoned.

'Quiet,' she spoke in a whisper. 'Quiet,' she spoke louder. 'Right that's enough, when I enter a room I expect to be at least acknowledged. Or have I been absent for so long that you have forgotten who I am?' She remonstrated in a voice that sounded alien to her. It was rasping – iron like, with a trait of anger. She would normally be calm, but not this morning, as last night she had come face to face with a murderer. And for the first time in her life she had felt afraid.

Someone giggled in the room. She did not speak. It was her military stance and her bulging eyes, which commanded the group's attention now. The officers who were not on her team then left.

'Thank you,' said Cadema, relaxing her posture. 'As you know we have only six months left to conclude these cases. From reading the notebooks, I believe that the dress we have from the trunk which Marriott discovered, belonged to someone called Ethel Redberry, the killer's sixth victim. From what was written, she was fifteen years old and not a prostitute. The dimensions of the dress fit perfectly to this age group. She may not have been a prostitute, however she did live in a common lodging house in the Whitechapel area. So, most likely, she was the daughter of a proprietor there. Which street, it was, is impossible to say.'

'May I ask a question, Ma'am?' said Marriott hesitantly.

'Go on, but please be succinct as I have an appointment with the ACC soon.' She looked at her wrist watch.

'It's about this Ethel. If she wasn't included in the five murders attributed to the perpetrator, then why was her clothing found in the trunk in the archives?'

'Obviously, I can't answer that. But it's a good point.'

'I think...' interrupted DC Galke. Cadema gave him a cold stare.

'Go on then let's hear what you have to say.' She sounded curt.

'I think that when one of the police stations was cleared, the whole lot, including the old trunk, were dumped willy-nilly into the archive room, without any formal cataloguing.'

'You're probably right, but it doesn't explain why the dress was in the trunk,' said Cadema. 'However, we can go on speculating forever and get nowhere. And there's no point. All we do know is the date when the station was cleared and everything was moved to the archive room. We will probably never know, who, why, or when the trunk was put in that station in the first instance.'

'But, Ma'am,' said Marriott defensively, 'regarding the content of the trunk. I think PC Marriott in 1888 could have placed the items in there along with his police pocketbooks, sealed it, and then it was forgotten about.'

'Any one of those accounts could be correct. But all this is speculation, and doesn't get us anywhere. So let's move on.'

'As you are aware, Doctor Lilly is currently examining the pieces of human tissue from the metal box in the pseudo-grave. If DNA can be found, then we may be able to trace the current relatives.'

'Is that wise, Ma'am?' said Pratt, his scepticism showing.

'Elucidate,' asked Cadema.

'Well, if I were a relative of a murder victim from then, I would rather not know.'

'I've considered that. But if we do identify them, then we are obliged, by the *Human Tissue Act 2004*, to inform them. But let's leave this subject for the moment and concentrate on what we need to do now. Are there any more questions?' Cadema asked as she looked around the room; no one else spoke. 'Good, so let's get on.'

As DC Galke handed photocopies of the notes Cadema had made, she instructed her team to read them as soon as they could.

'Now let's concentrate on the investigations we still need to do to solve these crimes,' said Cadema as Galke displayed a list on the board.

'This is what we need to do, and please, no comments, or questions, until I have finished.' She brushed a long strand of black, slightly greasy hair away from her face, and flipped it over her shoulder. 'As I've mentioned, I believe that the last female victim of the Whitechapel murderer was Ethel Redberry. From what we know, she was not mutilated, as most of the other women were. That is probably the reason why she was not considered to be the victim of that murderer. So, keeping this in mind, I will start with Ethel,' said Cadema as she turned and then began to read the list on the board: 'We need to know:

    1. Who was Ethel Redberry?
        a. Where did she live?
        b. Where she was murdered?

c. Are there any police records about her, or her murder?

d. Which morgue was her body taken to?

e. Who undertook her post mortem and where is that report?

f. What happened to the coroner's report on her death?

2. 'Where did the perpetrator live? He mentions Commercial Road, but I doubt this is the truth especially as he says he could see a common lodging house directly opposite his address. We have not been able to locate a lodging house in this road. Besides that, the road, as is now, was far too wide for him to see into another house opposite, as he claims to have done. To help with identifying where he may have lived, a geographical profile had been done. This map,' Cadema pointed, 'shows exactly the locations of all five murders. Here, lines have been superimposed from one murder location to the other. Therefore, where murder one and murder four took place, a horizontal line has been drawn between them.' Galke handed out a diagram. 'And where murder two and murder three occurred, another line from these two points has been drawn. As murders two and five were closer than the others, a dotted line has been added between these. Where the lines cross on the map, from east to west and north to south, this is most probably the location of his address.

'As you can see this takes us into the area bounded by Old Montague Street and Whitechapel Road to the north and south and Greatorex Street and Osborn Street to the east and west respectively. In the centre of this was Redgate Row. It isn't there now, but it is feasible that he lived there as it was mainly lined with common lodging houses but these were demolished in the nineteen-fifties.

Now a large portion of that area boasts luxury apartments and therefore, annihilating the history of its past residents. Any questions?' asked Cadema. No one spoke.

3. 'So, what was his name, and what were his real motives for killing, what we now consider to be, these six women? We believe his name is John Temple Ribley. He intimates that it was because the women, unfortunates he called them, sold their bodies. But did he have other motives? He does say that he murdered Ethel Redberry because she was blackmailing him.

4. 'Where did the killer go after he had completed his last notebook? He implies that he may have left the country, if so:

    a. When did he leave?

    b. How did he leave?

    c. Where did he go?

    d. Did he return?

5. 'To help answer the above, Sergeant Marriott has suspicions that he left the country on board a ship called *Bairnsdale*. We need to find out the date the ship set sail and its destinations. Then we need the passenger list to verify if he was on the vessel. If his name is on the list, we must also consider that it may not have been him who actually sailed – he could have sent someone else. I doubt this, but just keep it in the back of your minds.' The officers nodded, Pratt folded his arms.

6. 'If the perpetrator was on board, are there any records of missing passengers?

7. 'If he did settle in another country, are there any records of similar murders there?

8. 'We believe he was an apothecary; this needs verification.. So we need copies of his qualifications and identify where he practiced.

'That's all I have for now, but I'm sure we will identify many more questions as we search for the answers to these.'

Sergeant Marriott raised his hand. 'There is just one question I would like to add, Ma'am.' He hesitated as if he suspected another presence. 'Do you think the cross on your map is exactly the place where the killer lived?'

'I was hoping so, but on reflection, he could have been anywhere in that area. But most likely, he lived somewhere in the East End. He knew the area extremely well, but of course he could have lived somewhere else. However, on the night of the so called *double event*, he was heading in that direction. So, I believe, he lived somewhere near there. Are there any more questions?' No one else spoke. 'Good, so please continue with the work you're doing. Pratt and Marriott will follow up the ship theory. Galke and Clarke can follow up the actions you've been given. By the way, as we are short of a senior officer, you will be pleased to know that a new DCI will be joining us soon.'

Leaving the room, she could hear the usual rumpus from the officers and hoped they would find the answers, especially with another senior officer on her team.

Chapter 29

Two days later, Pratt and Marriott sat opposite Nathen Phillips, the maritime archivist. A tall thin man with a slightly bent frame. His metal-rimmed glasses, overhung by greying eyebrows, gave the impression that he was older than his high-pitched voice suggested.

'These shipping records are excellent,' said Pratt as he studied the papers that Phillips had displayed on the viewing table. 'Such a lot of information and so clear considering they were written more than a century ago.'

'Yes Inspector, people are usually surprised by that fact. And there's more,' said Phillips standing up and walking towards another table in the room. Pratt and Marriott followed. With gloved hands that shook with the rhythm of his voice, Phillips turned the pages of an enormous ledger. 'Here we are, the *Bairnsdale* – the sister ship to the *Ballaarat*,' he traced his index finger horizontally along the lines across the page.

'Wonderful,' exclaimed Pratt. 'Again – clear and precise handwriting.' He read the main headings:

Ship: HM Bairnsdale
Built: in 1881.
Owners: Peninsular and Oriental Steam Navigation Company.
Tonnage: 2679
Speed: 14 knots
Captain: Darrell Logan
Sailed from Tilbury: 30th January 1889.
Bound for: Sydney via Cape Town.

Crew:?
Passengers: first class: 160. second class: 28
Cargo: Mixed…

'There you have it, in black and white. Nothing could be clearer. And I've looked at the weather reports for that day. Apparently, the temperature was around seven degrees centigrade, and a south-westerly wind, and no rain.'

'That's excellent, and I was right about the ship,' said Marriott excitedly, 'it is the *Bairnsdale*. But I can't get over its small size; less than 2700 tonnes.' He shook his head. 'My sister and her husband travelled on one of today's passenger ships, and that was 80,000 tonnes or thereabouts. It took over 2500 passengers and travelled at 30 knots. I can't imagine a ship as small as the *Bairnsdale* travelling the oceans in rough seas, and especially to Australia.'

'Thanks for your reflections, Marriott,' said Pratt, sarcastically. 'What we need to know now, is how to find the passenger list for the dates we have in mind. And, is there a log book that'll tell us about the voyage?' Pratt looked at Phillips.

Phillips shook his head. 'It's been a long time, and I don't have a copy of the logbook or any other records to hand, apart from what you've seen already. But I may be able to find out who disembarked in Sydney, so that should help, unless the person you're looking for disembarked somewhere else.'

Pratt agreed and said he also needed to know about the passengers and crew on board, and who disembarked at Cape Town, in addition to Sydney. And whether anyone went missing during the journey. He tried to be as vague as possible as he didn't want to tell him too much about the investigation. It wasn't because Pratt didn't trust him, however he made it his policy not to give out more information than was necessary.

Phillips thought for a moment and then said he would contact the maritime museum in Sydney and speak to the archivist, whom he knew. He assured the officers that he would be able to find the information they were looking for.

'Good man, good man,' said Pratt. 'I'll look forward to that. I'm sure that anything you find on this will be helpful.' Pratt shook Phillip's hand with enthusiasm, but his eyes were cold.

'Thanks, but I would be failing my job if I didn't do that. Besides, the Australian authorities have always kept excellent records of people entering each state. They will no doubt be able to tell me when and where a person arrived in Australia and possibly where they settled. It's obviously much too early in the morning to telephone. I'll send McWilliams an email instead. He'll be most helpful, and timely I'm sure.' Phillips rubbed his hands together again. Seeing Pratt's emotionless face, he turned to Marriott who nodded and thanked him for his excellent work. Both officers said goodbye.

***

Reaching the station, they went straight to Cadema's office, and entered. Pratt took a seat facing her, Marriott stood to attention.

'That's what he said, Ma'am,' said Pratt. '"If McWilliams cannot find out, no one can."' Apparently, he's a member of an archivist network in New South Wales, so he knows who to contact. Phillips will send us an email when he has more information.'

Cadema realised how Pratt had developed since joining her team. She had certainly changed her mind about him. And he seemed to be working well with Marriott, and the investigation was on schedule, despite it taking a very different course than she had expected. This was especially the case now that the killer may have sailed to Australia. Most investigations in the past led the police to believe that he went to America or some other country – never Australia. And now there was a ship that seemed to have left London soon after the Whitechapel murderers ceased. Everything appeared to fit into place. The date was about right. And the notebooks found in the pseudo-grave also intimated that the killer was about to leave the country. But despite this knowledge, she still had some doubt in her mind. He could have gone anywhere; South Africa, Canada, but Australia was further than she expected.

If he did indeed go to Australia on the *Bairnsdale*, he must have bought a ticket soon after killing his very last witness, Reggie Bates – the person who dug the pseudo-grave. Whilst waiting for the sailing date to arrive, he could carry on with his job as normal. Then, believing no one suspected him, he silently sailed out of London into another world. There were no passports then, so no one would suspect anything.

Now Cadema needed proof that he was a passenger on that ship – assuming he used his own name rather than an alias.

Deep inside Cadema's mind, another, more serious debate, was taking place. What if the British and Australian Government already knew the identity of the perpetrator, but decided to keep it secret? If this were the case, the records at the time may have been lost or hidden away under the fifty-years, or hundred-years rule, then no one would ever know. The two collaborating authorities would have kept him under surveillance on the ship. Reaching Australia, he could have been incarcerated in any number of penal institutions, never to be seen again. She hoped this would not be the case.

However, if it did transpire, that John Temple Ribley actually went to Australia, and on his own volition, she needed to know where he lived there, and if he killed again. Perhaps he settled down, got married, and had a family. She had to find out which scenario was feasible, even if it meant taking a trip there to discover the truth.

Twenty-four hours later, Marriott received a message from Phillips on his mobile phone. "Got message from McWilliams, contact me immediately," it read. As Pratt was busy on another part of the investigation, Marriott went straight to Cadema. She decided they should visit Phillips together and see what the message was all about.

Phillips shook hands with both Cadema and Marriott as if they were long-lost family. Giving no time for collegial exchanges, he began to explain what McWilliams had discovered.

'Apparently, he spoke to a couple of his archivist friends, one of whom worked in Immigration. This is the email.' Philipps held up a sheet of A4 paper. 'McWilliams had, with considerable difficulty, eventually found the passenger list for the voyage in question, but that's all,' Phillips said as he cleared his throat with vigour. 'Mac says that there's much more research to do, especially concerning the voyage itself. He says a week should do it.' Phillips picked up the emailed passenger list and waved it like a white flag.

Cadema took hold of the paper and ran her fingers down the list – her hands shaking – mouth dry. She took a deep breath. 'We were right, he did embark on a journey to Australia,' she said, as Marriott eagerly looked at the list.

'Assuming he did arrive there,' she continued with some scepticism. 'We need to find out what happened to him when he disembarked at Sydney, and where he went from there.'

Phillips said he was sure Mac would be able to answer Cadema's questions, once he had probed the Sydney maritime archives.

After discussing the intricacies of research in general, Cadema thanked Phillips for keeping to the deadlines he had been given, and for finding the information she needed so quickly. As Marriott drove Cadema back to the station, he told her how he was feeling.

'This whole scenario seems futile to me, Ma'am. Why did we have to go to see Phillips when he could have just forwarded the email, and passenger list to us. After all, he didn't tell us anything else that we didn't already suspect.'

'That may be the case, Marriott, but it's useful to meet people who are helpful like that. Besides, if we don't liaise in that way, people become faceless bureaucrats, in a world of red tape. Breaking down barriers is as important as getting the facts. When we speak to Phillips again, there'll be no barriers. But I must admit, I did expect more from him than we received; perhaps next time...' Cadema did not finish what she was about to say. She had just read the text from Haady asking her out to dinner. That was a much better proposition than going out with Julia and Andrew Long.

***

Less than two days later, Marriott received a text message from Phillips:

"Exciting news from Mac. Come as soon as u can."

Cadema and Marriott did just that, and within an hour they were both sitting in his office listening to a report that they had never contemplated hearing.

Phillips explained that the captain of the *Bairnsdale*, a Darrell Logan, kept copious records in his log. They including information on the weather, the ports of call, and every incident that happened during the voyage. There were the terribly rough seas in the Bay of Biscay where the ship nearly capsized. But the most intriguing of all was that two women passengers, Martha Marksman and Louisa Baker, were "Lost at Sea." The captain detailed their descriptions and said they were travelling alone. Martha disappeared on the twelfth of February, 1889 and Louisa on the first of March. The record in the ship's log read:

1st March, 1889. Two women, both aged 25 years old, have now disappeared-presumed lost at sea. After making several enquiries as to their last movements, and interviewing all crew and many passengers, it appears that John Temple Ribley was the last person to have seen both women alive. Having locked the aforesaid passenger in the strong room, I ordered a detailed search of his cabin. Officers Bradley and Stuart found a piece of rope, two ladies' silk scarves, a very sharp knife, and a scalpel hidden behind the washbasin. They also found blood on some clothing. One jacket was missing from his wardrobe, although he had been seen wearing it the day Miss Marksman disappeared. In view of these findings I intend to keep him in custody until we reach Sydney. There, I will hand him over to the authorities. Signed; Captain Darrell Logan.

McWilliams explained that there were several other entries in the log concerning the prisoner during the journey to Australia. Reaching Sydney, Captain Logan wrote that he handed John Temple Ribley, and the evidence they had found concerning him, to the judicial authorities there. McWilliams said he would have to do more research to find out what happened to him next.

Thanking Phillips again, Cadema and Marriott left with a copy of the report. On the return journey to the station, Cadema told Marriott that she was contemplating a trip to Australia, if it was necessary. But that, due to her work and domestic commitments, she decided that if there was a need to go, then someone else from the team would have to go.

'Who are you thinking of asking, Ma'am?'

'There are only two officers who could go and that's you or DI Pratt. However, this needs much more discussion and a feasibility report needs to be done. Then permission given before anything else,' said Cadema.

'I'd be willing to go. A trip to Australia; awesome.'

'Now, Marriott, don't get your hopes too high. There's a lot of things to consider. And it will not be a holiday. It'll be a very tight schedule – no time for partying.'

'As if I would ever contemplate that. Never, not when on duty anyway. I'm too set in my ways now to go *partying* as you put it – too long in the tooth.' He sounded defensive.

'Sorry, I didn't mean to offend you. I know how hard you work and your tenacity to get things done; on schedule; is very commendable. Let's not discuss it any further now. But see what happens.'

Marriott nodded, and then smiled at the thought. The rest of the journey was made in silence.

Three days later, Cadema received a telephone call:

'Is that Superintendent Sharma? McWilliams here.' Cadema heard the broad Australian accent, with a hint of Scottish dialect, on her office telephone.

'Yes, it's good to hear from you.' She glanced at the clock on the wall. 'It's just past eight in the morning here, so it must be about seven p.m. over there?'

'It is, but I decided to wait, and when the time was right, phone rather than text. Hope that's okay? Anyway, I've discovered some great news about what happened to this Ribley bloke. You should be receiving an email with attachments. Sorry it has taken so long, but I had to clear this with the Police Commissioning Board and then the Commissioner had to sign all the papers. Now I've done this I'll be handing you over to one of my police friends. He's Superintendent Gareth Saxley, a good bloke. Originally from the UK, so he'll be on your radar, so to speak.' McWilliams eventually paused for breath.

'That's great,' said Cadema. 'I'll look forward to reading what you've sent and to working alongside Superintendent Saxley.'

'No worries, I enjoyed the challenge. So, I thought I'd give you a ring.' For the first time during the conversation, Cadema could hear some hesitation in his voice, as if he were embarrassed. She heard him cough. 'Anyhow, if you're making the trip to Oz I can arrange accommodation. All above board – and no hassle mind? And I've a mate in the force, female that is, who can arrange everything so there'll be no red tape. Hey, you still there?'

'Yes, sorry I was thinking. It sounds good, so I'll consider the offer. But as we have red tape here too, It'll take time, and of course I have other commitments.'

'No worries, the offer's there if you can make it. Perhaps even one of your officers...? But of course, it's up to you.' Good-day.'

Cadema was about to say goodbye when the phone went dead. Then, having procured a cup of tea, she switched on her computer and found the email.

Twenty-four pages were downloaded and printed. As Cadema began to read the attachments, she heard the voices of her teams in the building. One was laughing, another shouting, but the majority were quiet. The only one she had not heard was Pratt. He usually called out 'Good Morning' to her as he reached the top of the stairs, and before he entered the open plan offices where all the other team members were. Late again, she grumbled to herself, she would have to have a word with him.

Skim-reading the documents, she made the usual notes of the main issues. Starting with the file on Ribley from the New South Wales police department, she moved onto the records of the trial, his conviction and finally to his imprisonment. There was no mention as to why he did not

318

receive the death penalty, as this would have been the norm at that time; something did not seem right.

She picked up her phone and dialled Pratt's mobile number. 'That's all I need, the answer phone.' She began to leave a message. 'Where are you? Why are you late? When you *do* finally come in I *want* to see you in my office immediately.'

Just as she was about to put the phone down, a voice answered.

'Sorry, Ma'am, I pressed recent calls and saw your number. I'm in the building right now. I'll be with you in a few seconds.' As he spoke she could hear his heavy footsteps along the corridor. She switched off her phone.

A red faced and dishevelled figure burst into Cadema office. 'What on earth's wrong? Don't say someone landed on your bonnet again.' She offered a grimace of a smile.

'No, it's not that. My alarm failed to go off, that's all. I'll swear to you I'll get a new one asap.' He gesticulated with both hands in the stop position, then sat on a chair facing her.

'You'd better do that. It's nearly nine thirty, and that just won't do. What example do you think you're giving to the team? And look at you. I suggest you smarten yourself up before you see them.' Cadema paused for breath. 'Anyway, that aside, I have heard from McWilliams. He sent these.' She pointed to the documents on her desk. 'They are very interesting. And that's not all, he thinks it is a good idea for me to make a journey there.'

'Does he indeed?' His voice sounded a little cynical. 'So are you going, Ma'am?

'I've thought about it. But there are a couple of problems to consider. Firstly, I have to get permission, and secondly my mother is due back from India soon. Obviously, I need to be here for her.'

Pratt nodded in agreement.

'If that's the case, and we can get the authority to go, I'd be happy to go in your place, if there is a problem.'

'I thought you would. But, if I am unable to go then I will consider who the most appropriate person would be as a substitute. In the meantime, I'll put in a request for permission and funding.'

'So who do you have in mind to go?'

'I'm not going to speculate now.'

'So what's McWilliams said?' Pratt craned his neck to read the documents on the desk.

'There's no need for that. I'll give you a briefing together with the rest of the team. But it seems that we have found the killer. All we have to do now is find tangible evidence to link him directly to the crimes,' said Cadema dismissively.

Gathering up the papers, she marched with Pratt along the corridor. On the way, she asked him to give her one hour and then to assemble the officers in the briefing room. She would share the finding once she had spoken to the Deputy Commissioner.

***

Andrew Long was sitting at his desk surrounded by the usual array of files, which seemed to grow each time Cadema met him. He looked up, smiled and gestured for her to take a seat.

'Well I can see by the smile on your face that you're happy about something, so what have you found?' said Andrew who then brushed his hand across his bald head, happy to be doing something other than the work on his desk.

'You're right, Andrew, there is something. At least I think there is. Hopefully it's not all circumstantial. But I think we have found the perpetrator.'

'That's great news, isn't it? So why the frown?' Andrew asked, then gave a comforting smile. She smiled back. 'That's better. Now just give me the facts of the case, then I can make my own mind up about this miscreant.'

Cadema felt reassured now. Perhaps she should have taken up the offer of a meal with him and Julia, after all. But, at the time she felt it would have been an intrusion into the couple's time together. No, declining was the only sensible thing to do.

But if she had gone, and Andrew had become a friend, as Julia was, then her approach to him would have been different. She could tell him how inadequate she felt at times, and how difficult it was for her to handle Pratt. How she had to make a choice of either going to Australia herself or sending someone else in her place.

After these self-recriminations, Cadema decided to curtail them, at least for the moment. Now she was ready – head upright and shoulders back, she cleared her throat as Andrew's voice interrupted her.

'Are you all right, you seem a little preoccupied?

'I'm fine, thank you. Everything may have sounded a little nebulous before, but when I've given you the facts of the case, I hope you will be able to see what I mean.' Was she making sense, or did she sound a little strange? She didn't care.

'That's reassuring, so let's sit at the meeting table over there it's much more comfortable,' said Andrew as he walked to the other side of his office. Cadema followed.

After explaining about Phillips and how he had developed a rapport with McWilliams in Sydney, she placed the twenty-four-page document onto the table. Andrew frowned, but remained silent. 'Don't be alarmed, Andrew, as I've précised them for easy reference.' She took up her notebook and gave an outline on what had been discovered.

'John Temple Ribley *did* go to Australia on the ship called *Bairnsdale* – he's on the passenger list. He disembarked at Sydney where he was arrested for being involved in the disappearance of two women on the voyage from London to Sydney. The captain of the ship, Darrell Logan, handed him over to the New South Wales Police Authority together with the evidence found hidden in his cabin. But as there were no bodies of his victims, he was later given a life sentence and sent to prison, rather than the death penalty.' Cadema turned the page, just as the tea, which Andrew had ordered earlier, arrived. She took a sip, and then placed the cup and saucer on the table. 'One thing that is baffling me is the prison he was sent to.'

'Where was he sent?' requested Andrew.

'Well after a few weeks in Sydney, the records indicate that he was transferred to a prison in Tasmania. It's called Port Arthur.'

'So what's wrong with that?'

'I think this is a mistake as Port Arthur, according to the information I have gleaned, was closed as a prison in 1877. That's more than ten years before our murders took place.'

'No wonder you're sceptical,' Andrew frowned as he took a last gulp of his tea. 'So what are you going to do about it? He must have gone somewhere. Are you sure he wasn't executed?'

'There are no records of that, so I don't think so. I would ask McWilliams, but he has handed me over to a Superintendent Gareth Saxley. So it's a mystery for the time being. I'll ask Saxley to see what he can find out. Nevertheless, if Ribley didn't go to Port Arthur, he must have gone somewhere.' Cadema sat back in her chair and shrugged.

'It all sounds suspicious to me,' said Andrew. 'I'll look forward to hearing what Saxley says about it. But in my experience, these things are always the same. Over time, files go missing, or gaps appear. And of course, there's also the possibility that the two governments were hiding information, probably under some rule, or other. If that's the case, we may never get to the bottom of it.' Andrew leaned forward in his chair; his eyes seemed to be searching for an answer somewhere on the wall behind Cadema.

'Do you think so, Andrew? I believe that too, and with all the publicity about Jack the Ripper at the time, the authorities realised who he was. So when he reached Sydney, they arrested him. And although they didn't have the evidence, they couldn't risk releasing him. So when they did sentence him to life, it really would mean life.'

'You could be right, Cadema, something we must keep in mind anyway.'

Cadema felt somewhat dismissed by his answer. But she was determined to press the issue. 'I believe what I said; they just wanted him to disappear from all records, so they invented the story about Tasmania. He most probably rotted away in some prison in New South Wales, most people forgetting who he really was.'

'That's a very cynical view, and with nothing to substantiate it, I'm surprised at you.'

'I suppose it is, and I don't want to cast aspersions on the Australian penal system at that time, but it wouldn't surprise me if our government didn't know what was going on. Of course, there's no way of proving that.'

'You're speculating again. I've always considered you to be level-headed and sure of your facts before commenting.' Andrew smiled as he spoke. 'So we need to find out where they sent him.'

'Yes, we do,' said Cadema with renewed enthusiasm. 'And hopefully Saxley will be able to help as he should have access to the prison documents. It will be difficult for us to access them from here as McWilliams said most of them are on microfilm. But I'm not ruling out Port Arthur, after all it was a high security prison, with only one road in and out of it. And I understand that the terrain is similar to Dartmoor, so if a prisoner did escape, he wouldn't survive for long.'

'You seem to have made up your mind about that place; I hope you won't be too disappointed if you can't find him there.'

'We'll just have to wait and see.' Cadema smiled, took a deep breath and rolled her shoulders against the back of the chair.

'You've made many interesting assertions, so now we need the facts. Hopefully they will come in time. Nevertheless, well done.'

'Thanks, Andrew. But there's something I need to tell you. McWilliams has asked me to go to Sydney to investigate this with the authorities over there, and find the answers to the mystery. If I can get permission for that, I could view the microfilm and hopefully discover what happened to Ribley. If he went to Tasmania, I can find out why he was there when the prison was already closed and what happened to him.' As Cadema spoke, Andrew stood up and began pacing the floor.

'And what would your objective be? If the prison was closed when you said it was, then what do you expect to find? No, I could not agree to that, and I'm sure the Commissioner will back me up on this.' He paced faster and faster, his hands behind his back, like an old schoolmaster.

'Sorry to persist on this, but we have gone too far to stop now. If I go to Sydney,' she decided not to tell him she was thinking of not going there herself, 'at least I can see the files, and follow up leads. There may be something that's been overlooked which could lead to his whereabouts. All I want to do is to find out where he was buried, exhume the body and obtain samples for DNA analysis. If that DNA matches with the DNA we have from the dress, and to Ashley Ribley, we will have the killer.' Andrew stopped pacing and turned to face Cadema.

'I suppose that's a reasonable rationale. And your final aim is to get tangible evidence that proves, beyond doubt, that he is the perpetrator. But I'm not sure how feasible it is, especially with the exhumation bit. Just put it all in a business case and let me have it by tomorrow. Then I'll see what I can do. Don't forget that, apart from having permission from us, you will also need it from the Australian Government.'

Cadema jumped out of her seat, thanked Andrew for believing in her, and said the business case would be with him as requested.

Walking back to her office to drop off the papers before seeing her team, she wondered if she had left something out, but couldn't think what it might be. Everything was clear in her head. She had her plan, admittedly not a ten-point one. Something *was* missing from it, but still she didn't know what it was as she headed for the briefing room.

The corridor was quiet. Not a sound came from the room where the team were supposed to be. Expecting them to have gone somewhere else, she opened the door only to see them sitting quietly with DI Pratt standing there – arms folded. Seeing Cadema, he gestured to her to be quiet. Conforming, she tiptoed into the room and closed the door. On the whiteboard, Pratt had written some questions about the case. And it looked as if the team, sitting in examination conditions, were trying to answer them. Their heads bent over their paper, none of the officers looked up, or made a sound. All she could hear were a couple of sighs and the scratching of pens on paper. Cadema remembered he had done this before when he worked in his previous division. As she reached him, he pointed to his watch and gestured ten minutes. She nodded and sat in one of the seats facing the whiteboard. Notebook in hand, her pen hovered over the blank page. Nothing materialised, she felt as if a switch had been flipped off in her brain.

'That's it, I think you've all had enough time to come up with some answers to the questions,' said Pratt as everyone put their pens down in unison. 'Now I'd like you to rank order your answers, and then identify your first three.'

Taking up their pens again they began the task. Just like school, Cadema thought – but not the way to treat his colleagues.

'Now you've finished with that. Can you tell me, one answer from each of you, what you have thought about the profile of the killer? And give me the rationale for your answer where possible.' Galke raised his hand.

'Well, Sir, I think the killer lived alone in Old Montague Street.'

'Everyone else knows he must have lived alone Galke, so what's so special about that, and why that street? Superintendent Sharma has already said he lived near there. Not in the main street, but a narrow street called Redgate Row. Are you disputing that?' Pratt sounded curt. Galke shuffled in his seat.

'I'm not disputing it.' He coughed. 'I just think he lived at number 44.'

'You will need much more than that. Where's your evidence?' Pratt did not wait for an answer, instead he shrugged and turned to DC Clarke.

'What have you written?' She blushed and sat up straight.

'I agree with Galke,' said Clarke. 'I think he was single and probably lived alone. And I imagine him to be around thirty to thirty-five years old. And I don't think he wrote those letters to the press or to the police. But, it's just an assumption.'

'Good, so we have some agreements,' Pratt wrote the answer on the board. 'So let that be a lesson, and concentrate on the facts, not speculations. What about you, Marriott?

Marriott stood up, pushed his shoulders back and started to speak. 'I think he went to Australia and met his demise there. He was probably hanged as I don't think he would have stopped killing.'

Marriott was still talking when Cadema realised what she had forgotten. It was that if Ribley was sent to prison, did he actually die there? She began to speculate; what if he were released? If he was, where could he have gone – to London perhaps? She had to find out.

Pratt was just finishing, when Cadema tuned into what was being said. The room, now quiet, she explained about the information that McWilliams had sent from Sydney and that she had briefed the deputy commissioner on this. That there was a possibility of going to Sydney and then on to Tasmania. She then turned to leave the room, when she heard Clarke's timid voice.

'Can I accompany you to Oz, Ma'am?' Clarke giggled as she looked at her colleagues.

'There may be a possibility of two people going,' answered Cadema, 'but it must be done on merit and with equal opportunities in mind. I'm not speculating on who may be going just now. Nevertheless, as soon as I have permission, we will be discussing this in more detail. In the meantime, Pratt will allocate your actions.' Leaving the group, Cadema returned to her office.

Pratt instructed Galke and Clarke to find out more about the likely address of the killer. He sent Marriott to investigate if there were any similar murders between 1889 and 1930, either in London or other areas in the United Kingdom. Pratt did believe, that if Ribley did return from Australia, then he could have begun his killing spree again. But, that by 1930 he would have been too old to do so.

Once the officers were deployed to his satisfaction, Pratt decided to visit the Ribley family again to bring them up to date on what had been discovered. He would also ask Ashley Ribley if he had any correspondence that was sent to any of his ancestors from abroad. Before leaving, he went to see Cadema.

'Well that didn't go as I would have hoped, but at least they tried,' said Pratt as he walked into Cadema's office with the papers he had picked up from the briefing room. 'At least it got them thinking; hopefully they realise that police work isn't easy.'

'I think they already know. After all Marriott is an experienced officer, and you haven't given Galke and Clarke any merit on their achievements. So, your comment isn't valid on this.'

Pratt shrugged.

'Anyway, I've been thinking. When I write the business case I intend to ask for another police officer to accompany me.'

'Although you haven't said it,' Pratt fidgeted, 'it sounds to me as if you are asking. And you know there's nothing I'd like better than to go with you...'

'I wasn't asking….'

'Come on. I know you'd hate travelling alone on such a trip.'

'I…'

'Please let me finish, Ma'am,' Pratt interjected again. 'There's nothing I'd like better than to go with you. But think about the issues. You and I, I mean. I don't think it would go down well with the others. Besides I bet Andrew Long wouldn't agree to that. No, I think you should consider someone else – preferably a woman.'

'That's an antiquated way of thinking, I'm surprised at you. But in a way, I think you've got a point there.' Cadema gave a smug smile.

'I didn't mean it like that. I think it's all about rank not gender. Anyway, I think you would feel better being with a woman.

'You're being presumptive, how do you know what I feel?'

'Sorry, Ma'am, I didn't mean to offend. However, you need to consider the practicalities. At least you could share a room with a female, that would cut down the costs.'

'I realise that, so a female would be my best option.'

'Alternatively, and with appropriate funding, there's always Marriott. After all he's the one who found the trunk in the first place,' said Pratt, 'and his ancestor was a Marriott.'

'That's speculation...' said Cadema, as she wondered why he had suggested Marriott. Perhaps Pratt was avoiding telling her something – that he didn't want to go to Australia?

He interrupted her thoughts.

'I know that, but if you can't spare anyone from the team, there's always Haady – or perhaps you'd be better off with me?' He added the last clause quickly. He didn't want to mention how he'd noticed the way she had looked at Haady. That loving yearning look he had seen before when people wanted to be more than just friends. Haady had looked at her the same way. Maybe she should go with him? He decided not to say anything else.

'I'll consider what you've said,' answered Cadema, as Prat left. Then she sat for a while contemplating the alternatives. She thought of Julia Lilly. But would she be able to get permission to go with her? She certainly didn't want to go alone, and a female companion would be better. Johns was working elsewhere, but may consider it if she could be released from her current workload. That left Clarke, who was too inexperienced for the role. Just three women to choose from, and none suitable.

Sitting in her lounge sipping Merlot later that evening, Cadema began her business case. Three hours later she had finished and looked at the clock; ten thirty – too late to phone Julia.

Chapter 30

Showering the next morning, Cadema heard the telephone ring. Instead of getting out dripping wet, she let it ring, knowing the answerphone would soon activate. After dressing and making herself a cup of tea, she walked to the phone and pressed the play switch.

'Andrew Long here, sorry you were out. Give me a call on my mobile as soon as you get this. I want to speak to you before you arrive this morning.'

'So what's so urgent that you need to phone me at this hour,' Cadema said quietly, after glancing at the clock. 'It's only six.' She spoke to Cameo, as the cat circled around her feet. 'And that goes for you too, Cameo, no breakfast yet. I need to dry my hair first.' Cameo persisted as she headed for the bedroom. 'You'll both have to wait until I'm ready this time.'

Having fed Cameo, Cadema stood military style as she picked up the telephone and pressed button three of the stored numbers. She did not hear the phone ring at the other end, but there was no mistake about the male voice who answered it.

'Andrew Long here. Good morning, Cadema. It's about your proposal.'

'Yes, Andrew, I thought it would be. I've completed the business case. And I'm intending to...'

'Oh don't worry about that. I hoped you hadn't finished it yet.'

'But...'

'No, just listen. I had a word with the commissioner last night. He agrees that the best way forward is for you to go to Australia. There's plenty of funding left, and it would be insane not to do so.'

'That's great news. However, you need to be aware that my business case identifies the need for two people to go, rather than just one.'

'I thought that's what you would do, that's why I'm phoning you.' Andrew coughed. 'We can't spare anyone else from the team. You'll have to go alone.' His voice was firm and slightly apologetic.

'But Andrew, when I put the case together, I covered the workload with the remaining team. Someone else could go with me.'

'Who's that?'

'I've not actually named anyone. It's just the rank.' Cadema sighed and sat down – Cameo jumped onto her lap. 'Not now.' She lifted her onto the floor.

'What do you mean?'

'Sorry, I was talking to the cat.'

'Okay, let's hear what you've said in your document? Mind you, Duncan Mander is adamant that we cannot spare any other officers, especially with this current round of government cuts in the budget. Nevertheless, if you don't want to go it alone, you'll have to find someone, external from our team, who has the time, and the budget, to go with you.'

'I understand, but what do you want me to say in the business case?'

'Add a plan B, as a contingency plan. Anyway, at least you should be happy that you will be able to go.'

'Yes, of course,' her words stumbled out. 'Yes, I could go alone. I've just got one question.'

'Go on, I'm listening.'

'Do you mind if I come in later today, rather than this morning, so I can have more time to consider, and then write plan B?'

'That's not a problem, I'll ask Pratt to manage until I see you. And cheer up – it's good news. Bye.'

'Yes, bye, Andrew – thank you.' Cadema felt fatigued as she put the phone down and began stroking, and talking to, Cameo.

She could go alone; it wouldn't be a problem especially now she had managed to persuade mother to stay in India for another month. She opened her laptop lid.

Plan B, she thought. Plan B, there was always a plan B – Julia. She could not do plan B until she had spoken to her. She was just about to lift the telephone when she realised it was still too early to call her.

'Plan B.' She opened the document to see what she had written the previous evening. Plan B, she stared at the text. Plan B she typed. Plan B was not enough; there should also be a Plan C. Something even Andrew hadn't thought of.

She recalled that plan A was for her to go with an officer from her own team and find a replacement. Plan B was to go alone; Plan C was to go with someone else – someone connected to the case. Julia was the ideal person. Six-hundred and fifty words later, Plans A, B and C were tabulated, together with each rationale. Although she had not mentioned Julia in the text, she needed to speak to her now. Seven thirty, was it too early to phone? She pressed her number.

'Good morning, Julia, sorry to disturb you so early, but I need to discuss something with you.'

'Hello, so what's the urgency? Or is it an emergency?'

'Neither, I just need to talk to you, preferably before you start work.'

'Well, that's impossible today,' said Julia.

'Why? Are you off somewhere?'

'Not exactly. I'm off altogether, today. No work – wonderful. However, I'm going out later this morning. If you want to come around, you're welcome.'

'I'll be there in half an hour.'

'Too early, come at nine thirty.'

Agreeing to this, Julia jumped out of bed, dressed, and did her usual jog around the block. By the time Cadema had arrived, she had eaten breakfast, tided up a little, showered and dressed.

'Do come in and excuse the mess, haven't had time to clean everything,' said Julia.

Cadema couldn't see what the fuss was all about, as the house looked immaculate as usual.

'What can I get you?'

'Tea would be lovely, thank you,' said Cadema as she followed Julia into the kitchen and sat at the breakfast bar.

'I can tell by your eyes that something's worrying you, so what's the problem?'

'There's no problem. I just need to tell you what's been happening, and then get your view on something.'.

'Come on, don't be so hesitant. If that's all there was to it, we could have met at work. No, I think there *is* something else.' Julia sounded a little aggressive. Cadema ignored it.

'I'll tell you what the issues are.' Cadema began to explained about Australia, and that she did not want to travel alone.

'I can see your dilemma, but if they can't second anyone else, what are you going to do?'

'Well.' She hesitated, her eyes looked at Julia like a puppy.

'Oh no, I know what you're thinking. But I couldn't possibly. I've all this work to do and with Cox being relatively new, I couldn't leave her to manage.'

'I realise that. But as she's much more experienced than Bagley ever was, I thought that, if you wanted to go, you could get a locum in?' Julia frowned. 'And there's funding from the ring-fenced budget.' It wasn't really a lie – there is a budget, but insufficient to send two people.

'The cost is not a problem, but my time is.'

'So are you saying that, if you had the time you *would* go in principle?'

'Now you're putting words into my mouth. I think it is an excellent project and your objectives are sound, but I'm sorry, it's just not feasible for me to go. Can you find anyone else, someone not from your team, I mean?' Julia sipped her tea. Cadema sat in silence. 'How about Haady, you seem to get on well with him. After all he was a police officer and as he is now self-employed. Do you think he may like to go?' Cadema remained silent. 'What's wrong?' Julia could see Cadema's eyes were watering.

'Everything's wrong. I don't want to go alone. There's no one on my team who can go. I would prefer to go with a female, not a male. So, I can't go with Haady. And to top it all I'm feeling rejected.' Cadema began to sob. Julia moved closer and put her arm across her shoulder.

'Here, take a tissue, and tell me, what's really the matter?'

'I know it sound silly, but you're the only one who might understand. I feel threatened, as if my job is on the line; as if they want me to go to Australia to be out of the way. And then there's my mother, she's agreed to stay in India if I go, but I know she's desperate to get back. I feel I've abandoned her.' Cadema wiped her eyes with the tissue.

'Have you thought of sending someone else from your team, instead of you? Or do you have to go yourself?' Julia moved slightly away and gave what she hoped was an encouraging smile. Cadema smiled back.

'I've thought of that. There is one person who could handle it – DI Pratt. Although I'm not sure of him, he's the appropriate rank and could go alone. Yes, that would solve everything.'

'And you could communicate by Skype, and you'd still be in charge. What do you think?'

'Julia, you're a marvel. Anyway, Pratt did tentatively offer to go with me, but I didn't even consider it. I will speak to Andrew Long to see if it's feasible. Then I'll let you know.' Cadema smiled, dabbed at her red eyes with a tissue, and said she had to get home and complete the work on her business case, now she had a plan C.

'That's great, and it's good to see you smiling again. If you want a break, or need to discuss this further, let me know. You know I'm always here for you. And while you're at it, think about contacting Haady and have dinner with him again. You need to get out more,' said Julia as she helped Cadema put on her coat and then walked her to the front door. On leaving, Cadema thought of dinner she had already planned for Haady.

Chapter 31

'Cadema, come in and take a seat,' said Andrew Long, smiling. 'The Commissioner will be joining us. I'll let him know you're here.' He picked up the telephone and spoke to Duncan Mander's secretary. Turning to Cadema, he offered to order some tea.

'I'm fine, thank you,' she said, stealthily clutching the business case in her hand. 'I've finished this, but before you read it…'

'Sorry, Cadema, we must wait until Duncan arrives. Have you had a good day so far?'

'Very fruitful. Thank you.'

Andrew nodded and was just about to speak when Duncan entered the room. Following a brief acknowledgement from the two officers, the three moved to the meeting table. With his six-foot seven large frame, Duncan just managed to squeeze his knees under the table without injuring himself. He brushed his hand over his thinning grey hair while his dark-green eyes surveyed his surroundings. Since being promoted to commissioner, Duncan still liked to be involved in operational matters. He just couldn't let go.

'Before we start, can I get you some refreshments, Commissioner?' asked Andrew offering a wye smile.

'No, I don't really have the time. But cut the formality, call me Duncan.' He turned from Andrew to Cadema. 'It's good to see you again. How are you getting on with the case? You know I've agreed to your visit to Australia?'

'Yes sir, and I need to talk to you about that,' said Cadema. 'I do appreciate your decision to support this. But as for me going there, I've changed my mind. I don't want to go.' Cadema held back her tears, hoping her colleagues would not notice.

'Why ever not, it's a chance of a lifetime, and with such a high profile case. You should seriously reconsider your decision,' said Duncan in a firm but gentle voice. He knew he couldn't force her to go. Andrew nodded his head in agreement.

'It's not that I'm ungrateful,' added Cadema, 'I don't want to travel alone. And there's my mother to consider. DI Pratt intimated that he may like to go, so that's a possibility.'

'It's your prerogative,' said Andrew. 'Have you considered that someone else from your team could go? Marriott perhaps?'

'He said he could go, however it needs someone at the appropriate rank. DI Pratt is the obviously one,' said Cadema with determination.

Andrew nodded. 'That's a good point. But if you want to change your mind...'

'You've obviously thought it over,' said Duncan. 'It's your team, so I'll leave you and Andrew to sort it out. In the meantime,' he turned to Cadema, 'feel free to leave as I have things to discuss.

Cadema said a polite thank you. As she left the room and closed the door, Duncan turned to Andrew.

'How long has it been now, since Cadema's last breakdown that is?' said Duncan quietly.

'Let me see. It must be nearly six months. Why do you ask?'

'Didn't you see? Surely you must have noticed she was near to tears. I think she's on the brink of another breakdown.

And this whole case is getting too much for her. Australia would be the last straw.'

'I did notice she looked a little tired, but she's been working extremely hard. And even if she doesn't go to Australia, I've every faith in her to continue with this investigation.' Andrew's answer was firm, even defiant.

'If you're sure...?'

'I am. Cadema is an excellent officer and needs to stay in control – undermining her confidence will surely tip her over the edge. Just leave it with me, I'll keep an eye on her.'

'That's fine, I'll wait until I've heard from you. I must be off now – another meeting.'

***

Cadema walked slowly to her office looking sideways and behind her to make sure that no one was following her. Perhaps she should have considered Marriott's offer to go, but it was too late now. All she could do was go along with the plan. But now, she had to freshen up to clean the salt from her face.

Turning the junction in the corridor, she just managed to avoid colliding with DI Pratt. She coughed, mouthed 'Sorry', and continued. Pratt turned to follow her. She quickened her pace – he caught up. Without eye contact, she told him to see her in the office in half an hour. He stopped and agreed, as she sped on.

On time, Pratt took a seat in her office without being asked, then looked at her as if angry about something.

'What did the commissioner say about your business case?'

'I'll tell you in a minute.' Cadema's voice was harsh and hurried, as if she were running out of time, or patience with him.

Pratt nodded and then sat looking at her. He noticed how pale she was, and how red her eyes were. Not wanting to cause her any embarrassment, he averted his eyes for a couple of seconds. Then, standing up again, he looked straight at her, and coughed.

'Ma'am, you don't seem too good to me? There's a lot of it about.'

Cadema looked up at him, her face emotionless. 'A lot of what?'

'Tummy upsets, or something.' He shrugged.

'Don't insinuate illness, when there isn't any.' She took a deep breath. Pratt remained standing. 'As a matter of fact, I've discussed the case and it has been agreed.' Her voice was bland. She decided not to mention plan B or C, as he only needed to know about the initial business case.

'That's excellent news, so when will you be leaving. Not too soon I hope as there are lots of things I need to discuss with you first.' He sounded relieved and sat down in front of her again.

Cadema sat upright, swallowed and looked directly at him. 'I'm not going.'

'Excuse me,' said Pratt who sounded annoyed and frustrated. 'You said they both agreed with your proposal, so what's the problem?'

'I told them that someone else should go in my place. And as you said you might be interested, well…'

Pratt pushed his chair backwards and stood up. There was thunder in his whole face. 'I obviously gave you the wrong message then. It was just a throwaway comment, not a fact. I'd no intention of going then. And I don't have any intention of going now.' His voice raised as he punched his index finger towards the ground. He began to pace the floor, when he passed Cadema, he stopped and gave her a loathsome stare.

'There's no need for that attitude, or place for melodramatics. Just sit down and I'll explain,' said Cadema authoritatively.

'Sorry Ma'am, I'm just a bit angry that you haven't discussed it with me first. You just seemed to think I would go.'

Despite what Pratt had just said, she saw someone she hadn't seen before. His nostrils flaring, and the clenched fist. This was a man who could lose control, and his temper too. She watched as his fist sprang open at his side. She took a deep breath.

'I think you had better leave this room for a while, stand outside and take several breaths. Then, and only when you have calmed down you can come back and we can talk things over in a rational civilised way.' Cadema's voice was calm, but she emphasised every syllable. As Pratt got up to leave, she recalled what Jim Logan had said:

"Don't show any anger, it will only lead to a conflagration of emotions that will burn for eternity" – Jim was always right.

Reaching the door, Pratt took an intake of breath as if he were about to step into that fire. Glancing back at her, he gave her a strange look then walked out of the room.

Cadema sat back in her chair, her head leaning on the soft cushion; eyes fixed – staring into the abyss. An instant later they were closed. She slowly breathed in, filling her lungs to capacity. She breathed slowly out until every molecule of air was drawn from the dead space within. Every breath was controlled. Every muscle relaxed; the tension oozed from her body. Her demeanour calm. Her worries melted away. She took control. In her transient state, between consciousness and total absorption, she began floating upwards and upwards towards the clouds. Eventually she reached them; fluffy, white, serene. Her breathing – now shallow. Time – no consequence. Listless she floated, her hand casually drifting across the blue. A vessel in the sky of liquidity. Silently, safely, she drifted on – cocooned in a fluffy-white suit. Immune to everything – everyone. Calm. Restful. In a moment or two, she must return; slowly. Her landing must be controlled; serene. Downwards she went. Now she could feel the cold, her office, her chair. Still her eyes were closed. She savoured the moment.

Suddenly, in the distance, she heard something. Vague at first, then louder and louder. It didn't belong in the world she was in. It was alien. She tried to ignore it – it was relentless. Then, at that instant, she felt the switch in her mind trip. She was back in reality, sitting in her chair, in her office, at her desk; her telephone ringing. Trance-like she opened her eyes and reached for it. It stopped. In the distance she heard urgent footsteps, they came closer and closer to her office. Her door slammed against the stop. The figure of a man she knew stood in a haze at the doorway.

'Cadema,' he shouted. 'Are you all right?' said Andrew as he rushed towards her. She blinked and sat upright.

'Of course I'm all right. What's the matter?' She suppressed a yawn. 'Sorry, I've been up most of the night – just a little tired that's all.'

'Thank goodness,' said Andrew exhaling loudly. 'It's just that Pratt said you seemed a bit "out of it". And when you didn't answer your phone; you know what I mean.'

'He did, did he? Well as you can see, I'm perfectly okay. I asked Pratt to leave as he was being obnoxious. And rather than get angry, I decided to have a break.'

'Tell me then, what did he do to cause the problem?'

'As I said, he was obnoxious.' Cadema shrugged. 'It may have been a misunderstanding, and I overreacted. I'll handle it. Just let him in.'

'If you're sure? If not, I'll remain if you wish.'

'Thank you, Andrew, but that won't be necessary. I'll managed the situation in my own way.' Cadema gave a dismissive smile as Andrew shook his head slowly and headed for the door.

Turning again, Andrew was poised to speak as Cadema asked him to give her a few minutes before sending Pratt in to see her. Andrew nodded and left.

Washing her face and saying a prayer, Cadema opened her office door. Pratt was sitting on a chair in the corridor. She nodded for him to enter. As he did so, she realised she had to handle him very differently from the rest of her team. She had pushed him over the edge in not asking him what he thought before she assumed he would be delighted in going to Australia. From now on, she would consult him before making decisions that would affect his whole life. Going to Australia was one of those decisions. Nevertheless, she had not expected such an adverse reaction from him.

As Pratt sat facing her, she sensed the tension between them. He offered a brief smile – his face bland. She swallowed, then looked at him.

'I believe you were concerned with my welfare?'

'I can…'

'There wasn't anything to be concerned about,' interrupted Cadema. 'In fact, I think we both needed to take a break. Now we've had time to reflect, let's get on with things. I'll forget what happened earlier if you can guarantee that it won't happen again.'

'It won't. I just lost my cool, that's all. And you have my word that it won't reoccur. Besides that, I was thinking earlier, why don't we discuss this in a civilised manner over dinner perhaps.' Pratt sat back in the chair; crossing his arms over his chest he gave a conceited smile.

Now, Cadema was not with a colleague, but with a man. A probable admirer, or a predator, she didn't know which?

She frowned, brushed her hair from her shoulders, and sat, confrontational-style, before him.

'That is out of the question,' said Cadema as she experienced a hot flush and then shuffled in her chair. Pondering on what to say next.

'If you're too busy, how about lunch?' Pratt interrupted her thoughts. 'There's a café down the road.'

Cadema looked at her watch. It wasn't the time of the day that bothered her, or that she was too busy. It was just that he had the audacity to ask her out.

'I suppose, we could have afternoon tea?' she swallowed. 'I don't usually do that, but under the circumstances.'

'I'd much prefer dinner,' he interjected assertively.

'Oh no, afternoon tea, or nothing.' Cadema stood up and took her coat from the hook on the door. Pratt followed, finally leaving the building together.

Finding a suitable table for two in a quiet corner, Cadema ordered tea and cakes. Sitting quietly waiting for their order to arrive, she noticed how cosy the café was. Old fashioned in a way, with similar tablecloths she had seen in some Victorian house museums. For some reason, she felt at home as the tea arrived.

Pratt apologised about his reactions earlier, saying it was just a one-off and would never happen again.

'Okay, there's no time for reprimands, so let's move on.' She took a gulp of tea.

'Yes, I've come to that conclusion. And on reflection I think your idea of me going to Oz in your place, is a good one. I can go as soon as I've arranged some personal things which will only take a few days; if that's okay with you?'

'That will be okay, however, it's not just up to me. So, until I have permission for you to go, we'll have to be patient.' She gave a grimace of a smile, trying not to encourage him in any way. He had asked her out to dinner. She wanted a collegial relationship, nothing more. Besides, there was Haady to consider.

Pratt nodded, then forked at his angel cake. Driving it around and around the plate – deep in thought. Finally, he looked at Cadema:

'It's a pity they didn't have CCTV or VIVA back in those days, or even wireless, then who knows, the killer would have been caught then.'

Cadema smiled and thought of HOLMES, Home Office Large Major Enquiry System. Then she explained about her theory; that the UK and Australian authorities must have known who the killer was.

'When they notified the authorities in England,' she added, 'they must have agreed to sentence him to life imprisonment. And to him serving his sentence in Australia. I Think that is why the London police stopped looking for him so soon after the murders, and why he was never caught here.'

'That sounds a reasonable theory,' said Pratt. 'However, what makes you believe that we will be able to find him now. There may still be blocks on the records. So we may never be able to discover what really happened to him.'

'I've considered that possibility,' said Cadema condescendingly. 'However, I still need to see it though; hopefully we will discover the truth. Anyway, we need to get back to the station and to work.' Cadema asked for the bill, then let Pratt pay.

Chapter 32

'Yes Andrew,' said Cadema into her mobile phone, as she rubbed her wet hair in the towel, and gave a quiet smile. Now she was in control; nothing would upset her again. 'I'll be in soon.'

'No problem. When you do arrive, there's something I want you to see.' He placed a printed email on his desk.

Finishing the call, he busied himself with the mound of paperwork on his desk. Engrossed in it all, he almost missed the quiet tap on his office door. Frowning, and inclining his head to one side, he listened. 'Enter,' Andrew shouted. 'Good to see you, Cadema. Here, sit down and read this.' He pushed the email across the desk towards her.

'*Hi, McWilliams sent me your contact details,*' wrote Superintendent Saxley. '*I expect he told you that he knew me personally. Anyway, I've discussed your proposal with the Chief Constable. He's given the go-ahead. As for me, I'm originally from the Met, so I'll be on your wavelength, so to speak. I've left McWilliams working on the archives. If you send me the papers you have on the case, I'll see what I can find.*'

Signed: Gareth Saxley. Superintendent; NSW Police Headquarters, Parramatta.

'That's great, Andrew. I'll talk to him on Skype. And since DI Pratt has agreed to go there, he can also speak to Saxley. Once Pratt's there, hopefully he'll have the same positive support from the commissioner in Tasmania, that is, if John Ribley went there.'

'Let's hope Pratt gets his visa soon, so he can get going,' said Andrew, noticing that Cadema looked much better, especially since Pratt was going instead of her.

***

Four days later, Cadema heard the news. DI Pratt had been taken to hospital with a heart attack. As the blood seemed to drain from her body, she donned her coat and headed for the hospital.

'He's stabilized now, so you can see him for a couple of minutes, but that's all,' said Senior Nurse Banks in an authoritative whisper.

It was just as Cadema had imagined. Pratt was wired up to numerous contraptions measuring every breath, every heart beat and rhythm, pulse rate, and blood pressure. Through the haze of monitors and beeps, she could see he was conscious.

He nodded. His right hand waved, despite the tubes strapped to it. She returned his sombre smile and walked towards his bed.

Standing closely, she asked how he was. He nodded. From parched lips, he murmured he was okay and then drifted off to sleep. As she left the ward, she could still hear faint beeps from the monitor, while the smell of anaesthetic teased at her nostrils.

Outside, she stood for a moment slowly shaking her head – there's no way you can go now. As she headed for her parked car, she had already decided to continue with the investigation. Now she had to choose someone else to send to Australia.

***

'How is he?' said Andrew stepping into Cadema's office. 'Let's hope it's not too serious.'

'I think Pratt will be okay.' She took off her coat and hooked it at the back of the door. 'In a way, it's probably my fault,' she whispered.

'Nonsense, you're not to blame,' said Andrew harshly. 'After all, he was the one who took risks with his health. All that fast food and never exercising.'

'But the stress I probably put on him about the Australian trip.'

'That's nonsense, and you know it. I for one knew he wanted to go from the start. He was just winding you up. The whole station was talking about it. And were asking, behind your back, why you didn't you ask Marriott. It was rumoured that Pratt was ostracised when he agreed to go. I could not act on that as there was no proof. But if that didn't cause him stress, nothing would. And, as you and I know, Marriott was never really asked because he was studying for his inspector's exam.'

'Why didn't you tell me about this before,' said Cadema pacing the floor and taking deep breaths. 'If I'd known…'

'What could you have done?' demanded Andrew. 'Nothing. Anyway, you were also stressed.'

'I was not. Anyway this is not about me,' Cadema protested. 'I have a duty of care for my officers and now I feel responsible for Pratt's condition.' She continued to pace, faster and faster.

Andrew took hold of her shoulders and looked her in the face. 'Sit down. You're in no state now. Do your relaxation and I'll order some tea.' Andrew's word were spoken like an order, rather than a request.

'Tea's not the answer. I need to…'

'No, just sit.' He escorted her to a chair. 'Good. Now I'll handle the staff. You can postpone the investigation until

we've found a suitable officer who could go. Even Marriott?'
Andrew was firm but kind – caring.

Cadema took a tissue from the desk and blew her nose.
She had thought of asking Marriott, but what with his
divorce, the work and the studying, he too was stressed.
Perhaps that's what the job was all about – continuous stress.
Some self-imposed, some collegial, and some institutional.
There was nothing she could do about the first one, other
than counselling. But the other two…

'Marriott takes his exams next week,' said Cadema. 'I
could ask him after that.' She threw her tissue into the bin,
looked up and smiled.

'Good. I'm pleased to see that nothing's too complex for
you to solve. That's the spirit.'

***

Two weeks later everything had been settled; Marriott had
left for Australia. Twenty-four hours later, Cadema received
his text message.

'Ma'am, just stepped off the plane in Sydney. Feeling a
bit jet-lagged, despite sleep. Speak soon; Marriott.' He
pressed the send button with no idea what the time was back
in the UK.

Passing through border control, an excited dog sniffed at
Marriott momentarily then moved on. Standing at the
carousel for his luggage, he almost missed the second
suitcase as he transferred the first one to a trolley. Luggage
secured, he walked slowly through the customs area and into
the bottleneck of people being siphoned onto the concourse.
There, people with their relatives and friends, wailed,
screamed, laughed, hugged, and cried. Trolleys clattered,
watched by children's bewildered eyes.

'My, how you've grown,' said an obvious grandmother as she swept up a child of about five years old, from its seat on the pile of suitcases, and clutched the girl tightly in her arms. Marriott walked on.

"Harrison" was written on a board being held, head high, by a Chinese-looking man. Marriott kept on walking as he read the next boards. "Morris", "Wedekin family", "Maria Tollman". There was no board for him, but he hoped he would recognise McWilliams, and Saxley from talking to them on Skype.

He kept on walking. Cellophane-wrapped flowers and heart-shaped balloons mingled with the mêlée of heads that reminded him of the tail end of the Notting Hill carnival. All that was needed, he thought, was the steel band to authenticate it.

'Marriott.' He heard a voice in the distance. 'Marriott,' it was louder now. 'Marriott.' He turned and saw McWilliams waving in the crowd. Eventually they met.

'How you's goi'n.' said McWilliams vigorously shaking Marriott's hand, and smiling. 'This is Gareth Saxley.'

'Good to meet you,' said Marriott. 'I appreciate you picking me up.' He shook hands with Saxley.

'Good to meet you too,' said Saxley, towering over Marriott. Saxley's handshake was weak despite his large frame, with hands and feet to match. His receding grey hair, and thick eyebrows, along with his sallow completion, gave the impression that he was in his early fifties. Neatly dressed in a suit and tie, he stood military-like. Marriott wondered if he had been in the forces before joining the Met.

'How was the flight?' asked McWilliams, with the hint of a Scottish dialogue.

'Never been on a long-haul before. I guess it was okay, except now I need to freshen up and get some sleep.'

'No worries, that's what we'd expected. It'll take us about an hour to get to our destination. Then we'll leave you to sleep it off,' said McWilliams as he walked towards the airport exit door pushing the luggage trolley; Saxley and Marriott followed.

'By the way, let's cut the crap with formalities. You can call me Gareth, when out of the station that is. And McWilliams here, likes to be called Mac. What shall we call you?'

Marriott gave an embarrassed cough. 'I'm David.'

'Not Dave?' said Gareth. Marriott shook his head. 'That's settled then, David it is.'

As the three stepped outside, Marriott took a startled breath as his face caught the wall of heat. He stretched out his arms, took a deep breath, held his head backwards and whispered, 'Wonderful.'

'Thirty degrees,' said Mac. 'So I suppose it's hot to you.'

'We'll be heading for winter in a couple of month,' said Gareth. 'So, let's make the most of it while we can,' he added, racing towards the car park; Mac and Marriott did their best to keep up.

Having settled in the car with Gareth driving, they headed towards the city.

'I was going to show you the sights, but I can see you're dead beat,' said Mac. 'So we'll just drop you off at the hotel where you'll be able to get some kip. I'm heading off to the Beacon Hill after that. Gareth's going on to headquarters in Paramatta.'

Marriott stifled a yawn. Voices just faded in out. His head nodded as he jumped to wakefulness for a microsecond; his head nodded again as he tried to listen.

By the time they had reached their destination, Marriott was barely conscious. Helping him to book in to the hotel, and taking him to his room, they left him with a message to phone them once he had recovered.

On leaving, Gareth said he expected it would take him a couple of days to recover, and ordered him to rest and drink plenty of water.

Twenty-four hours later, Marriott was awake and alert, and having showered, was ready to do some work. Picking up the telephone, he pressed the numbers Mac had given him. Gareth answered immediately and said he would collect him and take him home for a barbeque.

Opening the curtains in the hotel room, Marriott was confronted by the most magnificent views he had ever seen. He blinked, turned, opened his suitcase and extracted his SLR. Standing at the window, he took several photographs of the panoramic view of the Sydney Harbour Bridge to his left, a flotilla of ships in the centre, and the magnificent Opera House on his right. Then, sitting motionless on his windowsill, he watched as a liner inched its way around the narrow waterways towards an estuary, which he assumed led to the sea.

The phone ringing made his whole body jump. The message was simple, so he picked up his coat, and his suitcases, and headed for the foyer where Gareth was waiting for him.

Gareth greeted him with a frown. 'It's thirty degrees out there, mate, so you won't be needing that,' he nodded to the coat. 'But you can leave it in the car.'

Marriott smiled and said thank you as Gareth explained that, on his way home, he would drive around the city and show him the sights.

'Then we'll head for the Hills; Beacon Hill to be precise. Everyone's dying to meet you.'

Marriott nodded, said thank you, then realised that he was still a little jet-lagged.

'Don't worry, a couple of beers and a good T-bone will sort you out. I know, I've done the trip many times.'

The one storey house in Beacon Hill was like all the others in the area with surrounding gardens which Gareth called 'The back yard'. Marriott could not help but notice the parched ground as he stepped out of the car. Despite this, each one had cultivated neatly cropped green lawns and borders of mixed flowers, some of which he didn't recognise.

Having been introduced to Gareth's wife, Angela, Marriott followed Gareth, along with his luggage, across the veranda, through an outer-meshed door, through the stained-wooden front door, and into the hallway. As a traffic police officer might, Gareth signposted to where the lounge, the dining room, bathroom and the bedrooms were. Then, dragging the suitcases, they entered a bedroom at the end of the corridor on the right.

'We've put you in here,' said Gareth. 'Feel free to make yourself comfortable. If you need to go to bed at any time, we don't stand on ceremony, just do as you need.'

Marriott nodded, and entered the room, saying he needed to change. Gareth nodded, and told him to make his way back along the corridor towards the rear of the house where everyone will meet him, when he was ready.

Half an hour later, Marriott headed along the corridor in the direction of people talking and laughing. Six smiling faces greeted him as he stepped through the back door and onto a veranda. His hosts, Gareth and Angela and their two grown-up children, Sarah and Boyce greeted him. Both had inherited their father's trait for height. A woman and man in their late forties, were sitting together on the couch. The women, Beatrice – sipping red wine and giggling. The man, Doug, drinking from a bottle of beer, a "stubby" he called it.

As soon as Marriott had been given their names, he filed them away in his brain, never to be forgotten. He smiled to himself, wondering where he should sit.

'Here, have a beer.' Gareth handed him a stubby. 'Must get back to the cooking though – just mingle as you can. We're all informal here.'

At the sound of the doorbell, a Labrador sprang into action. Barking like a ferocious demon and wagging his tail, he slid along the tiled floor leading to the front door.

'It's only Mac, you stupid creature,' shouted Gareth as Angela excused herself to let the visitor in. A stubby in his hand, Mac, along with his partner Clara, joined them. Marriott took a seat next to Mac, as Clara walked off with Gareth towards the barbecue.

During the meal Marriott, having only had one beer, felt light headed. By ten o'clock he had difficulty in concentrating, or even hearing what was being discussed. So, after answering some questions, he apologised for having to say good night so early, and then went to his room. Having had a shower, he fell into bed – exhausted.

A light tapping on his door woke him from a dreamless sleep.

'Sorry to wake you but it's eight-thirty,' said Gareth. 'I'm off to work. If you're up to it, you can join me so we can get on with the investigation.'

Marriott jumped out of bed and mumbled that he would be ready in a few minutes. Washed and dressed, Marriott appeared at the breakfast bar fifteen minutes later.

Setting out for Parramatta, across the Harbour Bridge, Marriott was amazed at the amount of traffic for the time of the day.

'What do you expect, after all it's a city. Just like London's rush hour and lasts all day here, too.'

Marriott didn't take much notice of what Gareth had said, he was too engrossed with the view of the Opera House on his left and the sky-scrapers in front of him as they crossed the Harbour Bridge.

'Lovely, isn't it? And if you look up, through the car's glass roof, you may be able to see the climbers on top of the bridge.'

Marriott leaned back as far as his neck, and the seatbelt, would allow. 'I can't see anyone.'

'Never mind, David, you'll have plenty of opportunities to see them another time. And if I can arrange it, we may be able to go up there ourselves. Taking into consideration that climbs are usually booked months, and sometimes years, in advance. But if they can squeeze us in sometime...'

Marriott shivered at the thought.

Travelling along the Great Western Highway, he read signs to places he was familiar with back in England. Surry Hills, Burwood, Enfield, Guilford and many more. Probably depicting the places where the early settlers came from, he reasoned. Then, closing his eyes, his mind drifting off.

'Hey, you with me mate?' Gareth's voice jolted him back. 'Here we are, so get a grip, we've got a lot of work to do.'

Marriott yawned, stretched his body and said he was ready for anything.

Chapter 33

Having introduced Marriott to his office staff, Gareth took out a file from the cabinet and laid them on the desk.

'This is the one I think you'll find interesting,' said Gareth, opening a bulging file and extracting a faded, flimsy piece of paper. 'Here we are. Your John Ribley was kept at Darlinghurst Prison. This says he spent nearly a year there.' He handed the paper to Marriott as delicately as his corpulent fingers would allow.

'I think this is his transfer paper to Port Arthur, and that letter, which was pinned to it originally, explains why he was sent there.' Marriott picked up the letter and began to read it.

The heading read: "Top Secret:1890"

Although the prison at Port Arthur is officially closed, and has been so since 1877, it still houses, in one wing, two political prisoners. These two prisoners, who shall not be named here, cannot be released due to national security reasons. There are six armed officers stationed there. They have been given orders to shoot if either of these said prisoners try to escape. The place is administered by two civilian staff. All staff have signed the Official Secrets Act. The wing will remain open until both prisoners have lived out their natural lives. When John Temple Ribley arrives, the officers will treat him the same as the other two prisoners. As the remaining parts of the prison are almost derelict, no one is aware of this wing being used. I have assigned three officers to escort the said John Temple Ribley to Port Arthur with immediate effect. They will be leaving at high tide tomorrow.

Signed Governor Kershaw.

'Do you know who the letter was addressed to?' said Marriott, 'or why it was written?'

Gareth shook his head. 'No idea. But at least we have proof that he was due to go there. Whether we can find proof that he arrived at Port Arthur, well that's another matter. Alternatively, he may have gone there, then later moved to somewhere else.'

Marriott gave Gareth a startled look. 'Let's hope that he *did* go there, and that he stayed there,' said Marriott.

'Yes, and there's another hope to consider.' Gareth frowned and shook his head. 'The sea around the Bass Straits is treacherous, irrespective of the time of the year. Hundreds of ships have foundered there in storms of hurricane proportions. You must have heard of the Sydney to Hobart Yacht Race?' Marriott nodded. 'As I recall, back in 1998 five yachts sank – six people were killed.'

'That's awful. I hope nothing happened to the ship we are looking for?' said Marriott despondently.

'There's only one way to find out,' added Gareth. 'That's to go there.' Gareth sat back in his chair with his hands linked across the back of his head. Then, turning his head towards the door, a smile appeared across his face as McWilliams entered.

'Hi all,' Mac blundered in – rubbing his hands together. 'Wonderful news.' He took an A4 wallet from under his arm. 'Oh sorry, good day,' Then he took a piece of paper from the wallet. 'Here we are. The passenger list from the steamship *SS Talune* when it docked in Hobart in January 1890.' Laying the paper on the desk, he pointed to the name Ribley. 'And accompanying him were three police officers, DS Glover, PC Richmond and PC Laurence.'

Gathering the papers together, they agreed to fly to Hobart as soon as it was logistically possible. Gareth would contact Superintendent Edward Baker in Hobart, whom he had met at a conference in Melbourne.

Marriott decided to sit in a quiet room and contact Cadema by Sataline, the new IT communication system, and update her on their progress. He switched on his tablet.

'Good evening, Ma'am. If my calculation is correct, we're eleven hours in front of you?'

'Yes, good morning. So, what's the news, Marriott?'

'We've managed to find out where Ribley ended up.' Marriott smiled at Cadema on his screen. He noticed how tired she looked, but decided not to comment. Instead he explained what had been found and that they were going to Tasmania.

'That's great news, just keep with it. I've got something for you too.' She explained that John Ribley studied to become an apothecary, but that he never completed the course. However, he would have studied anatomy. And, as his father was a registered apothecary, he may have learned from him too.

'That's why we couldn't find an address for his business,' said Cadema. 'But we did find records that suggest he was working with midwives at the time. And could have lived in, or near, Old Montague Street.'

After saying that she would look forward to hearing what they found in Tasmania. A few exchanges of personal interests, they said goodbye.

Cadema switched off her computer, and drained her glass of Merlot. Haady poured her another drink. Their glasses chinked together, and they kissed.

***

358

Stepping off the plane at Hobart, Gareth shivered and put on his coat. Clearing border control and customs, they entered the concourse. Gareth shivered again.

'Don't look like that at me, Mac, it's at least fifteen degrees colder here than Sydney,' said Gareth as he began to wave his hands above his head and the crowds. 'There he is, I'd recognise him anywhere.'

Marriott craned, then noticed a man of a similar height and frame as Gareth, waving back. Striding closer, the man now resembled John Wayne, the actor, including the hat. But unlike Gareth, he wore a short-sleeved shirt, and no coat.

'Hi it's great to see you again,' said Superintendent Edward Baker as he took Gareth's hand firmly.

'Great to see you too,' replied Gareth then turned to Marriott and Mac. 'These are the guys I was telling you about.'

As they walked and talked trivialities, they agreed to use first names except when at official meetings, or with lower-ranked officers at police headquarters. Superintendent Edward Baker preferred to be called Ted, he agreed to use Gareth, Mac and David.

As Ted drove to the police headquarters, he explained that he was trying to keep everything from the media for the time being.

'Anyway,' said Ted, 'I've found something interesting. But I'm going to keep you in suspense until we reach my office. That's only seventeen kilometres, so it won't take more than half an hour.'

'Typical of you, secretive to the end,' said Gareth laughing. The banter continued until they reached their destination.

***

Pulling into the car park, Marriott noticed that the police headquarters resembled the ones in England. Probably built in the sixties, it stood about nine storeys high. He had smiled when he saw *Liverpool Street*, and then *Argyle Street*. He would have liked to discover its history, but knew there was no time to do so.

Ted's office was about the same size as Cadema's, with a formal seating area with upright chairs and table for meeting. Two armchairs and a coffee table in another section, and a desk with two chairs, in another area.

After ordering coffee, Ted unlocked his filing cabinet and took out a battered cardboard shoe box. Removing the lid, he carefully placed the box on the coffee table and sat in one of the armchairs.

'Well, don't stand on ceremony – pull up a pew.'

'Come on Ted, tell us what you've found,' said Gareth as he sat in the other armchair as Mac and Marriott scraped two formal chairs across the floor.

'Hey, careful with that. This new flooring cost a bomb.'

Saying sorry, they sat and then leaned forward.

'Not yet, we need to wait for the coffee first. Then I'll show you.'

'Don't play games with us,' said Gareth with a hint of sarcasm. 'You can at the very least let us know what's inside?'

'Only when we have the coffee. You never know with these things.'

'Don't be ridiculous, it's not top secret. Just tell us.' said Gareth – his voice angry.

Ted raised his eyebrows just as the coffee arrived. Thanking the courier, he looked at Gareth. 'You know the prison, Port Arthur, was closed in 1877. And you said you have evidence that this Ribley guy was a prisoner there in 1890. I *know* he was – this box contains the evidence,' said Ted excitedly.

Gareth took a deep breath, his face crimson. Marriott and Mac leaned forward.

'You mean to say…' exclaimed Gareth.

'Let me finish,' said Ted. 'I don't know if he died there, or if he was discharged. But if he died there, then he's buried on the island.'

'The Isle of the Dead, you mean?' said Mac jumping up – eyes bulging.

'It's a possibility,' answered Ted. 'But there are no grave markings there for prisoners. And I haven't discovered any burial records, yet.'

'Come on then, no more delays, what's in the box, Ted?' said Gareth as if he were interrogating a suspect.

Ted stood up, donned a pair of cotton gloves, opened the box and took out a sheet of paper.

'This confirms Ribley was there. It lists his belongings and is signed by the governor general, so it's genuine. As it's damaged – I'll read it to you.' Ted opened the paper.

- *Prisoner Name, John Temple Ribley. Date of birth, first June 1856.*
- *Next of kin, unknown.*
- *Prisoner's belongings transferred from Darlinghurst Prison, New South Wales;*
- *One wallet containing five English pounds fifteen shillings and three pennies.*
- *One silk scarf.*
- *One silver and embossed plated snuffbox containing three brass rings, of no value.*

Marriott inhaled sharply, jumped up and stood over the open box.

'The snuffbox, where is it?' demanded Marriott. No one spoke as he picked up the empty box. 'The rings…'

'Calm down, David, the box was like this when it was found. There's no sign of the snuffbox or the rings,' said Ted quietly. 'Anyway what's all the fuss about? They were only brass rings; the snuffbox would be much more valuable.'

Marriott lowered his head and returned to his seat. Sitting quietly for a couple of minutes, he gradually explained about the significance of the rings. That three had been torn from the finger of Annie Chapman, and one had been found in the false grave in London. The killer had written in the notebooks that the other two rings would be found in his grave, along with another ring he took off Ethel Redberry's finger when he murdered her; three rings in total.

The officers all agreed that this was the most important fact that they had. Ted said he would authorise another search of the archives for the rings and for evidence which could identify where Ribley eventually died.

Two days later, a note was found. Written by one of the guards at Port Arthur, mentioning, that, when Ribley died, he was to be buried with his three brass rings. Apparently, he said that the rings had belonged to his mother, and that the authorities had agreed to his request. Ted agreed that the note was useful, but that it did not prove that Ribley died in the prison.

Marriott contacted Cadema again and explained what had been found. During the conversation with her, and the candid way she reacted, Marriott wondered if there was someone with her that she didn't want him to see. Or had she discovered something else about the case that she didn't want to tell him?

Chapter 34

'Yes, Mother, one of my officers took my place and went to Australia,' said Cadema. 'So I'm delighted you're coming home.' Cadema decided not to mention that she had found a partner. She didn't need to know, just in case it didn't work out. Nevertheless, she was almost sure he was the one, and tonight she was determined to find out if he felt the same way.

The smell of the tandoori chicken filled the house with an aroma of cooking – not experienced since her mother left for India some months before. Now it was like home again. But there was a hint of guilt in her elation at cooking for a man again. Since her husband... she glanced at his photograph. Reaching for a tissue, she dabbed her nose with the reassurance that she had to move on. Haady was helping her to do just that.

He liked tandoori chicken – so cooking it for him was like a thank you. And besides, instead of buying the usual bottle of Merlot, she lashed-out on a bottle of *Châteauneuf-du-Pap*, his favourite wine. And he, like her, only drank on special occasions; tonight, was that occasion – accepting the decadence.

As the doorbell rang, she lifted her sari as she rushed along the corridor, only stopping for a second at the mirror to tidy her hair. *Just in time*, she thought as she looked at her watch. Untangling Cameo from her ankles, she opened the door.

'Sorry to disturb you, Ma'am.' The police constable removed her hat. 'We've been trying to contact you – seems your telephone's out of order, and your mobile's off.'

'So that's why I've had no calls. But what's the problem?'

'There's been a shooting. The deputy commissioner sent me to take you to the scene. Armed robbery, I think.' She nodded towards the awaiting police car. 'I'll wait until you've changed, Ma'am.' The officer turned and walked away.

Haady, a bunch of flowers in hand, was crossing the road – his smile receding as he got closer to Cadema, she stepped onto the porch to greet him.

'Don't tell me. I can see that you've been summoned to go to something urgent. These jobs can play havoc with your social life,' said Haady handing her the flowers.

'Thank you, they're lovely. And roses, you shouldn't have.'

'Well I have, so no recriminations,' said Haady as they stepped inside the hallway – he closed the door.

'What a lovely smell. And you dressed for the occasion. How did you know my favourite colour is blue?' He smiled and gave her a kiss on her cheek.

'I think you mentioned it once. Anyway, I'm sorry but I'll have to go. You know how long these things take, but I'll be back as quickly as possible. Just help yourself to dinner.' Cadema stepped into her bedroom to change. On leaving she asked him to feed the cat.

***

Arriving at the murder scene, Superintendent Christine Ryan, from another division was there. After a few exchanges about how Ryan was getting on since leaving Cadema's team. Ryan briefed her about the armed robbery. That one of the duo had been shot dead by armed officers. The other was hidden behind the parked car and taking shots at anything that moved.

Doctor Julia Lilly, already dressed in her forensic suit, greeted Cadema as she approached her in the safety zone. Although Cadema was dressed in her usual working clothes in the form of a dark blue trouser suit, Julia noticed something else.

'I know you haven't made up just for me,' Julia smiled. 'So who's it for? Haady I presume?' said Julia teasingly.

'Right as usual. But I don't want anyone to...' Cadema whispered as a shot rang out. 'Better keep our heads down, or we'll be next.' She settled next to Julia behind a parked car.

'I did manage to have a quick look at the body over there. He's been shot in the chest at close range; died instantly. But when the bullets started hissing...'

'Very wise,' said Cadema with an air of sarcasm.

'Anyway, Ryan seems okay with the situation, so I suggest you go home and enjoy...'

Julia was right, she should go home. But it wasn't fair to leave Ryan. It wasn't her division, and Cadema needed to relieve her and take control. Besides there were other officers present from Cadema's division, some of whom had never been at a shooting before, and would need her support.

And now, over three years since her boss, Jim Logan, was shot by the sniper, Cadema didn't want anyone else to end up the same way. No, she had to stay, it was her duty. She told Ryan what she intended to do. She frowned at first, said she was happy to stay, but knew it wasn't the best idea to have two superintendents at one incident. And especially when there were more than enough officers present already.

At that moment, the sound of a single shot caused everyone to cower further towards the floor. Cadema, Julia and Ryan, held their breath. Silence. They breathed again – waiting.

Something metallic clattered on the ground. A creature screeched – they jumped, then sighed as the perpetrator, in the form of a stray cat, sprang passed.

'All clear,' a senior armed officer called out.

Cadema took up her duties. Then the sound of running feet, shouts, scuffles, and officers sprinting towards some figure across the tarmac. Then everyone resumed their previous roles. Three hours later, Cadema left with Julia and Ryan, leaving the remaining officers to manage the scene.

Entered her living room, she smiled. The smell of the food still lingering, and there, fast asleep on her sofa was Haady – Cameo on his lap. Tiptoeing, she sat on another chair watching him breath. Such a gentle breathing, his face serene, child-like. When the cat began to stir, she moved to the kitchen, the cat followed.

On seeing the note on the kitchen table, she began to read:

I decided to wait until we could eat the meal together, so I've put it in the fridge. She smiled, poured herself a glass of water, and quietly went upstairs to bed. Her relationship with Haady would have to be put on hold for a while – hopefully not for too long though.

Sitting in bed with her laptop on, she saw the message from Marriott. Reading about the rings, she smiled, snuggled down, and fell asleep.

Chapter 35

Superintendent Edward Baker, Ted to his close associates, screamed with excitement when he heard the news. He had been right all along and his tenacity to find it had eventually paid off. Now he was holding the paper that would lead to the actual burial site of the most notorious killer in history. All he had to do was to persuade the magistrate, Antonio Fusconi, to grant permission for an exhumation.

It sounded easy to anyone who didn't know Fusconi. No one, not even the commissioner, could make him agree to anything without lengthy debates and miles of red-tape. Although a little insignificant man on the surface, it was reputed that he could kill a kangaroo with this bare hands. Not that there were any kangaroos around to refute this – perhaps that was the reason?

Was the paper genuine? If there was a microdot of doubt, Fusconi would explode and then chastise the holder for wasting his time.

Ted hoped it were genuine, but he had doubts. Could they have made a mistake? Perhaps Marriott was right about a cover-up between the British and the Australian Governments when John Temple Ribley arrived in Sydney. The paper could have been written to divert suspicion? Speculation perhaps? But Ted knew there was always a hint of truth in any speculation. Nevertheless, he had to accept that the paper was genuine – there were no official records to refute it. Sitting at his desk, he began to write the exhumation request.

Next morning Gareth, Max and Marriott were ensconced in Ted's office. Gareth noticed that Ted, who had drained two plastic beakers of water in the last few minutes, looked flushed and agitated. Perhaps it was the heat, although Gareth still maintained it was cold despite the fire-ban there.

'Thanks for coming so promptly,' said Ted taking another drink and turning on the fan. 'Air conditioning's on the blink as usual.' He offered water to everyone.

'Thanks,' said Gareth. 'Now let's get on with things, otherwise I'll think I'm in one of those Agatha Christie novels, where everyone gathers togethers to hear the name of the killer.' He grinned.

Ted coughed, took another drink, then withdrew an A4 size file from his desk drawer. Opening it up, he spun it round so the others could read the paper he had placed on the desk. 'This is the document we found in the national archives,' he said, sitting back in his chair. 'It was in one of the stacks that hadn't been looked in before. It was probably filed after the last prisoners died at Port Arthur.'

The group moved closer, stood up and peered at the neat handwriting. Despite a few brown spots, and the obvious hallmarks of mites, the paper was decipherable. It was arranged in horizontal and vertical columns, each horizontal one carried a number on the left-hand side. The first was 6172, then 6173 and finally 6174, the rest of the page was blank. Headings on the top of the vertical lines identified the name, age, and any other information required. There were no names beside the first two numbers. They all agreed that they must have been the two political prisoners. The last one was John Temple Ribley. Further information revealed that Ribley died in 1902 and was buried on the island in grave number 6174.

'So, you're all as wise as I am now,' said Ted – his face relaxed, and he had stopped drinking the water.

After explaining about the exhumation request, and his appointment with the magistrate, Antonio Fusconi, in an hours' time, all three decided to go with Ted, "for moral support".

As soon as they entered Fusconi's office, Ted sensed the hostile atmosphere. Persuading the little figure, sitting behind an enormous desk, was going to be a challenge – Ted had to win.

With hardly any introductions, Ted slid the document onto the table until it was directly in front of Fusconi's eyes.

'You mean to tell me this is all you've got?' said Fusconi, his face red – cheeks bulging.

'That's all you need according to the request form,' answered Ted, holding back his anger at such an outburst.

'No, I won't agree to it, not like this. You need more proof. How would you feel if it were one of your relatives? Disturbing the sleep of someone deserves much more than this.' He picked up the paper flung it across his desk.

Ted took in a deep breath, his eyes penetrating into Fusconi's brain. 'It's not *my* relative, or *yours*. But think of this; *it* could have been one of your relatives who was a victim of this unscrupulous murderer. Wouldn't *you* want to know, without *any* doubt, the name of the perpetrator?'

'Even if you had a map, showing the exact spot where a pot of gold is buried, I would not budge from my decision without more proof.'

'Excuse me,' interjected Gareth. 'This *is* proof, the only proof there is. Our police services, and the Met in London, have together invested thousands to discover the truth. You're surely not going to stand in our way, now that we're on the brink of solving, what is considered to be, the most notorious murders ever committed?' Gareth spoke quietly, but with emphasis on every word.

The room went silent. Fusconi examined each face one by one. His dark eyes bulging, his mouth an ovoid chasm. Such an obnoxious man they had never encountered before.

Fusconi knew every argument – every counter argument, that had ever been written – he invented others. He knew the law as if he had written it himself. He guarded everything, as if it were his. He trusted no one. Everyone was corrupt, he wasn't going to budge. Even when Gareth argued that Fusconi was appointed by the state, and could be removed from office, he still held onto his belief that he was the guardian of humanity, and that was that.

It was only when Ted suggested that Fusconi should go to Port Arthur and visit the island, that his attitude mellowed for nearly a minute – his red complexion – blanched. Smiling, he sat in his copious chair like a child in a forbidden place. In a microsecond, he changed again sitting upright and bellowed.

'No, I won't go. I cannot go. It's sacrilegious – that's what it is, sacrilegious. To walk on someone's grave is blasphemy, let alone open it. This is the Devil's work. No, it's out of the question.' His face returned to its scarlet colour – eyes bulging.

'The Devil,' exclaimed Ted. 'How dare you. You're totally irrational.' Ted stood up, said he was leaving and headed for the door – his three colleagues followed, leaving Fusconi sitting smugly at his desk.

An hour later Ted spoke to the commissioner on the telephone.

'I realised you're annoyed, Ted,' said the commissioner, 'Fusconi *is* adamant. But I see what you mean about his attitude. Perhaps he's having some kind of breakdown. Leave it with me and I'll have a word with a psychiatrist friend of mine. He may be able to give some advice.'

The following morning Ted burst into the meeting room where his colleagues were waiting. 'We've got it. Permission for the exhumation, that is,' he said, waving the paper in the air.

'How on earth did you wangle that out of him?' asked Gareth.

'I didn't. Antonio Fusconi is in hospital. A suspected brain tumour they say; poor fella.'

'Yes, but at least he's in good hands.' Gareth could not think of anything else to say. The big "C", as he called it, had always been a problem to him.

By the end of that day, everything was arranged for their journey to Port Arthur for the following morning. Ted had completed his implementation plan for the exercise. He had organised the car for the journey, the ferryman who would be ready to take them to the island when they arrived. The ground scanning equipment was on its way, and the forensic team had been informed and would be mobilised once the grave had been located. The local police would help, and a priest was ready when needed. Two local gravediggers would be hired at the last minute as Ted didn't want the media to get wind of it. 'The least people that knew about it, the better.'

***

Having retired for the evening, Marriott set his alarm for six thirty. Hours later, he looked at his bedside clock – seven o'clock; his alarm hadn't worked. There was only half an hour to get ready. Showered and dressed, he turned on the radio.

'Breaking news,' said the female announcer. 'The famous murderer, Jack the Ripper, has been found in Tasmania. Jack cut the throats of at least five women, almost decapitating them, in London in 1888. One of our reporters is at the scene.'

'What the hell? How did that happen?' Marriott screamed at the radio. Then he decided to contact Cadema and tell her. He looked at his watch but could not remember if England was eleven hours or nine hours behind. He decided to call her anyway.

'Yes Ma'am, it's all over the news here, what about over there?'

'Not yet but I expect it will be soon. Wait a second.' She turned on her television. 'Nothing yet, as I can see.' She was just about to switch it off again when the BBC made the announcement. 'How on earth did they find out? Have you found Ribley and not told me?' She sounded angry.

After explaining that they had not found Ribley, he told her about the arrangements Ted had made, saying that they were all going to Port Arthur soon. But since hearing the news, things may change; he would let her know.

'That's all well and good,' said Cadema, 'but no doubt I'll have the Ripperologists knocking at my door when they discover what's happening.'

'Things will be difficult here too, Ma'am, especially as the press will indulge themselves in one of the biggest scoops of their careers.'

Cadema agreed and added that if the press flooded the scene, it would hinder their progress.

As he said goodbye, Marriott heard someone banging on his door. Opening it slightly, Gareth burst in, his eyes bulging and his nostrils wide.

'Have you seen...?' he yelled.

'Yes. Terrible,' replied Marriott calmly.

'Ted's wild. He's gone to the commissioner hoping to stop the press before they get there. He wants to set up road blocks – not too difficult considering there's only one major road there. He also wants to mobilise the military, and close the port. Talk about closing the stable door…'

'I know what you mean,' agreed Marriott. We'll just have to see what happens.'

***

Ted took a deep breath then barged into the commissioner's office. Standing to attention, and refusing to sit, he explained the situation and his solution to it.

Nodding on occasions, the commissioner sat back in his chair, and listened.

'Have you finished, Ted?' asked the commissioner.

Ted took a breath. 'Yes.'

'Then I can say that I agree wholeheartedly with all you've said but if the press are already there, I fear your plans are too late.'

'No, they're not,' emphasised Ted. 'There here, in Hobart; not at Port Arthur. So we can definitely stop them. Don't forget the eyes of the world will be upon us. We must do this right. We can't if we're crowded by the press. And there'll be hordes of sightseers.'

'In that case, you're in charge. Do what you think is right,' said the commissioner dismissively. 'In budget mind,' he added as Ted thanked him and then left.

By early afternoon, Ted had mobilised all he could, and contacted everyone from his implementation plan saying everything was still going ahead. That he would meet them in Port Arthur; three hours later than the original time.

On the journey, Marriott was fascinated by the terrain as he looked through the window of the four-by-four as they travelled along the main highway – A3. Once out of the city, across the bridge over the River Derwent, he noticed the airport and then a golf course. Soon after this, he held his breath as the car headed out towards a vast stretch of water. Here the highway metamorphosed into, what Marriott could only describe as a concrete platform, that stretched beyond the horizon. The Tasman highway, still the A3, became the "Tasman Bridge", announced Ted. Marriott closed his eyes hoping they would traverse the bridge quickly as he listened to Ted's account of the disaster in 1975 when a section of the bridge was hit by a ship and the bridge split in two, killing six people.

The looming disaster in Marriott's mind was soon abated when they reached the safety of "Midway Point"; a spear of land in the middle of, what appeared to be, a vast ocean. Marriott breathed a sigh as his eyes focused on the small town. All too soon the town vanished, replaced by another concrete construction, "The Sorell Causeway", a bridge from Midway Point, across Pitt Water. This, again, looked more like a sea than a river. Marriott held his breath again, waiting for tales of another disaster – none came. After Sorell, Ted turned the car south onto Arthur Highway: A9. Here, instead of the five-lane highway, it was now a two-way road lined with sparse trees, with shrub beyond. Marriott relaxed, pointed to various ornate birds and some minute hills.

'Termites,' said Ted, smiling as Marriott fidgeted.

As Ted sped on Marriott noticed that Gareth and Mac were catching up on their late night, so he decided to concentrate more on the terrain as they passed through Dunalley.

'Lovely, isn't it?' whispered Ted. 'You'd never know there was such a disaster here, would you?'

'A disaster?' cringed Marriott.

'Yer, January 2013, the whole place was nearly wiped out by the bush fires. Black Friday we called it, when the temperatures reached forty-one degrees Celsius. But the 300 or so residents managed to get it rebuilt. Looks good now, doesn't it?'

'It certainly does,' Marriott nodded as they crossed the narrow coastal strip of land and carried on towards Eaglehawk Neck, another strip of land boarded on each side by sea.

'This was called "Natures Prison Gate" in the past,' whispered Ted again. 'Prisoners at Port Arthur knew they couldn't get past here, not just because of the terrain, but because of the guards and chained dogs.'

Marriott nodded. He could see what Ted meant. It was then they saw the roadblock. Ted waved his warrant card as they passed. Now the area began to resemble Dartmoor, with its heather and wild undulating ground. Where amorphic legions conjured images in the fickle minds of humans. Where terrifying dogs with fangs dripping blood, and burning eyes that could melt skin – guarded the gates of hell. *The Hound of Baskerville*, thought Marriott. Where here, any escaped prisoner would definitely perish – dragged into the mire – never to be seen again.

Leaving the A9, Ted took the C 347. A single track road, more desolate than any other Marriott had encountered in Tasmania.

Two and a half hours after leaving Hobart they reached Port Arthur; longer than Ted's estimation, due to the road block.

Ted jumped out of the four-by-four and walked towards a tall, unassuming man of about forty. Smiling, the man flipped his thick blond hair away from his eyebrows and shook his head.

'Hello Simon, it's good to see you again,' said Ted meeting him halfway across the tarmac and vigorously shaking hands with him. Walking and talking, they entered the hotel lobby, followed by Gareth, Mac and Marriott. 'Sorry guys, this is DI Simon Miller,' said Ted, introducing his three companions.

Having booked into the hotel and then discarded their luggage in their rooms, all five met fifteen minutes later in the foyer for a tour of Port Arthur.

The prison was just as Marriott expected – a fortress. Spread out on undulating manicured lawns he noticed that one building was a ruin, while others had been renovated. Standing on one of the flat hills, he took in the keen Antarctic air and imagined what it must have been like to be a prisoner there. As they walked from building to building, Simon explained about the history of the area. Finally, they entered a cell block.

When Simon invited Marriott to step into an isolation cell alone, Marriott light-heartedly agreed. Simon closed the cell door.

The world stopped; darkness prevailed. Marriott stood – unable or unwilling to move, as if waiting for the floor to drop, where he would descend into the abyss at the end of a rope. Taking shallow breaths of the dank air, he listened – nothing. He couldn't even hear his own heartbeat – he couldn't think. Someone there? A presence, a movement of air; his hair. A breath; his breath. Another breath? It was standing close – too close. His body tingled with the nothingness of time. Taking a deep breath, his mind called out – his voice – consumed by the mortar of a lost time. He pulled at his collar, swallowed and wiped his forehead. When the door inched slowly opened – he squinted.

'You all right, mate?' asked Simon, half smiling.

Marriott stood tall, brushed his clothes with his hands, and coughed. 'Perfectly – what an experience.'

Simon nodded with a look that said he knew exactly what Marriott was referring to.

Chapter 36

The boat carried the five explorers, Ted, Gareth, Mac, Marriott and Simon, the crew, and two gravediggers, towards the infamous Isle of the Dead. The weather seemed to sense the sombreness of the occasion, as it drew a feather-like shroud over the peninsular. The boat sunk into it as if it were being engulfed by the fimbria of some gigantic amorphous creature. Until, not even the orange glow from the craft could be seen by the figures on the shore.

Marriott stood with the others on the deck, his eyes squinting – trying to see through the gloom. Nothing.

'How far did you say it was from the mainland?' he whispered – his body shuddered. Was it from that deathly cell he was compelled, by some force, to stand in that morning, or the cold weather, or perhaps a ghost coming to greet them from the island? No answer came as he watched the outline of a jetty come into view. He looked at his watch. The ten minute journey seemed like an hour.

'Just a few more minutes, then I'll have the boat at the jetty where we disembark,' said the skipper, Edward Drew, rubbing his black beard as the mist began to clear. 'Wouldn't normally have taken her out in this sort of weather. Instinct tells me it'll be a cracker of a day.'

'Hope you're right,' said Mac pulling up his collar – credulous of Edward's prediction.

'Thank God I managed to keep the press at bay,' said Ted sighing. 'Can you imagine the crowds if the vultures were here?' He turned and looked at Gareth who was standing at the bow. His eyes gazing – muscle twitching – alert – anxious to be the first to step ashore. Ted had other ideas as he pushed past Gareth, determined to precede everyone.

Marriott stood calmly, oblivious to the anxiety, then turned to see the boat nearing the jetty. Expecting to see a flat landscape he gasped at the steep cliffs and rough terrain. Alighting, he laboured with the others to the top of the embankment, disappointment overwhelming his senses. He had expected to see well-kept and regimented gravestones, like ones in an English graveyard. The topography here was part barren, part shrub and seemingly devoid of any human intrusion for many years.

The group moved onwards – feet crunching – insects scurrying away. Multi-coloured birds screamed overhead, as the sea screamed below as if in protest at their presence.

Walking further inland they eventually stepped into a forest of littered headstones. Marriott noticed that some were listing, while others stood tall, sentry-like, guarding their charges. Others, outlines of sculptured human forms, their stone heads looking out for life beyond the sea. A tomb stood among them – forlorn, morose, unkempt; as if it were about to implode. All were lichen-ridden, chipped, cracked – alone. Waiting for some caring hand to restore them. They appeared to be of similar age, certainly over one hundred and fifty years old. They told the story of lives in the harsh desolate penal colony; of the perpetual prisoners, never to be found or freed.

Marriott stood still and lowered his head, as did the others, in silent prayer. This was the place to honour the dead. Like the solitude of the prisoners' cell. No birds, no wind on the shrub-land, no thrash of the sea; silence – an island in mourning.

Moving on, they began searching for signs of the prisoners' graves. Some walked in silence, others talked.

Gareth crouched to read an inscription. Mac stopped. Traced his fingers across undecipherable words, and shook his head.

Further on, they came to a couple of indentations in the otherwise unassuming topography – devoid of headstones. Ted stopped to compare the rudimentary graves with a photocopied map he had been given of the area. Eventually agreeing on one of the graves, he set the gravediggers to work.

The weedy-looking one, Pete, stepped forward and plunged his spade, with vigour and enthusiasm, that seemed alien to his stature, into the earth. Moments later, there was a prang as his spade reverberated across a rock, just below the surface. Pete stopped and searched Ted's face for instructions, as the other gravedigger, John, moved forward.

Gareth was the first to recognise they were in the wrong place. 'I know I've said this before, but we must have a detailed map and burial plan. The map we have is less than useless,' he growled.

'Now, don't get heated,' said Ted. 'We need to be rational. It's here somewhere.' He looked at his map again and pointed to the other indentation. 'There.' He pointed and marched on. The others followed.

Putting Pete and John to work again, Pete stopped as he hit something that sounded like metal. Scraping some soil away, the whole group moved forward. Further excavation revealed a rusted metal box containing what looked like the remains of a dead cat.

'Great,' said Ted taking a deep breath and wiping his brow with a tissue. 'That's all we need, a bloody pet burial ground,' he muttered. 'But let's not dwell on it.' He examined the map again. 'Let's see if we can find anything over there.' He pointed and marched on again.

Ted was just about to tell the gravediggers to resume their work on this third site, when he stopped to listen to a female voice, he recognised as Stella's, shouting some distance from the group. Her voice became louder as a woman of about forty emerged from the top of an incline and marched towards them.

'This can't go on,' shouted Stella. 'This must stop, and stop now. If you continue to excavate in this fashion, you'll ruin the site.' Her face almost purple, her lungs heaving as she reached them.

She wore jogging pants, and a long-sleeved T-shirt bearing the logo "*PAHSMA*". Which; if Marriott remembered correctly, stood for the *Port Arthur Historic Site Management Authority*. He remembered seeing Simon wearing one when they had first met, and he had asked what the acronym stood for.

'Calm down, calm down,' said Ted, his hands gestured for her to stop as Stella stood before him, her chest heaving – hands on hips.

'I will *not* calm down.'

The look she gave Ted lasted far too long for his comfort. Nevertheless, he refused to move, or lower his eyes, as he stood in contempt.

'When we spoke yesterday, you said it would only take about a couple of hours,' she protested. 'I thought you knew where to dig, and would be methodical, but look at it now.' She gesticulated – making a three hundred and sixty degree turn as she did so. 'This is a heritage site, a museum in its own right. But look at the mess you and your team have created. If we had known, we'd never have agreed to let you on the island, let alone dig. Either you find exactly where the grave is, or stop and tidy it up, for the sake of future generations.'

Of course, Stella was right. But Ted still tried to reason with her. Surely, she would realise how important it would be if they did find the murderer there. The publicity alone would help to increase the number of visitors. That would offset any expense they had incurred.

Despite Ted trying to reason with her by saying that everything would be put back as it was once the work had been completed, it did not satisfy Stella. Following more outbursts, Ted agreed to call a halt on the dig, at least for the time being. At this, Stella huffed, turned, and headed towards the jetty saying they had to take better care of the place if they returned.

Watching Stella's full-figure disappear, Ted turned to the team and said, 'Sorry for that, but despite having everything agreed by the authorities, Stella always has to have the last word. This time, I believe that she is right, as without a detailed map, we can't continue. So, let's stop and resume later.'

As the boat headed towards the mainland an hour later, Ted took a phone call from one of the secretaries.

'You haven't? Well that's great news,' he yelled into his mobile phone. 'You can fill me in with the details when I get there.'

'Haven't what?' asked Gareth, as if he were interrogating a suspect.

'Haven't nothing. It looks as if we have found the solution to our problem, that's all. Anyway, we need to check it out first.'

'Don't be so evasive. So *what* has been discovered?' Gareth insisted.

'One of our researchers in Hobart has found a map that looks like a plan of the graveyard. It sounds promising. They're going to attach a copy to an email. It'll be there when we get back to the hotel.'

'Excellent,' said Gareth. 'Looks as if we're finally getting somewhere.' The group agreed.

***

Nearing the jetty at Port Arthur, Ted and the others could see a large gathering of people on the shore; lights flashing. *Bloody press*, Ted said to himself. Getting closer, he recognised Stella standing amongst them. *She couldn't have*, the words ground in his throat, his eyes fixed, face flushed; every muscle in his body taught as he waited, like a stalking lion, for the boat to dock.

Finally disembarking, Ted, together with Gareth and Simon, sauntered towards the group.

Flash on flash bombarded before them, like the bullets from a machine gun. Stella smiled, and walked slowly away, leaving the mêlée to sort themselves out.

'Have you found him?' a tall eager-faced reporter shouted.

'What have you found?' asked a young blonde woman holding an extended microphone above her head.

'When are you going to let us see the grave?' shouted a stocky man with a beard as he jumped up from behind other reporters.

As Ted moved forward, one of the reporter broke ranks. Rushing towards Ted, he thrust what resembled a gigantic sea urchin into his face. Ted clambered onto a rock giving him at least a foot above everyone else. Here he stood erect and silent on his make-shift platform – surveying the group. Then as he lifted his arms, as would a priest giving a blessing, everyone went quiet.

'Thank you.' Ted paused and strained to see the faces through the gloom created by the low clouds. 'You've all been very patient so I'll not keep you in suspense any longer.' He explained about the progress they had made. That they were about to identify where the grave was. And that once they had verified that the body was that of the perpetrator,

382

they would be informed. That any disturbance, at this critical stage, would jeopardise the whole operation.

The sound of muffled voices moved along the group of reporters. Then the tall man shouted:

'Do you expect to find the brass rings in the grave?'

Everyone went silent – craning their necks to see who had spoken.

'That's open to conjecture,' said Ted. 'Now please, let us get on with this work.' There were a few groans from the group, but no more questions.

As Ted stepped down from his platform, he scowled. *How had they found out about the rings?* Now, having refused to answer the question about them, he had probably aroused more suspicious. But that was life. He was determined not to give out information until it was going to be public knowledge anyway.

***

Lunch over and detailed map in hand, the group reassembled at the jetty, together with the priest, Father Cross.

All they were waiting for now was Doctor Natasha Brown, the pathologist. An archaeology enthusiast, she had worked on several excavations, and given many lectures on the subject to students at the local university. Now, nearly twenty-eight, she was hoping for a professorship. Perhaps this would enhance her chances of success in the field. Lumbering up with her equipment, her matchstick arms struggled with the weight.

'Sorry to keep you waiting,' said Natasha dumping her bag of equipment onto the ground. 'Can't believe the traffic,' she took a tissue from her pocket, wiped it across her brow, held up her mop of curly black hair from her neck, then wiped through to the nape. 'So what's going on?'

'Press,' said Ted.

Natasha nodded with a thought-so gesture.

'Anyway, good to see you again,' Ted continued, giving her a peck on the cheek just as Gareth moved forward and added to the greeting.

After Ted finished introducing everyone else, Marriott scooped up Natasha's bag, headed towards the boat, and stepped aboard with the others.

'We should have been on the island hours ago,' said Ted looking at his watch. 'Three o'clock. It'll be dark before we get going at this rate.'

'Don't think so mate,' said Gareth curtly. 'My reckoning is, we'll have another five hours before that. Unless it clouds over again.'

'You'd be right there, but I've booked dinner for six-thirty. By the time we set things up, we'll just have…'

'I *can* reckon,' answered Gareth. 'So when we've landed, we'd better get crackin'.'

Ted nodded. He wasn't about to argue, they were all tense enough as it was. Instead he stood by the exit – the first to disembark.

Gathered on shore, Ted held up the map, turned it around, nodded and marched forward; the others followed. Minutes later, he stopped. 'Here, we need to turn left here,' he flipped the map around just as the sun materialised from behind a cloud. 'Good,' he looked up. 'I'm sure we're on the right track.'

When Marriott noticed that Ted was scratching his head for a second time, he realised they were lost.

'Can I help?' said Marriott walking towards Ted, who was turning the map again. 'I used to be good at orienteering, and I know it's not easy out here.'

Ted made some excuse about there not being enough light, grunted, and handed the map to him.

384

Standing still for a moment, Marriott identified where they were on the map and asked the group to follow him. Five minutes later, Marriott stopped.

'This is the spot where we should dig – from here,' he made a mark in the soil with the heel of his shoe, and then moved on several paces. Stopping again, he made as similar mark as before. 'This is over six foot from one end to the other, big enough for a grave?' Marriott exclaimed.

'You'd better be right for all our sakes. Stella won't tolerate us much longer,' said Ted, Gareth nodded.

'If you would care to take the map and look for yourself,' said Marriott politely, 'you should be able to see that we're in the right place.'

'No worries, you appear to know what you're doing, so keep it,' Ted frowned. 'So let's start digging.'

'If you're sure,' said Gareth sceptically. 'We don't want to waste any more time.' He looked at Marriott.

'I'm almost positive,' answered Marriott. 'But we can't be totally sure until we find something tangible. Like a coffin or some bones.'

Everyone nodded, including Father Cross who was anxious to get back to the mainland for the evening confessions.

'Okay, let's get on with it then,' said Ted signalling to the gravediggers.

A few minutes later Pete and John had moved the top coarse grass revealing a conglomerate of earth and rocks. They stopped digging and ascended from the grave. Natasha stepped into it and began to brush the soil away – eventually dislodging some small rocks.

'I need these removed before I can continue,' said Natasha, motioning to Ted who put Pete and John to work again.

Other members of the group formed a relay chain so that when each rock, about the size of a cricket ball with other pieces of debris, were passed along the line and then stacked. As more soil was revealed, the gravediggers carefully removed it with their shovels until they scraped on what looked like a plank of wood.

Natasha took over again. Brushing further, she removed the remaining soil from an intact coffin lid. The group moved forward and looked into an obvious grave.

Everyone stopped. All fell silent as Father Cross stepped forward, said a prayer and gave his blessing. Then turning to group, he consented for the dig to continue. Reminding them to be respectful of the dead, he walked away in the direction of the boat. Some followed him with their eyes – others stood in silent prayer. Then, as if being woken from a dream, the work resumed.

Marriott looked into the grave: 'It amazes me that with these conditions,' he looked around, 'I'd expect the coffin to be rotted away,'

'It would have been,' said Natasha, 'if it were buried in a stack, especially at the bottom, as was reputed to have happened to other prisoners when they died. But this one was obviously buried last. Being just a few feet below the surface, and the acid soil, has obviously preserved it. But I'll know more when I've examined it.'

Natasha took some samples and placed them in labelled plastic bags. When she asked for the lid to be lifted, Mac and Marriott began, but stopped when the coffin lid started to creak.

Everyone took in a breath. No one dare breathe out. Lifting the lid further, the wood splintered – a piece broke off.

'I expected that to happen,' said Natasha calmly and shrugging. 'It's obviously going to be impossible to remove it intact, so we'll have to make the best of it.'

After carefully removing the lid, Mac and Marriott, now relieved of their task, climbed out of the grave onto the bank and watched as Natasha resumed her work.

Brushing away remnants of wood and soil, she exposed the outline of a skull, the clavicles and then the ribs. Removing the skull, she placed it on the protective sheet at the graveside, and continued with the exhumation. When she reached the pelvic area, and confirmed that it was a male skeleton, there was a quiet cheer from the group.

On further inspection of the skeleton, Natasha found a finely braided leather strap from behind the sixth cervical vertebrae.

'Looks as if he was wearing this.' She lifted it towards the group. 'I'll know more when I've examined it under the microscope.'

'Do you think the rings could have been threaded on it and hung round his neck?' asked Gareth.

'I'm not sure, but there's no sign of any rings. Nevertheless, if there are any here, I'll find them with the metal detector I have in my bag.' Natasha opened a small purse and took out an instrument resembling a pencil. 'All we need to do now is to keep as quiet as possible.'

They nodded as Natasha pressed the button on the instrument. A light appeared but no sound. She moved it from the top of the coffin, across the torso, down the sides, and then to the bottom of the coffin; nothing. She was just about to give up when the instrument gave a faint bleep. Simultaneously there were many intakes of breaths. Brushing further, she unearthed a nail. The group sighed.

'Sorry – not finished yet; there are still the corners.' She brushed the soil away from one of them. The sound was clear. The group moved forward, dislodging some soil. 'Hey, be careful, I don't need an avalanche.' She turned, took a pair of dissecting forceps from her bag, and resumed her search. 'Here we are.' She carefully lifted an object with the forceps.

'Although brass does not actually rust, nevertheless it can corrode.' She held up a ring-shaped object. 'Looks as if we've found at least one of your rings.'

'Brilliant,' said Ted with excitement, his voice croaking. 'Do you think the others are in there?'

'Not that I can see,' said Natasha. Placing the ring into a sample bag, she continued her search. A few minutes later she discovered a second ring in a similar condition to the first.

'Surely there was no doubt now that this is the grave we're looking for?' said Ted. 'The rings must have been tied to the leather twine you found around the neck.' As Ted verbalised these thoughts, Natasha had her doubts about the latter.

'You may be right, but leather also takes a long time to degrade in acid conditions, and as the leather twine was intact, the rings must have been somewhere else on his person when he was interned. But no matter now, at least you have the two rings.' She handed the bagged rings to Ted.

'But,' interrupted Marriott, 'there should be three rings, not two.'

'As far as I can tell, there are only two,' said Natasha shaking her head and trying to dismiss his obvious accusation.

Ted peered into the grave. Natasha stood there wondering what to do next, but was determined not to ask, after all she was the professional in all of this. She had done her best. Now they were questioning her integrity.

'Can you just take another look,' asked Ted as politely as his disappointment would allow.

'I can, and I certainly will do my best – as ever.' Natasha resumed her search. Five minutes later she was prepared to relinquish the search when she heard a faint sound coming from the thoracic cavity. As she moved the instrument deeper, the sound grew louder.

'It looks as if you were right, David Marriott.' She took up the forceps and held up another ring. 'It's much smaller than the other two. Probably small enough be swallowed, especially as I found it where the small intestines would have been.' She placed the ring inside another plastic bag and handed it to Ted.

As the group stood examining the three rings, Natasha took her last samples, including a small fraction of bone for DNA analysis.

The remains reinterred and the areas tided, the group collected their equipment, and headed for the jetty. Reaching the mainland, they had forty-five minutes to prepare themselves for the press and for a well-earned dinner.

***

Marriott turned his computer on at the same time as Cadema. She could tell he was excited by his exuberant voice. Managing to interrupt as he took a sharp intake of breath, she asked him to slow down and talk calmly.

Marriott tried to comply with Cadema's instruction. He explained about the grave and the three rings. That the two larger ones were probably Annie Chapman's, and the smaller one Ethel Redberry's, but knew that this could not be proved. However, he was hoping for a match with the DNA taken from the skeleton and the dress found in the archives. 'Hopefully,' he said, 'there will be a DNA match, and together with the three brass rings, it will alleviate any doubt that we have found the perpetrator.'

Cadema sat in silence as Marriott's pitch oscillated between calm to almost mania. It's all over, she thought. We've managed it. The DNA will prove it. There's no place for him to hide now. She calmly congratulated Marriott on his tenacity and dedication in helping to solve the crimes.

When Cadema explained that John Temple Ridley's address had been found but that the building had been demolished along with the others in the 1950s when the slums were cleared, she heard Marriott sigh.

'Don't be too despondent.' She frowned. 'The press has found some old photographs of the area and speculated on the type of property he lived in. Some members of the public have invaded the area, demanding to know the facts. But of course, there's nothing for them to see. Even the names of the roads there have been changed. The East End isn't the same as it used to be.'

Marriott nodded in agreement as he imagined himself living there in that decadent time.

After conversing about current work issues, Marriott's travel plans, and their personal trivialities, they both signed off. Returning to bed, Cadema looked at the diamond ring on her finger.

A week later, Marriott took a sip of sparkling wine, settled into his seat, fastened his seatbelt, closed his eyes, and then drifted off to sleep.

Now he was on the most famous bridge in the world, climbing ladders, traversing girders, and ducking under pipes again. He gasped in his slumber, as he had done when ascending a ladder, where his head became parallel with a train just a few feet away. Composing himself, he clambered on – finally reaching the arch of the bridge. Here he took a deep breath, his eyes scanning the panoramic view of another world. The boats and ships looking like miniatures at his feet below, the monumental majestic buildings reaching into the clouds, and the beacon – warning air traffic. It was all there. He thanked Gareth for organising the climb of his life.

Marriott yawned, opened his eyes, and looked down on the clouds below. Hours later, he jumped when someone touched his arm.

'Sorry to disturb you, Sir, but you must put your seat into the upright position, and prepare yourself as we are about to descend into Heathrow.' He thanked the steward, settled into his seat as instructed, and pulled a small package from his pocket.

'Home,' he whispered. 'Home.'

***

When he finally arrived on the concourse, Cadema was waiting for him and after a few minutes of greetings, and talking about the flight, they headed for the car park. Luggage secured in the boot, they got into the car and Cadema drove off. Turning the radio on, they listened to the broadcast.

'*Breaking news*,' the male announcer said. '*Today the file on Jack the Ripper is closed. On good authority, we are informed that the remains found in the coffin on the Isle of the Dead, in Tasmania, Australia is that of our infamous Jack.*

DNA taken from the remains of Jack's body has proven beyond doubt, that it matches with bodily fluids found on the dress worn by his last victim. His DNA also matches with a living relative in the UK, who, for legal reasons, cannot be named.

To authenticate this, two brass rings, torn from the fingers of his second victim Annie Chapman, and one smaller brass ring torn from his last victim, Ethel Redberry, were also found in the coffin.

Jack's remains have been reinterned on the island, and will remain there indefinitely.

By the time the announcer had finished, Marriott was asleep. Cadema smiled, her team together again at last. Now all she had to contend with was her mother.

Postscript

I believe that there is a box or trunk in some forgotten police archives, in a Government file, or in some ancestral attic, that contains tangible evidence relating to the Whitechapel murders of 1888. Where, with current police investigation skills, forensic techniques and DNA analysis, can be used to follow ancestral lines and discover the identity of the perpetrator.

This book, through fiction, tests this hypothesis.

S.J. Ridgway.

Appendix One

Family Tree

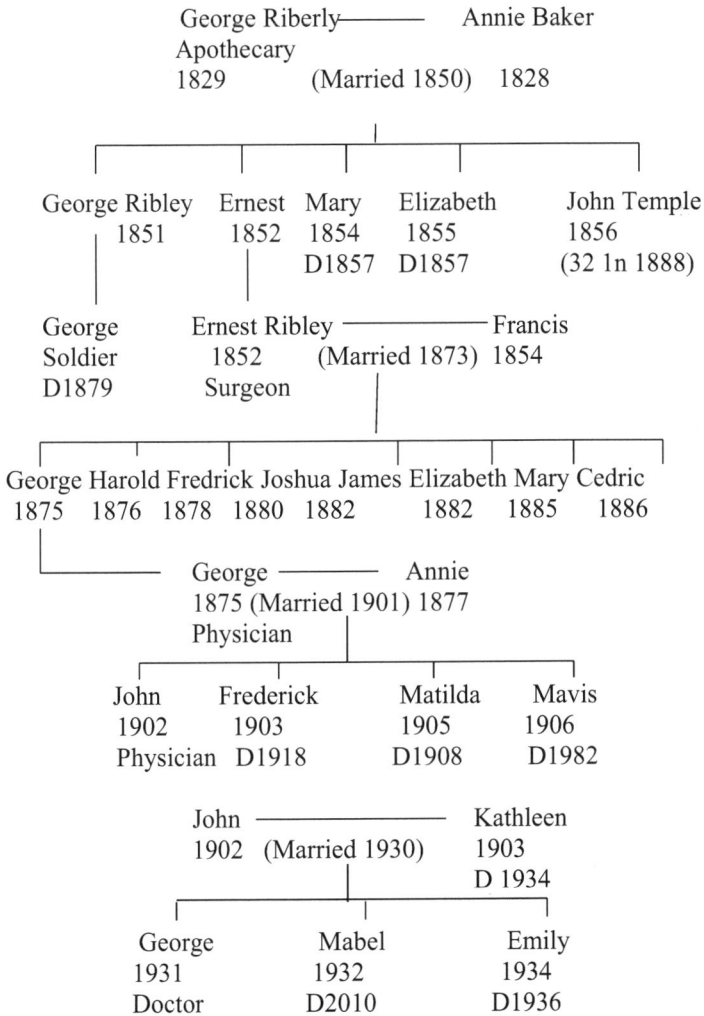

George Riberly———— Annie Baker
Apothecary
1829   (Married 1850)   1828

George Ribley   Ernest Mary   Elizabeth   John Temple
    1851   1852   1854   1855   1856
                        D1857   D1857   (32 1n 1888)

George   Ernest Ribley ——————Francis
Soldier   1852   (Married 1873) 1854
D1879   Surgeon

George Harold Fredrick Joshua James Elizabeth Mary Cedric
1875   1876   1878   1880   1882   1882   1885 1886

George ———— Annie
1875 (Married 1901) 1877
Physician

John   Frederick   Matilda   Mavis
1902   1903   1905   1906
Physician   D1918   D1908   D1982

John ———————————— Kathleen
1902 (Married 1930)   1903
                        D 1934

George   Mabel   Emily
1931   1932   1934
Doctor   D2010   D1936

George ———————— Elizabeth
1931   (Married 1957)   1931

John   George   Emily
1958   1959   1961
Doctor

        John ———————————— Susan
        1958   (Married 1983) 1959

            Ashley Ribley   Laura
            1985   1987
            Pharmacist

        Ashley Ribley ——— Sarah
            1985   (Married)   1986

                    No Children

Bibliography

Note:

Although this book is mainly fiction, it also included non-fiction. Areas of non-fiction, relating to my research on the Whitechapel murders, are identified in the following bibliography.

Primary sources:

The editor, The Daily Telegraph, 1888, page 3 including September 3,4,11,1314, 17,18, 19,20, 24,27,28 and October 2,3,4,5,20,24 and November 10 and 22. Most of these are on page three except the 4th October which is on page 5. There is no mention of the author in any of these reports, which were mainly from the coroners' inquests.

The editor, The Illustrated Police News, London September 22nd 1888:1, No:1284.

P&O shipping archives. National Maritime Museum, London. The steamship Ballaarat.

Secondary sources:

Canter, David & Keppel, Robert. *Inside the Mind of Serial Killers*. Harper Collins, London, 1994.

Cornwell, Patricia. *Portrait of a Killer (Jack the Ripper – case closed)*. Putnam USA. 2002

Evans, Stuart & Skinner, Keith. *Jack the Ripper: Letter from Hell*. Sutton, Stroud, 2001.

Fairclough, Melvyn. *The Ripper and the Royals*. Duckworth, London 1992 2nd edition.

Flanders, Judith. *The Invention of Murder*. Harper Collins, 2011

Harrison, Shirley & Barrett Michael. *The Diary of Jack the Ripper*. BCA London. 1993

Knight, Stephen. *Jack the Ripper – The Final Solution*. Treasure, London 1984 (revised edition)

Tully, James. *The Secret of Prisoner 1167 (was this man Jack the ripper?)* Robinson London. 1998

Rule, Fiona. *The Worst Street in London*. Ian Allan, USA. Impression 2010

Sugden, Philip. *The Complete History of Jack the Ripper*. Robinson, London 1995

S J Ridgway

After war service in the 8th Punjab Regt., Anthony Kirk-Greene graduated from Clare College, Cambridge and joined the Colonial Administrative Service in 1950. He spent ten years as a District Officer in N. Nigeria. He was ADC to the 1952 UN Visiting Mission to the Cameroons and was private Secretary to the first Nigerian Minister of Works in Kaduna. In 1957 he became the founding Supervisor of the Administrative Service Training Course at the Institute of Administration, Zaria, and was seconded to the new Ahmadu Bello University as Head of the Department of Government in 1962. He was awarded the MBE in 1963.

In 1967 he was elected Senior Research Fellow in African Studies at St. Antony's College, Oxford and became the University's first Lecturer in the Modern History of Africa. He was also Director of the Oxford Foreign Service Programme, 1986–1990. He has taught widely in North America. Author of 29 books and over 300 chapters and articles on African history and politics, his current research focuses on the Colonial Service.

His most recent books are *On Crown Service* (I.B.Tauris) and *Britain's Imperial Administrators* (Macmillan). He is married to Helen Sellar.